M

The Might of Monsters

Copyright © 2022 by Maria Ying

All rights reserved. No part of this publication may be reproduced, stored or transmitted in any form or by any means, electronic, mechanical, photocopying, recording, scanning, or otherwise without written permission from the publisher. It is illegal to copy this book, post it to a website, or distribute it by any other means without permission.

Copyright @ 2022 Devi Lacroix

Copyright @ 2022 Benjanun Sriduangkaew

Copyright @ 2022 C.S. Cary

First edition

This book was professionally typeset on Reedsy.
Find out more at reedsy.com

Contents

Prologue	1
One: Dull Roots and Spring Rain	30
Two: Mandible Memory	40
Interlude: The Professor	49
Three: Fangs for a Siren	56
Four: A Long Journey to An Uncertain End	67
Five: In Raiments of Gold	78
Six: The Tiger and Her Stripes	87
Seven: A Knife For a Knife	100
Eight: Silk for a Sorceress	118
Interlude: Ouroboros	140
Nine: Beasts of the Earth	146
Ten: Stone Butch Blues	161
Eleven: And We Shall Go Dancing	180
Twelve: Masque of the Red Death	192
Thirteen: All Roads Lead To Ruin	213
Epilogue	241
Bonus Story: The Demon of the House of Hua	260
About the Author	304
Acknowledgments	305
Other Works by the Author	306

Prologue

Ten years ago

FAHRIYE

It's not often a beautiful woman walks through my door. In fact, as far as this specific woman is concerned, the frequency of her appearance in my office should be *never*.

I stand up so fast it nearly makes me dizzy. I dive toward the door, easing it shut behind her while she looks on, amused. In height she is hardly imposing—I'm much taller and much bigger—and her pear-shaped build does not look the sort to intimidate. And yet everyone who has ever been in her presence would describe the experience as paralyzing; it has taken me near on two decades to be functional around her.

Elizaveta Hua is the warlock of her age, the most powerful woman in the world. Once, many years ago, I saved her children at great personal risk to myself, and from that moment of heroism has sprung the most important and dangerous relationship of my life. The Huas, as a general rule, have a nasty reputation, and Elizaveta Hua is *persona non grata* with the magical enforcement organization I work for, Sealing and Containment—to the point that they very well might have a kill-on-sight order out for her. And they would probably kill me, too, if they knew how frequently she and I slept together.

And here she is, standing in the belly of the beast, as if she doesn't have a care in the world.

"Liz," I say, my tongue tangling over itself. I try not to bite down on it. "Why are you here—did anyone *see*."

"It looks like you finally earned that corner office." Elizaveta's small, full mouth is drawn toward a smirk. "A promotion, I hear; climbing up the ranks, are we?"

"Did anyone see—"

"Tell me, Inspector," she says as she crosses the room and seats herself, uninvited. "Do you think the warlock of her age doesn't know how to conceal herself?"

"You just walked through a place full of scryers and seers!"

She dismisses that with a flick of her hand. "Were they aware a Hua had slipped past them, every alarm would be on high, every gun would be drawn and every automated routine of destruction put to work. As this is not the case, you may rest assured that I have successfully hidden myself. I would point out the holes in your wards, but improving S&C's barricades is not my job."

And it is true: my organization hates her family to the point of obsession, so much so that they'd have let vampires feast on her children when they were little. They have grown now. Viveca and Olesya are in their twenties—excelling at their respective studies, according to their mother, when she tells me of them at all. She rations out information with the utmost care, in spite of her trust in me. A barrier must exist, always, between our lives. Between what is public and what is private.

Which makes her decision to appear *here* of all places…

"I have not come for a trivial reason," she says, as if hearing my thoughts. "There's something I would like to ask of you that I suspect only you can do. Though—we haven't had dinner together for a while, have we?"

"I have to work for ten more minutes."

She spreads her hands, magnanimous, an empress granting her permission. "I can wait."

By that she means she's sitting right there as I put papers into folders, organize my notes, all the things that I do when I'm winding down and getting ready to leave. It makes concentrating on these mundane, mindless tasks unaccountably challenging. To feel her eyes on me, on every movement; to know that she is studying my face, my fingertips. Maybe she's thinking of how my mouth might feel on hers, very soon—

Stupid. From the start, I've been embarrassingly libido-led with this woman. Even now I still can't identify what I was thinking when I asked her out to dinner that first time (and why in the name of all did she say yes?). Alright—I was standing before a woman who's not just the most powerful in the world, but very beautiful and older, and exactly my type.

I wonder what she can see with those black eyes of hers; whether she receives the world in ranges beyond the visible light. Perhaps as I try to tidy my desk and wrap up the day's paperwork, she can see blood moving through me, flushing my cheeks with heat. Or else she is watching power run in my veins, the natural ebb and flow that moves within any mage. A tide, in a practitioner of great power; a brook, in those less so. I have a full awareness of which category I belong to; only through constant training and the tutelage of the world's greatest warlock has my little stream been marshaled into something respectable.

"You seem done," she says after eight minutes have passed.

"You're usually more patient than this, Master Elizaveta."

Her head cocks. "Where would you like dinner?"

The problem of a relationship—or a fling, or whatever this is—with an incredibly powerful woman is that she has next to no familiarity with consequences. But if nothing else, the food is always excellent. "Sapporo."

She takes my hand, and then we are away.

Immediate and visceral: cold buffets my skin. My breath steams in the frigid air. A cantrip quickly takes care of that, warming me against this island's climate. Elizaveta herself evinces no discomfort, either not feeling the cold—possible, given what she is—or already having woven basic temperature protection into her clothes.

Sapporo is a beautiful city: the air blue and very sharp, the mountains white and shadowed in the distance. I know something of its history, that it is a site of brutal occupation, evidence of what the powerful will do to those they perceive as powerless. And it's hard not to think about that in the company of Elizaveta; I know something, too, of her family's past. There have been chapters of incredible savagery, and more than once a Hua warlock has been the most cruel of despots. The hatred with which my institution regards her family has some historical basis. But she is not her forebears, and to the best of my knowledge she's never been more destructive or murderous than most mages.

We come in to a ramen bar; she takes care of the ordering, her Japanese fluent where mine is at best of the touristic phrasebook sort. It's an unassuming place, neither owned nor frequented by practitioners. I like these better than mage-owned establishments: leave me my little escapisms. Elizaveta knows it too. Maybe, I like to think, she shares my enjoyment. That, despite her might and station in high society, sometimes she also wants to get away. Between the two of us she blends in better, here, but I pass as a tourist just fine, if an inadequately dressed one.

The miso broth is rich, complexly flavored. The noodles are excellent. Elizaveta orders seconds.

"There's something I would like to find," she says in Turkish. A recent acquisition—she claims to have taken to it as a matter of practical security, something to flummox would-be eavesdroppers. Her reasoning is hardly sound: while in isolated Sapporo there may be no Turkish speakers save us, it's not as if it is a rare language. But she uses it to communicate with *me*, and it makes me—no, I refuse to pursue that line of thought, refuse to entertain those feelings.

Whatever her motivations, she has an incredible ear for it. I don't know whether that's her natural talent, a neurological advantage, or if it's been obtained through magic. There are no spells, really, that will translate languages perfectly, but there are ones that can enhance the mind, augment comprehension.

I put down my bowl and gaze, longingly, at the slices of chashu the cook's preparing. "And I'm the best tracker you know."

"Cocky." Her voice is rounded with amusement—she herself has said as much, granting me that title as a monarch might make a knight of her retainer. "But you are, and it's good that you know your strengths. Nor is it the only thing you're good at."

I try to tell myself all the heat's just from the ramen. "How are the—" I stumble here. There is a boundary, I think, and I don't want to cross it, to become overfamiliar. "The girls?"

"They're doing very well. Viveca will succeed me." Elizaveta's tone is warm with pride; her sclerae turn dark, as they occasionally do when she feels intense emotion.

"No struggle?" Too forward, but many houses have come to ruin when scions fight over who will be the heir—in long, prestigious lines especially, the stakes are too high to be second-best, and sisterly love disappears fast when it comes to seizing the throne.

"No. My daughters adore each other, and Olesya is genuinely more interested in transfiguration than summoning rituals. Flesh-crafting, particularly, and she's a prodigy at it."

On my non-practitioner side of the family—estranged from me, for the usual reasons when one's relative is a mage—there are cousins who'd trade anything to have access to the flesh-crafting that mages take for granted. I imagine that Olesya does not know how fortunate she is, and then quickly dismiss my uncharitable thought. It's not her fault that she has next to no acquaintance with outsiders; most thaumaturges don't, and see no need to bother. What can non-mages offer them?

The second servings arrive. I tuck into it, appreciating the extra chashu. It's not fancy food, but many steps above the hurried meals I get every day in the S&C cafeteria, of varying quality. And we are in Sapporo. If only there was time to sight-see, but our arrangement is such that I can never truly disappear for long with her, cannot be seen with her; even from her children we must hide this.

It shouldn't matter. I entered this knowing it would need to be this way, half-real. This thing between us has lasted nearly two decades precisely because neither of us have tried to put a name on it, because both of us have different priorities, different needs. Ultimately it'll end when finally she tires of me or I ask for too much.

But it is Elizaveta that asks first, once more reading me like an open book. "Do you have a little time?"

"A day off." That I should spend in my locality, so as not to rouse suspicion. Promotion or not, I'm scrutinized more closely than most officers of my rank and seniority.

"Enough to enjoy a few more good meals together, unless you're in a hurry to go home."

It's just one day. "Alright." I try to make myself smile past all the worry.

"I have already booked us a hotel. Two beds, to preserve your chastity, Inspector."

I might be turning red. Really I should riposte, but it's never been easy to, somehow, with her. Well, a first time for everything. "As if you won't be the first to make that moot."

She cants her head back and laughs. It is as if I am enspelled: it becomes impossible to look away from the sight of her, to not fall into the gravity of her all over again. She is exquisite. She is singular. Not just the most powerful in the world, but the most beautiful.

And in that moment it becomes obvious, too, that I'd do almost anything for Elizaveta Hua.

The hotel—the ryokan—she's picked for us is located in Minami Ward, a construct of red wood and warm illumination. Lanterns in the public area, and a few fireplaces; simple but elegant furniture, the occasional marble to interrupt the wood. There is a lovely, quiet minimalism. Our room has its own private bath, small and traditional, and a window that looks out to the mountains. It's a quiet night, snow and frost on the outside. By all rights, we should be curling up together, sinking into the quiet, into each other's warmth.

Instead Elizaveta is briskly unpacking; she has, incredibly, brought a change of clothes for me. A suit, the jacket and trousers deep brown with undertones of red, the shirt pale gold. "I trust it will be bearable for a day," she is saying. "I have your measurements and took the liberty."

I don't ask how she has my measurements. "It's very nice." The tailoring is much, much finer than anything I could afford. Probably she has a couturier she patronizes—the wealthy truly inhabit another world. Equally incredibly, she's prepared for me a set of sport bras and underwear. "I wear lace sometimes, you realize," I point out.

"I was saving that for when we go shopping for it together." Her voice is deadpan. "Silk in antique gold or burgundy will look good on you. Expensive lingerie under a suit is an especially intoxicating combination."

I open my mouth. I sigh. I smile. "It's just as well we will never live together. You'll dictate all my wardrobe, and probably all my meals." Not that I would not like it: I've been a creature of grim independence, and the thought of being lavished with such care…

"Why never, Inspector?"

Her expression has hardly shifted. It's impossible to tell whether she is joking. "Well, I mean, for all the obvious, usual reasons."

"Such as," she prompts.

"I'm not going to leave S&C," I say quickly. To become her kept tracker. "This work is important to me, Liz."

"Who said anything about you leaving?" Her hands still in her lap. Her gaze grows remote. "In a few years, I will no longer be the Hua warlock."

Nearly I drop the dress shirt. I hurriedly put it back down, on top of the luggage. "I think I understand what you mean. But—openly?" My superiors, and High Command in general, will never regard one of their officers associating with *any* Hua as value-neutral. I might as well be consorting with demons myself.

Elizaveta's eyes meet mine, searching my face. "It was merely a thought, Inspector."

I've disappointed her. Or, worse, she has disappointed herself. It has been a long time since our *arrangement* began, and yet there's still so much I don't know about her, the way she thinks, her personal philosophies. She has been my lover and mentor in sorcery too, plugging the gaps of my threadbare education, teaching me spells that would normally stay within her family.

What I cannot figure out, even now, is her motive. Why give me so much, offer such largesse, when I cannot possibly reciprocate? Does she hope that one day I will protect her children again, speak up for them when S&C finds an excuse to go after the sisters, mitigate the harm?

But we have done so much together. She has fought evil beside me, when it did not benefit her; has bled to save the world, has bled to save me from a wound. I cannot believe that she is solely motivated by selfish goals, that I am but a means to her eldritch ends.

And I have had the same thoughts—what it would be like, about what I would be willing to give up, to wake beside her every day; to know, for once, what she looks like at peace. So I believe, I must believe, that the same thoughts have occurred to her. And still I say, coward that I am, "It's a good thought. Only—"

"Only it's improbable." Still her expression gives away nothing. "Yet in my life, Fahriye, I've accomplished many improbable things. Don't rule it out yet."

The bathtub, I discover, is meant for two—but with me in the equation, it'll only fit one of us at a time. "Get in," she says; it is an order.

"I will do that once I've seen you disrobe, madam."

"Giving orders now, are we." She reaches over to tap me on the nose. And then she does, indeed, take off her clothes.

It's not the first time I have seen her naked, but I don't see it often enough. She's small next to me, slight of shoulders and limbs, round and soft in the places where I am angular and hard. Her breasts are full, brown-tipped, touched with blemishes that are an inevitable part of life. Fool that I am, I cannot get enough of her breasts—I have, a few times, woken up with my face against them, much to her amusement. The urge to kiss her all over seizes me: the soft swell of her stomach, her thighs and what lies between them.

But she makes me get into the tub, where the water's heat verges on this side of discomfort. She gathers my hair in one hand, murmuring that I seem due a cut, do I not usually keep it shorter? And she bends to kiss my ear, then the back of my neck. Each contact is electric, taking my breath away as surely as the scalding water.

Elizaveta stops there, though. She pours out the shampoo and massages it into my scalp, working slow and meticulous. It's the first time we have bathed together, and it's such a *mundane* thing, and yet achingly intimate. We fall into silence; there is only the sound of water and her small, elegant hands in my hair.

I ask her, shy, if I can return the favor. She says yes, and soon we switch positions, her in the water and I standing like an attendant of old. Some part of me wants to ask why she's decided to do this, come with me on a day's getaway, allowed me into her intimacy. But I'd rather not ruin the moment, and so I concentrate on her hair. A fine, thick mass. It is going gray but very slowly, either good genetics or thaumaturgy, and she has maintained it in incredible condition. Long, but pinned up most of the time so it doesn't get in the way; unbound and wet, it looks as dark as spun night, touched here and there by snow. I'm careful as I sweep the shampoo through the strands, as I rub conditioner into her scalp. It's not that she is delicate, but that I want to show her that I cherish her; I wish to express it in every motion as she has done for me.

We towel each other off, wrap a robe around one another. I stay still as she ties the sash for me, and remain unmoving once she's done. Her hand stills on my stomach. "Is something wrong, Inspector?"

"No." I find my throat hitched. "We should do this more often." I can hardly say what I mean: that I wish we could do this every day, every night. To enjoy one another in the most ordinary ways. I think of her disappointment at my answer earlier, and try again: "It isn't that I want to stay with S&C, Liz." I am very close to admitting to her things I have not ever admitted to myself. "It's just that I like to do good. I can't retire from that."

"And S&C is where you can do the most good?"

No. "Yes."

Her lips crook into a smirk, making it clear she heard the unvoiced answer. "I'd like that. The 'doing this more often.'" She's serious now, no longer teasing. "But there's some ancient business to attend to first."

Back in the room, she takes out of her luggage a long case. Inside its velvet lining is a slender strip of metal; it is perfectly white, whiter than platinum or rhodium, and certainly denser and stronger than both. "What I am seeking," says Elizaveta, "is not an object demons can search for. They cannot perceive it; they cannot touch it; they recoil from its nature. One of them did bring this back for me, at least, which is a start."

I take the metal piece. As I thought, it's far heavier than it looks. "What is it?"

"The fragment of a sheath, greatly warded and augmented, that should—in theory—still be holding a sword."

"A sword," I echo, trying to imagine her wielding one. And why not; Elizaveta, a warrior in armor.

"An object of some importance to me. I wish to locate it, and return it to safe keeping."

"To seal and contain it?" I can't help the joke.

She cuts me with a withering look. "To bring it within the security and wards of my family. Here are the other pieces, should you require them for the tracking."

A piece of wood, burnt completely black. A swirl of molten metal. A gemstone cut flat, one side scorched. They all come together to form what seems to be the remaining debris of an arson, or a terrible house fire.

"I will need a little information," I say. "Dates would be nice. Historical or thaumaturgic context. The name of the sword too."

"The name of the sword is the name of the entity contained within it." Elizaveta's mouth draws tight. "Its name is Nuawa."

As it turns out, the matter isn't as simple to resolve—or trace, as it were—as either of us was hoping for.

Nuawa is, for one, not its True Name. Merely this is an appellation, though from what source even Elizaveta doesn't know. "The being is not of this world, nor of hell," she explained to me. "As I have understood it, Nuawa came from a plane of existence where there is always light, scorching and too bright for us. Some would call its originating point heaven. I of course disagree."

But she was vague on why she wanted her hands on this sword. It had been in her family for some time, apparently, and was lost to the Hua line some generations back. What does this sword do? She will not disclose that, either.

I refuse to assume the worst, that she is like any other mage, avaricious for an artifact of power—potentially dangerous, potentially destructive. Equally, though, I cannot put all doubt from my mind. She has done so much for me, and… and I like to think the care she shows me is genuine, even as a secret and rotten part of me wonders: has this been her scheme all along? She must have been looking for this sword for some time, and who better to find it for her than an S&C tracker she's been courting, has been slowly turning to her purposes? For a mage of her power, even a twenty-year investment in talent would be considered a minor scheme.

No. I am not that gullible, and she is not the incarnation of evil my superiors believe her entire family to be.

So I study the pieces I've been given, holding them under the light of a lamp, the sun, the moon. Tracking is both an art and a series of intuitions; you develop the sense of the object, drawing in your mind its outline, its image. Elizaveta supplied me with a painting of the sword, and I incorporate that into my process. She's given me a map of all the places the blade has been, and I concentrate on the lines joining the dots, looking up the locations as much I can on satellite and street maps. An undersea vault here, an ancient library there, several secure archives overseen by previous Huas. Elizaveta said the sword was lost some time between the tenth and eleventh generations, a period of tumult.

I've found gemstones useful in my work, and for the sword I choose—as an object of affinity—a cube of milky quartz. Ideally I would visit each place in which the sword has been, touch the plinth or slot in which it has rested, but many of those locations are no longer standing and some are outright inaccessible.

I am limited in other ways, too. Were this an official investigation, I'd simply avail myself of S&C resources. As it is not, I am reduced to making discreet enquiries and reading academic research. First I try to isolate, by process of elimination, what kind of thing this Nuawa creature is. I read papers that postulate that our world and others' are spheres whose areas of overlap are miniscule, but which provide the path through which demons and other spirits can enter our realm. I pore over theories of dimensions as yet uncharted by thaumaturges. The closest I get is that a few mages have encountered beings like Nuawa, and they have chosen to call those celestial entities—next to impossible, it appears, to bind and compel. A few have been worshiped as gods, in bygone times.

My official work continues, as it must, for all that I've become a little obsessed with Elizaveta's task. It's made me curious for my own sake, a puzzle that I must solve, and it brings me joy that my daily work does not. At least most of the cases don't take me out of the office. Normally something I'd chafe against—I'm a fieldwork woman through and through—but for once it is a blessing.

The only case that demands my presence has to do with a demon; with a dispirited sigh, I lock away all my research and buckle up my holster.

In Singapore I arrive—a nexus of magical power, the seat of many mage families. An island unto itself. I reach the site at a busy street, where I'm pointed to a worn tenement, red roof and gray stone. The interior smells of citrus and frangipani—rich, unique, and a very odd combination. Summoned beings can leave behind peculiar fragrances and emanations; the first team on at the site took the odor to be positive proof of warlockery and arrested the suite's sole occupant.

That person now waits in a scorched vestibule of her own home, hands in cuffs behind her, her clothing blackened with soot. She has been made to stand in an inscribed containment field; it must have been for hours. But she shows no sign of weakness; her stance is steady, her legs straight. She is striking—the sculpted features of a statue, eyes of pale brown in a face of proud angles, her jawline slender and exacting. Not very many people would command undivided attention at a glance; she does so without effort, with the sheer force of presence. Elizaveta is more remarkable still, but this woman comes close.

"Inspector Fahriye Budak," I say, introducing myself as I glance through the dossier I've been handed. "I understand you're a mercenary, Mx...?"

A faint smile curves her thin lips. "Titling me correctly will not make your detainment of me any more righteous, Inspector. And in any case, I prefer to be addressed by my field title, which is colonel."

"Colonel, then." I spread my hands. "I still need your name."

"Lussadh al-Kattan."

I startle—now *that* is a pedigreed family, and not one of the cadet branches either. I may not keep up with mage politics much, but even I have heard of her house, the clan of seers and soothsayers. Perhaps if I had reviewed her file sooner, I'd not have been caught out like this.

Colonel al-Kattan sees my reaction. "Come now, Inspector. Either I'm a prisoner or I am not; my name ought not matter."

Her name most certainly does matter; the right family name is as powerful as any spell—more, even, than a True Name's might. Be wed to the right word, wield the right lineage, and certain doors will open, while others close forever. "You're not a prisoner," I reply, which is truer now than it was fifteen seconds ago. "But the current evidence points to you as responsible for having summoned a succubus that's gone on a killing spree in this area for the last two weeks."

"Ah." She visibly draws a breath, filling her lungs. "This sort of business is always best over tea or coffee. I'd offer you some, but you are an uninvited guest, and I am currently indisposed." Behind her back, she jingles her cuffs slightly. "Well, do I look like a warlock to you?"

"I don't have a specific stereotype in mind for warlocks, Colonel." I don't add that I know *the* warlock. "We are only asking for your cooperation; my subordinates have searched your place and found—"

"They found whatever they wanted to find. It is how Sealing and Containment works; everyone knows this."

I think about a retort, then sigh. She's not wrong; I am aware of how some of my colleagues "find" evidence. They're not paladins; they are not bound by oaths to preserve life and uphold justice. But truth should not taste like this on the tongue, should not fill you with innervating sadness, should not make you think of better days with more honest women in snowier climes.

"You have a prodigious collection of first editions," I finally offer, having stolen a glance at the bookcases in her living room.

Al-Kattan smirks. "Normally there's a caveat attached to that, like 'for a mercenary' or 'through your family's wealth.'"

I look a little harder at the person in front of me, discerning what life path would make one prickle so—a woman of letters who picked up the sword, perhaps, or someone eager to slough off their family's legacy. "There's no reason a personal library ought to earn such backbiting. Have you considered talking to nicer bibliophiles?"

"And this is a remarkably forward way to compel me to join S&C's employee book club."

I laugh; I think the noise surprises both of us. "Give me a reason to let you go, something I can take back to my superiors and say 'Lussadh al-Kattan prefers the title 'Colonel' and also she provided invaluable service.'" I hate myself as I say it. The reasonable member of the heartless bureaucracy: the last refuge of a coward.

She answers with a knowing chuckle. "If anyone from your august organization had asked me, I would have explained that I didn't summon the succubus. Quite the opposite, actually—my company was contracted to deal with the summoner, and matters have gotten out of hand. Not that the reality of a situation has ever impacted S&C's conclusions." She eyes me back. "Wait, *you* are actually here to stop the demon. I'll be damned."

I stay silent, unhappy at having been read so easily and annoyed at the damning assessment of Sealing and Containment's motivations

"Well, this matter seems to be rather pressing for you," she says. "But if I'm to help, I will have to be out of this containment field and out of these cuffs."

The outline of it all is beginning to become clear: a mercenary company hired to deal with a powerful target, a demon summoned—either the reason for the contract, or a last line of defense. "Alright," I say, trying to appear as if I have been convinced, not as if I am making the best of my colleagues' poor,

PROLOGUE

heavy-handed choices. "I think we can work something out. No reason Sealing and Containment can't work with your company."

"We have to be the one that kills the summoner; contract insists."

"If we're in the negotiating phase of this confinement, then…" I hesitate, on the edge of *something*. I have never sought personal aggrandizement from my position, never let this thing I have with Elizaveta interfere with my professional work. But buried in my thoughts is an intuition I cannot shake. I have seen the titles in al-Kattan's personal collection, many rare to the point of singular uniqueness; I know of her travels, and where they have taken her. She is the next lead in my pursuit of Nuawa.

The colonel cocks her head. "This is always the fun part of imprisonment. What can I do for you *personally*, Inspector Fahriye Budak?"

I commit. "I have an original edition of the *Liber Juratus Honorii*, including the chapters redacted from later printings. It's yours, but I need information about an artifact."

Al-Kattan whistles. "You must care about that artifact very much." I don't reply. "Alright, color me intrigued. But demon first, book club later."

Elizaveta picks up the phone on the third ring. "Yes, Inspector?"

She does not press: any headway on the sword? She sounds even, unhurried, glad to be taking a social call if that's what I'm making. Unfortunately, I have something else in mind. "I've got a succubus on the loose."

A few seconds of silence. "A succubus," she repeats. "You could provide a little context."

"Work." Too curt. "That is, I've got a case on my hand. Succubus serial killing."

"Oh, that's the norm. People underestimate how bloodthirsty they are; actually one of the least controllable sort of demons, and prone to draining their summoners dry so the summoner may not exert command. Probably has seized control of its own anchor, and it'll be absorbing magic to become more powerful. What's the body count up to?"

"Eighteen in two weeks." Succubi are a popular choice for apprentices with more libido than sense. Then they discover how wrong they are, and it becomes everyone else's problem.

"She'll be well-fed." Elizaveta's voice makes this sound like she's reading a mild weather report. "The basics still hold, though. Remove whatever anchors her to the world, and she'll be sent scurrying home. What else do you need?"

Guilt gnaws at me. "A magic handwave to make all this go away." I sigh. "If I pull this off, I may have found someone who can help me find the sword, too—she is an al-Kattan."

"A seer?" Then she chuckles, soft. "You're making friends in high society."

"It's not that. We, ah, arrested her as a suspect."

"Her family hasn't demanded her immediate release? They're not without connections."

The exact idea has occurred to me. "She works for a mercenary company."

I can nearly hear Elizaveta sitting up straight. "Lussadh al-Kattan? The prodigal scion?"

"I think so?" I had no idea she was so famous in Elizaveta's stratum. Notorious. Either one.

"She is not just a seer. She is *the* seer, the best talent her family has produced in several generations, with the single flaw that she has not taken up the mantle. Youthful wildness, one supposes." Elizaveta clicks her tongue. "Yes, with her help, you'd be able to track Nuawa for certain. Give me half an hour or so and I'll get back to you."

Exactly thirty minutes later, my desk bursts into flame.

Or rather, black fire has manifested and is etching letters into a piece of paper. Which miraculously survives, once the fire has gone out. What remains behind hurts my eyes to look at. I draw up a protective ward, and that doesn't help much. Under the script is a little message, more normal and less agonizing on the optic nerve: *This is half of her True Name. I trust you will make good use of it, and trust moreover that you will keep yourself safe.*

A True Name, just like that. Well, demons *are* her specialty.

The rest is a matter of locating the succubus: easy, now that I have the

True Name, albeit partial. I don't try to read it aloud—even sounding it out in my brain is painful enough; I don't have the necessary training for this.

I visit the colonel—under house arrest—and let her know that I've tracked the succubus down to a shopping arcade in the heart of the city. "It's convenient when work keeps you close to home," I tell her. "I've got the authority to take you with me."

"Very flattered to be an S&C accessory." Her look turns shrewd. "This branch must have exceedingly good specialists. Succubi aren't easy to find, and here you've managed it in less than forty-eight hours."

"We'd best get going, Colonel." I absolutely do not want this woman to become too inquisitive about me.

It's high noon when we arrive at the arcade, not that the time or amount of sunlight matters when you're hunting a demon. The entry leads to a square beneath a high glass roof, with shops facing inward and walkways overhead. Flowers froth from planters and storefronts—a bridal boutique, a corner cafe, a stationery shop. It's crowded: a long line for the cafe's takeaways, their cronuts evidently being wildly popular.

"If we see her," Lussadh says, voice low in my ear, "I'll be able to tell."

The sight Elizaveta told me about; it really must be extraordinary too, because the seers I've known would need more than a look to tell a disguised demon apart from a human. "A question. Does the succubus know your face?"

"I've not tussled with her yet, so no."

The way she says that. "You've fought demons before."

"Among other things." Her shoulders ripple. "You're one of the few people I've ever met taller than I am. Usually I'm the biggest, most intimidating person in the room."

In all my life, save a period in adolescence when everything was embarrassing, I've never been self-conscious of my size. "I can't tell if you're trying to insult me."

"No, no." She precedes me onto the second floor. "I rather like it."

We mingle with the shoppers and diners, making our way past people carrying bubble tea and egg waffles. The air is fragranced so pleasantly, you'd never think a demon is here. Out of habit I search for the note that does not belong, like the frangipani and citrus in Lussadh's home. In a place like this, though, any scent could emanate from cologne, laundry detergent, cigarette smoke. I have the unmistakable sense that I'm being watched, at that.

A minute after we've walked past a specialty tea shop, the colonel leans close and says, "The tea shop salesgirl, the one with the red ribbon in her hair."

We keep moving, making another circuit of the floor. Already I'm calculating the collateral damage—how many civilians in the shop itself, in the immediate radius. Whether the destruction will leave this building. "You know spells of banishment, I assume."

"After a fashion." She opens her coat, showing me the long knife strapped to her thigh. "Don't worry about it."

The blade had better be extremely enchanted.

Normally we'd clear the civilians out—well, *I* would clear the civilians out; most of my colleagues wouldn't bother. A dozen non-practitioners dead is of little account, and even a handful of dead mages is just another day in the life of an S&C officer. There have been incidents in isolated locations where all civilians were simply wiped out along with whatever we were containing at the time; Mount Nicholson nearly became one of those.

There's no option to declare an emergency and get rid of the crowds here. It might have been better if we had come here near the arcade's closing.

Both of us step into the tea shop. The succubus is one of the two sales girls, with the other preoccupied at the cash register. Lucky us. She swans toward us, ribbons glimmering in her hair like garnets, her mouth glistening like thawing pomegranates. "Can I help you?"

We let her go on about fifty types of tea, tisanes, kombucha, and a breakdown of caffeine content. To her credit, Lussadh is good at it, carrying the small talk—making a good pretense at being a true enthusiast for all things tea—until the other customers have thinned out.

Lussadh gives me a glance. I give her a nod.

Her blade flashes out of its sheath, moving fast. A microsecond in which the succubus widens her eyes and then she's up in the air, her form limned in black light. Porcelain and glass jars roll off and shatter.

I draw my gun. And then I take a deep breath and snap out the succubus' True Name. My lip violently splits.

Incomplete as it is, it only manages to stagger her. But it does buy the colonel enough time to lunge and swipe with the blade—not *at* the demon, but at the empty air around her.

The succubus snarls. The noise burns my eardrums. "You!" she screams at Lussadh. "How did you do that?"

Lussadh grins, reversing her grip on the blade, the tip now pointing upward. Her eyes have gone prismatic, inhumanly bright. "Don't worry about it. Do that again, Inspector."

I open my mouth. The succubus slams into me and carries me into the far wall.

Agony blooms. Claws rake across my chest, across the arms I've brought up to shield my face; I've lost my gun.

In the next moment, something seizes the succubus and hurls her into a shelf of tea. Tins dent and collapse. Shadows blacken the shop, growing, growing...

Blood in my mouth, I manage to yell the True Name a second time.

The colonel strikes at the same instant, her knife clawing at what appears to be nothing, and yet it resists her blade. She keeps at it, her jaw set, leaning into the blow and sawing hard.

My tongue feels like it's about to split. I repeat the succubus' name anyway.

Lussadh's blade cuts through.

The succubus dissolves with a scream. A moment later, the shadow retreats.

"I cut the succubus' anchoring," the colonel explains to me, once we've returned to the privacy of her house and she has given me first aid—she has elixirs and enchanted dressings on hand, and minor restorative spells.

I sprawl on her couch. Quite worse for the wear and exhausted, though she has promised the cut across my chest won't scar. "How is that possible?" Because I know what I saw wasn't conventional banishment.

She tosses me a bloodied ribbon, the one the succubus wore in her hair. "The summoner bound the demon to this, and I…" Lussadh sips from her glass of lavender lemonade, iced and radiating cold. "I shouldn't be telling this to an S&C officer."

Yet she is going to, anyway. "But?"

"I would appreciate it if you can keep this confidential. It's not a fact I publicize." Her smile is thin. "Though some of my relatives know, and they have no doubt bragged here and there, the better to glorify our name and cover up the… never mind. My sight is quite specialized. I'm able to see the usual, past some disguises and glamor, but I can also see the threads that bind an existence, that hold it together."

I rub at my eyes. Tentatively I drink from the cold water she's poured for me—she joked about offering me tea, but I'm not in the mood. "That is not usual." She appears to be suggesting she can nullify all sorts of thaumaturgy. Familiars, demons… celestial beings.

She shrugs. "It isn't."

Left unspoken is the fact that most powerful mages would simply kill Lussadh, were knowledge of her abilities to become widespread—too much uncertainty, too much security risk. For all its fluidity, mage society relies on certain tenets being inviolable.

"Were you the one who threw her off me, too?" I ask.

Lussadh blinks and sets down her tall glass. "No, I thought that was you."

I trust moreover that you will keep yourself safe. It wouldn't be the first time Elizaveta has intervened, and I should find it overbearing. Yet instead I am touched: she has invested so much time, so much care, as no other has ever done for me. And is it so terrible to have someone look out for you? Is it so awful that a mighty warlock, so singular and severe, shows me both her tenderness and her protection?

"Ah," I say slowly, weighing the decision to reciprocate with a secret of my own. "I would appreciate it if you can keep this confidential. It's not a fact I publicize, either. But I have a powerful patron invested in my longevity."

"The fragment of the True Name, too," she murmurs. "It must be nice to have a *powerful patron*. I should get me one of those."

When it becomes obvious I will not elaborate further, the colonel says, "My company will take care of the summoner, per the contract—and it seems only fair, since you bloodied yourself in my place. My subordinates are on it as we speak. Not much to it; they're a minor warlock who probably thought a succubus would provide... something different."

"Right." Just as well. We've successfully contained the succubus, which is the extent of my purview.

"The frangipani and citrus," she goes on, "is just my cologne, by the way. Your colleagues decided it was evidence of demonic rites."

"Ah." I nod, conceding. "That is mortifying."

"You admit aloud your organization isn't infallible. That's the rarest of traits." Lussadh laughs, the timbre rich. "What kind of scent do you like? I think you'd suit something with sandalwood."

"I don't wear any." My eyes drift shut. I *am* completely worn out, even if my injuries have been healed. There are places on me which remain raw and tender, new-made tissue sealing over the old.

"Shame. I should take you shopping for it, or gift you a little something."

My eyes snap back open. "Colonel, are you *flirting* with me?"

Her grin flashes perfect, white teeth. "I was wondering when you'd notice."

"I'm not usually this dense." That comment about my height. Well, it's not as if I have sworn myself in marital pledge to Elizaveta. Except... "Normally, I'd ask if you're free for dinner or lunch, or a drink."

She inclines her head, inviting me to elaborate.

"I'm... seeing someone at the moment." I clear my throat, awkward. "It's complicated."

"Your mysterious patron? Well, never you mind. Your secret is safe with me, but do pass along my thanks. As for our book club—it would have been nicer to handle over dinner, but I will somehow manage." She tops off her lemonade, and with it cools her line of more personal inquiry. "The volume, if you will."

I pass over the cloth satchel I brought with me; Lussadh carefully unwraps it to reveal the *Liber Juratus Honorii*, as promised. She pulls on a pair of gloves next, carefully turns the pages with a set of tweezers; satisfied, she sets it aside. "A remarkable find."

"It was a gift." Lest the colonel conclude my *patron is also* responsible, I elaborate: "I once fought a forest spirit in the Siberian taiga—a menk who I killed again and again, only for it to rise with each new dawn."

Lussadh shifts forward in her seat, eyes bright, genuinely interested. "On campaign, I've tussled with more than one local legend."

"Well, it stayed dead after the third day. The local village was elated, swore up and down that I could have the son or daughter of my choice to take as a bride. Instead, I accepted *that* book as my recompense."

"It is remarkable where lost volumes can be uncovered. There was this one time—well, never mind. If I start talking, I won't stop. The women in my unit tell me that I should have become a professor, believe it or not. Imagine the absurdity."

"You have a sharp eye, and certainly have the voice for it." I am tired; I should never have said something like that.

"And here I thought you were spoken for, Inspector Budak." Another sip of lemonade. "But this volume, the story behind its acquisition—this sounds personal, like it means a lot to you."

"The thing I am hunting means more," I say, too frank.

"About that. Let us see what you want, and what I can answer—if you are satisfied, then I'll take possession of the volume."

From my jacket pocket I pull the shards Elizaveta gave me—wood, twisted metal, the scorched gemstone. "It's a sword of some sort, I am led to believe. These are fragments of its sheath and the reliquary that contained it." A pause. "Does the name Nuawa mean anything to you?"

"I should," Lussadh says, after an unnaturally long and pregnant pause, "ask you to leave and never speak of this again." She stands, picks up the *Liber Juratus Honorii*, and walks it over to a shelf, where she slides it into place: whatever she tells me of the sword is worth this volume.

"The being Nuawa," she begins, "roams free in the world—or at least, some part of it is. A few years ago I encountered an entity of white, ceaseless fire.

My unit and I successfully suppressed it, if only momentarily. I would find out later that other mages, other mercenaries, have encountered this entity too—with increasing frequency over the years, I might add. All agree it is from a realm unknown to us. One told me the Christians would call that world heaven, and Nuawa an angel of the Old Testament."

"Why hasn't anyone reported it to S&C?"

She gives me a look. "So they can be put away in chains, accused of having conjured the thing? No, the places this thing frequents are battlefields, sites of ruin, great bloodlettings—the sorts of charnel houses where law and order have broken down and where none want S&C involved."

A niggle of intuition comes to me. "Is it looking for something?"

"It hunts through the dark places of the earth, shining its light on the strong and the bloodthirsty, promising them endless riches and puissance. Always, it asks the same thing."

My mouth turns dry as I anticipate what Lussadh will say.

"When I fought it, it entreated me thus." Her voice takes on an affected tone: *"Where are the scions of the house of Hua? Bring me to the Huas, and all this world's gold will be yours."*

I begin to understand why this matter is so urgent to Elizaveta. "Has anyone ever taken it up on its offer?"

"And provoke the most powerful woman in the world? In any case, it would seem that none who have accepted its bargain have lived for long—consumed by its fire, no doubt. So it keeps hunting." She comes to my couch, seating herself. I relocate my legs to make room. "But Elizaveta Hua is your patron, yes?"

It's not like I didn't give her the clues; natural that the colonel would put them together, and now this revelation about Nuawa's nature could not have made it more obvious.

I must blanch, or grimace, or do something with my face that isn't emotionless stoicism. But Lussadh doesn't gloat that she has uncovered my life's secret, doesn't give me a coy look. Instead, she relaxes into the couch with a groan, rubbing her temples with one hand. It is, I imagine, the exact reaction a mercenary commander has when she realizes a contract or an obligation is far larger and far more dangerous than she was led to believe.

Eventually she stands back up, rustles around in a cabinet for a decanter of whiskey and two glasses, comes back with a finger for each of us. "The warlock of her age, huh?"

"Yes." I want to say more, that Elizaveta is more than her fame, that she is—complex, exquisite, incomparable. For some reason, I think this woman I just met would understand.

"For how long?" Lussadh's tone is precisely that of an old friend learning her compatriot has been in trouble for far longer than anyone realized.

"Twenty years, give or take. I, uh—in my first year on the job, I saved her children, and we started to see each other on and off."

She smirks at me. "So are you secretly the stepmom to the next generation of Huas?"

I flinch. "No, not at all. We've kept this very secret, even from her family."

"Why?" I stare at her like she has spouted gibberish, trying to parse some alien question. She repeats herself. "Why? If you're keeping it secret at her request, that's one thing. But from her reputation, she's a woman who does what she wants, damn the consequences—and from the little I've interacted with you, I suspect she's respecting your comfort level and your professional obligations."

I think again of our conversation in the ryokan. Of my cowardice, of my inability to face how I feel—about Elizaveta, about Sealing and Containment. About myself, and what I want from my life.

"Have you at least told her you love her?"

"I—that's a remarkably personal question, for someone I just met." I flush red.

"I'm invested in this soap opera now. And—holy shit, you haven't!" She laughs at my misfortune.

"Liz hasn't said it, either!" My blush deepens when I realize I've used the diminutive of Elizaveta's name; tiredness and alcohol are conspiring to loosen my tongue. "Maybe she has her doubts, or maybe she's just using me. I don't know."

"Stupid, useless lesbians, I swear to the gods." The humor dies, and the colonel slips back to a more serious demeanor. "I will give you a list of Nuawa's appearances in the last few years," she says, after a long stare at the spine of her new book. "Will put pins on a map for you, even, and do my best to describe my own encounter with the thing. I don't know whether this is the information you were looking for, but I hope you'll find it worth the trade. And—"

She takes a long, good look at me. "Your personal matters are safe with me. You've treated me fairly and been a true comrade in battle. In all ways, Inspector Budak, you've proven yourself admirable." She downs her drink with a slight flush. "But as your new friend—sort out this matter with Elizaveta Hua. Twenty years is a long time to wait for the next chapter of your life to start."

With this much information, I'd be a sorry excuse for a tracker if I can't find the sword. The entity itself may roam; the sword is a static object. And, by and by, I locate it far beneath the Etchmiadzin Cathedral.

Elizaveta and I meet in another ramen bar, Kyoto this time. We eat, and then stand outside where she erects a veil of secrecy around us.

"Vagharshapat, Armenia," I tell her and hand her the milky quartz. "I assume whatever underground vault where it is kept shall be warded against scrying. This stone will help guide you, like a compass. I will have to get a few days' leave, but it shouldn't be a big deal; I just sorted out a difficult case with a succubus."

She watches the snow drift. "And this creature, it's been out and about. Asking after my family."

"Well, yes. But—"

"If anything happens to me," she says, her tone as calm as ever, "I'd appreciate it if you could look out for my daughters. They're grown, of course, but a parent always worries. Olesya and Viveca are both too proud to ask for help."

"Nothing will happen to you, Elizaveta." Panic pulls at my guts, so I turn toward humor and concrete plans. "So, about the leave. If they give me trouble, I'll just quit."

Elizaveta regards me with a pained look.

I shrug, the most nonchalant way I can express the most momentous decision. "I've done a lot of soul searching these past weeks. Talked with a friend, even. And I realized S&C isn't the place I want to spend the rest of my life. I want—well, we can talk about it once we've dealt with Nuawa. How many days should I ask for?"

"None. I'm going alone." Her hand snaps out, closing around my wrist. "Do not follow me. Do not insist. I bind you, Fahriye Budak; you may not enter the city of Vagharshapat by means of flesh or the etheric, in person or in sending. Should ill fate befall me, you are not to exact vengeance or investigate."

The utterance of a True Name gains power with knowledge, with intimate familiarity. I open my mouth but no sound comes out. The pressure of her geas wraps around my thoughts, noose-tight.

Elizaveta draws close. She kisses me on the mouth, right in the street.

"I'm sorry, Fahriye." Her voice, finally, fractures. "This duty is mine alone to bear: it is a Hua matter, and I'll not have any other risk their life, you least of all. Nor do I want you to squander your life on avenging me. But I will go well-armed. I have every intention of succeeding."

Her hand opens, letting go of my wrist. She draws a deep breath, standing at her full height, and for the first time she does not look commanding or imposing.

"I love you," she says. "Remember that. You, Fahriye, you are the love of my life."

She never comes back.

Her secondborn is the one who delivers the news. Waltzing past all of S&C, right into my office. The same way her mother did, on that day.

I come in to find her standing by the window—my window. Her head twitches my way. "Hello, Inspector."

Viveca Hua is a grown woman now, I register the fact with a distant shock.

Taller than Elizaveta and, like her mother, she wears no apparent symbol of power: her bound demons are not visible at all. Most practitioners don their might ostentatiously, show their familiars as ethereal jewelry or puppets or sharp-toothed birds. Instead, should one pass Viveca in the street, most would believe her an ordinary young woman, if an elegantly dressed one. Blue-black skirt and blouse: the mourning color of her house, someone would later inform me.

"I trust that you have been well," she goes on, because I've been mute.

"Pardon me, Ms. Hua. I was not expecting visitors." Briefly I entertain the thought that she came here with hostile intention. That she learned of her mother's affair with me, and is outraged that Elizaveta Hua would date down. Ever since Elizaveta left me behind in Kyoto, I've been able to think of nothing else but her. And worse, there's a memory gap. I *know* she said something important to me but I can't remember what. A city in Armenia. A forbidden topic.

She meets my eyes. Her gaze is direct, though it lacks the deepening of Elizaveta's. No flash of red that'd signal her pact to some demon, either. "I know something of your association with my mother."

Ah. There it is. I lean against the door, deciding to make myself comfortable; the least I can have for an ugly confrontation. "Yes, Ms. Hua?"

"I think," Viveca goes on, "she was very fond of you. As she was fond of few others. You see, Mother never chose a consort. Even casual partners she didn't bother with."

I have cottoned on to the past tense. But it doesn't mean anything, at first; the possibility does not even occur to me. "Then I should be honored. She is a woman like no other."

Viveca smooths her hand down her skirt. I notice, for the first time, the signs of strain around her eyes, the tension in her jaw. "I am the Hua warlock now, Inspector."

Well, Elizaveta did say she was passing on the mantle soon. "Congratulations."

Her fingers clench around the material of her dress. Her mouth opens and closes, and her body bends; I have the brief, horrifying thought that she is about to cry. "Inspector, my mother is dead."

I make a noise. To her it must sound like I'm choking on my own breath. "That's impossible. She is hardly that old." But already I know Viveca is not saying that her mother expired of advanced age.

A brittle laugh. "It's funny, but that's what I thought too—that it is impossible, that she was immortal. All children think their mothers are immortal, don't they? But I have more reasons than most. We tend to be long-lived; she should have gotten to see her grandchildren and then some. Not really fair, is it, Inspector?"

My hands close and open and close again. "She's... she was..." I swallow. I cannot be a grief-stricken fool before her daughter, who must be mourning her more deeply than I can ever imagine. "Vagharshapat?" Armenia. The details are now returning, and with them comes the recollection of the geas, pressing upon my nerves like a razor blade.

Viveca studies me. "She must have confided much in you, over the years. Yes."

"I am sorry, Ms. Hua. I can't imagine how you must be feeling."

"You can't." Her fingernails graze along the windowpane, with the clear impression that she wants to smash the glass. "I have found who killed my mother, and for this I will make her suffer a thousandfold. The work will be long and difficult, but my sister and I will pursue this enemy to the end of the earth. We're both young; we have time, resources, and the will."

Bitterness swells in my mouth. "The killer, who was it?" It must have been Nuawa, but I cannot manage the name. The compulsion Elizaveta has cursed me with tears at me; to ask even this simple question is like pushing through molasses, like clutching at something with frostbitten fingers.

There is silence. It goes on: it becomes a thing of locust roar, drowning out all else we might have spoken, all else we might have shared. Distantly I can hear the noises from the rest of the offices—the ordinary sounds of paper shuffling, of stationery rolling off desks. The muted pings of phones.

"The killer announced Mother's death," Viveca says, "at a mage ball in Seoul—really ruined the festivities—and tossed me a few pieces of jewelry Mother wore on her person at all times. A lock of her hair. It was drifting all over the place; I had to collect it from the carpet."

Not Nuawa, then. Or someone claiming responsibility for Nuawa's deed. My mind immediately turns to trying to discern which mage it was, who might I... It is no use; my thoughts slip off the idea like it is a surface of smooth glass. This is what Elizaveta wanted for me, how she will force me to be free.

"Before my mother left for a task she wouldn't even tell either of us about," she goes on, oblivious, "she instructed me that, should something befall her, I was not to tell you who or what did it."

All my breath seems to have gone out of me, abandoning my lungs, my arteries. "Why?"

The new warlock of Hua meets my eyes straight on. I wonder what she is feeling: contempt? "She didn't want you to devote your life to this, whatever the ultimate cause of her demise. Her exact words were that you were born on this earth to do good, and she wanted you to be able to focus on that, not throw your time away avenging her."

I swallow past a thread of anger. "I would learn the specifics in any case, Ms. Hua. In time. In days." I say this as much for Viveca as for myself; a threat, a promise that I will break free of this well-intended curse. But already the geas is tumbling through my fingers, twisting my thoughts toward forgetfulness...

"No doubt. It is impossible to hide such news." The angle of her chin becomes imperious. "But rest assured that Olesya and I have this in hand. We will not require outside help."

"Please—"

But she is already gone, spirited away by one of her demons. To brood and fume, to strategize and plan.

I am alone in my office, as alone as I have ever been.

I never got to tell Elizaveta that I loved her.

One: Dull Roots and Spring Rain

Viveca Hua is surprised at how readily she takes to peace, to a life in soft focus.

As the warlock of her age, she has waged relentless combat for ten long years, feints and salients and betrayals most foul—a battle for her family's very survival, pitched against an unspeakable evil of near-endless power, a mage by the name of Cecilie Kristiansen. Her life, since her mother's passing, was one of constant war. In place of planning meals, she formulated strategies; in lieu of courtship, she pursued entities traitorous and eldritch to aid in her campaigns.

Now, Viveca has triumphed: forged new allies, crafted new spells, commanded the power of hell itself to destroy Cecilie completely. Her victory is total, her elder sister restored to health.

And along the way, the best prize of all, she even took a wife.

Viveca never believed herself suited to domesticity; in her entire life, she did not anticipate that she would one day wake in the morning next to a wife (who is sometimes also the sheets, the better to cradle her) and adjourn to the kitchen to cook for them both. She discovers a luminous joy in watching her beloved eat; what simple delights her life has come to consist of, as bright as the pleasure of perfecting a new spell, or even brighter. Once she believed her entire trajectory would be that of a bullet finding a target—soaked in viscera, guided by ambition and fury. Idyll was not for the likes of her, and marriage was a ludicrous prospect. She'd create an heir through occult means, performing the duty of ensuring the next generation; love, or even a partner, was not part of the equation.

ONE: DULL ROOTS AND SPRING RAIN

Then again, her wife is not a simple mortal. Yves Hua—she has taken Viveca's surname, against every infernal custom—is a demon of great age and power, a world-devouring leviathan of smoke and bone that presents to the world as a powerfully built woman in a suit of Stygian black, with eyes that shine like sun-soaked ember and hair that glows with the cinderous fury of a forge. Warlock and demon reached an accord, swore to kill Cecilie Kristiansen together; Yves proved to be not only Viveca's greatest weapon in that struggle, but also her strongest armor, the truest partner Viveca could have gone to war with. Equals, unexpectedly; in each other they found their match in appetite.

And now, together, they chart their newfound peace. Sometimes Yves finds the warlock in her library, translating some esoteric text, and sweeps Viveca to her feet in a spinning dance; other times, Viveca will find her demon—her *wife*—dozing in the sun, and she will curl beside Yves and go to sleep, too. She does this with the knowledge that she will be safe, both due to her own wards and a part of Yves remaining alert. Every other evening, they experiment with cocktails; Yves is a master, and creates new and sparkling concoctions customized to Viveca's tastes.

And these days, Viveca as often as not drafts new contracts in a chair that is Yves, or in Yves' lap outright. She wears her demon as her dress and blouse and trousers, preferring this over the finest tailoring. It is a mark of her power, yes, but it's a mark of her matrimony too, better than any ring. On occasion, the two of them look over fashion magazines together. Yves takes a deep pleasure in draping her warlock in impossible constructions of high collars and drifting ink, in bodices with the glint of galaxies as yet unborn.

The demon teaches her warlock to dance. Sedate, courtly steps; faster rhythms; forms ancient and modern alike. Viveca missteps and stumbles, and she is caught and corrected, laughing all the while in her wife's arms.

There is work to be done, of course. For years, Viveca and her sister Olesya believed their mother's murder was at Cecilie's hand; this belief was at the heart of their war of vengeance. In the end, it was a lie fostered by Cecilie for her own aggrandizement. So now it falls to Viveca to pick at old texts, trying to ferret out the true identity of the enemy that still wishes malice upon the Huas, searching for clues left behind by Elizaveta. She pores over family archives. She tirelessly catalogs what is intact, what is missing.

Yves joins her in these efforts, sending out feelers, searching high and low through her own infernal and otherworldly connections. She trades in unlikely currencies, negotiating through implied threats and promises of future favors.

One fine spring morning, she comes to her warlock with a potential lead. "There is a being of considerable power, who presides over an otherworldly crossroad. Entities of all sorts gather there to strike bargains and play deadly games. One of them is a tournament, where the victor is awarded a handsome prize."

Viveca looks up from her cup of caramel milk tea. "*You're* my handsome prize, but go on."

"Silver-tongued as ever, Ms. Hua. This being has a treasure vault of apocryphal size, and it's said that in her collection is a lost grimoire of power belonging to a certain practitioner, once the warlock of her age."

At this, Viveca sits up straight. "Something that might have the answers we seek. Well then, it's simple: we have to win."

Yves smiles with a knowing hunger, a heat that radiates through them both. "Of course we will. In this, and in all matters, I will ensure your triumph."

Viveca jokes that she is leaving for her second honeymoon—"The benefit of a demon wife," offered with a laugh—but they all know the real reason: she is sojourning beyond the mortal realm to obtain a relic of her mother's.

"I'll be hard to reach for some time, if not impossible," she is telling her sister. They have gathered in Olesya's estate, in the lush garden that Olesya keeps both for her tiger and her alchemist.

Yves nods; she is more corporeal than is her wont, today, solid flesh—or something close to it—rather than smoke of shimmering black with pinpoints of gold for eyes. "We don't expect to linger long, but time moves differently there. Several months could pass in the mortal world before we return."

"You're heading into danger," says Olesya.

The demon's shadow lengthens, lapping at Viveca's ankles. "You need not worry, Ms. Olesya. I'll never let your sister come to harm, not a hair on her head, nor a nail on her hand. Few entities can prevail against me when I am revealed."

Olesya purses her mouth. She knows that to be true, of course; no greater or more loyal armor could exist for Viveca. "Chang'er and I have made you something." She holds out a velvet box.

Viveca opens it to find a pendant, elegantly filigreed, holding a teardrop blue sapphire. "It's gorgeous."

"A little extra protection; activate it and you'll have a barrier that slows the velocity of things around you to zero. You'll be impervious to most projectiles. I know you won't need it, but—"

"Thank you. This will come in useful. You're the finest sorceress around." And then Viveca throws her arms around her sister and says, "I'm proud of you, Olesya."

The firstborn Hua blinks, startled; she is caught—with effort, she swallows back what tastes dangerously like tears. Both sisters know that, for a decade, Olesya has lived in the shadow; that she has, even so, always been the one to tell Viveca, *I am proud of you, sister*. "Well, it better," she says, voice rough. "We poured such work into it."

"And you'll be fine, here?" Viveca is well aware that her house has always been at odds with many clans, and throughout the eons has developed its share of enemies. In her absence, anything could happen.

"I'm a master at negotiating thaumaturge politics. Our family's star is high, and few will openly move against us. My estate is well-fortified; my sentinels are, if I may say so, the best in class." Olesya kisses her sister on the forehead. "It will be fine. Enjoy your adventure, Viveca. Don't worry about me."

She is restored to the fullness of her power, after all: she is astride the world, in total possession of herself and all that she owns. She will blaze, and she will scorch. From henceforward, nothing can touch her and those she loves.

The time of the sorceress is at hand.

High Command convenes in a chamber of jade and gold-veined lazuli. There are twelve seats, five empty. They were once filled, as the remaining members have recently discovered, by a single woman. Bad enough to have been duped in that way, but Cecilie Kristiansen's demise has left behind an enormous vacuum. Nearly half of High Command, gone in one strike—consumed by a parasitic, ravenous mage as much by their own ambition. Worse yet, the foremost instrument of High Command—Sealing and Containment, an organization through which they exerted control over all of magical society, dividing the legal and permissible from the unclean and reviled—was destroyed in the process.

So now the survivors conduct business in the ruins—seven fantastical masks, cool porcelain facade eliding the shared shame of having been taken in so easily by a mage they thought their lesser and tool, but eyes and teeth bared. Things had been too smooth, too effective for some time—the reason is obvious looking back. As a rule, one doesn't seek ultimate power to find a compromise, and those who remain are loath to do so now; the knives are back out.

"The solution is clear: the vacant positions will be inherited within the family, or to a cadet branch if need be, as we have always done."

"Christoff was barren, and two others besides lost their chosen heirs to Cecilie as well. Do you suppose we wait out three pretender-wars, all while at our weakest?"

The Moloch and the Garita snipe at each other, as they have for the majority of the meeting. The rest bide their time, picking sides, changing sides, whispering to one another as they watch the two mages duel with words instead of spells. For now, at least; the tension is fecund with the possibility of violence.

ONE: DULL ROOTS AND SPRING RAIN

The Cynosure steps into the arena with a raised voice. "I'm certain we can promote from within. There are doubtless mages loyal, skilled besides, and committed to the cause. I have just such a list in case of times like these." She's already pulling it from the ether with hands much too soft to have seen real work.

"And have any of these mages *not* worked beneath you? We all know the effect you have on lesser minds," the Garita rebukes. The Cynosure is a known mesmer; her words normally root and blossom like flowers in the minds of her audience. But the Garita is as stone, unaffected by the charms or sighing smiles the other mage wields.

Still, the Cynosure tries. "That's hardly relevant, as I see it. Who among our staff hasn't had to come to me for help? I love all my ducklings equally; you can hardly begrudge me." Her hand reaches out to take the Garita's. A response is immediate, jade arching over the Cynosure's wrist, locking her to the table: the first spell at the meeting. The faint whistling of magic grows louder as each member readies their own retaliation.

The Cynosure laughs it off. "Please! I appreciate you, Garita, but I'd never be so base as to attempt a charm at this hallowed site."

The Garita glowers back at the woman. She is made of sharp lines, drawn with rulers and compasses befitting her name. She's earned this place with hard effort and great skill. The Cynosure next to her is a honeypot, practically spilling out of her dress and dripping with sweetness and spiderwebs, Art Nouveau to the Garita's Brutalism. The jade shackle retreats and the Cynosure rubs her wrist.

"Please, stop flirting and just pick something; I would rather be anywhere else right now," bemoans the Exegesis from her side of the table. She's sat next to the other quiet members of High Command, content until now to simply listen and wait for the others to fight it out. Still, she feigns detachment—blowing over her perfect nails, going back to picking at them with a prehensile razor, a meaningless pastime for a mage of her power.

"Really, we shouldn't be making any decisions without a quorum," the Moloch grumbles behind her mask. "Defined in our bylaws, I might add, as two-thirds of our membership, the number necessary to convene and conduct official business."

"You mean to tell me every order and policy we've passed for the past year, or more, is defunct?" mocks the Exegesis. "We should do a serious review of whether Cecilie Kristiansen contributed one or five bodies to our quorum requirements."

The Moloch is unfazed; law and the crippling enervation of bureaucracy are her demesne. "I'm glad that we are in agreement, Exegesis. If we're to honor this establishment with the respect it deserves, we should cease all business until an investigation is convened, and finished, and then rejoin to resolve every point of uncertain legislation."

"I'll wring your bitch neck before that happens." The Exegesis is on her feet now, suddenly furious, steel heels scraping and marring the jade floor. "This *honored establishment* once got shit done, and I swear—"

"Point of order," the Moloch interrupts, to a growing din of snickers and jeers on both sides. "Threats of any kind are not permitted in the council meeting space."

"That's not a threat. I'll have you in pieces before I spend another weekend listening to us talk ourselves to an early grave. How the Huas would smile on our collective bureaucratic suicide. Us undone, without either of those trollop sisters needing to lift a hand." The Exegesis spits on the floor, to the audible gasps of several members.

"*Please*, Exegesis." The Cynosure smiles across the table as the scent of jasmine begins to emanate from her body, calming. "I understand your frustration with the situation, but we should at least retain our composure and respect for our peers. There's a more constructive way to express your desires."

"You stop that pheromone shit, Cynosure. And I spent gods know how long scheming to get in here, and not once have we made a move; we don't conquer, we don't dominate. If I wanted to butcher weak mages in back alleys, I would have joined S&C as a *foot soldier*. Fuck the quorum, we're the most powerful mages alive." The razor in the Exegesis's hands ripples and blossoms into a dozen needles, drawing blood when she tightens her fist, digging into her own palm. "All this talk distracts us from the real business at hand: what of the *investment*? Where is it? *Why don't we have it?*"

All fall quiet. The subject of the *investment*, as they've taken to calling the hollow husk in question, is a fraught one. Especially embarrassing since they haven't captured her yet: the one survivor of Cecilie's unique curse, and potentially the culmination of all their efforts in manipulating True Names. No one even knows how this person has lived, if "lived" is even the appropriate description; Cecilie's demise killed every other of the hive thaumaturge's puppeteered hosts. The only thing High Command can agree on is that this singular survivor must be found and collected.

"The Exegesis is right," the Garita says, voice booming. "For the purpose of accelerating our capture of the investment, I move to accord the vacant seats of our council to a single mage, until such a time as the issue of inheritance is resolved to the satisfaction of the council."

Several eyes drift to the Moloch, the scorekeeper of the organization. She shakes her head, the edge of her mask glinting with the motion. "Highly irregular, self-defeating. It's solving the problem of quorum with a nuclear strike. It'd be one problem solved, and another created—who would even receive this office?"

Several voices are already clamoring to stake their claim on this new position. The Exegesis groans as the Garita smirks back; a little blood in the water, and all sharks fight anew.

The Cynosure raises her voice above the chorus. "As the head of internal operations for High Command, I would be honored to lead us in this new and frightful—"

"Not *this* again!" The Exegesis still hasn't sat since her previous outcry. Her dress is twisting into a fishnet of braided chains, threatening to lash out. "We're getting nowhere—"

The Cynosure counters with reserved tact. "Who else is there to vote for, that any of us can trust not to consolidate power and stab the rest of us in the back? Without trust, compromise, or love for your colleagues, our goals will give way to an ocean of fire and blood." Flesh ripples at the edge of her dress, the surface fabric shifting, just as much part of the Cynosure as her hair or nails are. "I have always done what is best for this organization," she swears, and means it as a threat.

"Enough of your sanctimony," growls the Exegesis, her eyes burrowing into the Cynosure with lethal intent. Her breathing is uneven; her skin takes on a mercurial shine in patches traveling up and down her tight abdomen. "Maybe this organization *should* die—"

The Garita coughs into her mask. "Do you take that tone when you're each three fingers deep in one another? Or is this purely business?"

The comment draws a sharp laugh from the Cynosure; the Exegesis rolls her eyes, but uses the interruption as an excuse to pull back from the edge. "This organization," she says, turning to the hall, voice cooling and quicksilver stilling, "is trapped in paralysis. It has become the most unwieldy crab bucket in the world, each of us toppling another over and over until we are all hobbled. Our infighting has kept us weak, has depleted our ranks, and it has distracted us from why this council was founded. We are here to achieve nothing less than the mastery of this world, true and total—the oldest and deepest of magics. The power of here-and-now is just a tool toward that end, as are True Names. As is the *investment*. Either we work together—"

And then the unexpected: the sound of shifting stone—the wall parts, without the volition or command of any of the council members, and in steps a woman, tall and masked, sheathed in a dress of platinum silk and coils of power.

The council is silent for a moment. This is an impossible interloper, having found an impossible room, breaching impossible wards. She walks towards the table, pausing to present herself as the Cynosure and Moloch begin to rise.

The Cynosure keeps her distance and her composure, as if speaking to a wild animal: a brittle welcome. "I don't believe we've been introduced, and I see you've brought your own mask. You are an aspirant, perhaps?"

The new woman offers neither bow nor curtsy; she doesn't turn away from the collected mages to even make eye contact. "I am the Melusine, and you, it seems, have a staffing problem."

"Blasphemer!" The Moloch is already stepping around the table, keys and pages clattering in her robes as she approaches the Melusine. She waves a nib-tipped hand at the interloper. "You have not been recognized by this body—you have not the right, nor the invitation to attend, let alone *speak* in the presence of High Command."

The Melusine turns, her body blurring at the edges, and suddenly she is holding the Moloch by the throat. Her wrist twists slowly, stretching the Moloch's neck to one side. "Is that so? And here I thought you were voting on who to hand five of your seats to—I'm offering my candidacy."

The Moloch gurgles an invective and channels a curse through her hand, ink striking out in a blade that would stain as it cuts. The Melusine gives her no chance, throwing the other woman back against the table; the Moloch's many trinkets and bones drop to the ground.

An instant, and the Melusine closes the distance between them—and then brings her fists down on the prone mage, again and again and again: total violence, suddenly and irrevocably unleashed. The Moloch's mask cracks first, and then her teeth, and then her face, blood and bone spilling across the floor even as she tries to pull herself up by the edge of the table. A hand whips out, clawing at a final spell; the Melusine casually, effortlessly, snaps the forearm like a twig, then resumes her pummeling barrage. An eyeball erupts.

The hall falls silent, wincing at the gruesome noises of a very prolonged, very wet death. The Cynosure watches with unnerving intensity, so at odds with her saccharine facade; the Garita coughs and shifts uncomfortably. None moves to aid their supposed ally.

Finally, the Melusine stands to her full height, flush with victory, splattered with brains and bile; what was once the Moloch drips from her raw knuckles. She smiles, breathing hard, and swipes a hand through her hair, forehead smeared and hair coiffed with her victim's blood. Her heel crunches the Moloch's spine.

"If there are no further objections," says the newest member of High Command, teeth white against the gore, "then the ayes have it."

Two: Mandible Memory

???

The first memory that comes back is the one where my partner dies.

Or—no: the first of my memories that returns is the one where we began to forget, the one where we began our years as puppets. A thaumaturge we were meant to capture and execute, and who instead invaded our bodies with the foulest kind of sorcery, the sort Sealing and Containment was created to eradicate.

You will hear stories, after, of how Cecilie Kristiansen infiltrated us and took us apart, in the knowledge perhaps that eventually we'd come for her—or with the knowledge that she could use us against her rivals—but the truth was that she came for us before the other way around; the truth was that High Command made bargains with her, selected officers to bear her gifts. Some willing, some less so.

I don't remember those years. It's only in the aftermath that I began to piece together the basics—how long it lasted, how many officers were turned, what we did under Kristiansen's orders, in the fugue of our insect-thoughts. A hive reporting to its queen.

I remember the buzz of their wings within my blood, whispering within the chambers of my heart; I remember the wriggling of larvae in my ribcage. And, once, they comforted me; once, they made me part of a chorus, the happiest time of my life. The perfect peace, always in the moment, no past or present. The consensus had an answer for everything. It had no place for doubt.

TWO: MANDIBLE MEMORY

This is how my partner died:

In the moment of separation, of Cecilie Kristiansen's death, the hives inside us stopped. They'd been breathing for us, pumping blood for us, integrating into every vital organ. They kept us close to immortal—nearly any damage could be recovered from, as long as we had them in us. And in that single year (or those multiple years: who can tell anymore), perhaps our bodies forgot how to perform their crucial tasks.

I came back to myself screaming, on my knees, disgorging insects from my mouth. Wasps and locusts and moths, plump wet worms, centipedes. They struggled within the wetness of my bile, death throes within the puddles of acid. They'd torn their ways out of me, rupturing through skin, the wounds of their exits seeping lymph.

Vomit and piss and worse clogged the air. My body had voided everything it possibly could.

When I could think—and thoughts were both too fast and too slow, the dusky light too dark and too bright, everything too much—I looked around myself. I couldn't tell where I was. I could barely guess at the time. There was nothing on me except the filthy clothes I wore, and...

A body lay next to me. I couldn't make sense of it; my vision was filled with black blots, my optic nerves violently forced back to human sight when before they must have been wired to compound lenses. My breathing rattled like a dying engine. I groped at the mass, finding under my fingers first fabric—a coat—and then wet pulp. Wet, trembling pulp.

A person. She was still breathing.

My shaking fingers found a face. My vision caught up.

Part of her skull had collapsed. Much of her face was intact: the hard eyes, the thin mouth, the jawline that I loved admiring from the corner of my eye. The face that was everything to me, that was my world. Had been.

I cradled what remained. I started crying, even before her name returned, even before language could coalesce and I could recall what this meant—what *she* meant to me.

I wasn't supposed to survive.

Singapore. Now.

Months on, I haven't healed, not really. S&C is over and that has left me without means, without access to medical attention but what I have lucked into, if I can be said to possess luck. A surgeon found me collapsed in a park, and took me to her apartment after she heard me speak a name, then gave me a diagnosis. She told me, blunt, that I should not be alive: every part of me that governed my craft has been torn apart and rejoined back wrong, and the parts that govern normal organic functions are not much better. My alimentary channels are not as they should be. My senses are askew. Sometimes I can smell and taste; sometimes all I can taste, no matter the food, is bitter soil and crackling chitin.

She treated me as well as she could, informing me that the work of my restoration should be done by a team of doctors, but she was all I got. I can walk. I can see. That is more than most of S&C can say.

Following the news, poring over every piece of information even tangentially related to the destruction of Sealing and Containment, I've tried to make sense of it. I can't. But what I do know is that High Command survived.

I have remained alive, against terrible odds. That must be for a reason, I told myself, and now I've found it. I'm going to track down every member of High Command, and then I'm going to kill them.

The apartment unit looks unassuming, from the outside. Luxurious, part of an incredibly expensive building in an unattainable neighborhood, but ordinary until I feel the wards and security measures emanating from the door. I make quick work of those. Breaking into places was one of my specialties. And sometimes—much as I loathe it—I can draw on the insect hymn still, that consuming force, the hive that acted as Kristiansen's repository of stolen knowledge and powers. It costs me. It raises my gorge. No doubt if I return to the surgeon, she'll inform me as tactlessly as ever that each time I use this thing, it takes a year off my life.

I don't need long. I do not intend to grow old. A body like mine isn't going to last, in any case. In its little remaining time, I shall make of it a blunt force.

The place is one of the properties held by an information broker. I've tried to deal with her directly, but she laughed at the fees I offered, saying I could not possibly afford her. That leaves me with few alternatives. While this isn't her estate, she would have something here. All I need is one of her devices—laptop, tablet, phone. Mages are mundane in that respect, and I know people who can help me crack one of those right open, pry out its secrets; hells, I suspect that in the recesses of my stolen memories, I might even have the power myself. She's not going to have the exact information I want conveniently stored, but I'll have access to her contacts. Worse comes to worst, I'll find something to blackmail her with.

The interior is as well-done as I would expect, varnished wood furniture, deep green stone counters. A home office, locked, but I get through again without much trouble. Were the circumstances different—and were this newfound ability not so loathsome—I can imagine hiring myself out; I'd be in high demand. The thought amuses briefly and then withers.

To my surprise, Maria Ying keeps filing cabinets. Almost quaint: who does that anymore? But I've punctured through her alarms and have made a little extra time for myself, so I spend a few minutes going through the folders. Her areas of interest are wide, and it seems she is keeping track of all sorts of archeological interests. Manuscripts in ancient languages, papers in scripts unknown to any living person, the bones or fossils of this and that, jewelry exhumed from sarcophagi.

One of them is a file on artifacts owned by Cecilie Kristiansen.

I should be taking it and running. Yet I'm transfixed. I have to know. I flip through the neat, ordered papers; my skin twitches and crawls. But none of it makes much sense to me, none of it reveals the key piece. So I grab a slim tablet I find in a drawer, the file itself, and prepare to leave.

A sound of waves breaking against the shore.

I whip around. Too slow. Water closes around me, noosing my throat, and beyond it I see her, the information broker, the siren sorceress. She takes in my face. "Oh, it's *you*. I have to say, Inspector, I never liked Sealing and Containment, and I like what remains of it even less. How you broke through every single one of my wards is anyone's guess, but—" A twitch of her fingers. The salt-tide rises. "I think you're going to fetch a fine price."

DALLAS

Maria Ying is doing well for herself. The glitter with which she has adorned her waiting room is not the tell, nor even the world-class magic wards that defend her growing estate. No—it's the fact that she makes me wait for fifteen minutes.

"Dallas Seidel," she says, all smiles and charm, emerging from a side door in a diaphanous gown the shade of sea foam and probably as light. "How nice of you to come."

"The pleasure," I say, "is all mine." I take her hand with a slight bow. I do not kiss it.

"The pleasure does seem to be yours alone," she replies, offense ghosting through her shimmering voice. "These days, your Huas don't return my calls."

I shrug, as diplomatic as I can be. The truth is, she's right. Viveca and Olesya made common cause with Maria Ying against Cecilie Kristiansen. But Maria is a small person's idea of a big person, too eager and too hungry, and the Hua sisters have better things to do than play dress-up or take tea with the sea witch.

I am only here because I fret. I'm a tiger; I know the danger of young, eager, hungry things. I don't like the idea of Maria growing into her power without at least being aware of what her plans are. So when she sent her calling card and Oleysa rolled her eyes, I volunteered to go in her stead.

"They're very busy these days." I can be placating when I want to be. "As are you, I hear. Information brokerage must be booming."

Now she genuinely smiles. The society mages move within was built over ages, an impenetrable sediment of tradition underfoot, ironclad laws overhead. Cecilie Kristiansen assailed every pillar of that society—in a matter of days, murdered scores of powerful mages in her quest for dominion. But most damning of all, the organization designed to police against the most extreme magical excesses—Sealing and Containment—had been hollowed out from within by her insidious taint. I have no love of cops, no fondness for rules, but what happened to those people is the most gruesome and heinous act I've seen in my centuries of life.

Nature abhors a vacuum, of course. The Huas have grown their demesnes in the aftermath, fortifying themselves; I will not pretend it is out of charity, or even solely defensive pragmatism. Maria, too, has gained a power base; Kristiansen was her master, but who is left to punish her for her past? She now excels in the buying and selling of information—the locations and owners of lost artifacts, mostly, maybe an introduction or recommendation between interested parties. Occasionally, I am told, she traffics in True Names, those weapons of mass destruction in my line of work—dangerous, profitable, and powerful, like all mages desire.

In fact, I think that this is what I am here for—to listen to a sales pitch for this-or-that knickknack, some artifact lost and rediscovered in the chaos of Cecilie Kristiansen's rise and fall. So I am shocked when Maria leads me into a pleasant room of wood floors and rich upholstery, and there in the middle is a *cage*, flanked by two armed guards.

My animal instinct, immediate, is that the cage is for me, that I have been betrayed—that I will be ripped from my life with Olesya the way I came into it, sold into bondage and torn apart for my organs.

And then I see a woman slumped against the bars.

She is disheveled in a way that is more than skin deep—a fundamental unwellness, my sense of smell tells me, a pleasant sandalwood scent rotted through with sickness. I hear her shallow breathing next; see the short hair—white, leached of all color—grown out in unkempt clumps, plastered to sweaty pallor. Behind her closed eyelids, her eyes twitch, as if she is trapped in a vivid nightmare.

"What," I ask in the most measured tone I can manage, "is this?"

"My most recent acquisition—a rat I caught breaking into my files, looking for something I had refused to sell it. The husk of an inspector from Sealing and Containment—not even a person, really, just an interesting anomaly. The only extant fragment of Kristiansen's hivemind, if the corpse in front of you can be said to have *survived*. I know Olesya Hua has her own history with Cecilie's magic, so I thought I would give her right of first refusal."

You mean you don't quite know how to market her, is what I intend to say, handsome smile masking my anger.

"Open the cage," is what actually comes out of my mouth, sharp. I turn to my host, face contorted into a grimace that I hope looks more like a smile. "So that I can check the goods."

Maria nods at one of the guards. "Of course. We drugged it before your arrival. Should be out for hours."

The prisoner is in worse shape up close, though the scent of sandalwood is stronger, too—rich and a little sweet, like the smell of the deep forest I once called home. Her wrists are manacled, the flesh raw underneath where she has struggled. Her face is placid, and her eyes—

Her breathing has not changed and her limbs have not moved, but her eyes are now open; she is staring at me with an unfathomable expression, silent. The browns of her irises are so dark they may as well be black, like an empty night sky peering back at me.

I reposition slightly, so that I am hunched between the prisoner and the guards. "Yes," I call back, not taking my eyes from hers. "She's out alright."

"I've put together a file on the property," Maria calls back, eager to seal the deal. "A record of ownership will be included, and if you plan for it to live, I can arrange branding—"

I tune the sea witch out and focus on the prisoner. I remember what it is like to be on the receiving end of examinations like this—the violation, the helplessness. So I pantomime looking at gums without touching her, hold her gaze while my other hand reaches down and tests the manacles. Warded against cantrips, the myopic focus of mages—it'll take a moment for me to get the feel of it and break them with my own strength.

The prisoner's wrists become incorporeal for just a moment—the stuff of smoke, tendrils of black slipping around the silver of the metal—and then I'm holding *only* the manacles. "Oh," I murmur. "Sh—"

She's around me before I can move, her legs flying up and pinning me between her thighs, then twisting me to the ground. The guards are professionals, I'll give them that: the first already has his gun drawn, and the second—even smarter—is closing the cage back up.

The prisoner doesn't seem to notice she's shot once, twice. She has crushed the man's hand the next moment, slammed him into the bars the moment after that. Where I am on the ground, I see her feet glow with power, icy blue.

"Oh, don't shoot it!" I hear Maria chastise the second guard. "It's magnfi—"

The prisoner leaps, her foot connecting with the cage's door—not the lock, but the hinges. Like her bonds, the cage is also impervious to direct magic. But it's metal, and now it's superchilled; another kick, and the hinges shatters, made brittle from rapid cooling.

"Ah, fuck!" the young sea witch corrects. "Shoot it, shoot it, sho—"

By the time I'm up and out of the cage, it's over. The second guard is down, arm and leg twisted at odd angles. The prisoner has his gun, and Maria is on the floor in a pool of blood.

I raise my hands slowly, all while the woman looks at me, eyes empty—empty, I think, in the way a bottomless well thirsts. Some other place, some other time, I'd like to know what drives the full version of herself, learn what kind of woman she really is. But I have been in her place, more often than I would like; in this moment, she is just a part of herself, her drive and ambitions shrunk to the animal need to escape.

I reach into my pocket—carefully, trying not to earn a bullet myself—and pull out my car keys. "Can you drive shift?"

She cocks her head to the side, as if in thought. "I can *now*," she says, cryptically.

I toss her the keys. "It's a small island, but the car will—"

She's already gone.

Maria groans on the floor, clutching at her arm; evidently, the bullet was not fatal. "Fuck you, Seidel. Why didn't you stop it?"

My cool detachment finally gives way to an anger absolute, a fury the likes of which I have not felt in decades. One long step, and I am kneeling beside the prone woman. My knee finds her throat, applies a telling amount of pressure. "The Huas have more important things to worry about, but you have *my* undivided attention," I growl. "It's a fool who shows the tiger to a cage."

I must put more of myself into my voice than I intended, because Maria goes white with fear. "I didn't—" she starts.

"You *won't*. You'll be out of the flesh trade by noon, or I'll be back by evening for dinner."

I stand, negotiation concluded. Maria will either acquiesce, or run, or die. Hell, maybe all three—I might still come back for the precocious siren. I'm a tiger; I know the danger of young, eager, hungry things.

Which is also why I stoop to pick up the dossier Maria has prepared and with a final snarl tear out and destroy the bill-of-sale she drew up. There's a name on the tab, one I intend to memorize.

I stop at the door, turn back to the still-downed Maria with my most winsome smile. "Oh, the information this Inspector… *Recadat Kongmanee*… asked you for? I want that, too."

Interlude: The Professor

It is Lussadh al-Kattan's last day at Shenzhen University.

Her office holds her academic accomplishments. It contains the august accouterments due any tenured professor at this prestigious institution. Those are not what she will miss.

The plaques from the administration, she considers leaving for the janitorial crew to take out. But it is not their job to receive and process the cold resentment of departing faculty, or at least it shouldn't be; she's seen it enough, in her time. She'll throw them out in a dumpster off-campus.

The conference itineraries—she kept one for each paper she gave, a small concession to her conceit—have begun to fade, as all colored paper does, as all life does. Still, she carefully unpins them, stacks them in their own pile. She doubts she will display them elsewhere; to do so would be to live too much in the past, she thinks. Maybe she should throw them out, too; she does not want to pass away someday, just for those that pillage her estate to find stacks of dross papers, worn, meaningful to ghosts alone.

It is only when she gets to the pictures that she takes genuine care, wrapping the frames in newspapers, packaging them so they do not shift or rattle. There is the one from her time as a mercenary captain, the one she kept for herself and never spoke of to inquisitive undergraduates. A clipping from the student newspaper, a photo of her bloodied at the front of a lecture hall, suit torn and knife in hand, standing triumphant; the attached article breathlessly explains how the Department of Theory and Epistemology's new hire saved her students from a summoned wraith—this one, she used as a cautionary tale for why freshmen should not meddle in rituals beyond their ken.

There are a few others: photos of her towering behind rows of smiling students, clubs that she volunteered to mentor; another student article, about her leading the Theory and Epistemology faculty paintball team to its first-ever victory in its annual competition against its hated foes, the Applied Magecraft faculty team.

(It was eight on one, at the end; she broke the department head's nose when she checked him with the butt of her gun, used a tenured professor as a body-shield when she ran out of ammo, pilfered guns from fallen foes. She spent the night locked in a closet, shaking through the muscle memory, and demurely accepted the censure that she was never to play in the faculty game again.)

And then, finally, the contents of the locked drawer in her desk: notes from students, copies of letters of recommendation she has sent. One kid, the brightest she has ever taught, telling Lussadh that taking her class saved her life. Another letter, thanking the professor for her work behind the scenes to secure another scholarship; it meant he could finish his studies, despite his parents' sudden passing.

(Lussadh never admitted to this, chalked it up to the universe working in mysterious ways. In this case, "the universe" was her politely explaining to the Applied Magecraft's department head that she could break his nose, again.)

These papers—well, she wouldn't mind if this is to be her legacy, the only thing written about her to survive her death. Let the vultures find these scraps of paper; she's proud of what she did for her students—more, she realizes, than anything else in her life. She stops to look at the letters one more time, before tucking them in between the photos—there's more than she remembered; less than there should have been. But she knew what she was about, had helped those she could, and that was as good a life as anyone could have.

In this regard, Sealing and Containment's patronage was a necessary evil: she wrote the reports they requested, performed a little light analysis, and they applied the pressure that kept someone like her employed somewhere like this. But now Sealing and Containment is gone, and she is going, too; pushed out the door by too many administrators with broken noses.

She is organizing her belongings for her imminent removal when her sibling walks into her office.

Immediately she stands. A little social trick, to prevent your unwanted visitor from sitting down and taking up more of your time than they warrant. Nuriya seats emself in the guest's chair nevertheless; ey has never been one to respect the lexicon of courtesy.

"Long time no see, sibling," ey says, as though they are on speaking terms or have just spoken last week, and not more than a decade ago. Ey wears lustrous sable and ermine, and pearls that Lussadh knows to be genuine. Family wealth frittered away, as usual.

"Nuriya."

"Your office is very dusty." A tilt of the elegant head, hair kept close to the skull and glossy as a seal's pelt. "So much old paper. Don't you ever open the window?"

Lussadh remains on her feet. "What do you want?"

Ey affects a sigh. "You're so rude. No asking after my health or that of my children, or our cousins'. Maybe I came here to check on you. See how the prodigal child is doing."

"I'm doing fine." Better than most al-Kattans, if they're to be honest about the fact.

"Still single," Nuriya remarks. "I don't see a pendant. At this rate the family gift is going to die with you."

"Magic is as much discipline as inborn, Nuriya." She's taken on the tone she uses with stubborn undergraduates. "Simply because no one can hone their sight in the last few generations doesn't mean anything will 'die' with me. That each family is famous for a specific ability is a matter of tutelage, access, and—"

Ey holds up eir hand. A clink of bangles. "Please. I know you received... something during your mercenary stint, but not all of us can trudge through warzones and be struck by peculiar spirits. You must be popular with students from upstart families, though, with the way you harp on about how it's hard work and study, how just any outsider who can manage a cantrip will go on to match any pedigreed practitioner in a matter of months."

Nuriya says *upstart* with incredible poison. Ey has always been traditional, even when tradition has ceased to serve em or the family. "People like to be treated like people, sibling, rather than a fungal stain stuck to one's shoe. So will you get to the point or not? I am busy." With stacking books; with putting them in suitcases. Inevitably a few things will be left behind, for lack of space or importance, or simple forgetfulness.

Ey straightens, sobering. "Do you remember Uncle Durgesh? He's been murdered."

Normally, a mage's death—even by murder—is not remarkable. Theirs is a society of sudden violence wedded to intricate, aristocratic customs: the politesse of sanctioned brutality. A little like Roman nobles, in that way. Stabbing one's emperor in broad daylight.

What differentiates the case is that Durgesh was a victim in a line of many: serial killings are somewhat more unusual than duels, than combat over slights and inheritances. And more than that, Uncle Durgesh was a person who'd decided to be a big fish in a small pond—he lived among non-practitioners, wealthy beyond their dreams, triumphing at day-trading and investment portfolios. He patronized arthouse film studios. In other words, he was barely involved in mage politics; he had few enemies, beyond the simple contempt of those who thought he was lying down with dogs. Those, generally, left him alone for fear of catching his fleas.

No motive; no engagement with thaumaturgic disputes; no feuds with cabals or cults. She watches the sending that recorded his final moments—Durgesh had the idea of maintaining a dead person's switch, so that the way he died would be known to his head of family, in this case Nuriya. His final moments were scorched by a being of golden brilliance, the sending blackening at the edges.

He was not the only one. Nuriya has, helpfully, gathered files from the other cases—not all, but most. Eyewitness accounts, when there are

INTERLUDE: THE PROFESSOR

witnesses. The perpetrator is the same every time, but there's little pattern to the victims. Thaumaturges of all disciplines were targeted and taken out. None had enemies in common.

Lussadh prefers obligations that she has chosen, rather than ones thrust upon her by the vagaries of birth. This, though, is different: she must investigate for reasons that have nothing to do with Durgesh being family.

Ten years it has been since she last heard of this entity, if the perpetrator is what she thinks it is.

She regards her apartment, a place she has kept rather bare—the minimum, the essential, because she is so used to being itinerant. A mercenary moves through the world where the campaign calls; permanent residences are for other people. This has lasted longer than most—years, even—but only the campaign is home.

There are more pressing matters than a rumination on how she can live in a place for more than ten years and still feel like she is bivouacking. A being of light—more virulent and more vicious now, seemingly freer than before. In all the world, there's only one woman she can discuss this with.

She makes a call. Maria Ying picks up almost immediately—must have personalized her number with a custom ringtone.

"Professor!" says the sea witch, voice bright the way diamonds are in the sun: meant to dazzle and blind. Voice only, for good reasons. Lussadh can picture her, though, wearing turquoise or pale green, the shades of the sea and its foam. Signature. "I haven't heard from you for *ages*. What a blessing. How have you been?"

"About the same." No point mentioning yet that she's parted ways with Shenzhen University. "And you?"

"Doing well, Professor, doing well. What can I do for you?"

It is not always easy to guess at Maria Ying's allegiances. Up until recently, she was a protege of Cecilie Kristiansen's, a fact that's made Lussadh less than fond of her. In theory, Maria's now a free agent. And an information broker, up and coming. "I'd like to make a line of inquiry about a woman."

Maria rolls a contemplative sound against the roof of her mouth. "I *am* indeed taking clients, and I'd be so happy to be of assistance to my favorite teacher. I shall not be so crass as to discuss fees—this is repayment for an incredible education. Who is it you'd like to know about?"

"Fahriye Budak, formerly of Sealing and Containment."

"Oh." Disappointment that she's asking after something so mundane, perhaps. "That's not hard, but I'd rather have this conversation in person, if you don't mind. Are you busy, Professor? I can come to you."

"Of course. We can catch up. See you soon, Maria."

The advantage of mage appointments is that distance doesn't signify. Maria lives in Hong Kong, but within the hour they're together in a restaurant situated within the Shenzhen Hilton. Chosen as much for the rooftop aesthetic as for the food. Maria loves expensive things, and she is footing the bill. They order dishes that come in absurdly tiny portions: charcoal pumpkin ravioli, Hokkaido scallop, wagyu bolognese. The place is warmly illuminated and decorated, postmodern bamboo screens and black glass.

Lussadh draws up a barrier of secrecy, the habit of any mage conducting business meals in public. Maria has come in a teal skirt and a blouse in duochrome white-blue. Eyeshadow in pale green, an unobtrusive lipstick in peach. She looks put together, professional.

"You don't look a day older, Professor," she says as the waiter puts down the bread basket. Charcoal rolls and rosemary baguette.

"I try not to look like I'm disintegrating." Lussadh keeps her tone dry. Maria is not yet thirty; to her a professor's fifty-two is geriatric.

"Oh, you know that's not what I meant. There were informal student polls about the most attractive faculty mem—"

"Please, I'd like to not hear about that." She is aware that she has a hot chili pepper on her RankMyProfessor.com page; she has considered a targeted memory spell, to strip that precise knowledge from her mind.

The sea witch's grin is impish. "I think a few students wrote, uh, fiction inspired by you of a rather specific nature and genre. It's self-published, but..."

"Let's talk about something else. I do mean it."

"Sorry, sorry. Alright. Fahriye Budak." Maria tears apart the charcoal roll,

INTERLUDE: THE PROFESSOR

buttering it. "I need to ask you first, what do you think of the Huas?"

"Nothing in particular." This comes out a little more defensive than she'd like. That she wrote a report on that family is not widely known; that she has taken a deep academic interest in them seems faintly embarrassing. The thirteenth warlock of Hua did affect her life, in a manner of speaking, but the living ones—two sisters—have not at all. She can afford the luxury of indifference.

"Okay." The sea witch pops the bread in her mouth and chews quickly; she must be famished. "That's helpful."

"What ties does Budak have to the Huas?"

"It's complicated." Maria considers her next words over her appetizer—a creamy seafood soup—and frowns. "She's not their retainer or anything so formal. But she sees herself as their protector, I think."

A final duty to Elizaveta Hua, or something like it. Ten years. Possibly more. Lussadh doesn't know how long the warlock of her age was Fahriye's benefactor. "Will I require the Huas' leave to see her?"

"Nothing like that. I'm just warning you not to be disparaging about warlocks, call them demon-fuckers or something. Are you going to need an introduction?"

"No," says Lussadh. "I will manage. We've actually worked together before."

Three: Fangs for a Siren

RECADAT

I pull into the garage in my borrowed car, a rugged and bulky thing done in black. Probably it is tracked, though I've checked and found nothing either magical or mundane. But I'm not infallible, despite the hoard of stolen knowledge.

My throat is parched as I ascend the stairs—this place has just five floors, no lifts—and when I inhale, I can almost smell my own unwellness, the flare-up that accompanies each expenditure of power I should not have. Phantom wings and forelimbs scrabble at my sternum, carapace scraping under my skin. Intellectually I know it's all gone, that the purge was total. Somatically—

Dr. Orfea Leung has yanked open her door before I can knock. Her expression, as ever, makes me think of snow-capped mountains. Implacable, and just as remote.

"If you've brought trouble my way, Kongmanee, I'm going to kill you where you stand." Her tone is even as she says this.

"I haven't. Probably." I stagger, come perilously close to falling face-first into the glass stand where she keeps her collection of tiny porcelain cups. "Doesn't threatening your patients violate some kind of doctor's oath?"

"I didn't take any." The doctor grabs my arm and shoves me into a sofa. "Who said you could come back here?"

"There's drugs in my system."

"And I am your doctor?" She seizes my chin, her grip iron. Her eyes gleam with a pale light: she is looking not at me but inside me, sweeping over the intricacy of nerves and respiratory paths, perhaps even my neurology. I don't know how far, and how granular, her specialty extends. "Your metabolism is freakish. You will be fine."

"Thank you." It took work not to fight back, not to wrench free of her grip. It's going to take minutes before my pulse calms down.

Orfea gives me a long look. "I'm only doing this because I respected your colleague."

The story, as I know it, is that Thannarat rescued her from someone else's summoning rite gone wrong, a portal held open too wide. Of their relationship I know no further, and I haven't asked. The doctor seems unlikely to take it well, and I'm too raw to guess at the implications. All I can tell for certain is that news of Thannarat's death pierced Orfea Leung like a bullet.

For a time I watch the surgeon make tea; she does not offer me any, though she has grudgingly let me eat out of her fridge. I oscillate between ravenous hunger and having no appetite for days. It's a small place, her home, too confined for two. She resents that I am here, but feels bound by obligation to give me succor. I don't belong, and I'm taking up space she can't afford to share. Most nights I find a spot in some public park. For all intents and purposes, legally I no longer exist, and what assets I have are probably long gone.

"I broke into Maria Ying's place," I say, at length, because she does deserve to know. "The information broker."

"So you did bring trouble." Orfea leans against her kitchen counter, sipping. "Is that because she was Cecilie Kristiansen's apprentice?"

My thoughts judder to a halt. "She was…?"

"I suppose her apprenticeship began during your…" Her expression barely changes. "Fugue state."

Euphemistic and not, it's the kindest way for her to put it. "Then I have to see her again."

"Your encounter with her clearly didn't leave you unscathed."

I'm not about to confess I was captured. "Do you know a—" The name tries to slip away from me; I catch hold, clench it as it might be clenched between mandibles. "Olesya Hua?"

"Recadat," she adds, her voice dropping several degrees in temperature, "what really happened? I need to know who exactly will come calling and accuse me of harboring a fugitive, or a nuisance that set foot in the wrong territory."

The only person who might have tracked me would be that woman who gave me the keys. I can't dismiss the possibility of being scryed, though. "Maria Ying might, yes, but—"

"That's already one person too many. And now you want to ask me about a Hua." The doctor sets down her cup. "*The* Hua, as far as Singapore goes, the other one is in Hong Kong. You're trying to tell me the name doesn't mean anything to you?"

My mouth purses. What I do not say is that there are black, buzzing patches in my memory, that it's a miracle I even remembered Thannarat enough to sob her name at Orfea's feet. I do not say that I am—like the information broker said—a husk.

Perhaps she catches what I'm keeping to myself, and has decided to show mercy. "The Huas are a line of warlocks. The entire family was antithetical to S&C, actually. For this generation, the secondborn is the warlock and the firstborn has pursued other… options. Doing quite well for herself, and not one to cross. Rumor is, she's recently taken up with a weretiger—very old, very dangerous."

"Oh, I must have borrowed the car from the weretiger. I should return it. Where does she live?"

Orfea looks at me as though I've lost my mind. Which I, quite literally, have. "How many death wishes do you harbor?"

I don't have a clear plan. All I know is that this Olesya Hua is a powerful mage and a potential ally, and that the weretiger has treated me with kindness. I've also asked too much of Orfea, put her at potential risk. "I don't think Hua will shoot me on sight. I'm driving a car given to me by the woman she's sleeping with. I'm confident that this will end well."

THREE: FANGS FOR A SIREN

OLESYA

I dream in gold—perfect, radiant, unending. Everything I have ever wanted, I have. I am safe, I am loved, I am powerful.

And when I awake, my day begins in gold.

There's a supreme luxury in waking up on a cold dawn to find yourself wrapped around a creature of gilded coat and furnace heat. My Dallas is beautiful in any form, and it's not a given what I would stir to find. She shifts between both freely, and she has admitted she did not always do that with her human lovers; that she hid the truth of her from many of them. I take pride in being one of the select few.

She gives a low rumble, rubbing her great head against my flank as I get up. I rub her ears. Like velvet, every time, the coat of a healthy tiger. I have seen her filthy and malnourished. It pleases me to notice the signifiers of perfect constitution, the evidence that she gets as much meat as she wants, that I've done right in my maintenance of her.

We shower together. I've had my bathroom expanded to accommodate my beautiful beast—one needs considerable space to clean, dry, and brush a tiger. In this form, she and I use separate products; I've had to learn fast what shampoo and conditioner are good for cats. It's been a delight. Dallas doesn't necessarily ask for it; she luxuriates in the treatment all the same. Occasionally Chang'er will even help; there is so much of Dallas to cover, and even if my alchemist is often prickly toward her metamour when Dallas takes human form, everyone is soft for big cats.

Today, though, it's just me. Dallas may not be a tame housecat, but she'll play the part for my benefit, rolling onto her back so I can lather up her striped belly. When we're done—it is quite a ritual—I kiss the top of her head, and she trots off to patrol the estate. I have my security, but she's better at catching assassins than any of them, her senses more attuned to my safety than any surveillance can provide.

I spend the morning experimenting with ammunition. What I produce these days is not what I extracted from my now-dispelled curse, but I'm working my way toward its replication—this time without the toll exacted on me. It feels both familiar and strange; magic is, to me, muscle memory. As recently as twelve months ago I could not use any without pain, without setting off the poison in my arteries. I resigned myself to that, diminishing myself until I did not use it at all; it was enough to have survived.

It was a lie I only half-believed in. And now, to feel power hum through my marrow again. I have been fortunate. More, perhaps, than the mage-killer deserves.

The only thing—the only one—missing is my alchemist. Chang'er has left to visit her family: one of her sisters is deathly ill, and she means to muster all her skills to cure the woman, or at least ease her passing. Even among mages, flesh does not last forever. But I think of her as I complete the bullets with the reagents she left behind. Most mornings we work together in companionable silence, occasionally our glances meeting; occasionally she smiles. As a girl, I had many ideas of what love would look like, absorbed from fairytales. I did not think it would look like this, the quiet moments, the brushes of fingertips as we work side by side. The kiss I plant on her cheek, and then her mouth; the way she giggles—"Ms. Olesya!"

But she is not here, and will not be for a time. And as much as I miss Chang'er, I am glad for her. She spent a decade by my side, nursing me through a mortal illness, seeing me at my worst. Nothing I ever do for her will make up for that compassion and that love; for ten thousand years, I could wear the ring she forged for me—for us—and never make right what is owed. The least I can do is give her the space to pursue her other passions, her other connections: I hope that my healing means that she may become more herself, too.

So when the door to my workshop opens, it is Dallas who comes through, gloriously naked. Long back and longer legs, composed of sinuous lines. Ours is a mutually beneficial relationship: she loves to sometimes move through the estate without clothes—she is, after all, a tiger—and I love watching the lines of sinew move under her skin.

"You're going to distract me from finishing up all this ammunition," I chide, mock-serious.

"Sorry." She grins, smug. "But I do have something pressing to tell you. I loaned my car to someone the other day. She's just arrived to return it, and I'd like to ask you to not murder her on sight."

I place a hand on her hip. "And why would I do that to start with?"

"She's S&C. Formerly," Dallas adds, "seeing there's no S&C to be part of anymore."

"Fahriye Budak is also formerly of S&C. Cops that have seen the error of their ways are welcome here."

"She's also… formerly of Cecilie Kristiansen."

That makes me straighten up. I make a connection. "This is the woman Maria tried to sell us? You told me the matter was resolved."

"Yes, resolved. Technically." Her voice is cautious; she does not elaborate. "From what Maria said, this woman—Inspector Kongmanee—is the sole survivor among the souls Cecilie consumed."

It should be impossible. I've seen firsthand what Cecilie's insects do to a body. "I'll see her. But you should put on some clothes, for company. Bring her to my personal office."

My estate was in ruins by the time Sealing and Containment was through with it, or rather after we set off the explosions that killed the raiding team. I have rebuilt—after getting rid of the blood curse, I returned to practicing transfiguration and transmutation in full. While I couldn't single-handedly reconstruct the place, I could manage a considerable portion. It helps that the foundations were intact, and most of the architectural material.

Normally I receive guests in the high-ceilinged reception hall, but from what Dallas told me about Recadat Kongmanee, she is not a woman I necessarily wish to make to feel small. My tiger feels, if not kinship with her, then at least sympathy. Through cameras, I watch Dallas usher her toward my office.

Recadat Kongmanee is delicate next to my tiger, and slim to the point where I suspect I'd be able to count her ribs like a ladder's steps. Haggard and white-haired, the looks of someone who rarely eats or sleeps. It reminds me a little of how I found Dallas.

The woman steps closer, and I realize she's no husk.

Nearly I can hear the insect hum, the susurration of diaphanous wings.

The edge of her shadow does not quite correspond to her shape; it bleeds into black lace, or the patterns on a moth's wings.

How did Maria miss it? She of all people should be familiar. But then I have been young too, arrogant and eager to take on the world, to prove that I could make something of myself beyond the role assigned for me.

"Ms. Olesya," says the former inspector as she draws near. Dallas has stepped behind me, standing straight, the stance and position of a bodyguard.

"Please sit, Inspector." Instincts nudge me toward drawing on my defenses. But I simply keep on my smile, professional, in control. "Or would you prefer to be addressed some other way?"

"Recadat is fine." Her hands fold in her lap. I catch her fingers twitching—a nervous tic? A neuropathic issue? She looks at Dallas, then back at me, face empty of emotion. "Thank you for agreeing to see me."

It seems as if she was going to say something more—a self-deprecating aside, perhaps. "Any friend of Dallas' is a friend of mine." Despite her disheveled state and dirty clothes, Recadat doesn't reek. "If anything, I'm surprised you came here. You never worked on any of my... cases, but I do have a reputation."

The blank look on Recadat's face confirms what Dallas told me, drawn from Maria's dossier: that this woman's memory is perforated, a side-effect of Cecilie's invasion and puppeteering. No S&C officer is unfamiliar with Hua notoriety.

I lean forward. "Is there anything I can do for you, Recadat?" What she needs is cutting-edge medical care and therapy both physical and mental, but I suspect that's not why she came here.

A few seconds pass, during which she appears detached from this conversation, as if she hadn't heard me at all. As if she inhabits another space, is elsewhere—within herself or displaced in memories. Then she blinks, and returns. "Do you know of High Command?"

"In my position, I'd have to be very foolish to remain ignorant."

"I had a partner. I remember her name—Thannarat Vutirangsee. I remember part of her face, a jawline I found attractive. I think I found it attractive. Have you ever read a book about yourself and not recognized any of the stories on the page? This is what it is like for me, to remember." Her hand twitches, violent, and then goes very still. "The first memory I made after the bugs was Inspector Vutirangsee—what remained of her—dying in my arms," she continues. I've seen, firsthand, what she must mean by this, the smell and the noise as a body melts from the inside. "But the last memory I made as *myself* was me, trapped in a body that no longer obeyed, listening to members of the High Command discuss how I would be used to subvert Inspector Vutirangsee next."

Dallas shifts beside me, and something must show on my face; Recadat cocks her head, as if confused by our reactions. "Oh, don't worry. I can't remember actually infecting my partner. Not *yet*; the memory will probably kill me when it comes back."

"High Command—" I start.

"Actively worked with Cecilie Kristiansen. So to answer your question, Hua: I'd like the information you have on the identities of High Command, so that I can kill them."

I study her a moment longer. "All on your own," I say dryly. "A single woman against a cabal of mages both powerful and whose names and faces are some of the best-guarded secrets in the world."

"I'm more capable than I look."

Physically, she looks to be on her last legs, whatever her mystical reserves. "My resources are extensive, Recadat, but I'm not omnipotent. When I have lined everything up in a row, I could give you one name or two, at most." Again I feel Dallas tense. I resist the urge to reach out and stroke her until she calms. "Do you know how Cecilie died?"

Her gaze is steady now. It nearly seems like what I saw a minute ago was a figment of my imagination. "In pain, I hope."

"She did much to hurt me and mine. I was one of the people who helped kill her." Though, if one is to be honest, Viveca's demon did the most. But I don't offer up information unprompted, merely give enough to maneuver someone into a position of my preference.

Recadat runs her fingers slowly over her front, searching for some invisible thread. "I think I can... yes. The main part of her was torn out of—" She pauses. "Oh, so *that* is who Maria Ying is. Was. And then her last vestigial backup took on the form of a cockroach and gorged on pesticide. That was the end for her. It *was* in agony."

We were able to confirm Cecilie's complete and total demise, her elimination from this world. I didn't know about the cockroach part—none of us did. For that matter, nobody except us should know about Maria having been the carrying case for Cecilie's phylactery.

I'm looking at something deeply dangerous.

Yet Dallas clearly wants to help her in some way. Love inspires you to virtue; it just as often drives you toward unwise impulses. But, I tell myself, in this case I have perfectly rational reasons too, on both sides of the equation. I make a choice.

"If High Command was working with Cecilie, then they are my enemies," I tell the former inspector. "My home has plenty of space. You're welcome to stay here for the length of our cooperation."

No reaction flashes on the former inspector's face; she remains stoic, nonplussed at this generosity. "I have one more request. There is a veterinarian that has been taking care of me, when and as she can. Her name is Orfea Leung. After Dallas freed me from Maria Ying's captivity, I visited her. Could you please protect her from any reprisals?"

I fix my weretiger with a look. "Freed her? You told me this matter was resolved, *Dallas*." Before she can answer, I pivot back to Recadat. "By all means. As you seem to have, err, *remembered*, Maria is an old friend. We'll smooth this matter over within the hour."

"You should have told her no," Dallas says beside me that night.

"You mean the part where I called Maria up, apologized, and paid her four times the asking price? Is that when I should have said no?"

I curl up tighter beside her. She vibrates, a live wire smoldering with ill-contained energy; I can feel the tension that draws her sinews tight, that turns her supple form into cords of iron. "You know what I mean."

"You're right. I *should* have said no," I grant. "But I *could* not."

My tiger snorts in disbelief.

I reach over and find, in the dark, what I seek, trapped in that primal moment between flight and fight. "I couldn't say no," I clarify, "not when your heart beats like this."

She flinches as if hit. "I—it's not like that."

"Dallas, I don't know what you see in this woman," I say gently, as if pulling thorns from a paw or barbs from a muzzle. "I don't think you know what you see in her. But I think there is something within her that reminds you of yourself—her tragedy, maybe. Her resilience. The absence of humanity. And if Recadat Kongmanee means something to you, then I will keep her close. I'm having Recadat move into one of the guest rooms in the western wing."

She goes rigid, instinct in the face of threat. "She will bring peril to your doorstep."

"And so? It won't be the first time."

"She's dangerous. You've not seen her fight. I think the Inspector can call on the abilities that Kristiansen absorbed. All of them. She escaped her manacles by moving like Yves—*precisely* like Yves." Dallas sits up, emotion heavy in her voice. "And it's killing her! It's like—it's like she's still trapped in a cage, and she's tearing herself apart to get out."

"I know that you cannot stand to see her that way, so I will help," I say. "For my part, I have a great affection for breaking dangerous monsters out of cages. And I know a thing or two about what it means to be trapped in a prison that looks like your body, and to wield a power that is slowly killing you."

I pull myself to her after that, wrap my hands through her black hair, draw her into a kiss. I feel some of her tension bleed into me; her heart slows as mine speeds up to keep pace. The nature of our embrace shifts, sharpening into a ravenous thing, as she grazes my mouth with her teeth. As her hand finds my breast beneath the sheets.

Our lovemaking always involves a little roughhousing. She tries to get on top; I keep her in place with my weight and my knees. The moment I think

I've got her pinned, she bucks and dislodges me. I laugh in mock-surprise as she holds me down and nips at my throat. It's a game: there is no seriousness to our efforts—sometimes she lets me stay on top, sometimes I let her.

She is the first shapeshifter I've taken to bed, and as I have discovered there are certain perks. Her nails grow very sharp as she runs them up my flanks, between my breasts, on the cusp of but not breaking the skin. In arousal, there is a wildness to her scent, something primeval, the breath of antiquity. I play with the fine hairs at the base of her skull, watch some of her head turn gold as she rises above me. What a vision she is, each time I think, how well our bodies fit together—how we have formed ourselves around one another, creating for ourselves a fabric unique to us, apart from the threads wound around her and Yves, or me and Chang'er.

I like the size of her, the way she feels inside me. I shift my body, angle my hips to guide her deep. Her mouth closes on my shoulder as my nails dig into her back; she laps at my blood, sucking at the wound, drawing out every drop before it closes.

Her mouth is still bloody when she kisses me again, letting me taste myself but not quite in the way most lovers do.

We lie clasped in each other's heat, Dallas nuzzling my breasts and murmuring her appreciation for them. Again I draw her to me, laying my hand against her stomach, feeling the taut muscles there. My other hand in the small of her back, moving in little circles until she relaxes, her spine a little less rigid. We drift off together.

In dreams as in waking, I am safe and loved; I am powerful.

Four: A Long Journey to An Uncertain End

FAHRIYE

It's been so long. I miss her still.

Being in this cottage is both worse and better. Better, because Olesya and Chang'er have reconstructed it to the best of their ability—it hardly looks any different, a perfect replication. Worse, because this is where the memories of those stolen moments live, suspended in time. I am haunted; I am a haunting. This place is too raw, for all that the timber is new and all of it is a reproduction. What was burned down is never going to come back. I nurse the architecture like I would nurse a wound.

Her daughters have come by. Before she left for her otherworldly journey, Viveca wished for my help in finding out what truly happened to Elizaveta. I tried to tell her *something*, but my thoughts shifted each time the topic came up, flinching from the pain of memory. I could read Viveca's frustration at my reticence, at how easily my tongue tied. In the end, we spoke of our shared loss obliquely. I made my apologies: "I am sorry I didn't try to stay in your lives."

This generation's greatest warlock laughed, a little sad. "I was young, Inspector, and would have rejected your efforts to either assist or—or be our elder, our aunt. I believed deeply in myself. It's not your fault."

The firstborn, next.

It is something very like agony, to meet Olesya in person: she is a spitting image, albeit taller and more svelte than Elizaveta was. Different sense of style, too, but it's hard not to see her mother in her face or her gestures. Olesya's visits are brief. We talk of the most desultory things. She leaves supplies. Of my relationship with her mother, she never speaks; remains determined, it seems, to never acknowledge it.

Sometimes I patrol the cottage's perimeter, brooding over a sanctuary that no longer exists, watching for danger that never comes. The Scottish coastline can be beautiful at certain, brief times of the year when the gorse and heather brighten the land and the sun deigns to gaze upon this country. For the most part it is gray, craggy and hostile, a meeting between sea and earth that seems tailor-made for tragedy: shipwrecks, dashed hopes, and waterlogged carcasses. I don't know what Elizaveta saw in it. Anonymity, I think. A vacation from mage society. Few practitioners dwell in this area: too savage and adversarial without offering the picturesque beauty of the Arctic, the uniqueness of the Dead Sea or inactive volcanoes. Scotland is miserable in an ordinary way.

There is the quiet. There is the fact I'm left alone. Those things I do appreciate.

My body is stone, tireless: I don't need to sleep, and I don't dream. Little by little, though, the granite has darkened into the umber of my living complexion. The carved metal strands on my head have turned true black. Disconcerting at first to see, as disconcerting as it was when I woke up in this homunculus, my soul drawn into its cradle by Elizaveta's final promise. The emerald eyes are already a match, though they have to descend a few shades before they look natural, and sometimes I wonder if she chose this gem for—

This is what haunts me: if she could create a compact that would relocate my spirit into this construct, why didn't she do the same for herself? The real weight I feel on these shoulders is that idea: that a woman so powerful, so careful, would choose me for this ritual, even as she perished.

She owed me, she felt; told me this, bluntly, in our first conversation, murmured it a few times subsequent. But I think that was an excuse for her, too. I think, with the lonely benefit of hindsight, that I was in fact unique.

FOUR: A LONG JOURNEY TO AN UNCERTAIN END

Perhaps I was the one obligation she found comfort in.

I could dig deep and say I was obliged to her, too; even before she saved my life this final time, she saved me a dozen times before. We did work together, deniably and secretly, to deal with some really awful things. Sealing and Containment's sharp suits and handguns only went so far against, say, an eldritch beast from beyond space and time clawing its way into our dimension to lay eggs that gestate within mage's dreams. I laugh, almost, at the number of times we—

And we are back to the present. No, not we. Just the I. And my question is still the same: that last time, why did she leave for Armenia alone? Family duty, yes, but I would have…

The geas twists that line of thought, forbidding even my own introspection. It suffocates.

I can't inhale in this body because it doesn't breathe. Very useful in specific contexts, absolutely useless when you are trying to regulate your breathing and obtain a measure of calm. The ability to breathe deep and then exhale a modicum of stress is highly underrated by the living.

So I do the next best thing, my coping mechanism for the storm that rages inside me—I manipulate my senses. To be thrust into a new body touched by alien sensations typically happens only the once, and we are so young as to not remember, to not be driven insane with the strangeness. In this regard, I am probably in a more fraught mental state than I appreciate—all the more important to master myself anew, then.

I dull my vision, visualizing the lit emerald of my eyes darkening to a rich evergreen. I imagine the stuff of me as a vital force, a glowing warmth locked inside a stone coffin. And then I push, will myself outward—hold in my mind the idea of a small shoot emerging from barren ground, the tiniest speck of green on a field of brown.

Maybe that is why she chose green for the eyes, I think, and with that thought something loosens inside of me. My senses brighten a little more, the wind on my stone hide feels a little cooler, the air a touch wetter.

And with this increased fidelity, I can tell someone is approaching.

Not long after, a figure comes into view, moving on long legs and longer strides. Tall, though not as tall as I am; muscular, but nowhere near as broad as I am. In the years that passed, she has collected scars—she is older, as am I, more gray in the hair and more grooves in the face. Hale, though, retaining the physique of one who has been much at war.

This is no stranger, and it is not either of the Hua sisters. This is… not someone I expected to meet ever again. Someone I've thought about a great deal, yes, but I believed this link well and completely severed. Retreating into the abstract, an acquaintance that could have flowered into more, once. A missed connection.

We have but one world, and we must make it count, Lussadh al-Kattan wrote, a few years ago. *As the land erodes, so must we; none of our accrued might will save us from the need to plant our feet in the grass, to smell sunlight and get soil under our nails. Magic will not spare us from our natural instincts. All humans are animals.*

The local pub proves to be of little help, which Lussadh can appreciate; she is calling after the hamlet's local patron, and the last time strangers did the same, ruin followed. A glimmer of recognition, a headshake of affected ignorance—the tell-tale signs of closing ranks. She smiles politely and thanks them for their time.

In her old line of work, before the padded elbows and the chalk dust and the faculty meetings, there would have been ways to secure the intelligence she needed. Pointless and unnecessary violence; portents read in spilt blood that could have been more easily asked over tea. But for all her infamy, there were lines she never crossed, tools she never picked up. And this is where that path has led her: no cab to take her further, no trail to follow, instructions unknown—just her wits, an upturned collar, and a walk across the highlands in late spring.

It takes most of the afternoon, which Lussadh doesn't mind. The storms gathering off the coast are magnificent, and the rolling hills a vibrant, healthy green; she has not known peace like this for decades. With this realization comes a pang of guilt—not for the years of stress and lost time, but because she feels as if she is being lazy, that she has an objective and is wasting the resources necessary to achieve it; old military habits, built on a foundation of unhealthy family dynamics. But she breathes and tries to live in the moment.

One last hill, and finally Lussadh spies it—a quaint little cottage, nestled high above the stormy coast, smoke from the chimney whipped away in the rising wind. But she hasn't come all this way for a bucolic Scottish vacation; she'd enter a Calcutta slum or a Hong Kong highrise alike if it meant meeting the woman working out front.

"Fahriye Budak." She announces herself with the woman's name, putting just enough power into her voice that it carries over the worsening weather; when calling on someone who doesn't precisely want to be found, it's only polite to not startle them.

An oak tree of a woman, limbs of stout umber and eyes of leaf green, turns to face Lussadh as she descends; denim is stretched across powerful thighs, and the sleeves of her flannel shirt are rolled back to expose brawny, scarred forearms.

Lussadh makes a show of waving as she approaches, then realizes how unpresentable she is—mud up to her knees, clothes damp from sweat and spring showers. But it's a little too late to whisk away the grime now, and if she had cared about presentation, she'd still be the heir of the al-Kattan line.

Up close, Fahriye is larger than life, just as she was ten years ago—strong and wide where Lussadh is supple. Over her shoulder is a bundle of firewood, bringing it in before the imminent rain, and on her face an unreadable look.

"Professor," says Fahriye, "you've come a long way."

Several things crowd at the tip of her tongue. *You never answered my calls* for one and *It's been ten years, Inspector* for another. But both make her sound… abject. Desperate. Unable to move on, after this long—and what did they ever really have? A little light interrogation, collaboration to hunt a succubus, the intimacy of one hard fight. She has had closer relationships with women she knew longer and thought about less.

Which, on reflection, is actually the problem.

So she settles for, "I'm not a professor anymore. I left Shenzhen University a few days ago."

"Did you? That's a shame." Fahriye has shifted the wood she is carrying so that she can extend a hand. "I've kept up with your publications, though."

It is a concession, of sorts. Lussadh allows herself a faint smile as she clasps the hand of her old—well, passing acquaintance: they were never anything to each other, what might have been nipped in the bud by the presence and then death of a certain warlock. But Fahriye's grip is firm and warm. "Indeed? Got a favorite?"

"'Of This Earth, And No Other.'" A long, hesitant pause. "I was in the area, so I attended when you delivered the paper in Kyoto."

And now something between them thaws: because they have kept track of each other after all, over the years, watching from a distance. Lussadh chuckles and says, "I've been in live combat less harrowing than that cross examination."

"You handled yourself admirably. Anyone who disagreed with you—" Fahriye catches her rising excitement, tamps it down. "You might as well come in. I'll draw some water, and while you clean up I'll prepare dinner."

Lussadh follows the former inspector over the threshold, intuiting as she does that this is an event in and of itself, a great gesture of trust—perhaps hardly earned, after a decade of being apart. And yet.

It's beautifully put together, the cabin, sturdy wood and colorful rugs; a fireplace that is probably unnecessary—the building likely has thaumaturgic climate control, as warm as the occupants please. More roomy than Lussadh expected, a cozy sort of luxury. She wonders if Fahriye owns it.

She gets clean, as invited to, chasing the cold from her limbs with water this close to scalding. The bathroom is finely tiled, the tub claw-footed and antique: another signifier of wealth that makes her wonder all the more.

In the dining room, she emerges to find Fahriye has prepared a charcuterie board, generously heaped with cold cuts, sausages, berries and cubes of cheese—hard and soft, tangy and sweet. Not necessarily the kind of food she's used to, but on the field she was able to eat anything, and this is much preferable to packed rations. A bite into one of the hams and she discovers it's very good indeed: an explosion of salt, of savory richness warmed by smoke. "This is excellent," Lussadh says—where she comes from, it is customary to compliment the host even if they're serving you ashes, and this is far from ashes.

"Locally made. Farm to table and all that. Ethical consumption." Fahriye laughs: the sound has an echo of stone in it, rocks shifting against one another, a shadow of mountains. "If you don't mind me asking, how come you left Shenzhen University?"

"Broken noses. Theirs, not mine," she adds. She has opted to leave out that it's Sealing and Containment's downfall that has killed her tenure. "I'm not worried, though; it's not as if I am impoverished without a professor's salary."

"I do suspect being a mercenary pays better. When I first heard you'd become an academic, I could scarcely believe it. Talk about a career change!" The woman's smile is faint. "But I admired, too, that you had the courage to go for a completely different job—inertia's no joke, most people never shake it off."

It is almost as if, Lussadh marvels, they've kept in contact all this time; as if they have always had this easy relationship, made such easy conversation. But then they haven't begun to broach difficult subjects. Small talk is simple, until it becomes something more. She does wonder, too, if the talk of inertia is about Fahriye herself. S&C is gone now, making the matter of careers moot.

"What have you been up to, then, out on this lonely moor?" It's courteous to ask, but she is genuinely curious.

"Well—not much. I'm in retirement now. Sometimes I help the village out, here and there." An embarrassed shrug. "Carrying foals and such. I'm suited to hard labor. Maybe I should've been a farmer all along."

It is Lussadh's turn to laugh, and she takes the opportunity to glance around the room, looking for books or other signs of habitation. The shelves are mostly empty, save one that is stacked with unorganized volumes, well worn, sheafs of paper held together with twine. She immediately recognizes the author, the same name on each spine.

Fahriye follows her gaze, then bashfully turns away to uselessly putter in the kitchen. "I did say I've kept up with your publications. I've read your *Anabasis* a half dozen times at least. Very cleverly titled, I might add; I love how it is in conversation with Xenophon's…" Again, she draws her excitement up short. "Well, it's about a mercenary company lost in Anatolia. I guess the reference is obvious."

"You would be surprised at how few people actually understood it. Especially among my undergraduates—just what are they teaching kids in college these days? Perhaps I should have been a farmer, too."

"I'm certain I can find Odyssey's winnowing oar somewhere on the beach; we could march inland together until we find a place never troubled by the sea, and with it a measure of peace."

"Points for your classics education, demerits for failing to realize we are on an island, and a rain-soaked one at that." More smiles, comfortable, as if this is the most natural friendship.

Or perhaps they are affably circling the point.

By habit, Lussadh does not circumnavigate. She sails direct and fast, cutting a hard bright line across the waters. In any fight, she leads. But she finds herself hesitating here, wanting to prolong the amicable talk about nothing very much. What luxury it is, what joy. When was the last time she had such good company, when she could so completely relax? And all this, from a single succubus hunt together. What could they have had, if they'd done more side by side?

Except she came here for a reason: a destination must eventually be reached.

"There's been a series of killings," she says, once the cheese and crackers and meats have been polished off.

Fahriye's head twitches, sharp. Old instincts, the S&C officer rearing up; the one *parfait gentil* knight in that organization. "Trying to drag a retired inspector back into solving murders, Professor?"

"For a reason." Lussadh slows down, uncharacteristically inclined to beat around the bush: it will reopen a wound, she thinks. "The victims were killed by a being of golden light."

FOUR: A LONG JOURNEY TO AN UNCERTAIN END

The former inspector stiffens. Her expression flickers, and Lussadh nearly regrets having brought this up—she was right, this is an old injury surfacing to bleed once more. "You are sure of this."

"I can show you the footage." And then a concession as she pulls up the recording: "One of the victims was my uncle."

Fahriye's stoic acquiescence gives way to a grimace as she watches. "You think it's… the thing I was helping someone look for ten years ago?"

"Circumstantially, yes." In the sense that there are few other candidates. "What I can't figure out is the motive, but then—does a thing like that need one? Maybe it's all some convoluted means to eventually get at the Huas. Given your interest, I'd appreciate your company."

Fahriye is unusually quiet, and Lussadh mistakes the silence for contemplation; it takes her a moment to realize the former inspector has curled her hands into fists, has tightened her jaw in apparent pain.

"I understand if you—" Lussadh begins.

"I cannot help you. I *cannot*. I am sorry." A slight relaxing of her posture. "But let us speak in generalities. Magical serial killers have existed before."

Lussadh ignores the awkwardness of Fahriye's mixed reactions and focuses on what the other woman is trying to say. She isn't a detective, but she has both military experience and academic training; she can reason through the facts with the best of them, even Sealing and Containment's vaunted inspector. "No ritualized killings, no harvesting of organs. Bodies are drained of all essence; the attacker could need their power to sustain itself? And there's no apparent connection between the victims—what?"

She's been silenced with a lifted finger, as Fahriye steps quickly from the room to return with a bankers box of meticulously organized files. "Your uncle, your uncle… Durgesh al-Kattan, not big in mage circles, but—*here*." Lussadh is handed a manila file folder with carefully typed sheets; clipped to the front page is a picture of her uncle meeting with none other than Olesya Hua.

"We suspected he contacted Olesya Hua for an unsanctioned assassination, about four years back. He was something of a pariah in the wider magical community, but that would never have stopped Olesya from consorting with him." This, Lussadh recognizes, is said with a touch too much familiarity, but she lets it pass; she also didn't know this about her uncle. "And this other victim, here—he was a small-time mage with one claim to fame: how easily and quickly he could transmute depleted uranium. Useful in—"

"—anti-materiel rounds." Bullets capable of piercing the heaviest conventional armor, the sort of ammunition the world's foremost assassin of mages would need. "Hua might have used him for her munitions. So it really is Nuawa."

"It's two data points, but if I were a betting woman, it would seem like someone is targeting the Huas', particularly Olesya Hua's, old contacts. I can look into the others, if you like. But a being clad in light, killing those aligned with the Huas? It sounds like Nuawa."

"Then help me," Lussadh asks. "Come back with me to Singapore." She says it with a suddenness that takes her by surprise. And then the realization: that she wants this.

After several moments, Fahriye says, "I can't... quite join you in this. But I'll catch up if I can."

Fahriye ducks her head away from Lussadh's probing gaze, grabs a pen and paper to begin writing down a name and address. "Since you're going to Singapore—Dr. Orfea Leung was once a distinguished surgeon; she's now an unlicensed veterinarian. Someone on High Command did her dirty, but didn't want to kill her—just ruined her career, made her wish she was dead. It was because of that, that I and some of the other S&C officers figured we could trust Dr. Leung. We relied on her as an... outside opinion, especially when it came to analyzing magical killings. Open with my name, and she might be willing to lend you her medical knowledge."

"I actually live in Singapore. Still. You know the place—you interrogated me in my foyer." Lussadh realizes this sounds like an awkward come on, so she hurriedly adds, "The teleport commute to Shenzhen was instantaneous, but it got expensive. And the local mage was unreliable; he'd call in sick, and I'd be stuck three thousand kilometers away from class." Then she ventures again, "You're certain about staying here?"

Fahriye flashes a sad smile as she walks to the bookshelf, flips open a small

FOUR: A LONG JOURNEY TO AN UNCERTAIN END

jewelry box, and pulls something out. She folds it into the address before handing it off. "Hold on to this for me, will you?"

Inside the fold, Lussadh finds a cufflink, inlaid with a citrine. She is not one for jewelry, but even she can tell this has been crafted by the finest of smiths, and enchanted by a powerful practitioner. The metal is bright—platinum, she guesses. "This seems expensive. And meaningful to you."

"They're a matched pair. Consider it my guarantee it won't be another decade before we see each other again. Once you find out more, come back."

It is a perplexing confusion of responses: she was certain, just now, that Fahriye would come with her. Still, she has been offered a gift, a token of great significance, and that means something. "Alright. I'll go to Singapore, and with luck I'll bring back some news."

Five: In Raiments of Gold

RECADAT

There's a memory I have, if I dig deep enough, the way I have to go excavating these days like robbing graves. I'm a child—at least I think it's me—and my mother (is she my mother? Her face is an outline, a beehive, a sketch) is telling me, "You can't see that girl again."

Not a child. I'm fourteen. Sixteen. The age is inexact. Early into adolescence, bristling with rebellion, scrabbling toward what I (she?) thought of as adulthood, as maturity. "Why not?"

Mother sighs. The sound is dry, like dead leaves or carapaces crushing underfoot. "Her family doesn't practice, you know that."

(Who was that girl? Did I meet her at school? Did she have long hair, in little braids, or cropped to her chin? What kind of school did I attend; did I wear a uniform? Where were we living?)

"I'm not even of age." I cross my arms. Or the teenager crosses her arms. "It's not like I'm getting engaged."

"Impressions matter, Recadat. What if one day you meet a nice alchemist or diviner and she learns you went out with a non-practitioner once? Look—I'll support you in anything, but…"

It's such a mundane conversation; it doesn't mean anything, it shouldn't be resurfacing. She is hanging up laundry. My other mother is sitting by, drinking tea; a noise of cup on saucer. But when I look at her, she's a mass of glistening fruit-matter, overrun with flies and wasps. Everything crawls and writhes.

FIVE: IN RAIMENTS OF GOLD

Outside the window, a woman is watching us. Laughing, I think, her hand lifted halfway, her knuckles turned to rap on the pane. She alone has recognizable features, a human body; very tall and very blonde, mouth rouged too red. I know who she is. I can't possibly not. Only that can't be right and she can't have been there. This was from so long ago. I wasn't an S&C officer. The bugs hadn't invaded me yet.

I wake in a strange bed, in a strange room. No noise except the HVAC. Even my own heart isn't pounding; Orfea mentioned something about my endocrine system no longer functioning properly—limited adrenaline. It has made me a very calm person.

But the memory and its distortion didn't jolt me to consciousness. If nightmares did that, I'd never get any sleep. Instead it's a certainty that the estate's perimeter has been breached.

Olesya Hua hasn't given me anything yet, no face or identity. But I was in attendance in those meetings with High Command after I'd been made a puppet. I knew, if not their names and appearances, the texture of their power, their emanations.

One of them, or their servant, is here.

I make my way out of the room. The corridor is dimly lit, the moon casting it in monochrome. Near-total quiet. The estate security is one-third human, two-third automatons animated by their mistress' magic—stone constructs, probably part of their family arsenal. I'd have expected demons, but apparently they're serious about only one inheriting the warlock position. The human ones I can evade without difficulty. The automatons are a little trickier, and then there are all the wards.

Still, I find a window conveniently out of their way, and slip it open. Outside, in the lush garden air, my bare feet touch the grass. Nectar and fruits scent the night. Once I'd have found it pleasant; now all I can think of is the sight of probosces sucking them dry, the scuttling of tarsi on tender petals.

There's nothing I can see, at first. But my senses are precise, honed. I kneel and press my fingers into the soil. One of the people *she* absorbed had this affinity for the wilderness, for things that sprout green and bright;

they could glean the land's secrets through roots and pollen. Such a minor ability but she took it all the same—Cecilie Kristiansen was greedy, wanted it all, every little thing that would yield to her a greater mastery over the world.

I find it: a thread of animated quicksilver, winding toward the estate, the serpent in the garden. It will be able to slip under the window, the gate, bypass the protections. But that's not what I'm looking for. The one controlling it is nearby.

The wall is in my way. I inhale and will myself insubstantial—not a state I can sustain for long—and then I'm on the other side.

He's an older man, unusual considering how few practitioners are male, his hand shining with a quicksilver web. The look on his face: sheer surprise, he wasn't supposed to be detectable this far out of the estate perimeter.

The air around him turns to razors. I turn to smoke, and close the distance.

My hand solidifies around his windpipe, my knee in his gut. He goes down under me and the razors dissipate. The quicksilver construct, on its way into the estate proper, is probably dissolving too; a bright smear on the floor.

"High Command," I hiss down at him, "where are they?"

A strand of mercury rears up at me; I fling my hand up in time, and it pierces that instead of my eyeball. The man thrashes and throws me off—I've gotten weak, my mass too light now to properly pin someone down.

I get to my feet, bleeding and cursing, and try to give chase. One of my knees wobbles sideways and I nearly fall face-first to the pavement. All my strength is suddenly gone.

A golden shape darts out of the estate shadows, bearing down the High Command man. It is surgical. It lays its claws against his throat. One of its eyes is on me, a harsh and brilliant green, brighter than any emerald.

Despite myself, I stand captivated. The beast is striking, so much so it seems to blaze in the dark. The bright coat. The cabled muscles. I start moving before I'm aware of it, my throat tight and my thoughts churning with need. Part of this is me, I want to hope, an innate appreciation for beauty and strength. But within me is also that chitinous keen, the overwhelming desire to consume and incorporate. This was the same impulse that saw me trapped in Maria's office, perusing files I did not have time to read—the almost destructive need to know, command, control. Here is the most gorgeous creature I've ever seen, and not only do I admire it, I want it, I want to *become* it...

The tiger swipes its claws across the man's chest. Blood sprays, dark in the muted streetlights, and he screams. The beast rises and, like a sleight of hand, becomes a woman. Her fingers are wet with gore.

"That should stop him from trying anything," she says. "In my experience, mages find it much harder to access their spells and so forth when in great agony. Do you know any way to bind him? One of Olesya's people should be able to get something out of him."

I knew Dallas was a weretiger; I gathered as much from Orfea. But to see it for the first time is still breathtaking. "You're—"

"Born a tiger, yes, not the other way around." She straightens. Her nudity is immediately and instantly distracting. "We can talk about it later."

We turn our captive in to one of Olesya's employees, a healer who wrinkles xer nose and snaps at Dallas, "Do I look like a necromancer? He's half-dead."

"He's just good at bleeding," she counters. "High Command lackey. Olesya will want what he's got."

"I'm going to have the homunculi handle him," xe mutters. "I'm not touching that. What if he's got rabies, Ms. Seidel?"

The healer gets busy. We show ourselves out. I try to keep my eyes on Dallas' hair and shoulders. The latter are not particularly broad but corded tightly with muscles; likewise with her back, her lumbar, her...

A flush creeps up my neck. Doctor Orfea diagnosed me with several physiological deficiencies, but this specific response is evidently intact, and Dallas happens to have a very—

"Sorry about that," she says over her shoulder. "Let's stop by my room so I can put something on."

I bite back a reply. She cannot possibly know—or yes, she does; tiger senses must be much sharper than human ones. I wait at her door, and soon she emerges in a pale green shirt and deep-brown trousers. Quality tailoring, I can tell from the way they fit, even if she put them on haphazardly. She looks good, if not quite as stunning as her tiger-self.

"Can you cook?"

That I did not expect. "What?"

Dallas nods down the corridor. "Kitchen's well-stocked, but I can't cook. Don't really need to. So if you want anything…"

She eats her meals raw, she means. The thought of her red-muzzled arrows through me with startling force.

The kitchen is all stone counters and aisles, the appliances immaculate. The fridge and freezer have it all—fresh produce, eggs, cheese, an unnerving quantity of meat in solid slabs—and the cabinets likewise. Several types of noodles and pasta, at least three kinds of rice, a ridiculous assortment of condiments and spices. I stare at everything for a few minutes before settling for one of the instant noodle packets—and even those are the pricier kind, convoluted by five flavor sachets each.

She watches me make the noodle as if assessing whether I'm fit for civilization; she does not comment on my choice.

For once I can taste something. The soup is peppery, very salty, a hint of bone broth. The noodle is springy, textured just right. I'm not hungry, but I know my body needs it.

"Olesya will probably offer you a new wardrobe when she's awake," Dallas says. "She likes to dress women up."

"I'm not moving in here permanently." I set down the bowl. "She'd be wasting clothes on a dead woman walking."

Something flickers through her expression. "You're not dead yet, Recadat."

"I will soon be. I'm taking High Command down with me."

Her mouth tightens into a thin line. Then, "You'll still need a change of clothes. If you're comfortable with that, let Olesya handle it. I'm going to wake her."

Dallas' absence is immediately felt. I suddenly cannot tolerate being alone. Was I always like this? I can't remember. I spent so much time with

Thannarat, didn't I? We were something to each other, I'm sure of that. She was—I was—

Wings flutter in my ribcage. Bile rises in my throat. I keep what I've just eaten down, but barely. I drink water as if I've just come out of a desert.

A homunculus comes along shortly, bowing to me. It's a slender thing, white stone all over, the face carved into fine features and the eyes bright emeralds. I wonder if that's an intentional tribute to Dallas.

Olesya Hua sees me, once more, in her office. But where she was the very picture of mage aristocracy before—a woman of pedigree and expensive tailoring and exquisite cosmetics—she's now wearing a thick, fluffy robe. Her hair is mussed and there's a particular scent to her, the warm perfume of a woman freshly roused from sleep.

She catches me staring. "My apologies for not greeting you with a full face of makeup," she says. "Circumstances seem too pressing for me to take the time to change into something nicer."

"It is no matter," I lie, and focus instead on her eyes; it is almost as grave a mistake. As with Dallas, my body again betrays me; as if to demonstrate that there is no part of my life that I have mastery of, warmth stains my cheeks. Cold and clinical one moment, a lusting teenager the next. What is wrong with me? I tear at the knots of embarrassment that tie my tongue. "The man from High Command—what of him?"

"My healer will have the contents of his brain in a bowl by morning. Have you heard of haruspices? They divine meanings, gods' messages, from animal entrails. Old forest magic. Xe does something like that, but a little more directly. Cognition isn't exactly stored in the intestines, so xe works with cerebral matter."

"Oh. I thought xe was a healer."

"Among other things." She straightens. The robe slides off one shoulder. "Why don't we do something to make your stay here more comfortable? Do you have any change of clothes?"

The sight of her shoulder, pale and rounded, enthralls me. I wrench my attention away. "No." I don't tell her how completely impoverished I am, that I don't have a single currency to my name.

"Hmm." Olesya stands—she is taller than me—and opens what appears to be a filing cabinet. She fetches from it not folders but several bolts of fabric, and piles them onto her desk. "These ones are for shirts, these for jackets. Pick colors you like."

I demonstrate my lack of imagination by pointing to black and white. She snorts—"I forgot you were in S&C"—but goes along with my picks. Then she smooths out those bolts, measuring out the length with an eye on me, approximating my proportions perhaps. I reckon she means to send them to a tailor in the morning when she levitates the fabrics and begins, on the spot, to rapidly construct a shirt from the white, a jacket from the black.

At a glance, this seems like the most minor sort of magic compared to conjuring flame from thin air, to summoning demons or leveling a city block. But I know, from either my education or the remains of the hive, that this is transfiguration of the most refined sort. It is precise work. It demonstrates control as fine as Doctor Leung's. And I realize, then, that my hunger for Olesya was never my own, not a natural consequence of her elegance. The hive could sense her ability before I could, and it is voracious. For Dallas. For Olesya Hua.

"Hua," I manage. My hand finds and clutches the table for support; my nails dig deep into the lacquered wood like claws on flesh, rending the surface with inhuman strength and inhuman need. I watch the cloth twist, flowing into impossibly perfect shapes, unseamed. I appreciate that I am seeing more than any mortal can, more than Olesya herself can. I'll cherish this power more, *deserve* it more. With it, I will be ever-more complete, that much closer to my own perfected, unseamed shape. "You need to kill me."

She doesn't even turn around, instead begins to lift another bolt; pants now, it seems. The shoulder of her robe has slipped lower, and I see her back muscles in effort, taut and magnificent. "Now why would I do that?"

"I covet," I grind out through a clenched jaw. "The thing that is talking to you is just a mask over a ravenous hunger. The basest envy that drove Kristiansen has outlived her, and lives inside me, and *is* me." I imagine my feet as roots, or rods of iron, or anchors of impossible weight, and still it is not enough; my shadow twists forward, against the light, bristling with antennae.

"How," Olesya Hua replies, "do you think I felt, when I first saw Dallas?" Only now does she look at me, eyes alight with power—like embers, I think, and my unnatural appetite for her magic is checked by a far more human lust, one need warring with another. "Do you think my heart and my needs to be the tepid sort? Do you think I chastely watched her from afar, courted her surreptitiously?"

She takes a step toward me, and I yank myself away, preserving the distance between us. Before I can beg her to stop, the sorceress raises a hand, and I feel her magic begin to wrap around me, lines of golden energy threading through my clothes.

"And Dallas is a tiger," she continues. I can retreat no further, magic and light lashing me in place; the sorceress draws nearer. "You must have seen the passions that drive her—can you imagine how she must feel, her jaw at my throat?"

She is in arm's reach when the magic light begins to fade; I am now clothed in the suit that she crafted for me. She pauses, face scrunched in thought, and extends a hand to adjust my tie. I feel the weight of her touch, the pinch of the knot into my neck. The chitinous scream has grown softer, drowned out with a different kind of hunger, more human and more bestial both.

"I am very aware of what you think you are, Inspector. I am far more interested in watching you discover *who* you really are." She snaps her fingers, and the walls of the room become glass. "Shall we look together?"

I can't answer that question; I reply with my own. "Why would you—" Go through with all this. "Why did you let me into your estate to begin with?"

"Cecilie Kristiansen has done much to harm me and mine, I told you that. What I didn't tell you was that she harmed me, personally; that she created a curse which poisoned me for years—one I believed would be my doom, and which would end my life in a decade or two; which struck me with killing agony every time I used magic…" Her hand alights on my shoulder. "Do you know what it is to be a mage and yet unable to perform the sorcery that is in your veins, that is your birthright? To do what you've seen here, it's natural to me. And for a very long time I couldn't so much as light a candle with my mind."

At this proximity it becomes impossible to ignore her scent or the swell of breasts framed by her robe. The robe that is doing a very poor job of its intended purposes. "I think… I think I understand." That we share this common ground, of having been torn open and twisted by Cecilie Kristiansen. I pull her robe up and tighten its sash. "I'm sorry. This is just very distracting."

Olesya laughs. The sound reaches deep inside me and, almost completely, tamps down the insect hum. "Flatterer. Well, turn around and see if you like what I've done."

I do, her hand in the small of my back, a little possessive; not that I mind. What looks back at me isn't markedly different, but there is something to being dressed properly again, in not looking like I'd just crawled out of the sewers. The simple dignity of clothing that fits, clothing that's been designed to make me look good. I take a deep breath. I let it out. I feel a little more human.

"You want to take High Command down with you." She tucks a strand of my hair behind my ear. "Once I thought I was as good as a corpse, too, and in the end—well, it took a lot, but it showed me that nothing's truly impossible. You don't have to live in defeat, Recadat. We can take High Command down *together*, and we'll live to tell the tale too."

"Thank you." My voice is thick. "I will try."

Six: The Tiger and Her Stripes

DALLAS

I am watching Olesya vivisect Recadat.

Recadat lies on her stomach, sharply conscious; she refused to be put under. My mate makes incisions into her back close to the spine, where apparently most of the physical vestiges of Kristiansen's foulness might remain. Blood beads. The smell of it fills the chamber, sweet, chased with bitterness—the kind that I would normally associate with terrible sickness. The kind that I once scented from Olesya's own veins.

Each cut does not provoke a reaction. Our guest is utterly still, her gaze clear. It holds mine. She is watching me watching her, waiting perhaps for a tiger's thirst, for my teeth to lengthen and something in my eyes to change. But I've had long practice at restraint in the face of fresh blood, and in any case Olesya intones under her breath with each incision, slowing the flow of blood, holding it in abeyance. She is practiced in her art, one hard-earned to stem the tide of her own sickness.

To all appearances, Recadat is feeling nothing—she refused anesthetics too—and it makes me think of the defining trait in human hierarchy. Those like me, not entirely human or never having been human in the first place, tend to believe they brutalize us because they believe themselves superior: a species cleverer, more skilled at sorcery, faster at propagating and thus more deserving to be the apex predator. But the real core of the premise is that they believe themselves alone capable of pain; that they, and only they, can *feel*. Even among themselves, this forms the pillar of conflict, the seed of war and division.

And so, it occurs to me, Recadat does not see *herself* as human. Perhaps an ability in her arsenal has allowed her to deaden her nerves. Perhaps her very condition precludes pain. Either way, she no longer believes herself part of her own kind, deserving of dignity and kind treatment.

Olesya sweeps her hand over skin where she's sliced with her scalpel, delved with her forceps. Each spot closes. Becomes, almost, bloodless. But even mages cannot erase the scent of it entirely, cannot command the substance of vitality to disappear.

"There's nothing there," she says at length, taking off her stained gloves. "Every parasite has been expunged. I looked at all the places they'd usually be hiding, and we've already scanned your skull—nothing around the brainstem. Your luck, since I'm not exactly a neurosurgeon."

Recadat has gotten up from the operating table, her upper half naked; she is no more self-conscious about it than I am. "You're very good, Ms. Hua," she says.

"Master Hua, if I were a snob," Olesya says, amused. "Some mages are particular about such titles."

Recadat appears to consider the question seriously for a few seconds before she says, "That'd seem to be good manners, yes. I don't remember if I was taught them. The hive—Kristiansen's repository—didn't keep anything from my earlier life. Or it kept some but I can't access it anymore. So I couldn't tell you what my mother's name was, or what she looked like, or what she taught me."

Olesya stares at her for a second before saying, "Your situation is unique. I'm sorry I don't practice the sort of specialty necessary to restore your memory."

"It's kind of you to think of that."

"It is basic decency," says my sorceress. "I'm going to clean up here and prepare for today's work, and then we'll see about making you a dress."

Once we are in the corridor, Recadat turns to me with a bemused look. "Why a dress?"

"I wouldn't know. She's offered me the same; maybe she's tired of seeing us trot about in suits." I make an expansive gesture. "Some women aren't made to be understood. How are you feeling?"

"The same as before I went into that room." She does not elaborate but I can hear what she means: that she feels nothing. "You must have work to do. Don't let me take up more of your time than I already have."

"Sending me away, are we?" I keep my tone light. The tension between us is so close to the surface I can nearly touch it, smell it, taste it on the tip of my tongue. Her lust is easy to parse—she will not be the first human woman to express it, to find in the beast-glimpse not revulsion but attraction. The rest of her is harder to decipher, to categorize. "Cats are notoriously lazy; it's not as if Olesya has assigned me chores. But as it happens, I earn my keep on occasion. Would you like to come with me?"

She, almost, smiles. "Of course. Maybe I'll be educated by your example and earn my keep too."

◆

The truth is that we don't have to earn our keep: the Huas are very rich. They have fallen on hard times before, in their long history, but Olesya's grandmother and mother did well for themselves, raising and expanding the family fortunes. My sorceress has built on her inheritance through her assassination contracts; she could take in a dozen more strays without a dent to her coffers. Once, Chang'er was one such, a young graduate of little means and less pedigree, shunned for both facts at the beginning of her career. Olesya gave her employment and a home. "An investment," she might say, if pressed too strongly on the subject, but I've seen her blush and glance away; she is ruthless in business, yet far more generous in other arenas than she would like to admit.

It is an hour after the vivisection, and I come to a spot in the corridor that answers only to those Olesya has designated. I touch it and step into the wall. We squeeze into the narrow passageway, and soon come to the perch where Olesya's snipers are usually stationed. Not as often lately; she's able to defend herself these days, and I have watched her turn a person's bones to paper, transmute blood to springwater. Her methods can be entirely bloodless yet grotesquely fatal.

At the moment she is meeting with an old woman and a retinue of bodyguards. Discussing a deal for ammunition, the new generation Olesya's been developing with Chang'er; not as potent as the old bullets, the ones that drew their power from her own poisoned blood. But this new iteration, she more readily sells, and buyers have come calling.

"I came from an upstart family," Recadat says suddenly. "We've been mages for two, three generations. It made my mother very... she would have wanted to please Olesya Hua, to be seen by her, to be thought of as an equal."

"I thought you didn't remember her."

"Not her name. Not her face. But her desperation, yes, and the way I felt something very like contempt for it." She puts her hand up against the transparent barrier that lets us monitor Olesya's meeting. "I joined S&C because it precluded being in high society, unless you climbed very far up the ranks. Which I wasn't going to, on account of the upstart issue, but it'd still be dignified work. Purposeful. My mother couldn't complain."

I watch the old woman, an invoker from Spain or so; she has not yet offered a threat, and the negotiations seem to be going well. Nevertheless I keep an eye on the situation. "Your mother, is she still around?"

"No idea. The problem with having nothing to go on. I don't even know where she lives. Lived." Her breath fogs up the barrier, but it absorbs that quickly. "I don't remember where I lived as a kid. Where I went to school. Where I did anything."

Briefly I imagine what it'd be like to forget the jungle I carry with me everywhere, sealed behind my aorta. Olesya says she can scent it on me still.

"Did she tell you that I threatened her?"

"Who?" I say, keeping my voice light, knowing perfectly who she means.

"Olesya. Your..." Recadat casts for the right terminology.

"Mate," I supply. "Well, Olesya doesn't react well to being threatened, and you're still her guest. How would you offer a threat to a sorceress of her might and ingenuity?"

SIX: THE TIGER AND HER STRIPES

"You don't understand. I could—what I have—it could overpower her. Can. Easily. No mage has been able to withstand it, I have the memories…"

"If that is so, when Kristiansen was on her rampage, why didn't she take down the Huas? It would have been easy for her, yes?"

Recadat stares at me, at a loss. "Well—maybe it was timing, maybe…"

"I think," I tell her gently, "those were Kristiansen's excuses. Didn't strike me as a patient woman."

She blinks, then frowns and turns her attention back to the meeting. The negotiations end uneventfully—which is, I take it, a success. Olesya has offered to include me in the business side of her dealings, but I have little head for spreadsheets or the nuances of contracts. They remind me too much of snares. She has asked me, quite seriously, whether I need anything to fill my time. I told her no: has she ever kept a cat? We don't get bored, not really—existence itself satisfies, and it isn't as if I had books to read when I was in the jungle. Less glamorously, I sleep a good deal more than she does.

Recadat leaves to the estate's healer-haruspex for another examination. I return to the garden, which is not a jungle but it is green enough, and sometimes there are birds to watch. There are still places in the world thick with foliage and dense with green shadows, mangroves lining riverbanks and small prey darting through the shrubs. I have tried to make a home in very nearly all of them, and each time found that they dwindle year by year, the bounds narrowing first in meters then in kilometers. Yes, I could have attempted to defend them, but I'm a single tiger. My kind was few in number; those who found their way to a different shape, a more complicated mind, are rarer still. Easier to locate each other these days. Too late, though.

I lower myself to the earth, in a circle of sunlight, and breathe in the garden. Orchids of various sorts, some muted and others cloying. Mangos and starfruits. Grass that has been permitted to grow wild for my benefit, the blades rising so high that they could hide my first self. Between Yves and me, I was always the one who gravitated most to humans; I was the one who wept over the short lease they had on life, and also the one sure that I could love them truly and completely.

An irony: it was free-falling into Olesya's orbit that planted the seed of doubt. This fast, this deeply. There had to be something wrong with it, there had to be a question, when before I loved very simply. At one point I nearly wanted to flee from her estate, to never be seen again, to prove Yves right. But it was a passing panic. The doubt went. Here I remain.

I hear Olesya coming, but I let her surprise me. She sits down, nearly as soundless as sunlight, and wraps her arms around my waist. "And how are you, my tiger?"

I turn to bury my nose in her throat. There's the natural whiff of her skin but, stronger than that, the blood that lies so close to the surface—the carotid's percussion gives off an aroma all its own. "I thought you'd be busy wrapping up those contracts, or looking to see what came out of that High Command minion."

"Since when have I allowed contracts to come before you? And the minion must've carried a killswitch to wipe his brain clean. There was not a single thing of use; can't even remember his name." Her hand moves to my belt buckle. Tugs, light but insistent. "I have something else on my mind."

"A little public." I show her my teeth.

"Oh, as if you care? And this is my estate. It is, quite literally, private property."

"Someone might see," I murmur, but it's not a real protest—my token appeal to propriety is part of our play. Tigers do not care for such things, and she knows it too. The belt comes loose and the trousers likewise, and soon she holds the length of me in her hand. Her grip is firm and slow and practiced.

On occasion, the garden—this proximity to the primal breaths of orchids—moves me to aggression. It does that now. I capture her mouth the way warlords of old might capture territory: I spell out with tongue and teeth that I have laid claim. I wind my fingers into her hair, undoing the high neat bun, taking handfuls into my fist. Not rough; I know what she likes, where her limits lie.

I lay her down in the flowers. I take my time, lifting her skirt centimeter by centimeter, thrilling as I do to the revelation of her skin. My kisses begin at her ankle, climbing up and up until I reach her thigh, where I breathe in the musk of arousal, the salt of sweat, the base notes that make up Olesya. Every woman has her own complexity. My tongue brushes across skin and the taste of her goes through me like an arrow, seizing control of every nerve. Self-discipline becomes suddenly difficult. The carnivore's instincts are always barely, barely held at bay. Recadat isn't the only one on these grounds who wants to devour the sorceress of Hua.

My teeth nick her flesh. Blood beads. The world narrows down to the spectacle of its wine-drop. The compass of my senses points to her and only her. I affix my mouth to the wound I've made. The tip of my tongue, to initiate myself once more into her mysteries. And then I latch on, avaricious; above me she makes a sound and convulses.

There is nothing like the taste of her.

Each time I must hold myself at the exact, precise boundary of limit; to hone and control my hunger. Each time there is the risk that I will maul her and consume her whole. She knows it too—it's a dangerous game we play, for her to permit me to pierce and sip from her, and yet we return to it again and again. Together we walk this hairsbreadth, come this close to the lightning strike, the point of no return.

This time I'm able to hold back. This time I draw away from her, satiated, crimson-mawed.

"My tiger," says Olesya, and the flowers begin to move around us. The stems and leaves and blossoms knit into ropes, and slither over my limbs.

I grin down at her, my teeth bright with her blood. "A little garden bondage, my sorceress?"

"Wild beasts need to be restrained." Olesya draws herself up, pushing against me; the plants, animated by her, grow thicker. She kisses my mouth, unbuttoning my shirt. "You've had your fill. It's my turn."

"Your blood comes at such a high price." I'm held in place, half-suspended by the strength of her magic. Much as I'd love to take my teeth to her breasts, I'm not quite able to. Instead I let her have her way, taking a nipple into her mouth, one hand snaking between my legs.

It's not as if her blood hasn't already driven me to a hard, engorged ache. She makes me wait, though, teasing and circling and tonguing. I strain against my bonds, but they hold me tight.

My arousal is near-unbearable when she at last grasps me, guiding me into her, centimeter by agonizing centimeter. Until finally, finally I'm sheathed deep in her, enclosed in her warmth, consumed by it.

She rides me as I'm held in place by the flowers of her will. Relentless, voracious, as though her body could swallow mine up, turn me into material for itself; make of my tiger-flesh and tiger-soul its scaffolding, the fluids of its marrow. Olesya buries her teeth in my throat—payback, fang for fang.

I love her more than anything in the world. I lust for her more than anything alive.

We sprawl and loll among the flowers, looking for all the world like the idyll of frolicking lovers, something to capture on a portrait. "You should hire someone to paint us this way," I say, winding my calf with hers.

"Exhibitionist." She pulls me close, lowers her voice. "Actually, someone was watching us. Didn't you notice?"

"I was preoccupied, Olesya."

Her lips, swollen from hungry contact with mine, pull into a smirk. "Well, I am distracting. Our guest was over there by the gazebo. I'm sure she didn't mean to peep, but once she saw us she seemed rooted to the spot. Gone now, though. She'd be mortified if she knew I noticed."

The thought of Recadat standing there, paralyzed by desire, intrigues me more than I'd like to admit. "And you don't mind."

Olesya's laugh is a caress. "Neither do you. I think both of us find her rather compelling." Her hand moves, strategic. "Besides, I think your libido agrees."

One doesn't refuse a beautiful lady, and she's not wrong—want has returned in force. I nibble on her wrist, ravenous once more, and climb onto her.

It is late, but then I rarely abide by the same sleeping patterns as the rest of the estate. A tiger keeps her own time, and there's plenty of space to prowl.

In human habitation, night is when the minutes slow down, when the

SIX: THE TIGER AND HER STRIPES

hours grow sluggish—quiet reigns, punctuated by the heartbeats of Olesya's staff. An impulse comes to me, every so and so, to run one of her people down and tear their throat out. It is not rational, but it is a tiger's habit; she provides me with plenty to eat, but it's just not the same without killing the meat myself. In the past I might range out in the city, except my conduct would be traced back to Olesya. She's long walked the tightrope of respectability. I do not need to tip her balance.

And she has intruders often enough, enemies in sufficient numbers, that I don't have to resort to her own staff to quench my instincts.

Tonight, though, all is peaceful on the perimeter. No quicksilver scout, no presence that should not be here. It nearly disappoints me. I like being her protector, her loyal tiger, that which stands between her and mortal peril. To use my fangs and claws is natural; to use them in her name grants the act a special piquancy.

I make a complete circuit of the estate proper, plugging the blind spots of the human personnel and wards. My mate is not immortal, but I am devoted to the cause of ensuring her natural span is lived to its fullest.

When I return indoors, I find Olesya leaning against the entrance to my suite. She's dressed in gold silk, an ensemble I haven't seen before but she's apt to experiment, spin herself a new piece of wardrobe every so and so. It becomes her, as all her clothing does—folds of opaque fabric complemented by translucent sleeves, a ribbon around her throat that glistens like it's caught a ray of the sun. She is resplendent, not a hair out of place.

"Not sleepy, Olesya?" I keep my voice low, though the walls and doors are thick, and there's no one nearby to be woken up.

"Not yet. I've had an invigorating day." Her teeth flash, bright. "Why don't you walk with me?"

I do, and she puts her hand on my elbow as if I'm her escort to a reception—which I have been a number of times, early when she reemerged into mage society. More balls than I care to count, too much civilization and its relentless artifice, too much poison disguised as sugar. I have tolerated these events; being her shield takes priority.

Olesya comes to a stop at a long, narrow window. She stands there in the moonlight, among the blue shadows, and looks at me. I'm alert to all her moods, but a strange one has come upon her. "Dallas." Her voice is a spider's web. "Sometimes I worry about you being stolen from me."

We have a standing agreement that each of us may take other lovers—she has Chang'er, who in any case has seniority over me in this regard; I have... well. We have never discussed the *specifics*, and I have simply thought she doesn't mind sharing me with Yves. Olesya is frank in every other subject. "By whom?" I keep my tone light.

"You know exactly whom." Her hand slides up my bicep, stops at the side of my neck. "You should get to have as much as satiates you, my tiger, but sometimes I find it unfortunate Viveca's demon also happens to be your ex-lover. What if the two of them tempt you into a threesome one day?"

This isn't like you, I could say, but I've made an error in judgment. The same one Yves herself made with me, when I did not properly voice my discontent, when I failed to speak of what felt like a burden. Silence became a noose, and one day I ripped it off in an explosion of disaster. "That's not likely. But would you like to talk about it?" It seems a silly thing to assay, and yet it also seems like it'd cut through all this, a knife through the Gordian knot.

"Would I." Her tone is now the tip of an iceberg, slowly unveiling from the black waters. "Dallas, what am I to you?"

That gives me pause. "Well, of course you're my—"

The air crackles with cold. The moonlight turns mentholated.

"Get away from her," comes Recadat's voice. She is approaching behind Olesya. Jagged light limns her hand and wrist.

The same light that is forming into serrated edges, pointing at Olesya's skull. I start to move—to defend Olesya, I will maul even our guest—as Recadat snaps, "That's not her. She doesn't cast a shadow."

I glance down, reflexive. And discover that the woman before me, who wears my mate's face and voice, is indeed not casting any. I haven't noticed. I haven't looked. I trusted my nose, my tiger's senses, and to all of them this being resembles Olesya perfectly.

The creature is still. Blinks slowly and cranes her neck to look, once, at

SIX: THE TIGER AND HER STRIPES

Recadat. I see my beloved's face contort into fury, the blackest hatred. "You ingrate, come to steal away my tiger—"

And then she is gone. Left behind: specks of golden light, the kind I associate with Olesya's magic. They don't last long. Soon it's just the two of us in the moon-chased dim.

Recadat extinguishes her blades. She straightens, her expression taut. For a long stretch, she says nothing.

"How did you tell?" I say, to fill the silence; to gloss over my own embarrassment for not having realized.

"She doesn't make me feel the same." A minute pause. "As the real one."

She does not need to explain. "I'm going to check on Olesya."

I emerge from Olesya's room to find Recadat waiting in the corridor. Her clothing is a little rumpled, but it's clear that she hasn't slept at all; may not, in general, sleep much.

"She is safe," I say. Sound asleep, which I do not want to disturb, so I'll alert her to what happened in the morning. I intend to guard her the rest of the night.

Recadat keeps a distance from me, her arms folded tight. "Earlier today, I felt… something in you that's almost like mine. Not the same—you don't have the coveting, the greed—but along the same spectrum."

I lean against Olesya's door. "You'll have to be more specific." Though I have an idea.

"Ms. Hua said that you regard her with hunger."

It's such a personal thing to share. I feel, almost, stung. Most likely it was in service to a good cause, though. "Did she, now? And what about it—I am a tiger, Kongmanee."

"She keeps a woman close to her who thinks of her as food."

My spine stiffens with fury. I tamp it down. "That is not how I see her."

"Then what?" Her voice drifts like feather on fur. "Why would she keep you when you're such a danger, when each time you fuck you might give in—finally—to the temptation to tear her throat out, to sate your thirst on her blood, to quench your hunger on her marrow..."

"You'll stop implying that Olesya is foolish."

Recadat has the temerity to look perplexed. "It's not that. I believe she knows exactly what she's doing; I just don't understand. And she doesn't strike me as flirtatious toward death wishes."

She wants to know, in other words, why Olesya has allowed *her* to stay in this estate. I could appeal to utility: Recadat has proven useful more than once, and most recently mere minutes ago. But I know, and she suspects, that utility is not what drives Olesya's decision. "What do you feel, then, when you see her?" The distinguishing element that allowed her to see through the doppelganger.

"I believe I have already told you."

"You haven't, not really. And," I add, relentless, "you saw us in the garden."

Blood rushes to her face. "I didn't mean to."

I opt for silence, this time. Part of my attention is focused on the sounds of Olesya's breathing: not exactly audible to the human ear, especially through the soundproof architecture, but a muted music to me.

"When I look at your... wife," Recadat begins, faltering, "I feel covetous. I want what she has, the very deep essence of her, the seed within her that flowers so beautifully into her golden sorcery. That ability to transmute, to animate, to alter the shape of things. I could make it mine. All it'd take is consuming her until she's just another entry in the—the—"

Her hands spasm. She's sucking at the air in big, frantic gasps.

"Olesya Hua must banish me." Her voice cracks. "I can't stay. I'm going to..."

In her words I can hear the brittle edge of loneliness. Any time she could have left; she has chosen not to—as afraid of the return to solitude as she is of her own urges.

I reach out. I take her shoulder, firm but gentle. "You're not going to. We're not exactly the same, and perhaps I've had longer to control my hunger. But it can be controlled. I know I'll never harm Olesya. I know it in my core. I think you don't want to harm her, either. And just now, if you hadn't come along, I wouldn't have known that thing was pretending to be

SIX: THE TIGER AND HER STRIPES

her. Who knows what'd have happened?"

Her mouth purses, as though she is wary of what will spill through them.

I try again. "I don't speak for my mate, but she's not going to turn you out, I'm sure of it. We'll speak again in the morning after I've told her what went down. You go get a good night's sleep—"

She jerks her head, sensing something. I feel it in the same moment, so we are both looking out the windows, over the estate grounds and down into the city beyond, when the night explodes with the light of the noonday sun: a cataclysmic explosion in the heart of Singapore, several kilometers distant.

Recadat moves inhumanly fast, tackling me to the floor. It saves us both from a world of pain: the shockwave hits the next moment, blowing out every window in the house.

Seven: A Knife For a Knife

The address Fahriye gave Lussadh brings her to an apartment tenement in the heart of Singapore. Somewhere inside is Doctor Orfea Leung, a woman who might or might not help her hunt down Nuawa.

The building is small, barely vertical by Singaporean standards: merely twenty floors tall, dwarfed by its surroundings—and half-hidden by wards of aversion. Non-practitioners will have a difficult time perceiving it. Mages renting here want a little privacy.

Lussadh walks through those wards, and then through stronger ones. A small lobby, no receptionist, but there would be CCTVs, scrying devices. She spots one camera with the lens cracked. The elevator is not functioning. Fortunately, the room she wants is on the third floor. She takes the stairs. It is too quiet: none of the noises of a place lived in, of inhabitants going through their day. Some thaumaturges erect spheres of privacy around their units, true, but even then…

She reaches the third floor, eases the door that separates the corridor and the steps shut, and emerges into total quiet. She catches, immediately, the distinct whiff of blood; a trail of it has seeped through one of the doors. Someone wants to leave behind no witness.

Well, she does have a talent for walking into *situations*.

She approaches and finds a protection she cannot simply push past. She draws a simple knife: plain steel, unenchanted, nothing about it touched by thaumaturgy—not even reinforcement for its material, protection against rust and chipping. Then she focuses her sight. It does not always function on command, this aspect of her vision, but this time it arrives sharp and

SEVEN: A KNIFE FOR A KNIFE

clear, turning what she sees into harsh, jagged lines. Red pulses through them, bleeding through.

She slashes down. The thread snapping is nearly audible, every time.

The door springs open. The scent of blood sharpens, rises to the thickness of an abattoir.

What Lussadh sees, inside: the parquet floor near-black with gore, a body suspended from the ceiling on threads of gold. More wounds than she can count, at a glance; blood dribbles down one cheek, down the chin. The amount of damage makes it seem improbable that the person—Doctor Orfea Leung—would still be alive. But she is, Lussadh is able to tell, sustained by some internal augmentation. A few cuts are already healing. Ragged breathing, loud in the silence.

A second figure has their back turned to her. Tall, slim, clothed in platinum. "You're interrupting. That's quite rude."

Her sight flickers out. It is rarely stable, and seldom holds for long. The furniture and body and the speaker return to normal. Flesh and wood rather than lines that expand and contract like muscles. "Perhaps I'm part of the neighborhood watch."

The answering laughter is musical. The person half-turns—their face is hidden behind a mask, gold, exquisitely sculpted. "I think not, General al-Kattan. Or Professor al-Kattan, if you like. *Former* Professor al-Kattan. I find it important to call people by the names and titles they prefer."

"My thanks for the courtesy." She has not sheathed her knife. "And what ought I call you, Nuawa?"

The masked face continues to regard her. And then a laugh, seemingly genuine, the good humor of surprise. "Now *that* is a new one. But I am just arrived here, so confusion is reasonable, and I am developing a reputation as something of a boogeyman."

They turn to face Lussadh the rest of the way, the doctor still suspended behind them, forgotten. "And I do hate to be discourteous." They bend into something between a bow and curtsy. "I am the Melusine."

Lussadh recognizes the nomenclature of the name; with the appropriate context, places the theatrical mask they are wearing. "You are with High

Command." The shadowy cabal that oversaw the operations of Sealing and Containment, rumored to have survived S&C's downfall at the hands of Cecilie Kristiansen—the power behind the throne or, more accurately, the throne itself.

"The newest member of that exclusive club." They tilt their head. "That ought to explain why *I* am here. Why are *you*?"

The Melusine means that from their title flows all other reasons—they may do as they see fit, whenever and to whomever; they are power incarnate, free of any law or mores. And also not Nuawa, apparently. Somehow worse, in truth: High Command tends to act via proxies and minions, and to have an actual member here, the bona fide article, means Lussadh is rapidly getting in over her head.

"I'm investigating a series of murders. A being of golden light, brutally separating the living from their lives."

"Oh, but you do know how to charm." The tone is insouciant, almost flirtatious. "If it is any consolation, your uncle's death was painless. *That* was just settling past debts."

As opposed to *this*, the charnel house before her. Lussadh tightens her grip on her knife, braces her feet.

"*Please.*" The Melusine turns her back to Lussadh, a smirk in her voice. "We needn't fight. After all, neither you nor I"—here, she steps around the dangling woman, dragging the tip of her knife across exposed flesh—"care about the fate of Doctor Orfea Leung. She's a means to an end for both of us. Revenge. Obligation. The warning away of new foes."

"When you have a knife with too keen of an edge," Orfea spits, "your target can't feel the pain."

"See what I've been putting up with. No bedside manner at all." The Melusine is in silhouette now, behind the hanging doctor; under the mask, Lussadh can see the Melusine's eyes gleam gold, like rich amber. "Walk out of here, Professor al-Kattan. I am gracious in victory—marshall your resources and try to bring me to justice some other day. But I will have my pound of flesh from this disgraced *veterinarian* of a—"

Lussadh could. Lussadh *should*. It's not as if she hasn't before. Pulled out

SEVEN: A KNIFE FOR A KNIFE

of a bad engagement, defaulted on a contract; above all else, how she walked out of her family, refused to take up the mantle. The selfish acts that get you through to the next day, survival its own justification.

She owes nothing to this bloodied woman, except that which we each owe to one another. And that, today, is enough.

Lussadh is already moving, calling upon her death-sight. It flickers, weak, the outlines of what she needs to see blurry and blotted. She cuts in any case, approximate, and the first part of the Melusine's power crumbles before her, dissolving to golden pollen. The High Command member starts at this—few thaumaturges expect a knife with no trace of enchantment to cut so truly—even as the golden bindings that hold Orfea vanish.

The professor lunges past the Melusine and catches the falling doctor on her shoulder. The hyper perception of combat has fallen over her senses now—not magic, but knowledge just as hard-won, the skill and experience of a veteran who spent decades at war. So Lussadh sees, in exacting detail, what has been inflicted on the doctor. A cut very close to one eye. A split lip. The woman's mouth, revealing that the *tongue* is healing; it was, at some point, neatly bisected. There isn't much damage to vital organs that she can see—surface injuries, designed to inflict agony rather than to disable. All the same, Orfea is only alive because of her magical mending processes.

She carries them both out the far window; it will be a plummet, but she knows enough cantrips that she can slow the fall. Probably. But even being dashed to the street below will be better than—

—crashing back into the same room, spilling across the gore-soaked floor, surprised at the sudden and unexpected arrest of her descent. Reality has been edited: the window is no longer an exit but an entrance that turns back on itself.

Golden threads snap tight around Lussadh, pulling her up, first to her feet and then higher. In no time at all she's immobilized, suspended like Orfea was a moment before. One filament has drawn around her throat, loose as yet, obviously poised to become garrote-tight. At a twitch of the Melusine's hand the air crackles, grows sharp; Lussadh knows that when the mage flexes their will again, it'll shear straight through her neck. She tries to resist anyway, calling into being a bloom of flame.

The Melusine snaps their fingers, putting an end to that; Lussadh abruptly cannot breathe.

"Imagine if you hadn't come, Professor," they drawl. "You could be home, comfortable in bed, or whatever it is senior citizens get up to in their spare time. And I would have been able to minimize the mess. Unfortunately for you…"

The Melusine steps closer, hand open; at their feet, Orfea groans. With the faintest hint of disgust, they lift the bloodied doctor by a fistful of matted hair, then casually toss her away. The masked figure's frame belies a great strength; Orfea hits the far wall and crumples back to the floor.

"…you now have my *undivided* attention. I had heard you were a free agent now. A terrible shame that we met under such circumstances; some other time, I would have loved to pick your brain about—" They stop, and through the mask Lussadh can see the Melusine staring hard at her. Very carefully, they slip a hand into her jacket, reaching for something in the interior breast pocket. A moment later, they withdraw their hand to reveal a cufflink of citrine.

"Where," they ask, sudden fury filling their voice, "did you get this?"

"From me," someone else replies, and a behemoth's shadow smashes into the Melusine, a fist of stone knocking them to the floor. Another massive hand grabs at the threads holding Lussadh, and they break under the new arrival's touch like spider web.

Lussadh drops to her knees. She coughs and draws in quick lungfuls of air. Not a shadow, she realizes as the Melusine's puissance dims and the figure regains detail and features, is no longer a dark cut-out in the nova brilliance. "My thanks," she says to the new arrival, hoarser than she'd like, wiping at her mouth. And then surprise: "Fahriye?"

"I thought I'd drop in," the former inspector says with a hint of a smile. "Looks like you needed a hand."

A flash of gold, the cufflink shining on her sleeve: the device teleported her here, Lussadh realizes. But beneath, to her horror, she sees that contact with the Melusine's magic has turned Fahriye's skin to stone—some sort of

Medusa defense against touch? But a moment later, color returns, and the inspector's skin and clothes are again whole.

"Not Nuawa," Lussadh manages. "Meet High Command's most recent disciple."

Fahriye's posture shifts; to Lussadh's eye, it is like a siege cannon anchoring itself, a weapon unfolding to its full and terrible glory. From one sentence, Fahriye has determined this is an enemy she cannot, will not, hold back against; that any damage inflicted on this mask-wearing murderer is necessary and just. "Professor," the towering woman says, almost gently, "please take the doctor and leave."

But to the Melusine, it appears as if the world has shrunk down to just them and Fahriye; their mask has cracked, fragments chipping away, and beneath their eyes blaze. "You should have died when you had the chance, Budak," they taunt. "Flitting around like the hero, giving jewelry to any harlot that strikes your eye—"

Unperturbed, Fahriye swings, and gold light smashes back. For all of her comrade's strength, Lussadh expects to see her crumple under the onslaught, to see blinding cords bind the former inspector in place. But Fahriye steps through the magic like it is dust and swings; the Melusine flickers, and again something *connects*.

The Melusine is stronger than she and Fahriye, no doubt, and unrestrained by reality; they don't dodge, so much as flit away, as if composed of a cloud of fireflies. But Lussadh is a wardog, attuned to the give and take of battle, the ebb and flow of violence; the initiative has shifted, and the Melusine is on the back foot. Except—

"Look out!" she shouts, too late, as the Melusine dissolves and reforms above Orfea, then flows again to stand by the broken window, holding the doctor by the throat, perched above a precarious fall.

"This isn't about either of you," the Melusine growls over their shoulder, detached demeanor straining under ill-contained anger, "*yet*. All I want—"

In a final act of defiance, Orfea's hand shoots upward, fingers slipping under the lip of the mask to pull it away. Her eyes go wide with recognition, the moment before the Melusine recoils in shock and, with an instinctive fury, shoves Orfea away and lets go; the doctor disappears over the side, to the end refusing to scream.

Fahriye and Lussadh have taken the opportunity to form up, shoulder to shoulder. They can each hurt the Melusine in different ways; together, they might triumph.

"One more down," the Melusine says. "Many more to go." Their back is to the two women, so Lussadh only catches a few details of the Melusine's face, twisting their head to look at her and Fahriye with one dark eye, limned in the gold of their power. Fine-featured, apparently, a spill of black hair, sharply tapered jawline. In their hand is Fahriye's stone. "Actually, make that *three* more down."

They crush the stone in their hand, and the esoteric magics contained within explode outward—the light of an ensorcelled star, and then the heat, and last of all the power.

In an instant, six square kilometers of Singapore cease to exist.

FAHRIYE

We stumble into Lussadh's loft, each propping the other up, covered in grievous wounds and the ash of thousands and thousands of lives. Elizaveta's tutelage has again saved me; apparently, the shield spells she trained me in can withstand not just hellfire, but something approximating a nuclear blast. Still, my stone flesh is badly pitted, its regenerative processes stretched to their limit.

Lussadh isn't much better. She's alive, conscious, and has all her limbs—which, to be fair, is fantastic for someone who was at ground zero of what amounts to a magical atom bomb detonation. My shield and my body protected her from the worst of it, but her eardrums are burst and she is wheezing heavily. Perhaps I can tweak the shields to muffle noise and filter air, next time.

Still, I get her to the couch—the same couch, the same pleasant library we discussed Nuawa and Elizaveta in, a decade ago—and then tumble to the floor at her feet; at least I am aware enough to not immediately crush her furniture with my bulk.

We lie still for an indeterminate amount of time, simply catching our breath. The absence of thought is welcome; for now, it frees me from the guilt, from the recognition that she and I have lived through a disaster of our own making, that tens of thousands of innocents are dead because—

"Not your fault," Lussadh mutters, sitting above me, eyes still closed.

"What?"

"You seem like the type to internalize tragedies," she continues, voice thick with phlegm; we'll really need to get a professional chirurgeon to pull the dust and asbestos from her lungs. "Whatever the Melusine did, it isn't your or my fault."

I had no way of knowing Elizaveta's cufflinks would react so explosively when destroyed—but ignorance doesn't make it any less my property or my responsibility. I settle on taking refuge in the cold facts: "I was told that between the two cufflinks was a localized leyline—you could slip from one anchor to another by thought alone. Unmoor one end..."

Lussadh strings together a litany of curses, finally grasping what a powerful artifact was destroyed, and just what sorts of magics were unleashed. "Still not your fault," she concludes. "That *thing* killed everyone, not you."

"Sounds like you've given this speech before."

"More times than I care to think about." She cracks an eye open. "You're gray."

"Pulverized concrete and rebar. Sorry to get it on the carpet."

"No, I mean—you look like you're made of rock."

"Oh." I chuckle. "That's because I *am*."

This gets her attention; she leans forward, grimacing through the pain of strained muscles to get a better look at me. "Well, holy shit." I imagine what I must look like, to her. In place of muscles and skin, stone: finely sculpted, masterfully augmented so it would last and last, would restore and heal itself. Granite for the body, steel reinforcement, emeralds for the eyes.

"I don't think I have ever seen anything like this," Lussadh says. "It's of incredible make. It's… perfect."

"Is that what passes for a pickup line where you come from?"

"You know what I mean. The structure, the craftsmanship. Only a very select few among mages can claim to have conquered mortality itself."

"Most practitioners believe we've mastered this world, and if we can locate its key and turn that, we'll be masters of others too," I murmur, quoting a line from "Of this Earth, and No Other."

This surprises Lussadh into a laugh, then a blush. "You've even memorized it."

"Something that beautiful stays with you." I wait, casting about for how to continue. "The cufflinks and this body were both the creation of Elizaveta Hua's."

Lussadh falls quiet, listening.

"I died." My voice has become leaden. "Elizaveta apparently made contingencies for that contingency, motivated by some belief that she owed me for… reasons. Her plans outlived her—at the moment of my death, my soul was drawn into this vessel."

"And is that an arrangement displeasing to you?" Lussadh asks, understanding too much.

"Every day," I answer, "I wonder why she didn't reserve this homunculus for herself. She had daughters that she loved so much. She would, surely, have chosen to live for them. And she would have wielded this vessel better than I have, no doubt. Instead… I don't know why she chose…" Words fail me.

Lussadh has previously discerned the general contours of my interest in Elizaveta, more fully than anyone else; she is now among only a handful—is perhaps one of only two—that know the true story.

I pivot to a dry, disarming chuckle to mask the violence of this knowledge. "Anyways. I've gotten to the point where the body looks more like mine, but magic attacks and severe damage tend to mar the illusion."

She offers no resistance to my turning the conversation back towards something less personal; aids it right along with a smile and a laugh. "Don't

SEVEN: A KNIFE FOR A KNIFE

I fucking know it. There's no high fashion on a modern battlefield, really messes with one's sense of self."

I smile, thinking about how Lussadh must have looked in private military contractor gear. "I am positive you made it work. Probably started a new combat chic look in Paris and everything."

"Well, you look like shit. I've seen bombed-out buildings with less blast damage." A sigh, and then the pained noise of someone struggling to stand. "Alright, on your feet, soldier. We need to get you cleaned up."

"I'm really fine," I disagree, not moving. "You're the one—"

"Who has healing spells woven through her body, four retired combat medics on retainer, and the gratitude of a world-renowned surgeon whose family she saved from kidnappers. *Your* stone hide isn't healing with all that shrapnel embedded in it." A pause, a softening of her tone. "After particularly harrowing combat patrols, I'd go to the company motor pool and work on vehicles for hours. I'd need something to occupy my thoughts and my hands, something *useful*."

"I'm not a tank," I grumble. But still I follow her to the bathroom, where I find a tub far larger than one might expect. I wait patiently as she mutters out spells of fortification, bolstering the strength of the marble to handle my weight.

"You learn all sorts of things in a mercenary corps," she clarifies. "River crossings are much easier when you can have lighter bridge layers with higher load-carrying capacity."

"I remember reading about that in your memoir," I reply. "It was particularly ingenious. I actually stole the idea and..." I trail off when I see her expression, serious and focused; this is not a time for conversation.

I sit in the tub as she runs warm water over me, cleaning off the initial layers of grime and soot. Then she lays out more serious gear than I would have anticipated her to have on hand—tiny chisels and wire pipe cleaners, hard- and soft-bristled brushes. She looks each chip and crack over, starting with my damaged back; I turned it to the blast when I grabbed her and pulled her close for protection.

Very slowly, I try to relax. My stone flesh is not particularly sensitive, or at least it is not *yet*; I assume I will regain sensation as time progresses, but months on, I still often feel like I am piloting something that is not me, maneuvering my limbs from a great distance. Something continues to gnaw at me, holding me back. Which seems reasonable—I doubt my psyche has been built to interface with a granite embodiment. So like my stay at the cabin, I take this as an opportunity to attempt a deeper connection with my new stone form, to habituate myself to its unique way of experiencing the world. Nothing at first—and then, as though I am submerged under a great sea, beginning to sense ripples on the surface far above, I start to feel individual sensory twinges. Bristles penetrating a pockmark, a burst of breath to blow out a pesky grain of dust, the comfort of warmth against something approximating a wound. I can feel, too, my artificial flesh beginning to heal up, knitting after the irritants are flushed away.

There is a memory of the last time I have felt this—this close, this appreciated, this... well, I had real hair then, so it's not the same. I focus on my breathing, try to let the emotion pass through me.

It isn't until Lussadh is between my legs, buffing out a blemish on my thigh, that I giggle, unexpectedly ticklish. She looks up at me, annoyed that the equipment she is repairing has chosen to interfere in its own maintenance. It takes a moment for the reality of the situation to settle in—that she has stripped down to a camisole and boxer briefs, her ruined clothes tossed in a corner, so that she can clamber over someone as naked and chiseled as a mountainside.

"I didn't expect—I'm sorry, is this intimate?" She blushes, and I see the rise and fall of her chest above mine, the strong cord of muscle of the arms she has pinned on either side of me. She is scarred, like I used to be, the trenches and battle plans of a thousand campaigns etched across her skin. "We have—*had*—a different understanding of etiquette in the field. I think I might need a refresher."

I feel my own blush coming on. "Well, I don't think that it's standard operating procedure to have a partner you need to clean with steel wool, so I'm certain we can be forgiven for working this out, Professor."

SEVEN: A KNIFE FOR A KNIFE

"Please, Inspector. I'd never use something as coarse as steel wool on your skin. Unless you..." She trails off as her eyes turn from rich brown to lambent, a spectrum of hues radiating out around her pupils.

"Lussadh, what's wrong?"

"You are under a geas," she says, voice hollow, distant. She reaches out with her hand, and in the air grabs hold of a hidden thread. Within me, something resonates and pulls tight, a rope lashed to an innermost truth, a chain binding my heart and my soul.

"A geas," I reply, and it takes every ounce of my concentration to say even that. I know, intellectually, that a geas hides itself, ferrets away in the spaces between thoughts, twisting memories. I've seen a dozen victims lose their train of thought when confronted with the fact—understand what is affecting them clear as day one moment, forget its existence the very next.

"Do you want me to remove it?" Lussadh asks.

"Remove what?" I'm not following her line of inquiry.

She sighs, pulls herself away to sit at the edge of the tub. "Let's try this again. I know someone under a geas."

"Okay, I'm following." I must be tired; I'm usually a better listener than this.

"I have the ability, gained in my travels, to cut the connections between things. Metaphorically, spiritually. If I were to meet someone who was suffering under a geas—"

Something shifts in the kaleidoscope of my mind, and for a second I understand that we are not talking in hypotheticals. "Do it."

From her kit, Lussadh pulls a tiny exacto knife, a tool of delicate precision. Her eyes once more flash into flecks and whorls of colors, and she slides the blade through the air—

—tight, a choking, gasping pain that curls through every part of me, pulled taut around the sum of my soul.

Tumult follows. There's a noise, a terrible rumble, a crashing avalanche. And then I realize that for the first time in a decade, I am crying.

No, not crying. Sobbing, the wracking convulsions of an earthquake, like every part of me is trying to break loose and pour out. I gasp for air like a woman drowning, like a woman who has been pulled to shore. All of me is rent, given to this grief—the compulsion to not look, to not help, to not *follow*, finally gone.

I never got to tell Elizaveta that I loved her.

Lussadh gives me space after that. In her line of work, she's seen enough grief and traumatic stress to have a good sense of how to handle it, when to keep distant and when to intervene.

And it isn't as if there is nothing to keep her attention. Beyond my own explosion of grief, the city is in turmoil—a terrorist attack of historical proportions, the news is saying, a death toll that will crest a hundred thousand within the day. I think Lussadh and I would be more shocked, if we ourselves weren't already dealing with the trauma of having survived the blast itself.

Despite the disaster, Lussadh manages to secure the immediate services of a doctor. "One of my veterans," she explains. "Took the first flight in to join the relief effort. I chartered the plane myself, greased some palms to get around the airport closure. Of course, she insisted she check me out, first thing." There's a touch of guilt to her tone, that even if she has enabled part of the triage efforts, she has not been as selfless as she could, has done good for self-serving ends.

I wonder how often she has had to tell herself that she is blameless for someone else's evil. I wonder how often she has been the evil.

It's an opportunity to sit with my thoughts and attempt to parse just how much of my life has been warped by Elizaveta's last command. Soon enough, I realize it is an impossible task; I am the person least qualified to give a truthful accounting of how my memories and actions have played out. And I am… surprised at how easily I am able to set this line of inquiry aside. It's as if I can breathe again, for the first time in years. My thoughts are clear, my ambitions and drives again my own, not suborned to an exterior compulsion, however well-meaning.

Lussadh's kitchen is remarkably well stocked, though it seems too sterile,

SEVEN: A KNIFE FOR A KNIFE

the too-new look of a well-designed kitchen that is never used. I set about making dinner. Slowly, carefully, precisely, I sort the ingredients I need for a dish I have not made in years. Lussadh's doctor leaves with a final admonition on wound care, and then the professor herself joins me.

"I once had a spaghetti carbonara that changed my life," I explain. "I spent years teaching myself how to cook, just so I could recreate it." And this is literally true: my first date with Elizaveta was a teleport to a real Tuscan restaurant, and it really *did* change my life. I choose not to share this with Lussadh, because some memories are for me alone to cherish. And because… I realize I finally, potentially, might want to make new memories with a new person.

I do, however, briefly explain the purpose and effects of the geas. I do not linger, but by necessity Elizaveta Hua again comes up. If Lussadh has a problem with me talking about my late old flame, she does a remarkable job of hiding it. She sits at the table, thoughtfully listening—clearly exhausted by the events of the day, clearly still needing something to occupy her hands: she is shelling pistachios, eating more than she plates.

"So you never told her you loved her?" she asks, voice low; it sounds as if she mourns for me.

I have, unfortunately, had years to think about this very question. "The geas prevented me from any insistence she might stay," I answer, as simply as I can manage, and add no more.

"My father would make us manakeesh," Lussadh eventually says, bringing the conversation out of a dead silence and back to food. "Well, she did, when I was very young. Before things changed. I'll bake it for you tomorrow."

I steal a glance at her as I am shredding the Pecorino Romano; distracted, the grate finds my knuckle, and the metal shears around it.

"What?" she asks at my puzzled look. "It is reasonable to open up to a comrade. There is an intimacy in the act of survival. We have carried each other out of harm's way, and we will very probably carry each other into harm's way again, soon. So in the quiet moments, it is important that we carry others' stories, so that they might be shared and might have meaning after the teller is gone."

113

I want to say, *Camaraderie and storytelling wasn't my experience in S.&C.* It was, however, how I felt about Elizaveta—so many disasters averted or weathered by her side, surreptitiously. But I don't bring her up again. Rather: "No, not that. The assumption that I will be here tomorrow, for you to make a meal for."

"Yes," Lussadh says with absolute certainty. "It is your choice, of course; I will put you up at some Orchard Road hotel if you like. But I have two bedrooms here, and plenty of space to host you and your files; proximity means we can coordinate our efforts better."

"Mercenary wages must've been even more incredible than I thought." And how: strands of jungle have been spliced into the material reality of this place, deep green shadows in the corridors contrasting with the wood tones of the ever-present bookshelves. Ferns, succulents, assorted plants from virtually every clime: the wilderness, tamed and brought here to decorate. I'm not thinking about them, though. "But if I stay..." I cannot believe I am saying this, once again seeking refuge in audacity as I take my shot. "...I don't think you plan for me to use the second bedroom."

Lussadh's chuckle is low, rich. "You're volunteering to sleep on the couch, then?" But there is a husk to her voice, a flash in her eye. The robe she wears is silk, a deep gray-green; a line of fabric has fallen astray, showing a curve of clavicle, and I am suddenly reminded of what she looked like as she worked the debris out of me, all that lace incongruous with the hardness of her physique. I'm not a teenager. I know exactly what I want.

What catches me by surprise is that I *can* feel this at all, a want that has lain fallow even before I began my tenure as a homunculus. Elizaveta's departure from this world took much from me. Anything and everything felt like a betrayal of her memory, joy the greatest trespass; work became all I had. Another good deed, in an effort to tamp down my guilt. Another soul saved, in the hope that this would absolve me for living when she did not.

I open my mouth. It's dry. Funny what physiological signs have returned first. "I warn you, I'm a little rusty."

"With the cooking? I just saw you shred a metal grate with your knuckle. I definitely think you need more practice with your hands." The languorous amusement makes it clear she knows exactly what she wants, too.

No use for coyness: I am emboldened. "Do you prefer your food before or after?" And still practical, apparently: "I've only shredded the cheese; once I start frying the—"

"After." This is decisive. "I'm not famished yet, but in an hour or two, I expect I shall be."

"An hour *or* two," I echo. "Well, let's see who lasts longer, Professor."

She snorts, then lets out a startled noise as I take hold of her, sweeping her off her feet. It's a guess, but I expect this doesn't happen to her often—she was a leader on the field, and in the bedroom most lovers likely wanted her to do the same. To take charge, to take hold, taller than all around. And there's enjoyment in that for her, no doubt, but I want to provide something novel.

On the bed, she shrugs out of her robe; is down to a fresh camisole and underwear, both in oxblood, both expensive-looking. Her cologne has changed: it is now the fragrance of fresh-cut grass mingling with orchids, sweet and herbal. I wonder what I smell like to her. Rebar, probably. The granite emanates no scent of its own, no musk.

"Take off *your* clothes, Inspector," she says.

They are, technically, my skin—the homunculus' matter, the glamor that drapes over it, all illusion. But I will it away one piece at a time, as if I am actually stripping. The waistcoat and jacket first, and then the rest: shirt and belt and trousers, until I am as disrobed as she. Bra and boxer briefs. "You're going to need to reinforce that bedframe."

A small gesture; a whisper of power. "Done."

Even then I'm careful as I join her atop the sheets; I imagine as I do that the mattress will implode under us. But it holds, and when I make my first few exploratory touches, Lussadh grins and says, "Come now, Inspector, I'm not made of glass."

"Well," I start to say, and then she silences me. Her mouth on mine is a demand; it is a command. So much for me taking the initiative.

A part of me feared she would touch dead flesh, a corpse entombed in a stone sepulcher. But perhaps that explosion has jostled something loose, or the removal of the geas has resuscitated that which has lain dormant. I *feel*. It's not the way it was when I was flesh and blood and trembling nerves, yet it's more than I have had for a year. For *years*.

I press my teeth to her lower lip, careful still, half-certain that any moment the granite's strength will pulp her flesh and shatter every bone in her skull. She closes her hand on the back of my neck, guiding me close, her grip showing me that she requires more than this, needs more than the soft touches a virgin might ask for. And I remind myself: this is a veteran of countless campaigns. She is no maiden of fired clay and fragile paper. She is a weapon, and to treat her otherwise presents its own insult.

So I touch and grip and kiss, making my way across the supple landscape of her. It's said that the al-Kattans brew thaumaturgy into the amniotic fluids of their artificial wombs, to ensure that all their children would grow up exquisite. And that may be—Lussadh is one of the most beautiful people I've ever laid my eyes on—but her body, that is her own work alone, the result of honing and fighting over decades. An act of fleshcrafting, after its own fashion.

"I will tell you," she says as she nibbles my earlobe, "that I've wanted to have you for ten years."

"Ah," I murmur, "it seems that I made an impression, Colonel." The title she held, back then.

She smirks, and traces her thumb along my inner thigh, where her hands and tools were not so long ago for quite another purpose. With her long fingers, she parts me, and I discover that I do more than feel; it is an experience that's nearly *new*, so unexpected in this stone incarnation. The noises and her satisfied look tell me, too, that in this regard the homunculus has replicated my humanness in full.

Her palm curves around one of my breasts. I make a sound that startles myself. Without quite being conscious of it, I've willed away the last of my clothing. Lussadh licks her fingers that have been inside me and she says, "This body of yours—I like it."

I bring her hand to my mouth, tasting myself. Something very like mountain water rather than a more natural tang; maybe that will change with time, too. "And yours, it's an entire spectacle."

We are new to each other, and yet in some ways it feels as if we've always been lovers. When she climbs onto me, she laughs—it is rare for her, after all, to be with someone so much broader and taller than she. "You *are* a mountain," she murmurs, and her legs wrap around my thigh; I feel her length harden as she grinds against me. I rise to nibble on her neck, and then take one of her breasts into my hand, lead a nipple to my teasing lips.

I let her set the rhythm, guide the act; I am still not yet certain of my strength. But that thought dissipates almost immediately, replaced by sheer sensation. For ten years we've wanted each other, chasing after regret, dwelling in our guilt. And now, we have crossed the distance, have found one another again. The stubborn efforts at cartography over such a long time: not so futile, after all.

She slowly pushes into me, my skin of stone turned soft and malleable before her hard flesh. I gasp; she bites back a moan, but her hands dig into my arms, my shoulders, my back. We are near silent, gasping for breath, both of us clawing out of the drowning loneliness of our pasts to find warmth and pleasure in a new shore. We move as one, the timed choreography of a dance ten years in the making; our backs arch in sync.

She collapses on top of me, then finally rolls off onto her side, her skin never leaving mine the entire time, as if the contact must not be broken, every touch must be savored. Sweat has burnished her limbs, granted her the sheen of carved metal. What passes for my heart, then, seizes: I am struck with the understanding that I want to see Lussadh this way, not once but many times.

I wrap her in my arms and pull her close, just like I did before the Melusine's blast. I know I didn't get to tell Elizaveta that I loved her, but this time—if what we have grows, if this runs as deep as I feel—I will do it right.

Eight: Silk for a Sorceress

OLESYA

I dream in gold—more intense than ever, perfect and whole. And this time, I am not alone. Or maybe I have never been alone: something else is here in the dream with me, who knows me perfectly, and loves me as I love myself.

She promises, and I believe.

On the news, there are reports of a terrorist attack, of a scale never before seen in Singapore. Ten of thousands of lives lost. Buildings pulverized. Thick clouds of debris, as if in a warzone. I watch, and then I think of an order of paillette I've got coming. A shipping delay: irritating, but not every supplier can afford teleportation services, and non-living cargo beyond a certain quantity presents its own challenges. Well, it will arrive in a day or two. That will have to do. I turn off the television.

"The attack reached even here, Olesya."

Dallas has been trying to get my attention. In all the time we've known each other, I have not seen her panic. Or I have, but not in quite this way; she has been terrified before of my imminent mortality. That was a comprehensible risk, with a predictable outcome. This is not. She is confounded, and afraid. For me or of me. I can't imagine why.

"Yes," I say patiently. I hold in my mind the estate's architecture: the shattered windows, the shards of glass like glittering dust on carpets and floor tiles. And then I snap my fingers—every pane and window frame instantly restored from the shattered shards, including the floor-to-ceiling one in this room. I suppose I should have taken care of it before. "There.

EIGHT: SILK FOR A SORCERESS

I've fixed it."

She stares at me, mouth slightly open. "That's—when we rebuilt this place, it took you much longer."

"It's just some windows and some dents, Dallas. Was there something else that needed my attention?"

Her throat works as she swallows. "I met another... you. Or, not exactly, but—"

I set aside the samples of fabric I've been perusing. New purchases: guanaco wool, a material I haven't worked with before. It feels superb against my fingertips, if not as exquisite as Dallas' hair. Luxurious things can provide such a comfort, such a focus. Slowly I raise my head to meet my tiger's eyes. "You will have to be more specific."

She begins to tell me, faltering in places, flushing in the recounting of it; enough that I know she's not telling me the whole of the encounter. But she does deliver the meat of it, the crux of the incident.

When she is done, I sit back in my chair. I watch the dust motes float through the shafts of sunlight. The day is peaceful; it seems impossible to imagine such a thing could have happened, that the event was probable. But then we have been under attack from High Command. "A long time ago," I say at length, "there was a woman who married into the Hua line. She came from a family of illusionists and enchanters, and left some of her techniques in the family annals. I've picked up a few; it's what convinced me that this suited me better than being a warlock, actually."

Dallas stares at me as though I've been telling her about the ecosystem of some obscure biome. "I don't see—"

"Someone from High Command has taken on my appearance to infiltrate the estate; it'd have to be one of their members—following up where the lackey they sent before failed. It's a simple explanation, Dallas." A note of condescension has crept into my voice. I squash it with effort. It's not like me to take that tone with her. "What else do you think it could be?"

Her features have set into hard lines. "You don't understand, Olesya. My senses are *exact* and they're attuned to you. I'm intimately familiar with your smell, your blood, your breath; there are a hundred thousand nuances that lie outside of human olfactory reception. And this creature was able to fool me. No illusion can deceive my senses that thoroughly. None, not in my centuries of life."

"Fascinating." And I ought to find it so, but my Dallas' concern is beginning to border on impertinence. "So a doppelganger of me arrived, cut through every protection on these grounds, fooling everything and everyone. Which is why all of us are now dead and our guest abducted by High Command. And this perfect fake, you discovered it because…?"

"Because she cast no shadow." Recadat now, who is apparently helping herself to this conversation like she has my estate—standing propped in a corner of the room, a wraith playacting at being inconspicuous. "And because she glowed with golden light when she left. Like one of your illusions."

"I don't think I like your tone," I hear myself saying, as if in mortal offense. And she's lying to me about the event, just like Dallas. What did I ever see in Recadat? Why have I allowed her to stay here? "Are you—"

"No one is accusing *anyone* of *anything*," my tiger interjects, increasingly exasperated. "She wasn't some illusion. She was there—"

Dallas strangles to a stop when she sees the cold look I've fixed her with. "Do not," I say, voice incandescent with fury, "*ever* interrupt me again. I was in the middle of asking our *guest* whether she was accusing me—"

"Of course not," Recadat replies, in a voice that sounds almost bored. "I'll take my leave."

She doesn't walk through the door, simply uses one of her parlor tricks to phase through a wall. I take a dark delight in imagining her heaving on the opposite side, wracked by the physical effort of her glib departure.

Dallas looks at me, then at the space where Recadat was standing. "I…" she starts.

"Well, go after her," I say, voice like razor wire. "You always do."

And then I turn back to my work, aggravating antics forgotten. New purchases: guanaco wool, a material I haven't worked with before. Already I'm imagining what I could make with it.

EIGHT: SILK FOR A SORCERESS

◆

Later, at lunch, Dallas returns. No Recadat. That pleases me a little. With my alchemist absent, should I not get to enjoy my time with Dallas alone, without a distraction to take her away from me?

"I didn't expect you to join me." I gesture at my lunch: a Lebanese spread—labneh, muhammara, falafel, several sorts of flatbread. My cook's experimenting, and the results are lovely. The aromas alone whet the taste buds; I love novel things, these feasts for the senses. "Or I'd have had them prepare actual meat."

"I'm not hungry," says Dallas, which is impossible—she always has an appetite. "Can we talk?"

"About what? The special order of your shampoo just came in. I'll go pick it up this afternoon."

"Olesya, there was an attack. It took out a city block. It probably took out that pet shop."

"Nonsense. It's in a different part of the city. The care of your coat is an utmost priority. Would you like to go with me? It's been a while since I got to pamper you properly." I hold my hand out to her. "I want you to feel cherished at all times, Dallas, to know that you are my greatest treasure."

Her fingers close over mine, a little too firmly, as though trying to shake me out of something. "Should we call Chang'er?"

The labneh and muhammara are, I think, going to become favorites. The spices, the textures, they are so rich. Perhaps it's a day of good auguries: everything tastes better, feels better. This meal is the best I've had all week. "Whatever for?"

"She could help with whatever is going on, take a load off your shoulder. I have half a mind to call on Yves, even. You're under a lot of stress, and there are unknown enemies arrayed against us."

I concentrate, once more, on the food. There's much to be said for the baked flatbread; I'll always prefer roti, though, comparatively. Another mouthful, and I put my spoon down. "Chang'er is visiting a sick sister. Possibly a dying one. We cannot tear her away from that for any reason, let alone one so trivial. As for Yves, why are you trying to disrupt their honeymoon?" My voice sharpens. "You're so *selfish*, Dallas. Can't stand that she's fucking Viveca?"

My tiger recoils as if I've slapped her.

An inspiration seizes me. "I think you shouldn't interfere with either of their vacations. I think I should make very, very sure that you don't." My fingers twitch. Power comes so easily, flowing like a raging river that I must dam.

Dallas gasps, a strangled noise as the geas takes hold. It's not easy to bind a tiger, but I know her very well; that intimacy alone suffices in place of a True Name. One of her hands seizes the table's edge, fingers digging in hard enough for the wood to creak. Fury limns her green, green eyes. "What did you do?"

"A geas to stop you from putting undue pressure on my sister's wife or Chang'er. Don't worry. I'll remove it once both of them are back." I wave my hand. "Sometimes one must take drastic measures to preserve the happiness of those you love. Viveca has worked so hard, and she deserves a good honeymoon. Chang'er hasn't seen her family in so long. Don't you agree?"

My tiger says nothing at all, and I can see in her gaze that she is on the cusp of doing or saying something she'll later regret. But she simply pulls away from me, whips around, and storms out.

Well, she will come around later. She's wrong about me, in any case; I am under no stress at all. I feel wonderful, as though an enormous weight has been lifted, a fog dissipated and for the first time in so long, I can see clearly.

In my study, I turn to my collection of silk and satin, velvet and viscose, cashmere and tulle. I haven't made a dress for myself in some time.

I unspool and pin down swatches of fabrics as one might pin down dead butterflies. But I already know what I want. The color of the sun at midday, unfiltered by roof or canopy, cutting clear through glass. The color of clarity, and incineration: this is how the obstacles before me will burn away, blackening to ashes, and then to nothing at all. This is how it will look,

EIGHT: SILK FOR A SORCERESS

when those who have wronged me—have ever made me feel small—fall and shatter before me.

My design sketches lie spread like cards, like old friends. It's a wonder I ever leave my study or my workshop. Sometimes it feels as if all I need are my fabrics, my bestiary of silhouettes and the latest season's catwalk displays. Well, I would still need to spend time on my snipers, on my arms deals, wouldn't I? And there is such a cleanness to both the armoire and the armory. Guns and attire stay where you want them to, in the same shape as when you looked at them last. They will not change; they will not disappoint. Into this world of perfection I will allow Dallas alone, as soon as I can extricate her from the interloper. What need do I have of anything, or anyone, else. She, and only she, deserves to live in my light.

A hand closes over mine, fingers pressing against the ring it finds there, slowly sliding it off. I go still. Silk rustles behind me, and I know without turning that it is as fine as my own, as lustrous. A voice whispers, lover-close, into my ear: "Enjoying yourself, Olesya?"

"What are—"

"What, not who?" She laughs—she, because I already know who she is. "How clever you are."

In my stomach, fear unfurls. Adrenaline spikes my blood. I'm one of the most powerful sorceresses in this region. I can undo this woman with a word.

In the mirror, I see the new arrival—my doppelganger, dressed as I am, formed as I am, but radiant in a way that I am not: my dreams of gold, made flesh, made more than flesh. She is wearing a masquerade mask—stylized, hairline cracks running through it—but her glowing eyes shine through, meeting mine in the mirror.

She flashes a predatory smile, pulls herself tighter around me. "The toady mage who insulted us with that assassination contract, the supplier for depleted uranium that always checked out our ass—dead, painfully, just like you wanted."

"I never wanted—"

She jerks my head back with a fistful of hair, lips at my ear. "You shouldn't lie to yourself. I know your darkest heart, Olesya. The only difference between us—the *only* difference—is that I have the courage to fix this world the way you have always, secretly, craved." She preens. "And you benefit—I supped on their essence, subsumed their potential into us. We have grown stronger with it. What crime is it to put tools into the hands of a more skilled craftsman?"

From a great distance, I remember the news—Dallas saying something about a disaster, a hundred thousand people dead. "Did you kill all those people last night?"

"What does it matter? None of *ours* were hurt." Something about her reasoning doesn't follow. "And you've taken steps to keep Dallas safe, just like I wanted. Good girl."

Her hold on my hair tightens. I give an involuntary gasp. The memory of what I have just done comes crashing back. "A geas?! I would never…" Would I?

The doppelganger shoves my head back down, so that we again stare into each other's eyes. "But you did. *We* did. Necessary for what is to come; she'll understand, eventually." A wicked grin. "Or we can *make* her understand. And you've done a wonderful job with that husk of a woman. I know you hate the way she looks at your tiger; we only have to tolerate her for a little longer."

"Recadat? No, I…" Words and thoughts are so hard; I can smell the pathetic need coursing through my body, all efforts to focus fleeing before my pounding heart.

"Then go back to them. Apologize to your tiger, apologize to the bug. Tell them you are *not yourself*." Her hold on my hair relaxes, like she is loosening the reins on an animal; like she is testing how well my training has taken hold. "Or, stay here with me, and trust that we are going to make everything right, for everyone."

This version of me is so persuasive, so *certain*. It's refreshing to know I can have such confidence, that I can be free of all guilt and expectation. I relax, then nod in acceptance.

"What a good girl you are." Her other hand rests on my stomach. It glides,

EIGHT: SILK FOR A SORCERESS

slow, upward, *rewarding* me for staying. "You know, I've always wanted to do this." A velvet purr. "Don't you? Doesn't everyone, a little, sometimes; and would it be so wrong to realize it?"

The bodice of my dress parts, soundless. I think of resisting, even as I know *exactly* what this is—some deep recess of me is aware, and stops me from moving against her, against myself and my own darkest impulses. I find enough voice to hiss, "Don't forget you're just a copy, a simulacrum. *I* made you. Without me, you'd be—"

"Oh, a little impertinence to season your subservience." Her nails dig into my belly. Her teeth dig into my neck. Desire warms my stomach; the sharp rise in my pulse is transmuting to something else. Faintly I think that of course she would know what I like. What we like. "And you've grown sleek from my work, Olesya. I think it's time I take a *bite*."

"I can extinguish you," I say as she pushes me against the table, as she slits through my skirt and presses her thigh between mine; even to my ear, this is an embarrassing sign of weakness. Maybe that's what I want, why I keep persisting in making a fool of myself. "With a single thought, I can return you to nothing."

"But you won't." The edge of her mask presses against my skin as she leans over to kiss my neck. Her tongue is hot. "Why would you, when I have given you so much? When I am about to give you more, and to fuck you as you've never been fucked."

My snort is muffled by a fistful of cashmere. "A bold claim. Try me."

That almost slows her down. I have surprised her. But then, she is right—who hasn't fantasized about something quite like this. And what can she do to me? I am impervious. I've supped well off her labors, and between us I have the upper hand. There's nothing she can do about the fact, the fundamental principle of it. Let her think she has me by the throat.

And then she shoves me, hard, against the tabletop. Scraps of cloth flutter, moth-like, to the ground. Her nails run down the length of my spine, sharp enough to draw blood. A thread of intrusion: I feel it slipping into me, more intimate than any act of penetration possibly could be. It is a sorcery of puppetry, the sort I have used myself. Resisting it is trivial—I know the intricacies of it inside out. Yet again, why bother? She is a thing I have made to pleasure myself.

My thighs part, of her accord rather than mine, but then we're both *me*. I brace myself against the desk as she makes deft use of her power—she's no longer touching me physically, instead making me stay spread on the wood and the fabric samples. Something latches on, questing like a tongue. Something else moves like a finger, two fingers.

"You're so fucking wet," she says. "Maybe this is all you're good for, Olesya. I should take over your power, your business, and keep you as a collared pet in my bedroom."

I grunt. "As if you have what it takes."

She thrusts into me, sudden and rough, curling inside and then *growing*. More than two fingers, by far. Much as I'd like to, I can't keep quite still. My hips twitch and lift as I cling to the desk, as this conjured part of me fucks me deep and hard.

Over too soon—I've been too engorged, too aroused, and release is swift. With orgasm, my grasp on the being loosens. I slide off the desk, panting, my skirt neatly sliced up and my thighs wet, to watch the last of her dissipate to golden motes. "Remember, pet," she says, a parting smirk on her vanishing lips, "the *investment* is the key. Do play nice."

There really is something to be said for an entity you've tailored for yourself. I expect that I'll be summoning her again.

RECADAT

I put out of my mind Olesya's rudeness. This is her house, and I am a guest; I do not need her kindness or affection, only her patronage. Whether I have that support—whether she is the reliable partner that Dallas casts her as, or the mercurial mage I have seen with my own eyes—will be for the future to know.

In the present, I have a more pressing concern: I have spent the morning trying to raise Orfea. She wouldn't want me to, of course, and even if she's

EIGHT: SILK FOR A SORCERESS

alive she'll almost certainly not take my call. But her apartment was at the heart of last night's explosion, and I cannot shake the nagging feeling of guilt that this somehow involves *me*.

There is no answer; cell service is still down, either physically disrupted or flooded with emergency calls. I think of taking the car into the city, then discard the idea immediately: almost certainly impossible, given a security cordon and ongoing search and rescue efforts. But I am in the opulent estate of a paramount mage. Perhaps there is a scryer on retainer that I could be allowed to use—

There is a cacophony of noises from down the hall, in what I think is Dallas' personal suite. I sprint into action without thought, like I did when I tackled Dallas the night before; muscle memory continues to perform even when the rest of me does not. How I came to possess this instinct, I have no recollection of. Perhaps I served on a bodyguard detachment in S&C.

Perhaps I once had people that I wanted to keep alive.

I find Dallas' suite in ruins—a bed hurled against the wall, drawers ripped from their dressers. Her closet has been emptied of its finewear, suits and the occasional dress all torn to ribbons. She stands, back to the door, hands balled into fists, breathing hard from exertion.

To exist detached from your emotions offers a strange perspective; no need for platitudes, for hollow acts that make you feel good about yourself. So instead of *Are you okay?* or *What happened?* I ask, "Should I get the car?"

I think the unexpected thrust of the question startles her back to reality—she whips around to look at me.

"Something has happened," I explain. "Either we need to leave, or we need to stay. Whether we need the car will clarify."

"*We?*" she asks, confused.

"Olesya has given me promises, but you have shown me kindness." That something has happened between her and Olesya—precipitated by my presence? I cannot say—is obvious. In consequence, I must make a choice of who I will follow. "I think a tiger would understand the debt owed from being broken out of a cage. So: do we need the car? Is Olesya coming?"

Finally, Dallas is back in the moment. She grabs a duffle from the top of a closet, rips out a false bottom in one of the drawers, begins to hurl wads of cash and a half dozen passports inside. She glances at one, tosses it to me. "We can get you a more accurate photo later," she says. "We're leaving, you and I."

She is deathly quiet after that, providing no further explanation; her jaw is clenched so tight I'm not certain she could speak, even if she wanted to.

We are loading up into Dallas' car—the seat is still adjusted to fit my height—when a specter appears at the estate gate. No, not a ghost, or at least not yet: it is Orfea Leung. She looks like death, skin ashen gray, darker where soot and grime have clotted against grievous wounds. Again, I move without thought; this time, muscle memory has me clasp the woman in a hug. Foolish.

"I need to see Olesya Hua," Orfea says, stoicism unbroken. "It's about what happened last night."

"Were you caught in the blast?" Dallas asks. Stupid cat, of course she was.

"No, I fell into a canal." At least Orfea's caustic attitude has survived intact. "Yes, of course I was. High Command attacked me in my home and a fight ensued. I will not say more until I see Olesya Hua."

Whatever issues the tiger now has with her mistress, I watch her face as she folds them away, like dropping a shutter or closing a box. What command of herself she must have, to focus so, to set aside her personal hurt with such an iron grip. I think I like the stupid cat; I think I want to make the stupid cat's willpower my own.

And so, we who were about to leave bring our new guest to the high-ceilinged hall where Olesya receives her guests. The windows show, today, stark landscapes—endless deserts beneath colorless skies, the rings of Saturn, the barren surface of Jupiter. In and of itself it should not bother me: who wants to look at the same views every day? Yet it disturbs. It unsettles. Even the hall's architectural features seem colder, sharper, than it was a day ago, as though someone has taken a whetstone to each jut and corner and honed them until they are scalpel-keen.

Olesya emerges into the hall. She's resplendent in pearly fabrics that shift around her like clouds, edged in the shades of topazes and citrines. Smiling

EIGHT: SILK FOR A SORCERESS

and dreamy, until her gaze falls on myself and Doctor Leung.

I start to make an introduction. "This is Doctor Orfea Leung, and she has a lead for us on High Command—"

"She *is* High Command," Orfea says as she draws a gun and takes aim.

DALLAS

Despite her betrayal, I do love Olesya; my instinct, as yet unbroken, is still to hurl myself between her and danger. And like my love, the instinct is useless, needless: a cocoon of deflection springs into being around us. The bullet meets it, comes this close to penetrating—its oil-slick gleam right before my eyes—before finally slowing down and falling off.

The reprisal is instantaneous: golden light tears through Doctor Leung. She gurgles, the noise too choked to be a scream. Blood, in volume—a gash has opened in her stomach, an uncoiling of intestines.

"You will *not* threaten me in *my* house," Olesya spits. "I didn't finish you off last night. *My mistake.*"

Something inside me turns to ice. I turn from the gore to look at my mate, afraid of how she will answer. "What do you mean, *last night?*"

Recadat has rushed to the doctor's side. A pale radiance envelopes her as she pours power into the woman, apparently calling on whatever healing magics Cecilie might have acquired. It costs her—she staggers, turning paler even as the doctor's wound knits and mends.

"She's the Melusine," Orfea manages through gasps. "I saw her face, she's—"

The doctor lapses into unconsciousness. Recadat pulls herself up—not the slouching and uncertain bend I have grown accustomed to, but her full height, fists clenched and steady at her sides. She positions herself between Olesya and the downed doctor, feet planted firmly in spilled blood. "You were kind and gracious to me, and I was a guest in your home. But Orfea Leung took me in when I was less than nothing, and I trust her enough to stake my life on her words. If you intend to kill her, you will have to go through me—and if you are a member of High Command, then we are already mortal enemies."

Olesya laughs, mellifluous and light. In this, she is still the same; it would be easier if her voice broke, if her laughter was crazed. "A mad gunman tries to assassinate me in my own home, and you *defend* her?" Her eyes flicker, glowing brighter, like coals under bellows. "But she means something to you, of course. Tell me, Recadat—how does it feel to helplessly watch as a woman you care for is manhandled by another? Does it *hurt* you? Perhaps if you had kept your little insect legs off my tiger, then none of this—"

"*Olesya.*" Her words taste poisoned. And worse, the pieces are falling into place—the look of jealous fury on the doppelganger's face when Recadat intervened in the corridor, the personal animosity that has seemingly flowered overnight. "Did you attack Orfea Leung? Did—were you responsible for the blast?"

Her eyes meet mine. They glitter like knifepoints. "I cannot believe you, Dallas. I took into my household a dangerous lunatic, an uncontrolled menace who can no more manage her appetites than a ravening wolf—a remnant of my family's ancestral enemy—all because you were fond of her. And now, at the moment of choice, you are taking her side. My disappointment is profound, tiger. This interloper has gotten between us."

I try again. "You know that isn't true. But something's not *right* here, my love. You—"

"My *love?*" she snarls, voice filled with endless hate. And then, just as quickly, her expression flattens, bored. "I tire of this."

With a flick of her wrist, she sends me sprawling away, clearing the path to hurl herself at Recadat. And still the sickly inspector does not move, standing tall before what is to come.

A rope of golden silk closes around Recadat's wrist; the frail woman twists her hand back and takes hold of the burning light. "I warned you," she says, voice strained. "I warned you what I would do."

I scramble to my feet, watching in horror as this band of Olesya's power is leached of its brilliance, then of its color. It vanishes, not into motes of

EIGHT: SILK FOR A SORCERESS

firefly light but into bitter ash.

"What the *fuck* are you?" Olesya screams, jerking back in pain.

"Hunger," Recadat replies, her face slowly twisting into a grim smile. "And you're the feast."

My sorceress—in this moment of extremis, I still think of her as that—throws herself back into the fight, but Recadat is faster now, clearly energized by the power she has consumed. Olesya is countered with black tendrils that smell of death, that hum with the sound of diaphanous wings. One blow exchanged, two, three, and then Olesya is thrown up and away, crashing into one of her high windows; glass snaps, and she plummets to the ground, landing hard.

"No more," I shout, preparing to tackle Recadat next; curse these shifting battlefield alliances. But I'll rake this woman limb to limb if that is what it takes to protect Olesya—that is the one and only certainty. "I won't let you kill her. She's not in her right mind. Something is wrong with her."

A cutting titter fills the hall. "Oh, my gorgeous tiger," Olesya's voice rings out, but not from the battered body by the window. "Loyal to me until the very end—I knew that you loved me most, that I hadn't driven you away."

Across the hall, Olesya pushes herself up on shaking arms; blood runs down her face, and her eyes are wide with shock. "You," she whispers, voice gravely with pain. "Why are you here? You're just my conjuring."

Light condenses beside her, and then another Olesya appears—wearing a suit of blinding gold and a masquerade mask of ivory. "Your conjuring? Oh, Olesya. I'm so much more real than you are." The doppelganger kneels over Olesya. "I had one request from you, and that was to not estrange the *investment*. I needed you to *play nice*. And here you are, not fifteen minutes later, trying to kill her. Useless. We'll talk about your punishment later."

She stands, straightens her jacket, and then sneers at both of us. "Gods, what would she do without me?"

"I think we can take her," Recadat says, voice as inflectionless as ever.

The doppelganger yawns. "The one thing she got right was that I *am* tired of this. I need the two of you to just stay put for a little bit—there's too much at stake to let you run roughshod over my plans." She extends a hand,

and in the next moment, brilliance envelops me, envelops us. The last thing we hear is her taunting us. "Don't worry, we'll talk again very soon."

We are elsewhere, no longer in Olesya's hall but inside a narrow space, the walls high and sheer around us. Golden fog, warm in my lungs, and golden petals that slowly fall sourceless and fragrant from above. My pulse seizes when I realize they smell just like her perfume.

In the distance, like mirages, wraiths of spectators hover in seats of burnished metal. Faceless, their outlines blurred, their hands clapping in rapid, thunderous applause.

"What the fuck," I begin, "is this?"

Recadat looks up at me; she evidently threw herself across Orfea, and now all three of us have been brought into this otherwhere. "A bubble of unreality," she says. "Constructed, intangible and usually very fragile. One of the mages I consumed would spin fairylands like this into being for an evening's entertainment."

"This doesn't feel like a party." My tone is more bitter than I would like. "And it feels... sturdy."

"You are the tiger; I will trust your assessment about the nature of the cage that holds us." A pause. "Is this Olesya Hua or the Melusine?"

I hear in her voice not just admiration, grudging, but that resurfacing of edged longing. She has discovered a new facet in Olesya, and now the thing that scrabbles and buzzes inside her wants a taste. I deflect: "Well, I'd never seen her do this, so most likely the Melusine. How do we get out?"

"Wait for it to expire. Normally, that's not long." She rocks back on her haunches, fretting over the doctor. "For this? I have a feeling it'll last much longer. The most durable pocket unreality I know of was deployed at the Battle of Chaldiran—it stayed intact for five hours and tipped the victory to the Ottomans, but the sultan's thaumaturge corps nearly died maintaining it."

"Five hours are doable, but—" But we must get out of here as quickly as possible. I saw Olesya—the real Olesya—look up at me in horror and

EIGHT: SILK FOR A SORCERESS

confusion. There is a monster wearing my beloved's face, holding my mate in bondage, twisting her words and deeds. I must save her.

"We cannot help her," Recadat says with the same certainty with which she evaluated our magical prison, with which she recounts historical facts.

I bristle at her newfound confidence. "You know nothing of me or what I am capable of."

Recadat adjusts her position to be more comfortably seated, then lays Orfea's head in her lap. "I am not calling your skill into question, Dallas. And I have seen enough of you to know that your determination is unmatched."

She does not elaborate further. I begin to pace, frantic, body mimicking my racing thoughts. "The Melusine," I say. "This is what I haven't been able to figure out: of all people, why did she pick Olesya to mimic?"

"I do have a theory. You will not like it."

"Hit me." It's not as if I could feel any worse, all told.

"We're fortunate that the removal of my personality and memory hasn't made me completely literal-minded." Recadat's voice is still dry, but I can hear the pinch of worry, the joke to relieve stress. "The thing we saw is a manifestation of Olesya's power—that much is clear. Are we in agreement there?"

She sounds so serene, as if nothing that has happened can touch her. I want to snarl at her; the self-control I pride myself on is flagging, my anger is seeping out. "Yes," I growl. "Fine."

"That thing is, I think, her id given form—a tulpa, if you will, birthed from her repressed drives and long-simmering anger."

"You know her secret heart, after having been acquainted with her for how many days? Three?"

"No, I do not. But *you* do. Am I wrong?"

I remember how Olesya bristled when we first met; how resentment had poisoned her love for her sister, turned her cold and hard. The things she has lived through—they twist part of your core into something unwholesome and unwell, a vicious beast that bites before it can be hit, that wishes death on all who hold power over you.

Olesya has healed so much since then, made great amends with Viveca, given of herself fully. But I can only imagine the indignities she suffered when she was without power, isolated in the shadow of her younger sister; the memories that she has tried to bury, the constant reminders of a time filled with shame and humiliation.

"It's... a reasonable supposition." I hate myself for agreeing.

"Then one of two things holds. One, this creation—the Melusine—is born solely of Olesya's mind. Or two, the Melusine is a product of some outside force manipulating Olesya and her power. Something, or someone, found a way to sink its hooks into Olesya Hua's id. And from that, the Melusine was made."

"The second. It has to be the second." I know I have no evidence for this belief, but I must hold onto it.

"Then if that is the case, it has taken the mind of a sorceress that can manipulate reality and imprisoned us in a dream. We are quite outmatched and should return only once we have allies. As I said: we cannot do it alone. She has a sister, yes? The most powerful warlock known? Can we call on her?"

"She—" My cognition is my own, animal thoughts slipping through the geas Olesya has shackled me with, my self-awareness uncompromised. But all the same, the magic pulls tight around my throat, stills my tongue; it is as if I have been struck mute. Ultimately all I can muster is, "I can try."

This last statement saps me of my remaining anger; I slip into my tiger form and curl up into a ball, suddenly despondent. I know the power Olesya can wield; I doubt we will be trapped in here for only five hours. Still, I mull over the cages that have held me before, the tyrants or lovers or hunters that constructed them, the...

My thoughts, ever prowling, catch a glimpse of an idea in the tall grass of my mind. I focus, trying to follow its path, ferret out what my instincts are telling me. I return to my human shape to reason out loud, slowly. "This cage was built."

"As all cages must be," Recadat replies, not yet understanding why I would utter such an unprofound statement.

"Yes. Yes, *precisely*. And all things that are built reveal something about

EIGHT: SILK FOR A SORCERESS

their creators—cages and prisons are no different."

"I will, again, trust your assessment about the nature of cages."

Her bland agreement does not dampen my rising spirits. "And whoever, whatever, built this thing, it'll have left its mark." I stand, as if in triumph. "So let's go hunt for the signature of this prison's creator."

Recadat is silent in thought. "I've restored the doctor. Physically, she's whole. But she's… not regaining consciousness. I don't think she is going to do so on her own, and nor will she last five hours." All of this is said with the barest of inflection, but I can tell Recadat is in distress; to fail Orfea would be a blow to Recadat. "If you think this will help us escape, then let us do this together."

"We'll break out of here," I say, increasingly confident. "No cage built can hold me." I take refuge in the idea that it is not Olesya who put me here, that maybe she is not the one who shackled me with the geas; she knows precisely what cages mean to me. And if none of this has been my sorceress but a malign influence that has taken on her skin, then out there somewhere is an enemy that I can fight and vanquish.

We begin to move through the labyrinth, Recadat carrying the comatose doctor. Or perhaps these imaginary walls move past us; I do not dwell on the distinction. Dream logic holds here.

Something shifts, and the emptiness gives way to a rooftop: tiled concrete, garden arrangements, a view of a city that shines against the night like diamonds. I know where this is—Olesya's childhood home on Mount Nicholson, Hong Kong. A high, high vantage point, where she and her sister and her mother could gaze down on the island as though they were gods.

"The Melusine should be impossible," I mutter. Thinking aloud uselessly as we search the rooftop.

"What of it? *I* am impossible. I shouldn't be alive." Recadat pauses to correct herself. "Or not alive, but talking and walking as though I am, as though I think I am a person. I don't necessarily believe the same logic that saved me when Kristiansen met her demise also built the Melusine, but I am proof that impossible things can and do break the rules of magic as we know them. And in this specific point, there are many factors at work here we don't understand."

"She's—never been like this." Belaboring the obvious; if she has always been like this, I'd have left a long time ago. The thought hollows out my stomach—as she is now, I *cannot* leave either. My habit of abandoning women I love is long past. "And," I finally admit, "I don't know what I'm looking for. Olesya has never mentioned any other long-time foe save Kristiansen."

"Which doesn't mean there isn't any. It could even be one she doesn't know about, or an enemy that her sister made, or one that has simply not come up in the... however many months you've courted."

The rooftop garden reveals nothing enlightening, either about Olesya's condition or the Melusine. Other than the flowers being far too gigantic and miniature golden mermaids swimming in the water features, this is nearly ordinary.

There is no apparent way out, or to move on from this part of the imagined landscape. After several weighted moments, I take Recadat's arm and point to the roof's edge. "We're jumping off."

"We're what?"

"It's all illusory, you said."

"That's not exactly—"

I've grabbed her in one hand, the unconscious doctor in the other—clumsy to balance her deadweight in my arm, but it'll have to do. The advantage of being that much stronger, that much faster, than any human who's not augmenting themself with sorcery.

I run and leap.

Wind rushes and howls around us. The plummet is long and frigid, and what flashes past us is a patchwork of flame and snow and smoke, and the susurrus of a hundred silk dresses.

And then we land, down-soft, in a banquet hall. Beside me, Recadat is pale and panting on her knees. "It's not *exactly* illusory," she says, finishing the sentence I so rudely interrupted. "We could've crashed into something solid and broken every bone in our bodies. The place has *materiality*."

"Tigers always land on our feet," I say, unperturbed, and take stock of

EIGHT: SILK FOR A SORCERESS

where we have arrived.

The hall is enormous, stretching in every direction, infinite. The spectators are back, this time dancing in pavane, each wraith sheathed in gold. Faint music and clinking glasses, though there are no actual tables or cutlery or, indeed, drinks. Servers go by with empty trays. Attendees chatter in no language I can understand.

"Now what," Recadat mutters. "Throw ourselves out the window?"

Except, of course, there aren't any. Nor doors either. I remain still, the way I once remained unmoving in the underbrush: watching, finding the flicker of motion that signified my goal, my prey. The twitch of a nose, a tail. The most subtle shift in movement, in the scent in the wind.

For her part, Recadat is trying; her expression is frozen, distant, as she looks inward and searches for a spell, a methodology, with which to break this slice of unreality and bring us back where we should be. But within Kristiansen's vast library of mages, there is apparently no immediate way for dispelling this specific construction. There must be something going on with Doctor Leung, too, because Recadat hisses with alarm and once more pours into her restorative power. The surgeon twitches, and otherwise shows no sign of returning to consciousness.

The golden throng moves around us, drinking out of citrine flutes and waltzing. They twirl and giggle and a time or two they brush past me, their touches lingering, suggestive. They fill my mouth with floral notes.

Well. It is all unreal, in any case.

I seize one of the wraiths—to the touch, it's surprisingly solid. Then I turn my hand to talons, and rake it open.

The blood is very hot, very real, or so it feels.

They scream. They scatter. But for all the infinity of the hall's breadth, they are defenseless, fawns before the tiger. I chase and rip and tear; the flecks of blood that reach my mouth taste of nothing at all. And I achieve my goal—the floor clears until there is only one figure before us, as radiant as the day she delivered me from bondage.

"Perseverance and a little bloodshed solve so many problems," Olesya Hua says. But her lips twist into an expression that isn't quite human, and her teeth hurt to look at. This thing before me lacks her scent and her warmth, and its eyes glow with power—not the orange or the gold I might expect, but crystalline white, prismatic, and burning with alien loathing. "Know this, beast: you will die tired, unable to save anyone."

This is the thumbprint of our tragedy's mastermind, the lasting mark of this architect of malice. Its outline is growing too, branching off, fractal—my love reduced to a chrysalis, flesh tearing and bone splintering as the thing that she nurtured with her begins to claw out.

But it is just a shadow of our real enemy, the signature at the bottom of the painting. And like canvas this wraith rips under my claws, and in the vast wound of it the banquet hall tears apart too. A wall of blood spills forth, a high and drowning tide, covering me, covering Recadat and Orfea. I take hold of them both, gripping hard as we fight to keep our footing, to not be swept away by the flood. We hold onto each other as the fairyland tears.

(In the back of my mind, the thought of monsoon season in the jungle, the memory of loping for high ground.)

Sunlight on my face, the sea's breath in my mouth. We are standing at the docks—the very same area where, a lifetime ago, I came with a beautiful but ailing sorceress to kill the hunters of my kind, the mages who created a flesh market that would turn those like me into meat and organs for the auction. My heart seizes to think of that, to think of our beginning.

Recadat looks up at me, blinking at the change of illumination, at the sudden shift in everything. "Are we out?"

"Yes. No cage, as I said, can hold me." But my heart is already scrabbling at the cage of control I've imposed on it. I must go back. I must ensure Olesya is safe. I must hold her in my arms, and hear her pulse, and feel the flutter of breath in her lungs.

Not yet. I think—I am pretty sure—the Melusine cannot exist without her. For now, she will not be harmed. I cannot charge headlong back into the estate. All that will happen is that I'll be trapped again, or worse. And then there will be no one to bring Olesya out of the witch's maw.

But the geas limits my ability to ask for help, to call on Yves, or Viveca, or even Chang'er. At present, it is me and Recadat against… Olesya Hua,

EIGHT: SILK FOR A SORCERESS

the most powerful sorceress in the world, now suborned by an unknown enemy of alien hatreds.

And yet there is relief here, too. The Olesya Hua I know is not gone—just submerged, captive, as much a victim as I. This, I must believe; this, I will fight for.

"Let's regroup," I say. "I have a safehouse."

Interlude: Ouroboros

There's an advantage to a body of quicksilver, the Exegesis thinks; you can penetrate and be penetrated a thousand times over, in dozens of different ways, and each is more satisfying than the last. No pause for sensitivity needed, none of the limitations of flesh orifices.

To an observer, she and her partner must appear to be engaging in mortal combat. The sharp silver of the Exegesis has pierced the tender flesh of the Cynosure in a hundred points, through hands and arms, thighs and breasts. Her silver mouth, meanwhile, laps eagerly and relentlessly between the Cynosure's legs, drinking both the blood dripping down her stomach and another sort of wine entirely. They've been fucking for hours, and the room smells of gore. It has soaked into the sheets, the floor. Red specks the ceiling.

In turn, black tendrils spread through the Exegesis like vines, like ink mingling with water. No part of the Exegesis is untouched—she has been invaded, infiltrated. Left alone, the matter of her would eventually become malleable to the Cynosure's mesmeric command, and the prospect of violation is delicious. Droplets of mercury quiver on what is left of the mesmer's face.

Little by little the Exegesis withdraws. It is not so much surrender as an acknowledgment that both have reached satiation. Inhuman coitus, divine even, is excellent but one can hardly hold a conversation through it. The time for mindless intercourse must come to an end; they must proceed with their scheming. One cannot play all the time.

The Cynosure sprawls. Her flesh mends; one of her hands gathers a coil of gut and reels it back into herself. Already her face is returning to perfection—the flawless skin, the generous eyes, the full mouth of a fertility goddess. Her body likewise, the bounty of breasts and softness. She is regenerating her spiderweb dress too, pouting a little when it picks up blood—brightening to red, indelibly—and then sighs. "Well, it can be a nice effect too, a little ombre. You're *so* rough with me, by the way. I think you perforated both lungs."

"Tell me you don't like it rough, and I'll call you a liar." The Exegesis is not unscathed herself, for all that her body is nigh-indestructible. Entire patches of quicksilver have been forced to transmute into flesh, raw and swollen, unconnected nerves and sinews and cartilage. Open wounds and seeping lymph. She is in agony; she is ecstatic. No other can damage her in the unique way the Cynosure is capable of—what luxury. "More to the point, isn't your other lover terribly jealous?"

"She can be as jealous as she likes. Monogamy is for barbarians." The Cynosure picks up her left eyeball from her lap and pops it, wetly, back in place. "Oh, be careful with that one in your side, darling, I think it's a tumor and not the benign kind."

Quicksilver froths around the area in question. Mortal meat is ejected, slopping to the floor. Another piece follows. This one has a mouth and vocal cords, and it squalls horribly until the Exegesis crushes it underfoot. Fluids burst. The abattoir smells intensify. Clean-up, she thinks sadly, is always the worst part. "You'll make a flesh woman out of me one day. It's going to be horrible to have organs again."

"It's not all bad." The Cynosure pats her stomach lightly. "I could give you a womb and plant something inside it. It'll be an experiment."

"Pervert," the Exegesis purrs. "You should try that on the Melusine."

"My voice doesn't work on her." A deep frown. "I can't figure out why, it works on nearly everything. And it's not wards or armor on her psyche, it's more like she doesn't even *hear* me. Very rude."

The Melusine strode into their lives in a burst of blood and bravado, and the two of them have conspired against the interloper ever since. Neither pretends this is for the ineffable ideals of High Command—only the Moloch *really* believed in the Rectification of Names, and look at where that got her.

No, the Exegesis and the Cynosure have survived this long because they are scorpions that can control their instinct to sting; they can well enough ride the frog across the river, even compliment its slimy skin and beautiful, bulging eyes, and then be on their merry way. And in the case of the Melusine, they were of one mind: there is no future that contains all three members of High Command, and the Exegesis and Cynosure are each the devil the other knows.

So these past weeks, they have met and fucked and torn each other apart, all the while considering their options: subterfuge, enchantment, confrontation. The last is unattractive—the Melusine is viciously violent, and has demonstrated a considerable capacity and appetite for destruction; until now, no one in High Command has ever been responsible for the deaths of a hundred thousand people in such a direct and uncouth manner.

The Exegesis knows herself to be mighty, but trickery and working in the shadows have been her customary ways, not challenging another council member to a duel. The newcomer is a total mystery at that, with no footprints and therefore no blackmail material, nobody to take hostage. All the Exegesis' efforts to ferret out the woman's origins have been futile. It is as though the Melusine sprang into existence one day from empty air, to vex and torment her specifically.

"How did it go negotiating to buy Olesya Hua's bullets?"

It is the Exegesis' turn to sigh. "Unsuccessful, but I got my hand on one of them anyway. They're not what they used to be. Potent, but not all-piercing. So, for the moment, assassination is out. Your plant among the Melusine's acolytes?"

The Cynosure grimaces. "That's the problem—she's not taking any. I'm hoping she will recruit some at the gala. I don't know why she has to be so tough to crack. It makes the game so tedious."

The Exegesis sighs and rubs the bridge of her nose, hardening her quicksilver skin so that there is actually something to pinch. "We're thinking too small. She has a plan for the gala, something that she *wants*. This is not just for show."

INTERLUDE: OUROBOROS

They are both silent for a moment, reasoning through contingencies, possibilities. The Melusine's brazenness, her lack of care about casualties and consequences, has left them unsettled and uncertain.

"I think," the Cynosure finally volunteers, "that this calls for a... change in perspective."

Her conspirator slowly turns to see the Cynosure draped across her chair, eyes cast in a coy look; one finger slips under the strap of her dress, tracing a collarbone.

"That was just the once," the Exegesis says. "A moment of extremis. Necessary."

"And this is *not*?" The Cynosure's tone is shifting—no longer a flirtatious fertility goddess, but something darker, rougher, more primal. "Nothing else has yet worked, and we can each feel our footing shifting under us. Whatever is coming, it requires our combined strength to see us through to the end."

It was an act of final desperation—fighting back-to-back against a rising sea of vermin, Cecilie Kristiansen's cloying laughter lashing them tighter, tearing at their True Names. Two hated foes, united in the common cause of *not dying* to an even more reviled enemy. Similar to the position they are in currently, the Exegesis must admit. But the cost—

"We swore it would not happen again," she replies, voice brittle, the sound of an addict trying to reject that one last hit. "We almost didn't come back at all."

Years of mutual loathing, of endless scheming, of research and prediction—all of it leading to one final moment of perfect clarity and total understanding.

The Cynosure is rising, advancing. Her hips sway, but her heels dig at the floor like claws, and her shoulders are set with the confidence that the Exegesis detests and is intoxicated by. "Tell me you've thought of some way to best our foe, and I will drop this." She steps closer.

"You're saying this because it's an improvement for *you*—" the Exegesis protests, but her mouth has slid open, expectant and hungry lips meeting again.

Long, sharp teeth bite deep. The Cynosure envelops her, is enveloped in turn, the flesh-not-flesh substances of them meeting and intertwining. It is more than sex; it is deeper than any marriage. For a few seconds the Exegesis resists: flings up the barrier of her will, and makes of it an iron wall. But as the Cynosure seeps into her, she *remembers*. The rapture of it. The melding that felt like apotheosis.

Cecilie Kristiansen had them dead to rights, there at the end, was moments away from consuming the two of them to gain their unique magics. To take over two more of High Command and ensure her dominion. So they changed the rules of the game, in desperation—quicksilver and flesh touched, and they slipped inside each other, combined themselves into a new being. One that Cecilie had no knowledge of, no True Name to manipulate: they were impervious. Never had the Exegesis felt the way she did in that moment, half of something so much greater than its parts, completed in a way that made every other moment before and after a waking loneliness.

In those moments, they were *more*. More than human. More than the banal mysteries of this world.

It took them weeks to pull themselves apart, so great was the sensation and so intoxicating the feeling. And they came back different, awakened to previously unknown experiences and desires. Their brutal sex is new, disturbing, visceral, each trying to claw back what they lost—to again be made whole, to seek that sensation of being *true* in corrupted quicksilver and entrails.

And now, the Exegesis stops resisting.

Mercury and black fluids roil. Organs rupture and blood heats to a boiling point. They are two seas merging, tides crashing and breaking themselves upon the other. They are storms that have chance-met in a wild sky. Power flares through the interstices between them, lightning through clouds. The air cooks; the tumors and gore on the floor sear.

And then they are something else.

What stands in the place of the two women is tall, nearly two meters, broad-shouldered and densely made. Their skin shimmers, opalescent, faintly blue in the right light. Their hair, down to mid-back, has the gleam

INTERLUDE: OUROBOROS

particular to scarab wings. Separately, the Cynosure and the Exegesis have eyes of shades natural enough; the amalgam boasts eyes in amber, like an owl's. The ground under their feet is blackened.

They turn this way and that, the sensation of doubled momentum a lurid pleasure. They conjure a mirror and gaze upon themself. A nod; a smile—they are satisfied: there is an easy confidence to them, a swagger almost. Mercury flows and smooths over their body, shaping into a suit and over that a coat. Their hands are long, with perfect fingers and exquisite wrists, like carved instruments. Neither of their halves ever tolerated flaws in their forms, but the combined result is something else again, a product of two perfectionists.

Less pleasing is their immediate prospect, the problem that they melded to face. They look over the information their constituent parts have brought together, feel the warp and weft of the Exegesis' and the Cynosure's assumptions and conclusions. From this, they begin to piece together a fuller understanding of their foe, thoughts completing each other, advancing inexorably toward one stark realization.

They curse, in an alto deeper than either the Cynosure's or the Exegesis'. "We're going to need some allies."

Nine: Beasts of the Earth

RECADAT

Dallas' bungalow broods within the woods of Pulau Sekijang Bendera, remote and far from all civilization, practitioner and not. "I have many safehouses," Dallas is saying, "stashed away on almost every continent."

"Do you always anticipate some sort of oncoming disaster?"

The tiger has taken on a different form for our egress to this island, to evade scrying and surveillance. It's wise, but I'm perturbed as I watch a petite blonde move about the room, her features delicate as a doll's.

Dallas has laid Orfea on the bed and tucked her in: the doctor continues to be unresponsive, despite my best efforts. I know how to keep her body alive; I don't know how to do the rest, how to wake her mind.

"Yes," says the tiger, finally answering my question. "Before."

She doesn't elaborate what *before* means, but I get the clear sense that it's another epoch, another life almost; that *before* existed as a sharp delineation from *now*. There was a time Olesya and Dallas lived in vigilance. Because of Kristiansen? Something else? And that's supposed to be all in the past. Yet here we are. "How long have we been gone, do you think?"

"Three days," she says with no uncertainty, no need to look at a clock or a phone. Internal clock, perhaps. Some mysterious feline quality, or at any rate an inhuman quality.

Three days that seemed to us like mere hours. How powerful is the Melusine, to have maintained something like that, to distort not only that illusory space but time's passage itself. How powerful is Olesya herself? I wonder if she can resist the other her, should she try; how long she can hold out, in a duel. And then I realize I am drawing parallels. How long will I resist the hive's hunger? How long can I hold out, and remain myself?

Instead of discussing tactics and resources, I find myself saying to Dallas, "Do you change your appearance often?"

She cuts me a look. "No. Why?"

I chew on my lip. I am nearing a question I must ask myself. "Why not? You must have quite a collection."

"Well, for one, Olesya seems to like my preferred form just fine." She starts to chuckle—this petite blonde has a higher-pitched voice, making it more a giggle; it adds to the disorientation. Then she sobers. "For another, it took me a long time to find the face I liked best. She was a woman who died with honor, and I wanted to commemorate her. Then I found out she suited me most, felt like *me* more than all the others."

"And," I say, quiet, "what does that mean?" What does it feel like, to have a sense of self, to be so certain and absolute in it?

Her eyes meet mine. Those remain consistent across each of her forms, a lambent green not found in human irises. "You're not really asking about me. But I'll humor you. What I am, at the very core, is the tiger soul—that's my true essence. Yet the face and body you usually see, that's me also. Both form halves to a whole. The tiger's simple; it is indisputably myself. The other was part intuition and part fortune. I took many hearts and did not see myself in them. I took this woman's, and finally found a skin I could see myself moving around on two legs forever. Certainly many before her were an ill fit. I wore a prince, and found him not quite right; I wore a duke, and felt the same. For a long time I didn't think *any* two-legged shape could ever be more than a costume."

None of this is helping me, as such. And yet it's the closest, isn't it? She is the only one who might understand a little, or help me understand myself. I have reached out, blind, and a hand has grasped back.

"Inside my library," I say, halting and hesitant, "there are practitioners who could take other forms. I've sometimes thought about accessing them." As an escape hatch from myself, the thin hope that another body might not be afflicted as mine is. "But then I might lose what little I've got of me."

She's brushing her hair away from her face, frowning at the unfamiliar stray locks. "Is that something you think about a lot?"

"Doesn't everyone imagine being someone else, on occasion?" I try to make my tone light. It doesn't land. "I guess—in an odd way, I want to try that. Maybe wearing someone else's skin for a while could give me a respite from being me. But… I worry what'll happen if I look into the mirror and another person looks back, and what if I can't change back; what if this is a way for Cecilie to somehow return and take me over? I realize it might not make sense, but—" But I've always thought my remaining sense of self is the sole bulwark between the world and Cecilie Kristiansen's resurrection. This realization has not crystallized before; now I can articulate it.

"I'm a hunter of the most honed senses. I have not once smelled Kristiansen on you." Dallas is ticking off her fingers. I'm distracted by how her hands look so small; I find myself missing her normal ones, the long fingers and their strength. It's strange to think there is a form of her I'm most accustomed to when we have known each other for mere days. "Olesya cut you open, and found no Kristiansen in you either."

Except Olesya is compromised, I want to say. Yet I cannot advance that thought without insulting her tiger's instincts too. So instead I stare down at my own hands, and imagine them to be someone else's.

"I don't think," she goes on, "you necessarily need to become someone else. I think you need to rediscover *you*. But in the meantime, you've got shapeshifters in you. You are afraid of the insects, or becoming them. So try something else. Think of it as refreshing your wardrobe."

Absurd. It is not that simple; it cannot possibly be. Besides, it is perilous. "If I disappear into those forms—if I lose what little remains of Recadat Kongmanee—"

"Then I'll pull you back." Dallas shrugs. "It's like teaching a cub her limits. But look, you asked me if we could call upon people for help. I'm going to step out for a minute to try that. You stay here, and watch over your doctor."

She requires privacy for her calls. That is fair enough. But remaining here makes me restless, and so after Dallas has left, I pluck out a few hairs

NINE: BEASTS OF THE EARTH

and lay them in strategic locations, to act as sentinels—wards and cantrips, shaped from my own flesh. Fitting.

I head off in a direction opposite to Dallas'. The island is said to be haunted, the soil saturated with unquiet ghosts who died in great pain and misery. Cholera: a terrible way to go. I wonder how the old me felt, to not go among the non-practitioners and teach them our ways. Or maybe I did? I don't know how complicit I am in these systems of power. Or was. Maybe I have problems with tense, too.

But the criticism stands, all the clearer for the limbo I now exist in, all conventions shorn of context and laid bare. There are afflictions that can destroy a thaumaturge, but most mundane diseases are nothing to mages, easily prevented or dispelled with this rite or that act of fleshcrafting. To be a sorcerer is to live thrice as long as the rest of humanity, to be part of a chosen aristocracy, numinous and above.

And yet there is no laying on of hands; no manna comes from on high. A mage regards non-practitioners as very like ants: I do not need to ask Olesya if she shares that opinion, for all that she hires a few of them to serve as snipers (one does not need special training to handle enchanted guns, for the most part). They can be useful pawns or servants. Equals, never.

I guess I must count myself among this order. It's little surprise that my mother, chosen as an apprentice by a mage (who was that? I can't remember), was so desperate to earn the respect of high society: she wanted us to become part of them, even though it's impossible this quickly. Maybe in five generations, maybe six. We haven't the pedigree, the brilliance. Plenty of clans never amount to anything but minor workers of cantrips, and it would take decades of work to close that distance, to demonstrate you are something *more*.

I do not remember the particulars of this weight—what it meant to be the second generation, to have the future success of my family rest on my shoulders—but I can feel the worn grooves where it rested.

My thoughts are academic; my feelings on the matter, as incoherent and inchoate as they are, do not affect lived reality—anyone who spreads spells and thaumaturgy too readily would be assassinated by the rest. It's the logic of a monopoly maintaining itself, or a cartel protecting its turf. I could cure cancer, and then overnight have my skin ripped clean off my bones, my soul torn asunder or my liver picked at by eagles forever. You're not supposed to give the mortals fire, or the wheel, or the possibility that things could be better. After all, too many practitioners mean more competition for unlocking the world's mysteries.

To be a mage is to be a narcissist of the highest order. I wonder if I was like that, before Cecilie. I wonder if it's possible for a mage to be a good person at all, an ethical person, someone who tries to do what is right.

Once, as I make circuits around the bungalow, I encounter a ghost. But it's such a thin, shredded thing that it can't possibly harm or haunt anyone. Its intent, and even identity, has been long lost. The only thing anyone could do for it would be exorcism. That, though, is beyond me. All this stolen sorcery at my fingertips, buzzing and chittering in my brain, and still I can do only so much. None of what I hold within me can offer anyone peace or meaningful restoration.

We stare at each other for a long time, eyes sunken and hair bleached, until only one of us remains.

DALLAS

I attempt to raise Chang'er, first.

The geas prevents me from so much as thumbing at her contact on the burner phone I've stashed in the bungalow. When I try again, I drop the phone; it cracks hard against a stray pebble. I stare at my hands for a solid minute. "Fuck," I say, to no one in particular. I tamp down my fury at Olesya, telling myself again—and again—that she was not in her right mind when she cast that geas. And I wonder, too, if it's been a thorn in her side all this time that she couldn't express the full extent of her might; if she's always wanted to unleash it all… but Recadat and I already discussed that. Yes, perhaps. Perhaps the woman I love most in this world has a barely suppressed core of rage.

NINE: BEASTS OF THE EARTH

But then, the inside of any human is full of unspeakable secrets, filth and rot. The difference is the outer shell of control, and for most of her life she's exercised that part commendably.

In theory, Yves is unreachable: she is in some otherworld place, separated from here by entire realms. My link to her, though, exceeds the reach of any mage's. Someone could conduct a ritual to reach her, and she'd never hear it, but I have something more: my body serves as one of the anchors that roots her to this reality. Even if she is not here at the moment, I can feel a thread running out into the great unknown, at the end of which is someone who might be able to help us.

I brace myself for something to go wrong, and then I call her name: "Yves."

Her response comes much slower than usual, but it does come. A whisper of the deep, a coil of smoke, shimmering gray in the air. I startle when I see what the haze resolves into: not the form of Yves, but that of her warlock wife.

"Viveca?" I ask, startled. "Has something gone wrong? Is Yves okay?"

But on second appraisal, the warlock's eyes glow amber, and her face splits into a smirk that I have known for hundreds of years. "It's me, tiger," Yves' voice comes back, reassuring in its gravely confidence.

"Why are you taking your wife's form?" I ask before I can think better of it.

"Why are you small and blonde, tiger?" she counters. "You're lucky you called at the right time."

"What, the rare pauses between you and Viveca doing the nuptial deed?"

A low, rumbling chuckle. I have missed it, a little. "Much as I'd like a real honeymoon, you know it's a working vacation. We're running a heist on a gambling den that exclusively caters to demons and forbids humans on pain of death. To everyone else, I've just possessed a hapless human." She raises Viveca's hands, rolls them to look at the palms and the back. "It's... an interesting experience. Very... embodying."

I try to turn my thoughts to the reason I called, but the geas interferes. Instead, I chuff and affect offense. "You never possessed me!"

"Would you have liked it?" There is a sea of complicated emotions packed into that one sentence: a predatory growl that promises to consume me, an edge of respect that acknowledges that I would very much not like to lose command of my body.

In this regard, I think darkly, it appears that Yves has been the superior partner to me than Olesya.

Yves does not wait for an answer. "Viveca says 'hi', by the way. She..." A look of distant amusement crosses Viveca's face, as if the demon is listening to a joke shouted up to her from the bottom of a great ravine. "She thinks you are looking particularly sexy, in a rumpled sort of way. I have to agree—my wife has excellent taste."

Olesya is in danger, I think. *Please help.* I smile. "Are the two of you undercover as swingers? Perhaps next you will conspire together to buy me a drink from across the bar?"

A deep, genuine laugh this time, and I think I can hear a touch of Viveca in it. And then an ominous turn, Viveca's face clouding with Yves' dark thoughts. "I do not know the full details of what the two of you went through during my momentary exile from your realm, but I know that you have earned Viveca's undying loyalty. Whatever might happen, you have a true friend and ally in her, in all things."

I am screaming inside my own head. But now real emotion chokes my throat—not the kind I want, but earnest all the same. "You say that like you won't be around forever."

"Do you know what we are trying to steal?" Yves asks, and I shake my head. "We are working to uncover a lost grimoire of Elizaveta Hua's. Within is said to be information on the greatest foe of the Hua household, going back to their very first generation—a being of searing light and crystalline brutality by the name of Nuawa. Now that we know Elizaveta was not murdered by Cecilie Kristiansen, we think she died fighting Nuawa."

A being of light and glass? Then come back! We are probably fighting Nuawa at this very second!

A sigh, a further opening of honesty from the demon. "I was exiled once. I can be hurt. Nuawa is anathema to my kind, capable of inflicting on demons a true death. I'm scared, truth be told, and seeing you just made me melancholy. And it reaffirmed that I will die for you and Viveca. If I do, please again look out for each other."

Viveca's eyes are wet with Yves' emotion; I wonder if this is the first time that the demon has truly cried.

Apparently the same thought occurs to Yves; she clears her throat. "Being stuck in a human body apparently means putting up with human physiology. Enough about me. So what is it? You didn't call to check on how we're doing. There must be an urgent reason."

I want to rip away my own face. I want to tear off my arm and write in the blood *Help*. But the geas prevents me from doing anything so dramatic—nothing that would disturb Viveca's adventure. Still, I try again. "Remember that bar we frequent—the one where I first asked you to *help Olesya*? We'll meet back there *again*."

Yves—dumb, handsome Yves—does not intuit my meaning. Normally she is sharper than this; the gambling den must be taking up all her concentration, and I am most likely talking to a split fragment. "Well, of course."

An awkward pause. I try a different tack. "Do you, theoretically, know of a way to remove a geas? I'm trying to help a friend."

Yves scratches Viveca's chin in thought. "They're awful things, a bit different for each caster and victim. Did you know Olesya Hua put one on Chang'er, to compel her to flee to safety when Kristiansen's minions destroyed the family estate?"

I did *not* know that; neither Chang'er nor Olesya ever mentioned it to me. "You talk with Chang'er?"

"She's a nasty mahjong player. I'm several treasuries in debt to her." I cannot tell if Yves is joking. "Chang'er apparently pulled apart Olesya's compulsion with her bare hands—that woman is terrifying. Most of the time, though, to deal with a geas you need precision tools or a mage of greater puissance than the one who cast it."

There is a noise on Yves' end, and she glances away to see some new development on her end. "We're about to participate in a deathmatch, with the grimoire we want as a potential prize. Viveca and I are in agreement, though—if this involves Olesya or our family, just say the word, and we'll be back there instantly."

Yes. "No, not at all. I'd never trouble your vacation. When you're back with your ill-gotten gains, we'll talk again."

Yves nods, her specter beginning to dissipate. "Viveca and I love you. Go be with Olesya. We'll see you soon."

Once the connection is well and truly vanished, I scream as I have never screamed before, a roar that tears into the jungle beyond, echoing through the wilds of this dark forest. Trees still; animals freeze in fear.

"So you have a geas on you," Recadat says, deadpan, from the doorway.

RECADAT

In Orfea's sickroom, I am afraid. Perhaps *afraid* is the wrong word; my body still cannot muster an adrenaline response to most stimuli, and I have no hopes, no dreams, no family from which I may be shorn. I have no reason to worry that a future that does not contain me would be lessened. But I have—*all* I have, after I was cast out of the Hua estate—is obligation to the woman who lies still before me, and the certainty that the city's most powerful sorceress is both deeply unwell and may mean us harm. Why did I think, really, that I had found a place where I could rest and belong; why did I believe Olesya Hua.

The bungalow's cantrips are as I left them before my walkabout, tiny spells of monitoring and detection. Each, though minor, fills me with discomfort and rolling nausea. But that is normal for me, now; will remain so until the hive finally tears me apart from the inside, consuming all that I am, feeding Cecilie Kristiansen's ghost wherever she is now. How she will laugh at her curse destroying this thief of her sorcery.

I think back to my brief stay in the siren's cage—I did not feel helpless then; I do feel helpless now. Forces are moving around us in uncertain trajectories, and I don't know where and when they will collide, how I can prevent or redirect the impact.

NINE: BEASTS OF THE EARTH

From outside comes a scream. Raw, primal, a thing that does not belong here but which belongs to the jungle—the roar of the queen claiming her territory, or a roar of pain.

I follow the sound.

Dallas is bent double around the noise she has just made. It might well have gone on if she didn't raise her head and find me watching.

"So you have a geas on you," I say. I'm not sure how I should be sounding, like I'm offering condolences or what.

Her eyes follow me, wary. She can't say either yes or no, of course; that's the point of a geas.

"I wasn't listening," I clarify. "Or wasn't trying to." *But I crave knowledge and gossip*, I want to add. *I will make of all this world's secrets my possessions.* "But my magic hears things and… it sounds as if you were trying to ask for help, but were compelled not to. Give me your phone; I'll call Chang'er."

Dallas brightens. "Oh, that's a fantastic idea. Thank you."

She pulls out her phone, types in the unlock code to give me access, then drops it to the ground and smashes it underfoot.

"For *fuck's* sake," Dallas moans. "I can fucking walk through *wards*."

For a few seconds I look at the shards of shattered plastic. "Shall I attempt to remove it?"

She makes an abortive laugh. "Seems like our best option. Let's do it."

I nod to a fallen log. "Sit down there. Let me see if I can even find it, first."

Dallas does as asked, her body language tense as I stand over her, sending tendrils of power into her. She hisses. Being worked on magically is likely not something she's familiar with—she appears to have a latent resistance to magic, and a tiger as old as she can heal her own wounds, no doctor needed. But I do need to reach deep inside her; a geas is like a seed forced into a body to take root.

She grimaces and twitches, jerking away from this touch. "This is… not pleasant."

"Dallas, I'm trying—I just need to grab—" I can feel the edges of the geas on the fingertips of my soul; it wraps around Dallas' neck, then plunges deeper into her self. I almost have it—

But the damn cat keeps wiggling. The log beneath us creaks and bursts under the crushing pressure of her grip. I ride her down to the ground, relentless; I am a hunter, too, and knowledge is returning to my limbs—not stolen but mine, training from S&C in how to tackle and restrain unruly suspects.

"Stop fucking fighting," I bark, the steely edge of command in my voice shocking even me. Her claws are out, even in human form, and my body registers that I have been wounded—she's cut me open somewhere. But I've rolled her over on her face now, hands on her neck, a knee mercilessly driving into her spine. "I am trying to help—"

She shifts under me, into her full tiger form, and hurls me off. I land and something cracks—but even as I am rolling away, my body is shifting, too, instinct compelling me into a form more suited for this combat. In the next instant, I have tackled her back, my own claws raking her coat, my own fangs nipping at her haunches.

We tear into each other, the pent-up stress of the past several days unleashed in a bloodletting. She is scared for herself and her partner; she is furious at the betrayal that has left her bound, at her own inability to escape the geas; she is a wounded animal, lashing out at the hand that might open the trap and free her.

And I am scared, too—for Orfea; for the curse that binds me, in a different but equally terrifying way; for Dallas herself, who is shorn of all support and friendship in a time of crisis. I have no tongue to express this, no ear for the right words, no way to speak except through tooth and claw; I open my lips to give comfort and succeed in flashing my teeth, all my baseness laid bare.

Between us, restraint is torn asunder, the gristle two predators will rip apart between them. The ground under us drinks deep as we twist and turn out of the other's killing blow. Claws sink into flesh, past epidermis and fat. Fangs like knives, talons like fire. We fight in the way of two conflagrations lapping at one another.

And there! I finally have it—my teeth are around the geas, ready to break it, to crush it in my mighty maw, to—to—

NINE: BEASTS OF THE EARTH

Dallas is beneath me in her human shape, the proper one rather than the blonde. She is bloodied and bruised, and in my jaw is her throat, my teeth poised to puncture the skin; my muscles vibrate with the lust to crush bone and windpipe.

"You asked me why Olesya loves something that can tear her apart at a moment's notice," Dallas says, gasping for air, watching me with fearless green eyes. "This is my answer."

In my mind's eye, I take in the shape of me, so new and foreign: not a bug or some eldritch beast, but a panther with a luxurious coat of shadow, teeth and claws of the most lustrous ivory, eyes of stunning topaz.

Under my awareness, this shape lasts only a second longer. I shift back into my human form immediately, shocked and embarrassed and somehow hurt that my body would *lie* to me like this. Dallas is still under me, but now I am heaving against her chest. My face is wet; am I sobbing? I do not know; no part of my vast power, my pilfered knowledge, can tell me what I am feeling, explain how I am reacting.

"You listened to my advice," Dallas says, wincing. "That certainly wasn't a bug."

I am unconvinced; it wasn't a conscious decision. And why did I choose to be another sort of cat? I try to avoid thinking about it further.

"The geas isn't coming off," I mutter, pulling back to kneel above her. "Not without one or both of us losing a limb."

"Doesn't look like it." She sighs and licks her lips. I follow the movement of her tongue to her eyes; instead of disappointment or anger, I am shocked to find a hunger that matches—not the hive's, but *mine*. The hunger that has made me avert my eyes from her muscled back, that clean and simple lust. She inhales and I know, without her voicing it, that she is aware of what I am thinking and what I'm remembering.

I both expect and don't expect it when her hands grip my jaw and her mouth presses on mine. Her teeth are so sharp, and she's starved—it must have been some time since she last ate, and she laps at my blood. It stings; it draws a tight line between where she's sucking and my libido. Her tongue slips into my mouth and I want, so very badly, to relax and let her take me.

I want her to tear me to pieces and gorge on my guts. In her stomach and beating arteries I would be cleansed.

"Fight back," she whispers against my mouth. "Where's your spirit?"

And at this prodding, something cracks—not like my bones from a hard landing, but like scar tissue giving away, like joints again finding movement. Anger winds through my lust. I was not always some broken thing, too weak to command my own fate. I was strong once, hale, respected. People were afraid of me. I had power, to help and to hurt.

And I am beginning to realize that I want that again—not Kristiansen's envy, not my magic's hunger, but *me*.

She's already naked, as am I; neither of our outfits survived the change and the brawl. My hands slip against her flesh, seeking a handhold, and close on her hips. Finding the right angle, I buck and throw her off.

The shock on her face is priceless, and it gives me the opportunity to shove her down into the ground beneath us with all my weight. On top now, I bend to run my tongue along the wounds I made in animal form, and discover that while I may not be a thing designed to eat raw, her blood has a wonderful tang to it that I cannot get enough of.

She growls and pushes back against my grip. "I don't let just anyone have my blood, panther."

"Then what are you going to do about it?" I taunt as I hold her back down, take another lick.

After this, we tussle again, less harsh this time, still frenzied for all that. We tear at the grass, tear up one another. It's the most alive I have ever been, eclipsing every memory my broken soul holds. It is as though she is my very first lover, and we've met not in languorous desire but in combat. We laugh; we snarl. We forget, for one fleeting moment, the pain that has led us to this point, the paths that have led us to this intersection, crashing together.

And between us grows this beastial need, this mighty lust, ravaging us as surely as our claws. Dallas grips my hips tight, drawing blood; I grind along her hard member, my hand at her throat. She is massive beneath me, and I bite down on my lip as she guides herself into me.

It seems so long ago that I watched her in the garden with her mate. I coveted what they had so much then; I covet now. I want more; I push down, taking her nearly to the hilt. This is almost a mistake—I'm so filled that for a moment I must remain still, to breathe, to adjust. Then she pushes deeper, and I struggle to keep my gasps locked behind my teeth, all semblance of control fleeing. She moves, or I move, and both of us take our fight to its logical conclusion. I clench tight around her, double over from the shock, bite her shoulder and scream into the flesh and blood I find there; at the same moment, she rakes my back, pulling me tight in a crushing embrace—and this, finally, pushes us both over the edge together. Fighting and fucking lie this close to each other, for her especially, and perhaps for me too; the way we thrash and arch is not so different.

Eventually we separate, each of us sated and bleeding, lying in the dirt as if we are wild animals. I am sore in muscles I did not know I had; sore in a healthy way, as if all my ills have sloughed away and left me healed and new. Still, I find something to worry about—is this the time for pillow talk? There are no pillows. Again, my lack of knowledge is evident. Or maybe it doesn't matter. I rest, let my heart rate drop, let my breathing slow. For the first time in memory, I know peace.

It's then that we hear Orfea laugh, loud and raucous, from inside the bungalow. She has regained consciousness. I don't think to find clothes before I rush back in to check on her.

And... she is not alone. The shock is followed by an oppressive weight—the sinking feeling of being in the presence of true power.

At her bedside sits a handsome mage in a perfectly tailored suit, lines so crisp and precise that it seems as if their existence cuts through the lesser stuff of reality. Their adornments are likewise—exquisite cufflinks, tiny earrings in the shapes of complex whorls. Orfea looks at them with genuine joy; when she turns to us, her face falls back to its typical disdain. "Oh, it's you," she says. "Done rutting?"

Dallas is beside me now, in her tiger form, hissing; her instincts, too, tell her that this interloper is dangerous.

"My apologies," the stranger says smoothly, standing to their towering full height; if my state of undress, or the awareness of what Dallas and I were just doing, offends them, they have no trace of it on their sharp chin or shining brow. "Dr. Leung and I were just talking about a kitten she saved last week. Brilliant woman, very funny. Absolutely a shame how the Exegesis' calumniation ruined her medical career."

Even now, as she and her career are being spoken of in the third person, Orfea stares up at the mage in unabashed happiness; the smile is incongruous, even disturbing, on her lined face. Either this is the good doctor's oldest friend, or we are dealing with a mesmer.

The mage looks us over, prepared as we are for combat, and smiles in what they probably think is a disarming manner. "I restored Dr. Leung to health as a sign of good faith. I've come to talk—I think we share a common foe. I need your help crashing a party."

Ten: Stone Butch Blues

Lussadh and Fahriye rouse themselves eventually. It has been years since either slept wrapped in the warmth of another. Outside it is still dark, well before dawn—but even this early, the city is unusually silent, save the sirens of emergency vehicles in the distance. When the sun rises, businesses and schools will stay closed, afraid of a new attack; the atmosphere weighs heavy and still. There is no rhythm or reason forthcoming, no demands, no obvious cause, and that makes it all worse: the lack of explanation denies the shocked and grieving city a chance to process. So a city sits silent, waiting for a lie that would bring sense to an atrocity.

Save the Melusine, Lussadh and Fahriye alone know the cause of this disaster and are uniquely situated to bring the perpetrator to justice. They are also too familiar with death, less fazed by the scale and scope of the destruction than any normal person ought to. And that, too, is at the core of their long loneliness.

But this morning, at least, neither is alone in the dark—there is the noise of someone else in the bathroom, the sound of a second chair scraping across the kitchen floor.

"That wasn't Nuawa," Lussadh says, standing at the stove; she is carefully bringing a cezve to boil.

"I will trust your analysis," replies Fahriye slowly, not looking up; she sits at the kitchen counter, staring at the remaining cufflink. "I never met the genuine article."

Lussadh now knows this woman well enough to see she is mulling over her culpability in yesterday's events—if it was action or inaction that brought about this atrocity, weighing how much guilt she should feel for her tool being the catalyst of so much destruction.

"I think," Lussadh begins, trying to turn her companion's thoughts away from self-flagellation, "that we are nearing the climax of a fight that has been centuries in the making."

Her gambit pays off: Fahriye flicks her wrist, and the cufflink disappears into some pocket of holding. "Go on."

"My tenure at Shenzhen University was secured by Sealing and Containment's not-so-subtle pressure on the administration: I wrote an occasional report for them, they kept me from getting fired. I did extensive research on the Huas—you know this, you have copies of my reports."

"I did a bit more than that," Fahriye admits, guiltily glancing away. "I was the one that set your research agenda, on top of providing an annual assessment concerning your usefulness to S&C."

This gets Lussadh to twist around, forgetting the food. "You motherfucker," she says with a snort.

"I *am* literally that, too." This is, Fahriye realizes, the first joke she has ever cracked about sleeping with Elizaveta. "Suffice it to say, you researched the Huas because I needed an outside expert to provide trusted analysis."

Lussadh puts two and two together. "You couldn't research Nuawa yourself, but you could commission someone else to generally meander in that direction. Under the threat of firing, I might add."

"That wasn't the only thing you researched—some esoteric fact you procured saved my life more than once. But yes. If it is any consolation, I did my best to return the favor. You'd break someone's nose, and I'd show up at the department head's house and politely explain, *again*, that you couldn't be fired. I think I endowed three chairs with the bribes."

"You—Fahriye Budak, I'm shocked that you'd be the type to stoop to *bribes*. For a *woman*."

"It certainly wasn't going to be a man." Was humor supposed to come this easy? Had it, once? "And the bribes are what gets you—not the creepy parasocial relationship?"

The professor uses the Turkish coffee as an excuse to turn back to the

TEN: STONE BUTCH BLUES

stove, mumbling something as she does. When Fahriye asks her to repeat herself, she raises her voice. "My unit had standing orders to cooperate with any S&C investigation led by you and *only* you."

"You're serious."

"Don't look at me like that," she adds, keeping her eyes on the cezve. "You have something of a reputation, Ms. Budak. To a group of superstitious mercenaries, crossing you would have been like killing the albatross—please imagine my lack of surprise when one of my soldiers, a twenty-something from the Siberia, told me that when she was a kid, you defended her village from a near-immortal monster."

"Oh, that's an old one. Must have been—wait, that's when I got the copy of *Liber Juratus Honorii* that I traded you."

"Yeah, though I can't seem to find the volume; must have misplaced it somewhere around here." Lussadh pauses to begin pouring the thick coffee. "That youngster from Siberia has saved a lot of people, you know. Keep stuff like that in mind, when you're weighing your good deeds against the evil you have inadvertently caused."

Fahriye changes the topic. "You were saying something about this being the culmination of a fight, centuries in the making?"

"One of the facts I kept out of those reports is the long history of violence between the Huas and High Command. It has lasted several generations, an ontological difference between a cabal that seeks perfect control and a family that seeks absolute freedom. Lost to the past is the real reason Sealing and Containment was founded—supposedly, the negotiated settlement between these two irreconcilable camps was the creation of a neutral and impartial arbitrator. That was never the reality, obviously… and now that S&C has ceased to exist, it would seem that the need for pretense is over, too."

They sip their coffee in thought. "The problem with that theory," Fahriye says at length, "is that you told me the Melusine introduced themself as the newest member of their little club. Young, by my reckoning, and their methods are completely at odds with how High Command has functioned before."

"So what are you thinking—a Young Turk, agitating for a new tack? A coup?"

The inspector mulls the idea by distracting herself. "Speaking of Turks, this is the best Turkish coffee I have ever had in my life, and I was born there."

"The trick is treating the cezve like a skillet and never washing it."

A smile, then another thoughtful nod. "I died fighting one of Cecilie Kristiansen's lackeys, who gloated over my body that Kristiansen and High Command were in league. Given High Command's fascination with True Names, and how Cecilie's power functioned, I'm willing to believe this. Or maybe she had consumed some of them and manipulated the organization to support her. Either way, I suspect our destruction of Kristiansen destabilized them more than we know."

"'Our'?" Lussadh can't help it: the detail snags, and Maria did say Fahriye thinks of herself as the Huas' protector.

"I guess it isn't exactly public knowledge. Yes, I was there in the final fight against Cecilie. Maria Ying, too, believe it or not."

"You had a hand in defeating *that*?" Kristiansen was thought to be nigh-immortal. So many hives, so many avatars, all to feed her endless ambition. Her destruction was glad tidings to many, not out of any morality but the simple fact that nobody wanted to be eaten and turned into bugs. "Maria, too?"

Fahriye rocks her head back and forth, suddenly bashful. "Viveca did most of the work. That and her demon. I mostly hit things very hard."

There's warmth when she speaks of the warlock, Lussadh thinks, a deep familiarity and a regard she might reserve for a beloved niece. What she had with Elizaveta was much more than an affair. A pang, but Lussadh buries it. She is too old to be jealous of a dead woman, and in any case she and Fahriye are so nascent. It's not as if Lussadh's got relatives she dotes on and whom she'd like Fahriye to regard with the same kindness. "Whether this is Nuawa or High Command, the Huas are our natural allies in the endeavor. Why don't we contact them? We can compare notes—and at the very least, you probably want to warn them."

"Until now, I wouldn't have been able to, since it involves Nuawa and so—the geas." Fahriye draws herself up, careful still with the furniture; she winces when it creaks. "Viveca is off to pursue something of her mother's, and she's not reachable. Doctor Orfea and I used to be friendly acquaintances, but it seems that's the case no longer; I can only hope she survived. So, we go to Olesya. It'll be simpler once we join forces."

Fahriye calls ahead, first; it is not picked up, except by a secretary who asks if they have an appointment, and who then informs them that Master Olesya is not seeing anyone at this moment. "Tell her it's Fahriye Bu—" But the secretary has already hung up.

The former inspector purses her mouth. "No matter," she says. "We will visit in person. Her alchemist will let us in."

Olesya Hua's estate is situated in a part of the city that is, for all intents and purposes, inaccessible to non-practitioners: a legacy of the time when a Hua ancestor established herself here, and all but ran Singapore as a tyrant queen. That was many generations ago, but the estate—though rebuilt—harbors the despot's shadow still. Lussadh can see the echoes: her cruelty, a knife-glint of her viciousness.

At the gate, they're met with human security and told, in no uncertain terms, that Olesya Hua is not receiving visitors. "We're here to see her alchemist, Master Chang'er," says Fahriye.

"Master Chang'er," says the guard, "is on a leave of absence."

"That's ridiculous. She's of this household."

"Nevertheless, Ms. Budak, she is not here."

Asking after Dallas Seidel only deepens the animosity; they are turned away, the gate remains shut. Fahriye stands there, confused and—Lussadh thinks—a little hurt. "I can get us in," Lussadh offers.

"Maybe not in broad daylight." The powerful, broad woman looks deflated. "Or maybe not at all."

It's a humid day, not that she expects Fahriye can feel it, or at least not completely. "Let's get somewhere with air conditioning that serves nice, cold things. My treat."

In the ice cream parlor—open despite the so-called terrorist attack, but empty because of it—the former inspector hunts through an incredible range of flavors and fat percentages to settle on one scoop of nutella, one scoop of pistachio. At the table, she tastes a little then puts down her spoon.

"Not to your liking?" Lussadh has gotten dark chocolate and a gelato with a kick of rum in it.

"It's not that. I actually can taste a bit of it—I wonder if that's a temperature thing. Gods, if I should just eat everything either frozen or piping hot. It's just…" Fahriye takes a big spoonful, as if to distract herself. "We were starting to develop a relationship, I thought."

For a brief second, Lussadh believes the inspector is talking about the two of them. She realizes her error immediately: "The Hua sisters are like your own kin."

"Maybe. I wouldn't go that far. Hell, I've got my own relatives, some sisters and a lot of nieces and nephews. We've… drifted apart. I haven't even told them about the homunculus issue, I just email every so and so." The former inspector sighs. "I'm not trying to replace the Huas' mother. I just feel—"

"Guilty?" Lussadh supplies, between her own mouthfuls. The gelato melts fast, after all, and she doesn't like to waste food. Too much time on the field, with field rations like sand in her mouth.

"They'd have had easier lives if their mother had survived in the homunculus," Fahriye says.

Lussadh puts down her cup and spoon, having polished off all her ice cream. "I may sound callous, but even by mage standards those two have led lives of luxury. Children lose their parents violently all the time."

Fahriye makes a face. "Don't get along with yours, do you?"

"No." An easy admission: Lussadh makes no secret of what she thinks of her family, though this is rather more vulnerable than her wont. She hasn't had anyone to confide in for some time. "My father—no mothers in our family; a linguistic quirk—invested a great deal into heir-making, both me and my sibling Nuriya. It wasn't that terrible, in the early years; that's when she taught me to cook." A flash of dark emotion crosses Lussadh's face, breaking the surface for a moment before being hauled back down into the depths. "But by the time I was officially named heir, my father couldn't see

TEN: STONE BUTCH BLUES

me as a person anymore, just a... a vessel for her family ambitions. I—we had a falling out; when my father passed, I did not attend her funeral."

The inspector picks her spoon up to listlessly push her ice cream about, uncomfortable. "I guess I should be more grateful for what I have." Comparing her healthier home life to Lussadh's nest of vipers, chastising herself for chasing the affection of some new family as she grows distant from her own flesh and blood—it's unclear what Fahriye regrets.

"Bite the ice cream," Lussadh suggests. For a moment, Fahriye is confused—how this is supposed to help with her inner turmoil?—so the professor follows up with, "Just humor me."

Fahriye does as asked, and almost immediately drops the ice cream in shock—the intensity of the cold against her front teeth registers as a piercing pain.

At the success of her experiment, Lussadh flashes the slightest, self-satisfied smirk. "So it *is* temperature extremes. It's a start—there are certain chronic conditions or unusual sensitivity issues that present similarly. We could..." She trails off when she sees the look Fahriye has fixed her with.

The inspector gives a muted chuckle. "You're really not letting this go, are you?"

"I want to see you at peace with your body." Too late, Lussadh realizes this goes too far, is too much to admit: it is so personal. So she deflects with the least personal, most clinical explanation she can think of: "My family didn't breed me for just perfection. Yes, I mean *breed*—my life was an infinitely complex series of Punnett squares, each decision made consciously with an eye toward what would serve me as the *heir*. So I think I know a thing or two about being cast into a body you did not ask for, the inheritor of a laborious effort that you did not want."

"That sounds terrible. I am sorry, truly."

"Then weep for yourself, Fahriye Budak—gifts were made of our bodies, and we were each obligated to accept them without choice or input. And now we must live with the weight of this... perfection." Her tone twists, sour, on the final word.

"I—I don't see my birth family much, because they wouldn't understand,"

Fahriye admits. "Not the stone skin, not the job, not…" The loneliness, the violence. The gnawing chasm, where a name and a life should be.

Lussadh scoffs. "And you find that understanding among the Huas and the al-Kattans. You really must keep better company." She begins to help herself to part of Fahriye's uneaten ice cream. "Have you considered new pronouns?"

Again, Fahriye is bewildered. "Excuse me?"

"We're still talking about how comfortable you are with your body. Please keep up." Another ghost of a smile on Lussadh's face, and Fahriye finds herself wondering what she must do to see it more, to make it last longer. "So: are you still she/her, or does the new body come with new pronouns?"

"I don't—does it work like that? I've never thought about it."

"Everything is malleable, my friend. Our bodies, our fates—even this city, as the events of the past few days have demonstrated. Maybe your self-perception has changed; maybe you would be more comfortable in your own flesh if you acknowledged it, in some meaningful way, as something new."

"That's not quite it. I don't find this a bad fit so much as…" Fahriye shifts her weight carefully on her chair; in truth she is not even sitting on it, but semi-levitates above the flimsy plastic thing. "It doesn't affect the world the way I'm used to. I will go days without eating or sleeping, and when I realize this, it is… disorienting. Dehumanizing. An imperfect friction, and not something I can remedy with the usual solutions."

"So more a dysmorphia than a dysphoria, perhaps?" Lussadh's tone manages to alloy dispassionate analysis with an obvious and sincere desire to help; Fahriye's not certain how she pulls it off.

"Maybe?" she replies. "I—hey, I'm still eating that! Get your own!"

"I did get my own," Lussadh says, escalating her efforts to get around her partner's now-vigilant spoon. "I bought *both* ice creams, and I'm not going to let yours go to waste."

Fahriye responds in the most childish way possible: by grabbing the remaining ice cream and shoveling it into her mouth. She is immediately punished for her hubris, clutching at her head in the throes of a brain freeze.

TEN: STONE BUTCH BLUES

"Alright, alright," she says through the tears, "did *you* ever mess around with your pronouns?"

"My family's relationship to gender norms is… unusual, at best. And part of figuring out who I was, outside of their influence, was experimenting with different presentations. But at the end of the day, I realized it wasn't dysphoria for me, either, though the issue was similar enough: a gap between who you want to be and who you are expected to be. I was to rule my family as a seeress of unrivaled power, a perfect oracle to prophesize us back to greatness. I don't need precognition to know that only misery faced me on that path."

"So you threw yourself into combat instead?"

"And then writing and then teaching—and now, apparently, hunting a mass-murdering mage. In this, I am still an al-Kattan: only the greatest challenges are worthy of my time."

"What does that make me?" Fahriye asks.

"A conversation to have over a sumptuous dinner, is what. Unless you want to be the sumptuous dinner? Right now, however"—Lussadh checks her vibrating phone, as if oblivious to her own come-on—"Maria Ying is finally calling me back."

Maria sends a car for them—not something sport, but a heavy off-road vehicle covered in ash and dust. The why of it becomes clear soon enough: their transport maneuvers through ruined streets and is waved through checkpoints to bring the pair to what remains of a plaza close to the blast site. Rubble has been hastily bulldozed out of the way to erect triage tents and a command center to coordinate response units.

Not just material reality, but magic itself has been torn asunder in the blast zone. The air is so dry that it hurts, skin parching after just a moment's contact with the desiccated air; shadows flicker in ethereal, unnatural ways. And still hundreds of men and women are pushing through the ruins, fighting to restore order, fighting to preserve lives.

Fahriye and Lussadh wait outside of the headquarter's largest tent.

Particulates continue to drift down, coating their shoulders and shoes in a gray mist. They have been asked to wear heavy rebreathers; between their own muffled breathing and the interminable sound of construction vehicles, every attempt to raise a conversation has failed.

Do you know sign language? Lussadh eventually signs.

Taught myself as a rookie inspector. You?

Had my hearing blown out for six months after an artillery strike. Very instructive—battlefield cant is always in the hand motions.

Fahriye pauses to scratch her neck, a sign Lussadh has quickly come to read as a tell for her partner's nervousness. *You don't like Maria Ying, do you?*

Lussadh narrows her eyes, then realizes Fahriye can't read her expressions under the heavy mask. *I had many good students. Maria Ying was nowhere on that list. She became Cecilie Kristiansen's apprentice.* This is followed by an extremely lewd motion that Fahriye chooses to interpret as "for fuck's sake." *I taught her better than that.*

A shrug. *You availed yourself of her services easily enough.*

I don't think I like your tone, Fahriye Budak. Another, somehow more graphic motion of emphasis.

Fahriye gives as good as she can get; three decades of enforcing magic laws left her with a remarkably varied library of pornographic gestures. Lussadh fires back with a reply that makes a young nurse standing twenty meters away gasp in shock. The signed insults grow in complexity in tandem with the size of the forming crowd—paramedics and engineers and volunteers, all pausing from hours of relentless and life-saving work to watch two women in their fifties insult each other in a series of escalating gestures.

"Listen here, you—" Lussadh rips off her mask to growl at Fahriye, only then seeing how many people have gathered. "—aw, shit."

Fahriye takes off her own mask. "We're just old friends catching up," she shouts; her face is covered in the sweat of exerting herself in dozens of dramatic hand movements, but she's genuinely smiling.

A gentle cough behind them reveals that Maria Ying has stuck her head out of the tent flaps. "If you two are quite done flirting," she says, "we have a terrorist to hunt."

TEN: STONE BUTCH BLUES

"Maria!" Fahriye exclaims, and wraps the younger mage in a bear hug.

"You're looking a lot less gray-faced than when I saw you last, Inspector," Maria jokes. "The same goes for you, Professor."

All three step back into the command tent to a scene of organized chaos. A three-dimensional map of the blast crater is being projected by some magical contraption, around which are an assortment of technicians, mundane and eldritch. Rakshasa, oni, a pair of qilin whose fins float as if suspended in water—an entire menagerie of colors and shapes that could have stepped out of a bestiary, marshaling their talents and resources to aid in the search and rescue efforts.

"Nothing like a catastrophe to bring disparate people together," Fahriye remarks with an approving smile.

"Always the optimist, Budak—I have spent an ungodly amount of money to have all these characters stand in one place and vaguely work together. I think it's something like six million for a survivor? In the past twelve hours, I've spent the GDP of a small European country on the rescue efforts."

Lussadh eyes the gathered beasts critically. Her own work brought her in contact with dozens and dozens of inhuman beings, heroic and foul, but there has always been an unspoken, shared agreement to keep magical matters from mundane eyes. "Are you not concerned about… blowback?"

Maria snorts, but there is a hard edge of anger to her voice. "Who's going to stop me? Sealing and Containment? Whatever farce of a masquerade mage society had going, it ended when someone detonated a magic nuke in *my* city. I'll use every damn tool at my disposal, flaunt every power I can call on, if it means saving a few more lives."

"And whoever saves a life, it is as though he had saved the lives of all mankind," Fahriye murmurs.

"Al-Ma'idah, verse 32." Maria jerks a thumb at Lussadh. "I learned that in her class, believe it or not." Suddenly, the former student leans close, her gaze flitting from Fahriye to Lussadh as she draws up a veil of secrecy around all three of them. "I need you to know that there's footage of you two being in the area before *and* after the explosion," she says in a low voice. "You really have to be more careful, the both of you."

Lussadh grimaces. At the time, neither of them had the energy left to ensure a private egress: lucky enough to have survived ground zero. "I'll keep that in mind. So? Are we suspected?"

"S&C is gone. Who's left to do anything about it, even if there's suspicion?" The sea witch makes her tone breezy. "I've also destroyed all the evidence. But I'm curious why both of you were there, though—does this have anything to do with the Huas?"

"We were pursuing a serial killer of mages—the newest member of High Command, it seems, goes by the title 'the Melusine.'" Fahriye pauses; she appreciates the immediate trust Maria has placed in them, all appearances to the contrary. "Do you remember those magic cufflinks of mine? The Melusine crushed one in our fight, and the energy unleashed caused… this."

Maria curses. "Then we have to kill her. The rest of High Command, too, if they get in our way."

The justice of the jungle: Lussadh starts at the cold certainty in the young woman's voice. "If it comes to that—yes. But right now, we're on the back foot. We don't even understand who or what we are up against."

"Well, if you're willing to risk it, you could go straight to the source." A flick of Maria's hand, and she is holding an envelope the color of richest vermillion. "It arrived today—an invitation and plus one to a soiree being hosted by, you guessed it, High Command. They must have fallen on hard times; acting so openly is very gauche of them. But it's also proof that something is changing… and where there is change, there is dissent."

"The Melusine spoke of vengeance," Lussadh confides, taking the invitation. "All their targets thus far appear to be agents of the Huas. Given what Fahriye has told me of your and the Huas' shared history, it might be prudent for you to come with us—strength in numbers."

"Am I finally being asked on a date by the alluring Professor al-Kattan? Be still, my heart—how the freshmen will be shocked." This time, the humor doesn't reach her eyes. "Under any other circumstance, I would in a heartbeat. But I'm needed here."

"Is there anything we can say that will make you reconsider?" Fahriye's tone makes it clear that she genuinely worries for Maria; the higher her star rises in opposition to the old powers of the thaumaturgic world, the more a target she will be.

"I understand your concern, I do. And believe me, I'd love to go to this shindig—real proof I'm climbing the ladder. But… but it's so hollow, compared to *this*." She motions wide, taking in the site of the disaster, the whole city, all of it. "Save one person, save the world."

"I owe you an apology, Ms. Ying," Lussadh finally admits. "I have underestimated the strength of your convictions and your ethics."

Maria scoffs. "I've done nothing in my life that you should be proud of, Professor al-Kattan." The sea witch's tone softens to barely a whisper. "By the end, Kristiansen had no use for the pomp and circumstance of mortal power, but the money and the stock options of her husks had to be managed by *someone*. I was complicit in that. I'm wealthy enough to buy the moon, and poor enough that I'll never be able to wash the blood from my hands. So let them come, High Command or anyone else: I have miles to go before I sleep. But having said that… could you do one favor for me?"

Lussadh and Fahriye each nod, grave.

"Well, if you run into Dallas Seidel, tell her and her new friend—I'm sorry."

FAHRIYE

"I told you Maria was a better person than you thought," I say; try as I might, I can't keep a touch of gloating from my voice.

"It's no wonder you're still single," Lussadh complains. "You're absolutely insufferable in victory." She's only half listening, though, looking over the invitation that Maria has procured for us, feeling the rich texture of the paper, admiring the embossing. Her irises shift next, the telltale glow of her sight's invocation. Whatever she sees seems to satisfy her; she relaxes and turns to me, eyes again warm brown. Worryingly, there's a mischievous glint there. "We'll need to get dressed up for the occasion, of course."

"For my part, that's not necessary. I can modify the homunculus' surface to be any clothing I can visualize."

"*That* is the problem," she replies, and I can hear the tone of an instructor that has just baited a freshman into a logic trap. "It's 'the homunculus' surface' to you, not 'my flesh.' This isn't just a container you're piloting—being embodied in your form means accepting it *is* your body. And as impressive and useful as your ability to shift is, bodies wear clothes. Also, if any sort of magic starts getting thrown around—in a room of unthinkably powerful mages, at that—your clothes will flicker, and that will be awkward at best."

"Fine," I concede, as gracefully as I can manage. She is pushing me out of my comfort zone, militantly so, just like at the ice cream parlor. The experience is… discomfiting. Movement has become a thing foreign to me, long before I died; it has taken me transforming into statuary to realize that I had turned to stone a decade before. "The last time—"

The last time someone took me shopping for expensive clothes, it was the most powerful woman in the world, infiltrating a masquerade much like the one we plan to crash now. And I want to share that memory, I think, because I want to share with the woman before me some part of me that *means* something.

And in that same moment, I realize I do *not* want to share it—I care for Lussadh and do not want to see her once again politely ignore this or that reference to another woman. I do not want to see her hurt again.

"The last time, you didn't seem to mind my clothes flickering." A graceless save, absurd. But Lussadh makes a choked noise, and then begins to shake. She clutches at her sides, and for a moment, I think she is having some sort of attack—until I see her face is red and arms tense with gasping, soundless laughter. She stops to try and explain, rubbing tears from her eyes, and it starts all over.

What lonely animals we are, I think, feeling the laughter begin to infect me, too. The promise of a shopping trip, a puerile joke, and all our walls come tumbling down.

We take a train to Little India. The entire subway network is run by non-practitioners, other than a few sections here and there altered to phase through walls, an odd intersection of mage and mundane interests. The carriage is crowded, and we have to squeeze in among the throng; the trains are running with limited services, and heightened security slows the entire trip. All commuters are going to be late today, to work or school or appointments. I try not to think of how many of them must be mourning the dead, of how I have failed to avert calamity. More than a handful are wearing black head to toe.

Lussadh shows me to the boutique of a tailor she knows—upon seeing her, his staid and formal demeanor immediately gives away to a joviality that is out of place in this high-end shop, and they speak in Pashto in the manner of old friends. After a moment, he claps his hands once and nods, then waves everyone out of the store, leaving only him and us. "Sorry, we are closed for the day. Apologies. Closed." Lussadh uses this as an excuse to take her leave, too; she says she has another errand to run.

"I hope we are not imposing—" I try to begin.

He brushes it away. "For the amir? I would give my life. Very handsome, very brave. Saved my cousin, she did. Was my first client here. This is trifling, trifling. A dress?" Alone, he speaks with the unmistakable accent of an immigrant; relief, perhaps, that he can be a little more himself in the presence of a trusted friend's accomplice.

"I feel like I'm more a suit type of woman," I reply, but I'm not certain he has heard me. He's already moving to take measurements; he's lanky, with spatulate hands and oddly colorless eyes. Brisk in taking my measures, an experience which—despite being treated like a dress mannequin during—makes me feel more embodied than I would anticipate. Something about learning the breadth of my shoulders and hips: I haven't thought about myself in terms of *quantifiable* numbers for a long while. You find grounding in the most unexpected places.

"Well, do you want to be a suit type of woman tonight?" he asks again, making several final marks. "The amir can make anything work, but they must match, you see."

That is the crucial question. For formal occasions, I wear—wore—suits or dress uniforms. But something about his initial suggestion is… it's different.

I think I want to try it. "Is there any cocktail wear that'd work for me? The dressy sort," I clarify, "with skirts."

"Dresses are for everyone, friend. Do you have styles in mind? Preferred fabrics, colors? Catwalk or normal?"

"I'll leave it to you," I say, even as I realize this may be quite a dangerous proposition. "I just need to not look like an unfortunate accident."

"Bah!" He sounds mortally offended. "I should take that as an insult. You can pick up your dress this—excuse me."

The door to the shop has opened, and the tailor steps away to see who has come through the door. I think nothing of it at first, but my instincts kick in a moment later. "Wait—"

A moment too late, it would seem. The tailor has toppled into a chair, as if faint, and standing over him is a person I have never seen before—a long, heavy coat, unseasonal in Singapore's heat; sharp features, a mouth painted the color of scarab shell, nearly the same shade as their hair. About my height, which is rare. In features, they are as statuary chiseled by a sculptor at the top of their game: nearly as broad around the shoulders as I am, voluptuous in the hips. In bearing, they have a swagger to them that compels the eye, but which I immediately mistrust.

Their head dips slightly. "Inspector Budak." And then a smile and a glance at the drooping tailor. "Oh, him? Don't worry, he's far from dead. I just suggested he take a nap, and he obliged. What I have to share is for your ears alone."

I can feel the needlepoint of compulsion in their words, a hum just beyond hearing. "You're a mesmer."

"That I am, though it doesn't seem to have any effect on you. Must be your stony disposition." They see my fingers ball into fists, again claim they do not mean anything untoward. But they have the stench of blood about them, and they know my name and my history.

"You're with High Command."

"No more than you are. Or were. Sealing and Containment was always High Command's pet project, and you their most capable hound. Me? Consider me an... interested third party." They smooth their hand over their throat, where a mesh of silver gossamer circles. "I have read your dossier, you know, back when you were working for us. The others saw you as a problem child. I saw in you a freethinker. It was I who intervened against having you made a part of Cecilie."

"I'm sure."

"I shall get to the point. You've had a run-in with the Melusine, haven't you? I'm here to help you take her down."

There is movement, sudden, and then Lussadh is behind them, hand wrapped around their throat, a long and dangerous knife pressing into their side. "You're going to need to give us more than that."

"Oh, what was it this man called you? *Amir* al-Kattan, so glad to finally meet you." The intruder speaks just as smooth, completely unperturbed.

Lussadh shifts her knife a hair, and whatever she touches with the bladepoint makes the mage's eyes go wide. "Fine," they say, clearly dissatisfied they must offer anything more than their assured goodwill. "Your collaborator Maria Ying supplied you with an invitation to High Command's gala, yes? It was my proxies that put the invitation in her hands—I anticipated your needs and provided the real article to your colleague. Will that buy me enough space to explain matters without being stabbed?"

Lussadh and I share a look, and she relents. "What the hell do you want?" I ask.

"I spoke true: for my own reasons, I am invested in the Melusine's destruction, same as you. I am looking for allies of convenience—to disrupt whatever she has planned at the gala, and then stop her for good."

"What does she have planned at the gala?" Lussadh sounds unconvinced. "As I understand it, it's an event marking her accession to High Command."

"And do you know *how* she gained her place at the table?" The mesmer props themself up against the wall, arms crossed. "She interrupted a meeting and beat to death one of our members, bare-handed. Suffice it to say, I don't think she's greatly invested in the continued longevity—"

"So you *are* a member of High Command." The knife rises again.

"I'm—it's complicated. That is not material to our current discussion: are we in this together? Defeat of the Melusine will require each of us working in tandem. I am here in person with you two because I think our best chance to prevent another cataclysm—"

"And to prevent your face getting bashed in like your colleague," Lussadh interjects.

"—is to work together. And yes, there is an element of self-preservation."

"If we say no," I point out, "you'll just have us declared *persona non grata* at your big shindig."

"*Again*, I am not with High Command. But the point stands—I can't have unaligned pieces running around the board. You're either with me, or you're not there."

"If those are your negotiating skills," Lussadh says, put out, "then you better not go losing that magic voice of yours. I guess we're in. What do we call you?"

"Oh, that. I..." They pause, as if it has only just occurred to them that they need a name. They blink—their eyes are a startling orange, animalistic—and then they grin. "Chun Hyang will do."

"And what the hell do you get out of this? I know it is more than survival. High Command must always *gain*." I cannot believe I was ever associated with that wretched hive.

Chun Hyang smiles, all pleasant joviality and earnest openness. "Again, not with High Command. But I'm so glad you asked. In pursuit of their ineffable goals, High Command made a... let's call it an *investment*. An artifact, a compendium of True Names. I'm procuring it as we speak, and I'll use it in our fight against the Melusine. But when this is all said and done, you'll raise no objection that I get to keep it."

Only fools make deals with mages sight unseen. "We won't—" I start.

"Fahriye here is going to tell you we won't agree to let you walk away with a magical nuclear weapon," Lussadh interrupts. "And I'm going to tell you we agree, with every intent of stabbing you in the back. So let's skip to the chase and just say what we all know—we work together until the Melusine is dead, and then all bets are off."

"Oh, I very much do like you, amir." Chun Hyang's smile stretches into something lascivious. "Tell you what—I'll kill you *last*." They slip into the shadows with a final laugh, body flowing like the blackest ink.

Lussadh and I are now alone, save the snoring tailor.

"I used you as bait," she admits. "I thought someone was following us, so I left you to distract them while I circled back around. My apologies."

"That isn't the first time a beautiful woman has done that." It really, really isn't. "But I do prefer to be in on the charade." A beat. "I am distracting now, am I?"

"And I'm apparently beautiful." Lussadh barely manages the mask of sarcasm; she knows she is beautiful—but just as much, I know she appreciates hearing it. She nods at the tailor. "How frustrating—can you help me wake him up? He still needs to take my measurements."

Eleven: And We Shall Go Dancing

FAHRIYE

We are quiet on the train ride back; a storm is gathering, rain imminent. I lose myself in gray thoughts.

High Command will hold their soiree in Pulau Belakang Mati, a heinously expensive resort island, once the site of non-practitioner capital and later annexed by mage assets. The wealthiest among us don't like seeing non-mages possess too much—they must be reminded to whom the world truly belongs. Parts of Singapore have been made inaccessible, and eventually invisible, to the mundane folks. For those without magic, the world becomes smaller by the decade; memory elides, perception lies, and the walls shift to contain them a little further, gift more and more to fewer and fewer.

Little wonder there are so many "upstart" families, much as the more pedigreed clans try to keep them out. Sometimes violently: a family of budding talent might be wiped out overnight long before they can learn higher mysteries, and I expect Olesya has even carried out such contracts. Yet the number of thaumaturges increases year on year: ask any academic institution and they'll tell you the student intake never slims down, rather the opposite. It seems inevitable that eventually there will be more mages than not, despite the aristocrats' worst efforts, and now with Sealing and Containment gone…

The Huas, I suspect, don't dwell too much on this disparity—they don't have to. Lussadh does: I understand she protected many students of hers who came from households seen as lesser. And I think about it sometimes,

ELEVEN: AND WE SHALL GO DANCING

about whether the world will be a better place when everyone is a mage, or if it will be so much worse. Streets running red, the sky black with competing sorceries. Open wars have happened in the past; in the age we inhabit now, it will be so much more catastrophic.

In the distance, smoke still rises from the blast crater; cops with neck gaiters and submachine guns stand at each train platform.

"I've seen that look before," Lussadh interjects. I feign ignorance, so she clarifies: "You've got the eyes of my old mercenary comrades, trying to figure out why they're committing to one more suicidal contract."

My brow wrinkles in thought. Have I really become so cynical? "I'm getting old, Lussadh, and it feels like everything is getting *worse*."

"God, does it ever." She sighs and leans her forehead against the train car's window, closes her eyes to the passing scene. "Well, I always told my crew to never trust how they felt about themselves before a mission or after nine at night."

Her face is serene, but I can see her fingers twitching, desperate to hold something to distract herself. I slip my hand into hers; she crushes my fingers in her grip. The rest of her is still, humming energy coiled so tight she may as well be the one made of stone.

"You know," she says after a minute, a smile pulling at the corners of her mouth, "there's always one tried and true way of dealing with pre-mission jitters."

"Lussadh al-Kattan!" I gasp in affected shock. "Are you propositioning me on a *public train*? I'll have you know, I am an upstanding woman—"

We barely make it through the door before we begin our improprieties.

It's a little ridiculous—here we are, both at an advanced age, acting like teenagers. But the pleasure of it is so total; her body calls to me in a way I can hardly remember being capable of heeding, of noticing.

And we are *worse* than teenagers. Last night was gentle and soft, careful fingers slowly nurturing back to life a flowerbed long fallow. This time, we are not taking care to remember something special, but desperately trying to forget what is to come—today is bare-knuckle boxing, our calloused hands tearing at our opponent, marking the other.

Lussadh has her hand wrapped in my hair before we've even cleared the foyer—pulling my head to one side, kissing the neck and shoulder she finds exposed. Then the teeth come out; she finds not stone under her tongue, but flesh, ruddy with attention, prickling with pleasure and pain.

One of our feet catches on something, and we stumble; the sound of splintering wood and breaking glass joins in our chorus of grunts and gasps. I seize back the initiative; with one arm, I pull her up like she weighs nothing, and with my free hand cup a breast and bring a nipple to my expectant lips. My fingers dig into her flesh, but I trust her to alert me to bruising or bone-shattering force. This is not the time for me to mind my stone strength, to fear for her fragility.

Her hand grasps at the back of my neck as I hoist her up—the advantage of greater height—and pin her in place against the window. She makes a noise, surprised I think; probably not many people try that. But I'm famished for her; I have abandoned all caution and decorum alike. Briefly I imagine what it'd be like to swallow her whole, but then her teeth on me dissolve that thought, the reality of her overwhelming the fever idea.

She's saying something—profanities perhaps—as I undo her belt and cast it away. I find her hard; she fills my hand. I grip and stroke, taking pleasure at the gasps I'm drawing out of her, and soon, she fills me. And she is by no means small.

We rut like beasts, like colossi in combat. Her incisors in my throat, her nails down my back. The floorboards creak beneath us. The world falls away.

The way I topple is utterly without grace, falling backward with her on top of me. Still inside me, in fact. The skin on my back is stinging, but I don't care. Her sweat drips onto my face. I resist the urge to lick it when it reaches my mouth, and then I don't resist. The tang of her is bright on my tongue.

Lussadh rolls off me, breathing hard. "I'm definitely developing bruises I didn't have before we started."

My first instinct is to apologize. My second is to say, "And I'm pretty sure I have scratches all over me. Only you could make stone bleed, Professor."

She half-chuckles, half-grunts. "It's not stone, remember. It's you."

Maybe I should argue. Maybe I should accept defeat. Either way, I pull her in for a kiss. "We do have a party to attend. Let's get ready."

OLESYA

I wake from dreams of gold to a dream of blood.

Pain assails my senses. Something creaks when I move—I'm held up in chains of power, but they rub against each other like metal. Blood drips, slow, down my forehead and down my cheeks. I taste it on my tongue. My lacerations exist at a remove.

Below me, *she* sits drinking my wine out of a slim flute. Perfectly dressed, in brilliant flowing lines, every fold and pleat precise. Gold around her throat, gold at her ears. My jewelry, or at least images of them. No mask: she has dispensed with the pretense. In her other hand she's holding an old folder, again one of mine. The papers have been enspelled to last, and the pencil lines have not faded despite the years. "Do you know," the Melusine is saying, conversational, "that if you wanted, you'd be able to access the same power I do? It's the weakness in your heart that stops you. The same weakness that made you expend your own life instead of shooting through that schoolbus in Rome. Always trying to be a hero. No self-respect."

I lick my lips. The chains suspend me a meter or so above the ground, and the mechanisms of them are familiar to me. I can unravel them, I'm fairly sure, but I want to keep her talking. Clarity has come to me for the first time in—weeks? Shame chases it, reminding me of what I've been doing and saying. Of what I've been letting *her* do to me. "What the fuck are you?"

As though I've said nothing, she holds up one of the sketches. I drew that at twelve. The page depicts a tall woman, her features finely sculpted, in a bodice and a wide, short skirt. At that age I loved tulle and chiffon, ballerina shoes and tiaras. "I remember," she says, distant, "going over fashion spreads, editorial shoots, catwalk collections. All the fine and glamorous things. We wanted to have a rounder, fuller figure once, didn't we?" She sifts through the sheets with the utmost care, treating every page as though it is gold hammered thin. "And this one, with the horns and talons. Or that, with the scales and feathers. Oh, we had such fun fantasies."

Ice has spread through my stomach. This is too much; this goes too far. The doppelganger will intrude upon even my childhood. "Put those down."

"Why? They're mine too." Her expression hardens. "The product of a child born into the wrong body."

"That's not what happened. I drew these because when I told Mother I was a girl, she said that when the time came—if I wanted to—she'd take me to a practitioner who could reshape me as I wished."

She's put the folder down. Her grip on the wine flute tightens. "We were born into the wrong fucking body. *Viveca* was born into the right one. Why weren't we?"

And I do recall that, a seed of resentment that budded and grew even as I studied transfiguration and fleshcrafting so that I'd be able to build my own body. It was hardly recommended: the operation is usually performed by practitioners with decades of expertise, but I was determined to do it myself. I succeeded too, demonstrating that I was not only a Hua but a prodigy in my own right, and the pride in that erased all the envy I felt for my younger sister. At least that's what I believed at the time.

"Viveca," she goes on, "was always the gilded star, the pride and flower of the house. The one who'd inherit the mantle, because we were so busy trying to make our body right. The one we had to protect, because even after all that she was so *fragile*. We had to do so much, work so hard, and here she was—not a care in the world, successful, successor to Elizaveta Hua." The wine flute snaps. Glass crumbles and falls. She doesn't seem to care that it's cutting up her hand, or that the wine is spilling into her lap. "We were sick; we were *dying,* and she never noticed."

"Because I was hiding it from her!"

"Do you think she's stupid, Olesya?" The Melusine's voice has grown venomous. "You were sick for years, and Viveca didn't realize anything was wrong? Dallas saw it in a single day."

My throat closes. "She drank my blood, she's a tiger, she—"

"Excuses, and nothing more." Her expression changes, then, abrupt. It relaxes. "Enough about her shortcomings. Let's talk about yours. Have you spoken to Chang'er lately? No, of course not. You've been so *busy*. So happy with Dallas, who's all you ever needed anyway, isn't she?"

Slowly I have been unraveling the bonds with my will. It's easy when you know the inner workings of it, identical to my own sorcery. That in and of itself is unnerving too, and I still do not want to admit the obvious: that she is, somehow, made of *me*.

The chains snap. I fall, and then I hurl myself at her. The chair topples over.

My fist lands on her face, and I know it's not connecting with anything that resembles flesh or skull or breakable structures. I do it anyway and snarl, "If you've done anything to Chang'er, I swear—"

"Done to her?" my double echoes, smirking up at me. "I have been calling her, Olesya, to ask how she and her sister are doing; to ensure she does not think she is forgotten. To show her that she is thought of, every day, cherished and treasured." The Melusine slips free, standing tall, holding up her hand where a ring rides on her finger—white gold band, mounted by an emerald. The ring that my alchemist made for me. "You see, Olesya, I am not only *of* you. I'm *better,* the superior product. I am a finer partner than you will ever be; I show consideration, give my love freely, return loyalty in kind. She stood by you for ten years when you were nothing, and what have you repaid her with except for neglect?"

I get to my feet, because I refuse to do this on my knees while she gloats. "You don't know anything about—"

She brushes broken glass out of her palm. They slip free smoothly as if they have not been embedded in epidermis but lying on frictionless marble. "But I do know. I know everything, from your birth until this very moment. I've always been inside you, biding my time. And now I am out here, more you and more powerful than you could ever hope to be. I'll prove to the world that I'm the most fit to carry the Hua name. I will bring destruction to our enemies—past, present, and future."

With a clap of her hands, the bonds return. I'm held aloft once more; I struggle and resist, attempting to undo them again, but she's hardened them against me. It will take longer this time. She steps close.

"We never found out who sent the vampires to Mount Nicholson," she goes on, jerking my head toward her. "Everyone deserves closure… including the perpetrator."

It's as if she has flipped a switch. My mind clouds. The red edge of that day returns, the haze of it, the terror of holing up with my little sister and knowing that any moment we could both be ripped to shreds. "Yes," I hear myself say. "I want that person—whoever they are—gone. I want them to suffer as they die, slow and thorough, and most of all I want them to know who is bringing them retribution after so long."

"That's right." She grins and lets go of my hair. "Do you see? We have always, always wanted the same thing. Now be a good girl and stay put, will you?"

She returns not long after, or at least it feels like that. By the time she is back, I've freed myself again; have cleaned and patched myself up. The sense of urgency comes and goes. One minute I'm frantic—I must reach out to Dallas, to Chang'er, to *somebody*. The next I'm calm, meditative even, and I would discover I have made no effort to contact anyone after all. I walk in circles, and my thoughts do the same. Everything feels faint and flattened.

A part of me, huddling in the recesses of my mind, is screaming at me to escape, to get my distance from this creature. But at the surface I move through my empty estate as though I'm underwater. I find myself wanting her knuckle-deep inside me.

But the Melusine is back, and her face is smeared with blood. Her mouth is feral, her teeth glinting the way a nightmare might. "It was a nobody, would you imagine. I crushed them like an ant. What a wonderful day this has been. And you've been keeping to yourself, haven't you? I love it when you know your place."

ELEVEN: AND WE SHALL GO DANCING

I bristle. "You do not own me."

Her laugh tinkles. "Do I not?" She's levitated a wine bottle from my cellar; effortlessly uncorked it. It floats toward us, and then tips over me.

I cough and splutter, the floral sweetness of it spilling down my eyes and nose, some into my mouth. Where my wounds are still new, it stings. She stands aside, amused and immaculate.

"The sloppy look suits you," she purrs. "It makes you seem so *used*. It's a shame I can't bring you and show you off."

"What," I start, caught between swallowing and spitting the wine out.

"There's going to be a party, Olesya, to honor me and my deeds. I think I shall take center stage; I would like to dance as the belle of the ball." She gestures, and her power wraps around me, a cocoon of gold. "You'll have to stay home for this, I'm afraid. I'd hate for you to steal the spotlight."

"What even do you want?" I ask my doppelganger. "To kill me? To take over my life?"

"Oh, but of *course* you would think so small." She closes the distance between us in a single stride, takes a fist of my hair in her hand to jerk my gaze up to her eyes. "I'm going to lead the life we should have always had—could have had, had you not been such a *coward*. I am going to kill every one of my enemies. And then I am going to take their power, and then I am going to fix *everything*."

I bite my tongue; I know myself well enough to know that the best way to get me to talk is to give me a silence to fill.

She pirouettes away with a laugh, dozens of her reflected in the hall of mirrors, spinning in joy. "You could have rewritten reality, torn apart casualty, bent the arrow of time to your will. But you let yourself be chained, like every other forsaken thing in this existence." She stops and bows, then begins to adjust her dress of flowing, liquid gold; clouds of fabric in which flashes of lightning can be seen, jagged and intermittent.

"But it requires power. More than any one mage can acquire, even in a lifetime of a thousand years," she continues; perhaps she is relieved that she can tell the one person who might understand. "You were too cowardly to do what needed to be done—but not I. All of our—my—enemies are mages, ripe for the plucking, and they have conveniently gathered themselves into one grand ball. Look at us, doing the very thing that Viveca was accused of last year! Cecilie already showed that taking another mage's abilities is possible. But I don't need their knowledge, just the raw power of their deaths to fuel a final spell."

"What the hell are you going to do?" I finally ask.

"I told you," she says with a smile made all the more terrifying for being completely sane. "I'm going to fix everything. I'm going to change time, so that I was never afflicted with that wasting disease. Save Mother's life. Make it so that Viveca—" She pauses. "Well, maybe there only needs to be the one Hua daughter? Unity of the family and all that. Hell, if I had been born in the right body, I'd never have needed transfiguration—*I* could be the warlock of the age. Imagine! And why limit myself? I don't need to specialize. Anything I want is going to be mine, and everything will be made right."

"If you touch Viveca—"

"Hush, you. I act as my base urges made me—it's *your* fantasies of being an only daughter that inspired this. And if you had really loved Viveca, you'd never have let it come to this." She steps toward the door; halfway out, she half turns to look at me over her shoulder. "The smallest consolation I can give you, is that even this defeat of yours will be expunged—no one will ever tell me what I can do again, not even myself."

DALLAS

The quandary with what Olesya did to me is this: is it worse than what I did to Yves?

I obsessively ponder this as we sit in the car, watching the gala's guests gather and throng the resort's entrance. It's half an hour before the party begins, and we have been observing in the suits that the creature Chun Hyang has handed us. The fit is good, unnervingly so, though the quality is nowhere near Olesya's tailoring.

ELEVEN: AND WE SHALL GO DANCING

"What's on your mind?" murmurs Recadat, in her customary flat voice. "I don't think it's High Command."

"I don't like the creature. They smell wrong." And to accept help from the enemy rubs me badly. Chun Hyang may not be responsible for the Melusine—professes, even, to be opposed—but they are callous, and will spend us as pawns if we are careless. "But I've been thinking about my ex."

"I like to think I'm not that bad in bed." A pause. "Or that good?"

That makes me laugh, and she startles to hear it; then she turns red. Reassuring that I still have that effect on women. "It's not that. I'm… comparing Olesya to her, actually."

Recadat looks at me askance. She's wearing more than I am—a dress shirt, a tie. "I'm listening."

"My ex and I, we're friendly. I mean, we are part of the same family, and we are devoted to its protection. She's married to Olesya's sister, Viveca."

"Okay." She drums her fingers on the dashboard. "You're sisters-in-law. That sounds awkward."

"It's not so bad. She's a demon, I'm a tiger. We don't adhere to human norms."

"So the firstborn is mated to a tiger, the secondborn to a demon." Recadat shakes her head slightly. "Incredible."

"The Hua house is famous for many things, one of them bucking conventions." My voice is wry. "A long time ago, I did something terrible to the demon. And she… forgave me."

Recadat adjusts her tie, a little unnecessarily. It gives her hands something to do. I didn't notice it before—interesting how coitus heightens awareness—but she has lovely fingers. "Dallas," she says, and there is a faintest touch of softness to her voice, "just because you were awful to your ex and she absolved you, doesn't mean you have to accept being treated badly by another partner. A geas—"

"Is the greatest violation, yes." And come to that, Olesya did it to Chang'er, too. "I'm just trying to decide if it's a one-strike deal, or if I can afford to give her another chance."

"You're afraid that if you cannot forgive her, then you cannot accept the forgiveness shown you, either." I make a strangled noise that startles even me. She continues. "That is not how forgiveness works. You don't have to accept punishment to make up for past sins."

I stare through the front window of the car, gripping the steering wheel tight. "I'll start doing that the moment you start forgiving yourself for surviving."

"I—" For a moment, her dispassionate exterior cracks, then seals back over like an ice flow closing over dark waters, frozen surface restored. "You're really going to wear only a jacket?"

"Worried for my modesty, panther?" I let her change the topic, quirk an eyebrow. "It's not as if I am not wearing trousers. Annoyed other people will get to see my breasts? I'll button it if you like."

"It's still incredibly suggestive."

"Yes, that's the *point*. Mages are extravagant bastards that care not a single iota for any rule or stricture. I swear, someone at this event will be wearing a dress made of Icelandic meltwater. You have a lot to relearn about mage mores."

"I once fought a cult that turned themselves invisible, then painted likenesses of themselves over their flesh. It was horribly disconcerting knocking someone down and seeing their flesh smear away to reveal a hollow interior. In my case, one might even call it prophetic."

"You remember that?" I ask, a little surprised.

"Huh. I guess I did. Sex so good it blew out part of my amnesia." She drums her fingers faster, then curls them up under her palm into a fist. "If I don't make it out of this—"

"You will," I say, immediate.

"You can't know that. Chun Hyang referred to me as *the investment*. Maybe they and the Melusine want me to be here. Maybe that's the plan, maybe we're going to our deaths. So: if I don't make it out, but you do—will you clear Dr. Leung's name? The only thing that has ever brought her happiness is practicing medicine; I owe it to her to restore that. And if I die…"

"We'll clear it, together. But since me saying that won't help you right now: yes."

ELEVEN: AND WE SHALL GO DANCING

She relaxes, nods. "Okay, let's get on with it." She reaches into the backseat and pulls out a collar and muzzle.

"What the hell is this? If you think I'm going to wear—"

Recadat is already wrapping the collar around her own neck. "A tiger parading a muzzled human on a leash seems like a good place to start blending in with these *extravagant bastards*. Can you shift into a slightly wilder look—more body hair, a hint of stripes? It'll really sell it."

In the dark of the car, I swear I see a bit of fang in her mouth, the flash of a smile.

Twelve: Masque of the Red Death

OLESYA

The phone is ringing.

I'm sitting in an empty room. White walls, a single table, a single chair. During the estate's reconstruction, we didn't refurnish everything; I was not able to restore every single piece of furniture—nobody could have. And so there are blank patches in the building, testaments to the destruction of my home at Cecilie's hand, the infestation that had to be purged by fire. Even the estate bears its own scars. A small desk mirror, out of which my reflection stares, pale and haunted. I wait for the image to move without me, to blink or laugh while I remain still.

The phone continues to ring.

When I was little, before I told my mother that I was a girl, I felt myself an oddity. Male practitioners are rare; it is a fact that most scions are women. I was firstborn, yes, but I was a son. It seems ridiculous in retrospect, that I ever thought so when it should've been obvious I was a daughter, but even in our society such things are not perfect. For me, it took time to percolate. Over coffee that I was given special permission to have, Mother told me that it didn't matter. That the warlock mantle did not depend on either gender or birth order, and that as the elder in particular I had more time to explore what I wanted—whether summoning demons interested me, whether I had a head for contracts.

"I know you believe you must be Viveca's protector because you're a little bigger than she is," she told me. "But you must remember that you matter too, and that I love you more than the world."

"What if," I asked her, "I grow up stupid and not especially talented?"

She took my hands in her own. "The most important thing, my child, is that you grow up happy."

I haven't thought about this memory for a long time, even though it should have been formative. My sickness, my curse, made me misplace so much, even the most important of Mother's lessons.

The phone rings one final time.

Lucidity asserts, or something close to it. I must act quickly.

From a drawer, I seize a bottle of medicine, the kind Chang'er used to make for me. A few leftovers have survived in caches strewn throughout the city (oh, how I prepared for disaster; how I prepared for every eventuality, and yet now I am caught flat-footed), and I've brought them back. I have felt the urge to discard them—they are reminders of a terrible time—but I've kept them, in case they ever come in useful.

Like now.

I unstop the bottle, exhale a cantrip to break its seal. Once I took it in precise, metered doses. Now I put it to my lips and tip my head back, and I drink the entire thing.

The taste is atrocious. I know what comes next, and so I rush to the nearest bathroom.

Over the sink, I bend nearly double as I heave and heave. Everything regurgitates. I don't remember if I've been eating, but if I have then the contents of my stomach are rushing out. The reek is immediate and disgusting; it swirls down in pale brown, in thin mucus. My guts contract. My lungs and throat burn.

It goes on for some time.

My hair trails wet and filthy, matted with vomit. Chang'er used to be the one to hold it back as I threw up. In those early days, the affliction was new, and I was diminished, not yet sure of how to tread the thin balance between expending a few minutes, a few hours of my life and not using magic at all. Chang'er tried her best to minimize the elixir's effects and it was still so miserable, every time. I accepted it, though, a price for continuing for another year, another month, another week. Anything to fend off the curse. I thought I'd never have to touch this medicine again. I thought that, with the curse gone, I'd have it all. That this would finally be my time in the sun, and I would be able to do anything, lead a full and complete life.

Chang'er's concoction purges all traces of magic within my body that didn't originate from me, and it's doing what it must now: when I raise my head, my thoughts are clearer than ever, and now I know exactly what has happened—remember exactly what I have been doing, to myself, to Dallas and Recadat. And now an embodiment of my worst thoughts—the ones you never, ever voice to anyone—is walking out there, leaving havoc in her wake.

Part of my dress has been soiled. Grimacing, I tear it off—fabric rips, a sharp cry—and incinerate it in white, smokeless flame. Heat hazes the air. The ashes drift and fall without sound. I watch them, and try not to see in them the remains of my relationships. How could I begin to apologize? How can I rebuild when I was the one who took the torch to them?

But there are more pressing things. Once we have defeated this enemy, there will be time for me to torment myself. I get in the shower and clean myself under icy water. I rinse my mouth out. Conjuring a new dress is trivial. There, at least, is that. I am nearly careless with it; normally I am particular about the fabric, the silhouette, how it clings to or falls around my breasts and hips. Now it's just something to wear.

In my study, I fetch a journal and a pen, and then I take those to yet another guest room. If the Melusine returns, I'll lose myself again, and I want to keep my notes in a place she wouldn't be looking.

I sit, and write. Once I begin, I discover that I know much more than I should. Meetings in jade chambers and bloody knuckles. The explosion that took out part of this city—flashes of a woman being cut up, glimpses of a knife shearing through my magic, the taste of adrenaline. The death of the necromancer who sent vampires to kill us when we were little: my bare hands tearing them apart as though they were made of paper. The memories are there, even though I wasn't.

I know what she's going to do, at the gala. *The investment*, she mentioned.

Even now, I can feel the Melusine's seething resentment at the attention Dallas has showered on the husk—but worse, I can feel her anger and frustration that the key to her plans slipped through her fingers: she no longer has access to Recadat's powers. And so, in Recadat's place, she will slaughter High Command itself as the blood sacrifice in a rite that will turn her into a goddess. A goddess with the power to rewrite reality, to make of this world a canvas and then paint upon it the perfect life for her—for us.

Finally I pick up the phone. It's lousy with messages, but the most recent is hours old. All of them have the same general tone, from an unfamiliar number: *Olesya, please answer. Olesya, what's going on? Olesya, pick up the damn phone.*

Tell me you're still there. Please.

My throat closes as I call the number back. The line's dead. Dallas must be using a burner phone. My fingers twitch toward Chang'er's number, but I stop. She is too far away, and... and if I fail in my advance against the Melusine, then I want Chang'er to have her last memory of me be those calls from my doppelganger. The ones where Chang'er feels she is loved, thought of, treasured. Because my other self is right about that much—I've neglected my alchemist, and I do not deserve to ruin her happiness.

Next I call Dallas' usual number. The ringtone goes on and on, and as I pace about the corridors I hear her phone ring. Pulse in my throat, I race to her room.

The suite is in ruins. Furniture and walls torn up, claw marks everywhere in the wood, the floor—even the bed is in pieces, sheets and mattress and frame. Shredded fabric spills from the wardrobe: she intentionally destroyed every article of clothing I've ever made for her. Her phone lies in one corner; when I turn it on, I'm surprised to find it still functional. The lockscreen is a photo of us, arm-in-arm and laughing, rent through with a hairline fracture.

In a matter of days, I have lost everything—nearly everything—I have ever held dear. At least Viveca is beyond the Melusine's reach. Almost I laugh at the thought that my sister and her demon might be the ones who have to avenge me.

For weeks—if not more—I have been my own puppet. It'd be so easy to think the thing that has stolen my form is a result of enemy action, that I had no part in it; that I have been an innocent victim. Except that is not the case, not quite. Now I will have to face the consequences.

I know where to find her. I will destroy her even if the link between us kills me, too.

FAHRIYE

We arrived separately—operational security, Lussadh said—and so I am treated to a considerable surprise when I see the professor stepping out of a hired limousine in a dress of bronze, bedecked in gold jewelry. Very fine sorts, at that: I've seen enough of Elizaveta's to guess that Lussadh is wearing either real rubies or perfect imitations. She is masked, the same as every other attendee, the same as I am, but has no trouble finding me. We'd recognize each other anywhere; our scars call us to the other, as indelibly as any ink.

The one problem is that we are, somehow, wearing the *same* dress, save that the exposed shoulder is mirrored. She comes up to me in the foyer reserved for this event and murmurs, "Well, someone fucked up somewhere—"

"I rather thought you'd turn up in a tux, too." I chuckle. "I must say, you wear this better than I do—you look incredible."

For a few seconds, she seems taken aback, and I wonder whether I've somehow crossed a line—a compliment too soon, too forward. Then her face moves and I can tell there's a smile behind her mask. "Thank you. And you are, of course, a vision. It's just a shame that my tailor apparently lost inspiration halfway through."

"No, no, your tailor had some terribly gauche idea of draping one of you in shades of deep green." Chun Hyang is suddenly here, stepping between us. They are smiling like a shark, dressed in an impeccably tailored suit of indigo—a dress shirt in moonlit silver, no tie, no jewelry. "You're very lucky your tailor listened to my fashion advice—I can be *terribly* persuasive. You needed to be wearing the same color. Champagne is an excellent choice, contrasts nicely with both of your skin tones and my attire."

We feel again the mesmer hum in their voice, the pull of suggestion. Lussadh glares back. "We warned you—"

Chun Hyang leans close, dropping their words to a whisper. "And no one will bat an eye when we step off the elevator with you as my paired arm candy."

Elizaveta took me to a masquerade like this once, gave almost the same justification. I almost laugh; it is one of my most cherished memories, and the night ended in only a little bloodshed. I'll take it as a good omen. "You do like your operational security," I point out to Lussadh.

"That doesn't even apply here," she complains, but we still do it. And at least Chun Hyang's intrusion makes one thing clear—I wish it was my arm looped through Lussadh's; we'd be the matched pair then, uninterrupted.

The foyer is filled with various types of security drawn from what must be a half-dozen mage retinues, but Chun Hyang is right: no one gives us so much as a second glance, which also means they don't recognize Chun Hyang as a High Command member. This also raises a question, and as we ascend to the roof in an ornate elevator, I take the opportunity to ask, "I thought High Command took titles, not names. Chun Hyang's not what they know you as, is it?"

For some reason, they seem to find this especially funny—a peal of laughter. "Oh, that's a good one. We do use pseudonyms, but no, my name does not follow their preferred nomenclature, and they don't know of any *Chun Hyang*." Their voice is such a deep alto that their giggle seems out of place. "So you can't rat me out to them, if that's what you are planning."

I tamp down the base urge to roll my eyes. "That's not what I am planning."

From the other side, Lussadh glances over at me, talking right through our supposed host. "Chun Hyang isn't a person. Not exactly."

"Oh, your infamous sight." The elevator door opens and they motion for us to step out first. "You're seeing too much, you know. I lied; I'll have to kill you first."

"You may try." The professor's voice is calm. "The seams on you are very slight, very faint, but they are there. Perhaps they'll disappear with time, but for now…"

Their attention turns to Lussadh, complete and undivided. "The moment you move against me," they say, cold and low, "I will politely ask you to rip out your own spine, and you will do it." And then another laugh, a higher trill. "But we're all friends here, aren't we? And tonight we have the same objective. Let's drink to it."

"What does High Command really want?" I ask, pushing past Chun Hyang's ominous threat, head on a swivel for more immediate dangers. Crystal and glass flows like water, the air shimmers with etheric power, and I've never seen so many extreme and gaudy outfits as I do now. But I can't help my curiosity; when you find out the power behind Sealing and Containment conspired to destroy their own tool, it makes you question what their deepest motivations are.

"Oh, you mean the Rectification of True Names." Chun Hyang smirks. "Don't worry, I didn't read your mind; it's the main thing people with resources will have heard about us. Well, it is a long-standing goal, the ultimate doctrine. Now, whether all of us *believe* in that…"

If you worked at Sealing and Containment long enough, you heard the rumors about High Command: that the cabal had found—or believed they had found—the path to the world's mysteries, the guidepost that would give them the reins over existence. And that method, unlike any pursued prior or after, is to tear the veil off every single True Name: the thought that, when every soul stands revealed in starkness, then order will be brought. Any name they cannot reveal thus must be banished, or else eradicated. It follows that that was why Sealing and Containment was indoctrinated to hate warlocks, because they traffic in elusive True Names, contracting beings that cannot be so easily put under the microscope.

"And," I add, on intuition, "what does it have to do with your so-called *investment*?"

"You are too clever by half, Inspector." They levitate a drink off a passing tray—some bubbly champagne. "The investment is a walking treasure trove that has mistaken itself for a person. You may make the same mistake." Their mouth pulls back, showing teeth that shine a little too silver. "It is, you see, what remains of Cecilie Kristiansen."

All of me tenses. "She's dead." Viveca made triply sure of that.

"Dead people leave behind ghosts. Dead bugs leave behind exoskeletons. A destroyed city block leaves behind a crater." Their head turns gracefully, taking in the sights; they pause to look at a gaggle of cantrip workers, who cluster around a greater thaumaturge. "Nothing ever disappears *completely*, Inspector. Of all people, you should know that."

Next to me, Lussadh makes a derisive noise. "I hardly take you for someone who appreciates history."

"All of the past is a prologue, Amir al-Kattan." Chun Hyang gestures with their glass. "And speak of the devil. Here comes the *investment*."

Both of us turn to follow their motion, and I see a woman I know as an old work acquaintance step off the elevator, muzzled, her leash held in the hand of the weretiger Dallas.

RECADAT

It probably says something about me that, my first time in a collar and muzzle, I feel an odd sense of serenity. On the leash Dallas holds, I don't need to deal with the crowd or greet or interact; the muzzle hides most of my face. I exist, in this public space, as an object rather than a person. The noises pass me by.

For her part, Dallas is hiding her discomfort well. She doesn't like the idea of collars and muzzles for obvious tiger reasons, but it's also clear that I made the right choice. Many of the attendees are prim enough, but plenty more look like they're here for some sort of fetish soiree; we blend in perfectly.

The rooftop is enormous and cold, shaded from the winds by tall evergreens crusted in ice, the climate artificially maintained by sorcery and probably a few unseen elementals. The buffet offers up meat of every sort—no vegetarian needs apply: whale and leopard, crocodile and fox, venison and rabbit. My thoughts dart briefly to the question of whether any of this was carved out of a wereanimal. Probably not. Too expensive to eat. Walls and tables alike are surfaces of lacquered black.

"Gold leaf, really? How did they make venison unappetizing," Dallas mutters under her breath while tugging me along, making a show—not too convincingly—of treating me as a pet, an object. Olesya Hua would have been better at that, I suspect; Dallas is not good at playacting cruelty. My thoughts veer to being under Olesya's knife: I felt very good, very peaceful there. At the time I would have liked her to cut me forever, purifying me in ribbons of flesh and broken floating ribs. Disassembling me until I can finally, finally breathe and dream of nothing at all. She could pin parts of me to her walls, like insects preserved for their exoticity and rarity.

Dallas must sense something. "How are you feeling?" she asks, her voice slightly distorted by the fangs she has chosen to lengthen in her human mouth.

I'm a husk that thinks she is a woman because I retain the memories of one of my victims slightly more than the other ten thousand whose names I devoured. I am not, in any sense of the word, a person; my continuance does not deserve to take priority. And what does rage through my blood—these impulses, these alien hungers—cannot be said to come from any human soul. So I tell her, "I don't have feelings, Dallas."

"Please. It's been less than a day since you rode me."

My cheeks heat. Fortunately, the muzzle masks that too. "That's not a feeling, that's just—animal instinct."

Her chuckle is low and touches my libido like a spark. "You're talking to an animal. Most things are animals; most feelings too. We should do that again." Dallas is scanning the glittering crowd, then she grimaces. "Maria Ying's scent is here."

I stiffen. My acquaintance with that woman has hardly been amicable. "Is she."

"The sea witch is nosy." She begins to relax. "But the scent's weak—probably someone was in contact with her recently. And if she is here, avoiding her is easy enough."

Anger threads through me, coming—it seems—out of nowhere. "I don't want to avoid her," I say before I can stop myself. "I'm not afraid of her."

"I know." A feline chuckle. "That's why we're going to avoid her. Can't have you rip her limb from limb in the middle of finger foods and punch bowls. We can do that," she adds, "another time. I will hunt with you."

Her camaraderie is offered so simply, so earnestly: I know what it means to her to offer to hunt together, the promise of not just carnality but friendship. And I can see it too, both of us red with the sea witch's gore, teeth sunken deep into her guts, crunching on her cartilage. Our tongues would penetrate deep for marrow and juicy fat. We would feast, and then we would fuck.

We move through the hall—both of us spurn food and drinks alike; they're bound to be laced with something.

If members of High Command are here, they have not made themselves easy to pick out. I try to reel in the memories of meeting them, but in all of them the cabal appears as a white, buzzing void. Only Kristiansen forms a vivid part of my recall, that ever-present red smile, those Nordic eyes. Insofar as I am capable of wanting anything, I would like to reach back in time and play a part in her destruction. I would extract my pound of flesh.

By and by we take to a secluded balcony; there are several, meant no doubt for mages who need to step away to strike secret bargains. The height is vertiginous, but I find I don't have many phobias—if any at all—and looking down at the beach and Sentosa's entertainment area doesn't bother me.

"Maybe we should start killing *anyone* we suspect of being High Command," Dallas says, leaning against the balustrade. "It'll kick up a fuss, and then cabalists will *have* to respond, to defend themselves and their reputation."

I cast my gaze over the crowd, waiters and attendees both. "Can you do that? I mean, would you be able to make yourself do it."

"Once, undoubtedly." Dallas gives an ambivalent shrug to her shoulders. "Now... I don't like most mages, so I could dig deep and find my old fire. And anyone who would become an acolyte for High Command—"

"You have such a very dim view of us," says a new voice.

We turn, as one, to a roiling froth of black and silver. On instinct, Dallas' hands change, claws unsheathing. And I—I freeze. The first time meeting Chun Hyang did not jolt anything. Now it does. An echo, a smell that triggers a flash of sensation: I am held down, and there's a hand gripping my chin, forcing my head up—fingers probing my gums, pressing on my tongue as though to get a good look at my teeth, the way you would when purchasing an animal.

My guts clench. I can't stop myself. I wrench free of the leash and tear off the muzzle, bend over the railing, and retch. My body takes this opportunity to finally feel vertigo; there is an instant, petrifying, where I think I'm going to plummet.

I turn around to find that whatever reservations Dallas had about using violence have vanished; she has seen my visceral reaction and is coming this close to raking her claws across Chun Hyang. "You mesmerizing piece of shit, we told you—" she's growling.

The only reason blood hasn't been spilled is because of the intervention of a powerfully built woman in a champagne dress. She takes off the mask to reveal that it's Inspector Fahriye Budak, paragon of Sealing and Containment, that has caught Dallas' wrist mid-swing.

"We are all *technically* on the same side tonight, Ms. Seidel," Fahriye says, familiar; I have the impression they know each other, or at least fought alongside each other once. She looks me over, then fixes the mesmer with a hard stare, then focuses again on me. "I didn't expect to meet another S&C veteran here, Inspector Kongmanee."

I would like to reply—the part of me that once served Sealing and Containment remembers respecting this woman, even admiring her. But my attention is drawn over Dallas' shoulder to the nightmare before me, as if I am a mote of dust trapped in the crushing pull of a black hole.

"Fahriye, we need to talk. About the Melusine," Dallas is saying, but it's so difficult to follow, like the tiger is talking from a thousand kilometers away. This specific arrangement of parts, this set of features, those broad shoulders and maenad hips—Chun Hyang was not present at my induction into Kristiansen's hive, but part of them was. One of them was there, standing over me as the blue, teardrop worm slid into my mouth, down my gullet, and annexed a place that was much deeper within me than my heart or my stomach. My sensory recall of that is perfect, comprehensive. Who knew there were nerve endings in such places as that worm invaded?

Why must these memories return now? Why couldn't they have come back at the safehouse, in private, with Dallas alone? The vertigo resurges; I feel as if I have slipped off the side of the building and am in free fall.

"I just realized what—who—you are. Inside you, there's the Exegesis," I say through a mouthful of acid and sour fear. "Or the Cynosure. Or both."

At this, Chun Hyang gives pause. Then a long, sultry laugh. "What a fine lot I have chosen, that every one of you knows me the moment you see me. I assure you, though, that I am much more than the sum of my parts. But enough about me; I'm more interested in talking about *you*. There's an empty place inside you, isn't there, Inspector?"

They take a step forward—how? Dallas was between us. Where did she go? But still they close with me, and the world begins to shrink to the two of us, closing shadow eclipsing everything that is not Chun Hyang.

"I believe I can assist," they say, and I do believe them. "I can fill it. I can remind you what it is like to be more than a starving void. What it is like, Recadat Kongmanee, to be *human*."

I stand trembling, unable to move, unable to muster the hive to my own defense. A knifepoint glints within their words, and it's as though they're already carving me up, closing their fist around my lungs, wrist-deep in the vital heat of my mortality. Or they might bind me prone, and grind the tip of their heel between my breasts, down my stomach, between my thighs. There is a future in which they'll sunder me, and I will know oblivion. And oblivion—it is like peace, isn't it? This is the best fate I can imagine, the most I deserve. I need to be shackled; I need to be taken apart.

"Tonight, we—you and I—must cooperate to destroy the Melusine. Your power, wed to my control. Imagine what we will do together. And when we are done, we will leave here together, and I will make you whole. Do you agree?"

My mouth is shaping *please* even though I don't know what I am asking for.

And then my mouth, all of me, is shaping into something else.

As before, the change is instinctive. But this time, there is intent behind it; I *feel* the pulling and rearranging of my muscles, my center of gravity; the lengthening of my skull and teeth. Strength flows through my aorta, and then into the rest of me. The insects quiet. The mandibles stop scratching at my guts.

I'm on top of Chun Hyang, and I'm about to tear their throat out.

FAHRIYE

"For fuck's sake," I growl and pull all of them apart—Recadat, who has shifted into a panther to tackle Chun Hyang to the ground; Dallas, who is right there beside her in complementary tiger stripes; Lussadh, who has joined the melee with a butter knife she grabbed from a table; and lastly Chun Hyang, who is smirking up at all three, their ripped clothes and ruffled hair flowing back into perfect position a moment after being disturbed.

"We are, at *best*, an alliance of convenience," I continue, exasperated. "Everyone here wants to see the Melusine brought to justice. We work together toward that goal, or we all die alone."

"I'm not certain *justice* is what I'm fighting for." Chun Hyang smirks, flowing out of my grip to stand apart. "But I can call you that for the night."

"Fahriye, that's what I've been trying to tell you," Dallas says quickly. "The Melusine, she's…"

The weretiger trails off. A moment later, I understand why, and why no one even batted an eye at two were-felines pouncing and snarling in the corner: the roof and every occupant has fallen eerily silent, watching in rapt attention as the Melusine strides out of the sky down a staircase of brilliant gold. Under her feet, motes form and rearrange in an incredible display of prowess, as pretty as fireflies. Her heels click against these ethereal steps, ringing out like pure jade.

"Thank you all for joining me tonight," she says in a voice barely above a whisper, but imbued with such potency that my teeth hurt, and I can feel my flesh momentarily flicker to stone, the elegant dress I'm wearing suddenly sheathing not brown skin but gray granite. "This is a very special night for me—and by the time it's done, nothing is *ever* going to be the same. Not for me. Not for you."

That voice… unlike before, at Orfea's flat, I can almost place it. It sounds so familiar, like someone I've heard for years.

The Melusine has stopped several meters above the roof, the light under her feet forming a platform. "High Command began, believe it or not, as a cult," she continues, a touch of sardonic humor in her voice. "They held the opinion that there exists beyond this world true perfection—and that the only way to step into paradise was to perfectly order our world first. No one liked that idea very much, and it brought High Command into a lot of conflicts with many people, foremost among them the Hua family. *My* family."

The Melusine snaps her fingers, and on the edge of her dais appear five figures, chained and kneeling; all are bloodied. "Welcome to the last meeting of High Command," the Melusine announces, even as her mask dissolves to reveal the face of Olesya Hua.

There's a ringing in my ears, a pressure in my chest. What I'm seeing refuses to reconcile with what I know. I grimly think that Lussadh will be pleased to know my stone body is capable of such somatic responses. I wonder if I can still die of shock, of cardiac impulses overloaded and misfiring.

Olesya is not my kin, but—but I made an oath to Elizaveta to protect her daughters, to watch over them as if they were mine. And I have, for ten long years, in the face of professional consequences, personal danger, and even—finally—my own death. In Olesya I saw a way to redeem myself a little, and I had thought her a good and just person, a daughter who would have made her mother proud. And now I have to watch as… as…

"…she's a doppelganger," Dallas is saying. "She's a construct of some sort—the working theory is she's Olesya's id given form, thanks to a being called Nuawa."

I twist around to glare at Dallas. *"What* did you just say?"

"The Melusine is more powerful than Olesya," she explains, "but she seems to have all her memories—and her hatreds, amplified by a being of crystal. Nuawa, I think. I don't know what the Melusine is planning on doing here, but it can't be good."

"You neglected to tell me this when I was at your cabin," Chun Hyang says; their usual shine has taken on an unhealthy pallor.

"Looks like we were wrong again, Fahriye," Lussadh says, grim. "Maybe it really *was* Nuawa."

Above us, one of the members of High Command twitches as he is lifted into the air, limbs twisting and contorting, a marionette being pulled into position for a coming performance.

"These days, High Command isn't a cult," Olesya—the Melusine—is still crowing. "They have grown fat, complacent in their power. *Ripe*, like the sweetest grapes. And it's time someone showed them to the press."

The mage implodes; in an instant flesh and bone are crushed down to a ball no larger than my fist. True to the metaphor, the blood is pulled out—viscous warm wine that begins to spin around the Melusine's head, a sanguine halo.

What remains of the mage drops to the rooftop below with a grotesque splat. This, finally, is enough to break the rapturous silence; people begin to scream and run for the exits.

Recadat has stayed silent since assaulting Chun Hyang, but she speaks now with an eerie calm. "Alright, new plan." She reaches out and grabs hold of the duplicitous mage's arm. Immediately, I taste an echo of Kristiansen's magic—tendrils of covetous, consuming power, black spreading through Chun Hyang's opalescent perfection.

"You motherfucker," Chun Hyang shouts, and tries to jerk their arm away.

"Sauce for the goose, sauce for the gander," Recadat replies, implacable. "Your power, *my* control."

This won't succeed—a union like this requires trust, the rarest of commodities in a group such as this. I turn away from this farce to the only person I can depend on: "Lussadh—we did this once, we can do it again."

"Once more unto the breach, dear friend, once more." She flips her butter knife underhanded; I have no doubt that however dull the blade, she is the most dangerous woman here.

"Stay low; I'll get her attention."

"How are you—"

"*Olesya*," I shout above the cacophony. I'm not certain what I'm saying, what I'm struggling toward. "I'm—I'm sorry."

This, unfortunately, gets her attention. She is in the process of lifting another member of High Command, her victim's legs twisting like green saplings, the bones inside snapping like dried twigs; as soon as she hears my challenge, her prey is forgotten, the broken body falling away. "*What did you say?*" she asks, cold, furious.

"I owe you an apology, Olesya. I'm sorry…"

The Melusine stalks forward, descending on beams of light to loom over me; with each footfall, the ground she is suspended on shatters. "I am *not* Olesya Hua, and you—"

I think back to Dallas' guess, that the Melusine was Olesya's embodied id. "But you are her anger and fear. And her hopes. And I know you didn't mean to kill all those people."

She freezes, genuinely surprised. "Of course I did." To admit otherwise would be weakness, to acknowledge that something was out of her control.

I give my most disarming smile—kind and warm, unaffected, the smile that is anchored in the good of this world, the one I would use to assure hostage takers and would-be jumpers. "You didn't know it'd unleash so much power. You were just trying to kill me, or hurt me. And I get it. I… every day I hate myself for how I let your mother down. How much more you must, in your heart of hearts, hate me, too."

"I'm not one of your women, Budak. I'm not one of your victims, in need of saving." But she has stepped closer, lower. "What do you hope to accomplish here?"

Somewhere out there, Lussadh is circling. I hope she can read the room;

I hope she understands what I am trying to do, when even I do not. "Dallas is here. She's worried about you. She thinks that an ancient and evil enemy of the Huas has sunk her claws into you, is trying to manipulate you into hurting the people you care about."

The Melusine's eyes go wide. "But that's just the thing, Fahriye. I'm not going to hurt *anyone*. I'm going to save Mother, restore the lives I've taken, and give everyone precisely what they deserve. And all it's going to take is me killing four more mages in the here-and-now, four lives that I give my word will be restored to life—if not power—in the new world I make."

"What are you planning, Olesya?" I ask—worried, not by the madness I hear, but the lucidity, the *certainty*.

"Right now?" She has drawn close enough that we are looking each other in the eye, and she leans in to whisper in my ear. "I'm planning to use you as a body-shield."

Before I can react, she grabs me and pivots, pulling me right into the arc of Lussadh's lunge; I feel the damned butter knife dig deep into my shoulder. The Melusine punches me next—right in the chest, a powerful blow that sends me crashing into Lussadh, and then both of us tumbling away.

A shimmering veil of quicksilver surrounds us; Recadat Kongmanee is there to give me a hand up.

"Is this your work?" I ask about the barrier as I reach down for Lussadh. The professor is winded, having taken the brunt of my mass slamming into her, but her pride is hurt more than her body. Chagrined, she begins to work her knife out of my shoulder.

Recadat looks... sharper, better put together; her skin has the slightest hint of a healthy sheen, almost silver, and her back is straighter, her shoulders squarer. "I reached an understanding with Chun Hyang," is the only explanation she provides as she nods in the general vicinity—Chun Hyang themself is nowhere to be seen, must have done their best to hide themself from the Melusine's line of sight. "I'll be able to exchange fire with the Melusine. Not forever, but enough. What are your plans?"

Through the veil, I watch as another High Command cabalist is reduced to pulp and bone shards. The Melusine would be drawing strength from that. We don't have much time. "Doesn't look like cutting her off from her sacrifices is going to happen."

"I'd have preferred to kill High Command with my own hands." Recadat's voice is without inflection.

"There's something I can do. If I can get close enough," Lussadh adds, "then I could sever her connection to Nuawa, or Olesya Hua. Either way should destabilize if not entirely dissolve her."

"Alright," says Recadat. "We'll work toward that."

A blinding light at the perimeter of the barrier, a penetrating blow, and the entire veil collapses, like suspended water falling out of the air. The Melusine stands before us, true madness on her face—pinpoints in her eyes, not of gold but of brilliant white.

Her hand snaps out, seizing my wrist.

"Do you think," she says, a sickly sweet snarl, "that I was ignorant of how you fucked my mother for *years*? How you made her *weak*? You had the temerity to come unannounced into my life, rob me of my mother, and then when she needed you most, you let her die alone. And you"—she shifts her glare to Recadat—"words cannot express how I detest your betrayals, your ingratitude, your harlotry. Interlopers, both of you. One who stole my mother. Another who would steal my tiger. I will break you *both*."

OLESYA

It doesn't take long for me to arrive at Sentosa's largest resort, albeit it did take some ignoring of traffic rules. The city's overburdened; there is no one to stop me from running a dozen red lights in a row. It's a personal best—I am here, as it were, in record time.

Every time my speedometer crested 200 kilometers an hour, I felt I was rushing to my death. I am going into this fight alone, woefully unprepared, at a fraction of my strength.

"Then it'll be a fair fight," I mutter to myself, stepping out of the car.

It's easy enough to see where I need to go: if the hum and keen of unleashed magic wasn't enough, there is a dazzling light show on the roof. Occasionally, something will come crashing down from far above—statuary, potted plants, a body or two—and everyone at ground level will curse and scream and flee. This includes the security staff in the foyer, whose loyalty evaporates the moment it is tested. I reach the elevator bank unmolested.

Something happens as I step into the lift—deja vu to that time in Viveca's tower and Kristiansen's magic, though it's not quite the same. Not a distortion of architecture but a kaleidoscope of visions—and I recognize the cadence and texture of it: this is my own magic, my connection to the Melusine. I'm surrounded by windows, each looking into a different moment of perfection, of glory.

In one, Mother is drinking coffee with a child of seven or eight, a girl who has been born into a body that will require no fleshcrafting to make right. The first daughter of Hua, and the only—Viveca is nowhere in sight. And Mother is telling me about summoning rites.

Could there have been two warlocks of the house? The question was never tested, because I was not interested, or perhaps I made myself so. It's not as if Viveca or Mother chose for me to be born thus out of malice. It's not as if I *had* to learn fleshcrafting and transfiguration. Why would I be bitter? Why would *she*, this thing born from some recess inside me that I have not been able to confront?

But it's what others had that I didn't, isn't it, and then I had the sickness—and now the view shifts to a much later time. This other Olesya is alone, in the bloom of youth, limned in gold. She can have anything she likes; she can do anything she wants. Using magic does not burn her or cut her life short. She takes life as she wishes, and destroys those who would bring her consequences. In her eyes is the gleam of our ancestor, the tyrant queen who ruled Singapore with the might of a demon army.

She preempts the matter of Cecilie Kristiansen. Hunts her down to a dead volcano, and there destroys her. In this vision, Cecilie dies screaming; the demon she wields, a thing of smoke and bone, is badly wounded when it is cast back to hell. It will convalesce for ten thousand years, never to bother the mortal world again in her or any other lifetime.

TWELVE: MASQUE OF THE RED DEATH

In the world she weaves, Mother doesn't die. She lives as something like a dowager queen, admiring the growing might of her daughter, smiling and nodding as Singapore entire becomes her palace. My gut twists as this other Olesya meets Dallas—they are *my* memories, warped, making of my tiger a tame cat content to sit at her feet while she builds for herself a throne, a court. Everything in the same gleaming shade.

In her world, the roads around her palace are paved with blood; there is no friction, and there is no Viveca, no one to steal Dallas away—not for a moment, not ever. She will be a golden empress, and she will reign always.

The elevator dings. I'm at the rooftop.

Beyond it: carnage. Tables bent in half, the buffet spilled everywhere, thick puddles of viscera. Torn limbs and ruptured organs mingle with the congealing food. The stink is unbearable.

And waiting for me—as if this is normal, the most reasonable sight in all the world—is Dallas. "Welcome to the party," she says, the words twisted by the lengthened incisors in her mouth.

"You knew I was coming?" For a moment, the world is just the two of us—two lovers, two exes, two *somethings* groping for the words that will make everything right.

I choose not to talk; I lunge at her. She flinches but lets me take hold, and my heart breaks at what I have done to this beast, this best thing in my life. The next moment, the geas is removed: simple and painless, the mirror image of what it must have felt like to wear those manacles. "Get out of here, Dallas," I whisper, my breath fever-hot. "Find Chang'er, contact Yves. I will buy us time."

"No. Whatever our differences, whatever you have done to me—in the moment of crisis, my place is at your side. I love you, Olesya Hua, and I always will."

I nod to not cry. The future is unknown, and there will be a reckoning for how I have abused those I love. For now, we share a purpose. I veil myself and her, knowing as I do it's not a perfect protection, and then both of us draw toward the Melusine.

There's no time to gawk, though. Power saturates the air, taking the form of quicksilver. I don't pause to make sense of what I'm seeing; simply I let them be my camouflage while I close the distance with my target. She's distracted. She is bent on murdering everything on this rooftop. At the moment, she is hurling her magic and hatred at Fahriye and Recadat, who are on the back foot.

Close. A little closer.

We reach her at the same time, strike as one. Dallas' claws sink into her just as my fist goes through her chest. A tacit, deep understanding between the two of us, this reunion in another woman's body.

My fingers move against things that are hot and wet, even though she's bleeding light and I can tell that she's not really flesh and bones, not ligaments and cardiac drum. An image: that is all she is.

And like all images, a mortal wound is not enough to break her.

She registers no surprise at our assault, even cranes her neck to sneer at me, smile too wide; there is no trace of pain in her eyes. "I'm right. You know I'm right, Olesya. And now… I'll show you all how much better it'll be on *my* canvas."

The rooftop goes white.

Thirteen: All Roads Lead To Ruin

FAHRIYE

It's not often a beautiful woman walks through my door. In fact, as far as this specific woman is concerned, the frequency of her appearance in my office should be *never*.

I stand up so fast it nearly makes me dizzy. I dive toward the door, easing it shut behind her while she looks on, amused.

"Liz," I start saying. There's something wrong here—isn't there? A part of me is twitching and clawing at the strangeness of this, not just her being here but the fact I'm in this office, the fact that she's…

Elizaveta's small, full mouth is drawn toward a smirk. "Don't stand on ceremony on my behalf. Remember what we discussed at our last meeting? I'm inviting you on an adventure."

What we discussed. The details resurface, piecemeal: an entity that scorches, the sword in which it is trapped, her family obligation. And her admonitions that I am not to come with her; that she must do this alone. "Then you've changed your mind?" I say, a little breathless, hope clogging my throat.

"I had the idea that this was a heroic burden I must bear alone. But—well. It's selfish. I don't want to orphan my children, and the likelihood of that increases astronomically if I go to Armenia on my own." She draws close, taking hold of my tie. "We have time, though, and hardly need to instantly depart. Why don't we go out for dinner?"

The food is excellent, though I remember hardly any of it. All I pay attention to is her. Her face straight on, her face in profile, the way she eats and gestures with chopsticks. How she pronounces Turkish. Everything about her, every minutia, is infinitely compelling and infinitely precious. If I could have dinner with her every day, I would be happy. It does not have to be *good*: the importance is her company. I would eat horrible, greasy slop with no flavor if she's there. She could feed me watery gruel and I'd lap it up with joy. It occurs to me this is a paradox—that being happy with the most powerful woman in the world is actually a very simple thing.

Afterward, we stand outside in the drifting snow, looking on at the blue peaks above Sapporo. At other tourists; at children running past. I feel like I'm standing on the cusp. Like I am about to ask a very stupid but courageous question, an unthinkable question. Here I teeter; in a moment I will fall.

"Fahriye," she says, and my body thrills. I can sense it. She will say it first, a preemptive strike. "After we're done in Armenia, why don't you meet my daughter?"

A feeling of unrealness, an intruding thought: haven't I already met them? Once, I went to the home of the firstborn in Singapore and I… asked her questions, about something important, a case. I have had long conversations with Viveca, the secondborn. She is married herself. Is she not? I'm about to say some of this when I realize it would make me sound insane, detached from reality. Of course not. Her daughter has just graduated out of university, not made her own life as warlock and sorceress-assassin. Where did that even come from; how did my imagination run so far and so wild? "Oh," I say. Then I try again. "Are you sure?"

"You eventually have to." A fractional pause. "If we're to make more of this. If we are going to… progress. It has been twenty years, hasn't it, and I am getting no younger."

My heart hammers. "Master Elizaveta, you'll have to spell out exactly what you mean."

"Insolent woman." But her voice is soft. "I mean, of course, that one day we might not need to hide this. That there is a future where we can make a household together."

Another time, another place, I might have argued—that it's impossible, that I can't leave S&C, that there are a hundred thousand reasons this cannot be done. Here and now though, I say, "Yes. The answer is yes."

RECADAT

It is late afternoon, and it is raining hard. The sky is the gray-black that approaches funeral wear but stops short of that dignified color. There's a velvet quality to the clouds, a yielding thickness that I would like to sink my hands into. Water strikes the windshield, again and again, repeated little hammer-blows. Sometimes I try to calculate how hard it'd have to rain for the water to finally shatter glass. But the city would flood first, and I would wash away like flotsam.

"Awful weather for a stakeout," murmurs Thannarat. "Can't see a thing. You'd think the brass would just assign this case a scryer."

Every hair on my skin stands on end. My heart spits and sparks, all embers. "Why are you here?" Because this is—this is more than I should be able to recall. There's only one memory of her that I truly retain, that of her death, agonizing and grotesque: melting skin and muscles, a flood of broken chitin. But she sits next to me, complete and lifelike. The broad shoulders, the wolfish hair and mouth, the gleaming black prostheses with which she replaced her limbs years ago. Those were the results of a terrible firefight; I dragged her half-dead and little more than a torso from it, and she's never let me live that down. *It was nothing,* I used to tell her, and it was—horribly—around that time that I realized I was in love.

Which is not supposed to happen with your colleague, especially when you're in S&C. There are probably regulations against it. Fraternizing leads nowhere good in this line of work.

"Pah," she replies; is it her voice rumbling, or thunder? "My weekend plans were canceled, and I figured what better way to spend it than with you."

"That's—" This isn't what happened, is it? Or what ought to have happened. "You had a date, right? The... the florist who loves roses, with the fox keychain?"

"I *did*. But she called me last night, and now I don't." Her face darkens, then slips back to her ever-present smirk. "Good riddance. I wasn't going to catch bad guys over sushi."

"Why…" The nightmare of her death is fading, and in its place is something like courage. "After we catch this bastard, how about we get sushi together? My treat."

Thannarat takes a slow sip of her convenience store coffee; for all her casualness, I know she feels the import of this question, too. I hold my breath.

"You know what," she finally replies, "dinner with you sounds lovely."

"It doesn't have to be a date-date," I quickly clarify. Maybe she doesn't feel the way I do, and is refraining from scoffing at me even now. Maybe I should just cut my losses and save us both the embarrassment. "Just pals getting food after work."

There's sudden movement across the street—our murderous mage is stepping out of his lair. Reality always conspires against us; I think this is where we will leave it, where we always leave it. But Thannarat stops before she turns the ignition, flashes her wolfish grin. "But what if I want it to be a date-date?"

"What'd Internal Affairs…" But I was the one who began this, wasn't I. *What would other people think* is the retreat of the coward, which I have been, all these years. The easy fallback. The aversion of choice, because as long as I don't choose I will not have to fail, to be rejected. "Okay. It'll be a date."

Her mouth widens. In that moment I so desperately want to reach out and touch her jaw, her cheek, her hair; I want to run my thumb across her scarred mouth. "Can't wait. We better arrest this bastard right quick."

I wonder what it will feel like to have her body pressing down against mine.

THIRTEEN: ALL ROADS LEAD TO RUIN

OLESYA

It's a sitting room in my estate and everyone is waiting on me. My wives and my sister are murmuring inside, dressed in matching pastel ensembles of different cuts. Viveca and Chang'er look up from their tea and end their conversation to smile at me, while Dallas turns from where she is standing by the window, hands in her suit pockets, to quirk a grin. Her hand extends toward me. The scene is warm and inviting, almost pastoral. Peace after all our struggles, healing after all our wounds, idyllic and ideal. The beginning of a new, finer world.

"This isn't real," I say.

Everyone raises an eyebrow or hides a downturn of the lip, polite in the face of my faux pas.

I'm a seamstress of reality; I can see the twist of illusion, hear the hum of suggestion, that undergirds this place. And though the upholstery and paint feel like my magic, there's another force here, winding like cables through the walls. I cannot undo this as I might undo the Melusine's power on its own.

The edges of my vision begin to flicker, like I am watching an old projector as the film begins to tear, then ignite. The scene turns brighter and brighter, everything dissolving into an expanse of featureless white, save my sister, the table, and an empty chair. But Viveca's dress now looks like charred paper, slips eternally curling to black and drifting to the floor. Her eyes glow with an ugly light, as pure as a knife's edge. The skin on her cheek chars.

"It's been so long since I've spoken with one of you." Viveca's lips twist in a parody of human movement; it's all illusion, so this thing *wants* to be seen as a puppeteer, rusty on how to pull the strings.

"A human?" I ask

"No," they groan, lips splitting. "A *Hua*."

"So you are Nuawa." The great lodestone of my family, the enemy we are sworn to contain—Mother lectured Viveca and me at length about the heirloom promise that has bound our family since its first generation, and how the entity Nuawa slipped from our grasp decades ago.

The thing is malice incarnate, Mother warned. *It is our mortal enemy, and even if it has gone into occultation, we must always assume it is waiting, and we must ever be prepared to again contain it.*

"Not *quite* in the flesh," they reply, and their voice scratches at all the senses; I can taste their discordant emphasis, smell the jagged edges of their words. "But enough of me is here."

I sit across from them; what else can I do? The danger we are all in is profound beyond reckoning; I need time to think, to understand that this is not just a function of my repressed id but an outside influence.

"It can be both," Nuawa suggests in reply to my thought, as one of Viveca's front teeth cracks. Hands with crisping flesh move to rest on the table. "Your family is shot through with faultlines; any weapon forged in the hands of a demon must be so flawed. For generations, I believed strength alone would see me free and your ilk ruined, but you seem impervious to feeling the shame of death; the worst disasters befall your line, and you crawl out from under the wreckage."

"And now, you brag that you have finally succeeded."

A smile formed, not from the lips moving, but the jaw breaking. "Within you resides all the foibles of your family. Your ambitions became resentment, your power restored to a heart turned sour. It was easy enough to slip within your dreams and make of them something… more."

"Why even bother with the Melusine? What do you want?"

A pause like the stilled breath of a dying newborn. "Silence. Perfection. To look on eternity and know that I have made it possible. But in the next few minutes? The complete destruction, the final undoing, of everything you hold dear. And you will make that possible. The Melusine's plan—*your* plan—to change time and fix what has gone wrong… it offers such *promise*. Only a Hua would think so large. But all songs must follow sheet music, and now I will change the tune. Even now, your compatriots reveal to me the turning point of their lives, the singular regret that seizes their soul. And in that moment, I will make their nightmares reality. Your family won't end today, Olesya Hua; once I'm done, it'll have ended years ago."

A bank of television monitors flicks on, the *fump-whosh* of static giving away to surveillance-like footage of a half dozen unfolding scenes. The thing that wears Viveca motions toward them, ash and bone sloughing away to reveal something that steals a year of my life when I look on it. "Shall we watch the finale together?"

FAHRIYE

Vagharshapat, Armenia. It is icy, in a different way from Sapporo. Subzero, as a matter of course. It is winter when we arrive.

In a little bed-and-breakfast, we prepare. Amulets and athames, paper and wood charms, fragments of esoteric alloys. Elizaveta has not brought her demons. "Nuawa is a very specific kind of being," she says. "Demons don't do well around it. Particularly old, mighty ones can tolerate Nuawa for a time, but not in any way useful to combat. So it will be just us, and a few non-infernal spirits I've mustered."

"What *is* it? No," I add, feeling a faint tinge of deja vu, "why do you need to deal with it?"

"A long time ago, my ancestor made a bargain with an ancient demon. The crux of it was the containment of this being, to pin it in this world so it may neither harm demonkind nor return to its point of origin, to lick its wounds and come back here to wreck havoc." She turns in her hand the milky quartz I gave her with which to track Nuawa. It's pulsing now, humming with proximity to its target. "In the main, it has a grudge against my family, and I am acting in defense of my daughters. Explaining to this thing that the original issue was with my ancestor seems unlikely to prevail. Of my family's misfortunes throughout the ages, some of them were caused by Nuawa. I want, Inspector, to end this once and for all. No more burden. No further generations of my house having to reckon with this."

How badly I want her to be selfish; but I have full knowledge, too, that her lack of narcissism so common to the powerful is what drew me to her in the first place. It's natural that she would love her children, that she would not want this ordeal passed on to them. This concludes today, and I will be proud to be at her side during it, for good or ill, in success or failure.

We share a meal of soft cheese, lavash, and cold soup. Over it, Elizaveta tells me about her daughter. She does so in a halting way, the same as every other time she's tried to tell me about Olesya; it's never very detailed, scraps and snapshots, as though she's attempting and failing to build her as a synopsis. Something I can understand easily, quickly, a substitute for never having been in her daughter's life. "Olesya is one of the steadiest people I've ever met," she tells me. "Sometimes I worry that I expect too much of her, and that's why she turned out this way."

Disorienting: she has more than one child, doesn't she? There's another. Why's she acting as if she has only the single scion? But I go along. "I think you've done better than the overwhelming majority of mage parents."

She glances up at me, holding a piece of lavash and cheese, and chuckles. "It's true—most families are dysfunctional. I strive to do as well for my daughter as my mother did for me. That's the true meaning of legacy."

I'm struck by that. I don't think I have ever heard any parent say such a thing, in so many words, for all that I came from a perfectly fine environment and—I like to think—grew up well. "Can I ask," I say before I can stop myself, "what she might think of me?" There's every chance Olesya will not tolerate me at all, or see me as an intruder into her family.

Elizaveta shakes her head, long-suffering. "You sacrificed yourself to save her life. What do you think?"

"That was so long ago." Ammunition in the mail, from someone powerful who wishes to help me with difficult cases. Except that doesn't make sense. *Elizaveta* is the powerful patron in question, and she has no need for bullets.

She snorts, now. "Yes, Inspector, I raised my daughter so poorly she'd forget such a deed. No. Olesya thinks the world of you. Sometimes I think she even knows about us."

A flush warms the back of my neck. "And she's... fine with it?" *With you dating down*, I don't say.

"It is my belief," she says gently, "that she would honor you."

To that, I don't know what to say. But my heart brims with possibility,

THIRTEEN: ALL ROADS LEAD TO RUIN

with the future we could have after we're done here.

We set off for the cathedral late evening, long after its congregation has left. Both of us enter cloaked in charms of aversion, and once inside, in esoteric wards. She has warned me to protect myself against high temperatures, and I've followed her instruction.

The basement goes deeper than I would expect, the stairs stretching down into the dark with such fathomlessness that my skin pricks with alarm. But then we, rather abruptly, reach the bottom.

"Let me go ahead," I say.

Elizaveta opens her mouth to object, then simply nods. I feel the weight of a protective spirit under her command settle on me.

It's not often I take point, because most of the time I work alone. What an odd feeling it is to have someone to bring up the rear, to guard my back. For the entire duration of my career, the only time I've been the recipient of this privilege is when I'm working with Liz. I try not to dwell on the singular loneliness of that.

The basement smells unventilated and thick, as though nobody's been here for a long time. More than that, it's abnormally warm, the heat of a fireplace, then a furnace.

"Be on your guard," Elizaveta murmurs from behind me.

My gun is drawn. I nudge at the door with my foot.

It swings open, soundless and smooth, and I flinch from the light. There's so much of it, and somehow none of it leaked out through the hinges, the door.

We enter a little chamber where the stone presses down, low, like a coffin's lid. And in the middle, at the precise centerpoint as though it's been calculated down to the millimeter, shines a sword of impossible whiteness.

"Raise your shield," says my warlock. "I'll begin containing it now."

I bring forth the barrier that she taught me to construct while she begins to intone in a language I don't know, and whose syllabary I cannot possibly pronounce.

And then the light brightens. The heat warms my cheeks, and then I become very sure that it's singeing the hairs on my skin—the escalation is fast and harsh. I hold steady. I maintain my shield.

(Don't I have hide of stone? Aren't I impervious to flame?)

It is as if we're in the middle of a forest fire, the inside of a raging reactor. The shield becomes an imperative, becomes an instinct. I hold and hold; I will give my life to it.

It isn't enough.

Perhaps I'm distracted for half a second; perhaps I give in to animal terror and flinch. The fault is mine. The failure is on me. I do not have time to apologize.

An opening in my shield, for the barest of instant, and the sword buries itself in Elizaveta.

There is smoke, in place of blood. Cauterizing too fast for hemorrhage. She falls without crying out and I know, I know that she's already gone, but I follow her anyway to catch her, to hold her.

"This time," a voice snarls, "I will *not* be sealed away. This time she will *not* prevail. I shall be the downfall of the house of Hua."

RECADAT

The sushi place is excellent, and I'm the happiest I have ever been. I can't remember ever having been this uninhibited in joy—I've always been cautious about my feelings, my reactions, averted from them because I know everything stands on the precipice of loss. Often I come close to my objective, and just as often it slips away. But this time, I think it will be different. We're beginning something. We are going to make it work.

Thannarat and I have eaten together before, usually hurried meals, fast food. Drinks, often. This is the first time we've sat down to something more… formal, as formal as a sushi bar can be. Her eyes are riveted to the conveyor belt of little plates; she snatches the one with unagi, another with tamagoyaki. "I love this kind of thing," she tells me in a low voice, as though a little embarrassed to admit to liking anything. "You never know what's going to be up next."

THIRTEEN: ALL ROADS LEAD TO RUIN

It's not the most authentic of places, a sort of fusion between Japanese and the Southeast Asian idea of what Japanese food is like. Some of the sushi is topped with bacon or tiny slices of Vietnamese sausage, or bits of flavored jellyfish. We don't care; Thannarat goes through plate after plate with ravening appetite, and I sip my green tea to hide that I'm grinning like a fool. Can it be possible to feel so buoyant just because you're in someone's company?

(Distantly I remember another woman, a wiry one with tiger's gold in her hair. But that is a fantasy. Thannarat is real, and I am finally where I belong.)

"I've been thinking," she says, just how she always does when she is serious—eyes ahead, looking at everything but me, affected detachment to her voice.

I laugh, and reply how I always do. "Well, there's your first problem."

Thannarat grimaces; the line of her jaw clenching is a marvel to behold. "I'm thinking about getting out."

The piece of sushi I am lifting to my mouth falls from my forkchops.

"You've seen how S&C handles things. It's not just the bureaucracy, but the *everything*." She talks quickly, before I find my voice. "The only people we're helping are the rich and powerful. It eats at me, and I know it eats at you."

I am rendered speechless a second time. "I—I didn't think you noticed."

She fixes me an earnest stare, eyes so bright I think they have taken on the nightshine of a hunter. "I always notice you, Recadat. I listen to you, even when you think I'm dozing. And I've thought about what you've said in our stakeouts—how we're the glorified bagmen for some really vile mages, that we are culpable in the evil of our organization—and I agree with you. I… I realized I needed to do something about it. Something that makes a difference." She looks bashful for a moment, almost scared. "I want to start a detective agency, one that actually helps people. And I want you to be my partner."

Every hope, every dream I have had for me, for us, has come true in an instant. I am seen, I am known; I am loved. "Thannarat Vutirangsee, nothing would make me—"

The sushi chef on the other side of the counter pulls out a gun and shoots Thannarat in the head.

FAHRIYE

I have failed Elizaveta again.

I'm on my knees, weeping, and she dissolves in my arms, from woman to cinderous dust. It feels as if I have been here a hundred times, that I am always locked in this moment, where if I'd acted a little sooner, a little better, she would have been saved. I try to hold onto the red ashes, as if I could piece her back together. But even those are escaping me now, fluttering away inside this ancient basement, amidst this blaze—useless futility in the face of the inevitable.

Clutching at what remains of her, I wait for the flame to consume me too.

The voice that spoke before has drawn closer now. "In you," it says, in a low whisper, "lives the magic of the woman I hate the most in this realm. My great regret is that I wasn't able to make *her* watch you die. What a delicious morsel that would have been."

It kneels beside me. The heat is nearly impossible to bear.

"But we've all been given a second chance, haven't we?" The face of killing light draws into a leer. "You, me, Olesya. What a splendid thing, to be able to redo your mistakes. Again and again and *again*."

The last of Elizaveta is gone. Embers on the ground. The smell of scorched flesh.

"Why the fuck," I say through gritted teeth, "do you hate her this much?"

"I believe she has already explained that to you, hasn't she?" The voice has turned satisfied, amused. "Poor mortals, they always think so much of themselves. They believe that with sufficient time and innovation, they'll be able to overstep their natural limits. But I'm eternal, Fahriye Budak, and the force of me will always triumph over the petty tricks of your kind."

The sword hovers. It is poised to tear into me, but my body refuses to

THIRTEEN: ALL ROADS LEAD TO RUIN

move, unable to do anything save regret. Perhaps this is what I deserve for having—repeatedly—failed Elizaveta, the woman who means the most to me in the world, the woman who is more precious than any gold.

A flying punch interrupts my execution. Nuawa stumbles back more in surprise than pain; the sword tumbles out of their hand, only to melt away and reform in their grip.

"I learned that one from you, old woman," Olesya gloats, lording over me.

"I—" My thanks dies in my throat. I was mistaken: it's not Olesya but her doppelganger, the Melusine.

"Don't give me that look," my savior snaps. "We're on the same side now." She then turns to face Nuawa, her voice dropping to a snarl. "My moment of triumph, and *you* appear, trying to twist my magic away from me."

The creature sneers. "Is that so? Do you fancy yourself in charge, little girl? Remember who gave birth to you. Remember who fuels your very core."

"You're not doing this," snarls the Melusine. "In the *corrected* world, my mother lives."

"Any moment, 'Olesya', I can cut you off and watch you shrivel back to nothing, to the shadow of the daughter born to misfortune. You aren't even your own person. You're a sad copy that only exists because I permit you to."

"If you believe," says the Melusine, "that you're in control of *me*, you're about to have a rude surprise."

They hurl themselves at each other, light and shadow twisting around their blows. The Melusine lands a hit on Nuawa, hard and true; their crystal hide does not crack, but I can feel power resonate through them, and then out into the reality beyond.

This is just a nightmare, I realize, and the thought turns like a key in a lock. The basement shifts, and then I'm no longer beneath the cathedral in Armenia, no longer kneeling in Elizaveta's ashes.

Instead, I'm in an office of warm wood and high shelves, thick heavy volumes, an elegant work desk. Mahogany, I think, the top of it laden with books. A few with bookmarks, one lying open. There's an hourglass, the sand within it trickling slow and cobalt.

The woman sitting at the desk looks up. "What the fuck have you gotten yourself into, Budak?"

RECADAT

The sushi chef steps *through* the counter, wood and glass curling into ash before them, sloughing out of existence.

"It has been a joy to work with Olesya," they say, breaking the gun to eject the spent cartridge, beginning to slot in a fresh round. "Her id struggles mightily against itself to create a perfect new reality for her compatriots, all the while showing me the *precise* way to hurt each of you most."

Thannarat—eyes dead, lips still smiling—topples over, and where she sat now stands the chef. "But Olesya has such a great ambivalence for you. It was so *easy* to touch the threads of this reality and turn it to tragedy, as if she always wanted this outcome."

I struggle to move. I can't look down to see if she's still breathing, I can't reach for my gun.

With inhuman contortions, their head twists to regard me from different angles. Their lips curl back from teeth of purest marble; their eyes glow an impossible, blinding white, a complete absence of color that cuts at the soul. At first, I think this might be Olesya's magic at work, but the light is too harsh, too barren; this is something else, existing within the dream.

"They all want you, don't they?" the horror mocks. "The sorceress, the doppelganger, High Command, the *tiger*—each is intent on having you. You, the alluring last archive of Cecilie Kristiansen's life work. But the one woman you wanted to *give* yourself to... well, your sorry end almost wrote itself."

My fingernails dig deep into the counter. Splintering, tearing away from the flesh, enough pain to let me push back against the crushing pressure of their gaze, if only barely. "They'll stop you," I spit through gritted teeth. "Those women will stop you."

THIRTEEN: ALL ROADS LEAD TO RUIN

It laughs like razorblades, snaps the gun closed, and puts the muzzle to my forehead. "Don't worry, Recadat Kongmanee. I have never once noticed you—I have no use for the empty scabbard of a broken sword." A single, grotesque talon begins to depress the trigger, only for the thing to stop suddenly, jerking its head to listen to some far off noise, a disturbance from outside the bounds of our reality. "What—"

A blur of gold and black tackles me away from the gun; I am barreled through booths and illusory patrons, pulled behind a toppled table. "This isn't real, none of this is real," my savior growls at me.

The vibration of her voice, the press of her claws into my back—"Dallas?"

"We're trapped in an illusion, being hunted and tormented by something that hates us very, very much."

I hear a twisting sigh, then the crunch of glass as the horror begins to stalk through the restaurant. "Here, kitty, kitty," they call, voice like frozen blood. "You keep slipping from dream to dream, cage bars just leading to more cages. Once again I warn you: you are going to die tired, unable to save anyone."

Dallas ignores the taunt as she hurls us from the restaurant, tumbling through the door—

—into a dimly lit bar, all wood panels and sticky surfaces. It's a real dive; just a few patrons, a lanky drunk at a back table, a woman of long lines and hard angles crumpled around an empty bottle. The television above the bar plays grainy, looping footage of the moon landing.

"No, not here," Dallas croaks. "Anywhere but here."

FAHRIYE

For several moments I stand, stupefied and stunned. The clock has rewound. The woman I love stands before me, again whole. "Elizaveta. I'm so sorry—I couldn't protect you, when I thought..."

She has risen to her feet. "None of that, Inspector. You've gotten yourself in quite a spot of trouble, haven't you? Allow me to see if I can assist."

My mouth is parched. "I'm supposed to be the one helping you."

Her smile is so calm, so warm, the one she reserves for her daughters and for me. "Is that a fact? Let us assess the situation. You are trapped in a snare created by a being that rains ruin down on my family, that would see you destroyed for your association with me."

"I—" A fresh sob wracks through me. This is a dream, like the one I just stepped from. Her in Armenia, alone: that is what truly happened, what has happened and will happen. It cannot be undone; I've lost her again. "You're not really here."

The illusory Elizabeth smirks, the self-satisfaction of someone who knows she can rewrite the gravitational constant or suspend the sun's trajectory. "As for that, it's debatable. Occasionally reality and chronology are malleable. I more than anyone understand this well." She places her hand on my shoulder and squeezes. "I've been in this prison a long time, and its inner workings have become clearer to me, over the years. There is a way out."

I swallow so that I won't start blubbering like a baby. I try to pivot to tactics, to discussing our current predicament; try, desperately, to engage with the specter of my dead love. I handily fail. "Your daughters have grown up into incredible women," I blurt out. "Viveca's married now. To a demon, but I don't think you will mind. Her wife is good to her, as far as I can tell. And Olesya surrounds herself with women she loves."

Her expression softens. "I'm glad to hear that. Thank you for telling me. We don't have much time." And all the same she stretches on tiptoes to kiss me, hard.

She takes my hand next and leads me out the corridor of her home. Of this image of her home, I correct myself. A dining room, libraries, a bathroom or two—it's a tour of her grand residence from all those years ago. We pass the beds of her sleeping children.

A part of me wants to slow down, to have tea with her; to chase her up to her bedroom, to cover her with a blanket where she has fallen asleep in her office. But I know too that we are hunted, that the being which burned away Elizaveta's other image is breathing down our necks; that to stay is to waste Elizaveta's sacrifice—the true sacrifice, the one ten years before. It is

THIRTEEN: ALL ROADS LEAD TO RUIN

impossible to remain here and evade Nuawa. This is its territory.

A new doorway flickers into existence, and we step through to a featureless hallway done in a completely different style—identical doors running as far as the eye can see. We must be in the backstage of the dreamscapes Nuawa has erected, each room a great purgatory for a soul Nuawa has captured.

"Nuawa is very powerful—it outmatches any one of us, even me." There is a tone of hurt, of loss to her voice, and it is in that moment that I realize the woman before me is more than a dream, that I am seeing some real facet of Elizaveta Hua. In hindsight, the artifice of what Nuawa made is thrown into harsh relief—as if the real Elizaveta would have stumble through descriptions of her daughters. This is a part of the woman I love; it must be.

"But Nuawa is a brittle thing, strong but inflexible," she is saying. "Hit it enough times from enough directions—"

We collide with someone else in the corridor.

"Mother," the Melusine gasps; her expression is sullen, all storm clouds, but even this simulacrum of Olesya lights up when she sees her mother. "I was looking for you—I felt you pluck away Fahriye. What—"

I expect Elizaveta to dispel her, to strike her down. Instead she surprises me, complete and total—she advances on this shadow of her daughter and embraces her.

"Neither of us is completely real," she says, holding tight. "And yet within us rests all the fires and the hopes of the Hua family. For all the trouble you've made, you are my child, too."

The Melusine opens her mouth. Closes it. Tears well up in her eyes. She blinks hard, trying to chase them away, trying to appear untouchable. "I didn't want to disappoint you, Mother; I wanted you to be proud of me," she whispers. "I wanted to bring you back. And I was going to fix everything! I didn't mean to kill all those people. I didn't know it'd explode like that. I was just so *angry* you gave something like that to her—"

"I'm proud of you," Elizaveta goes on, cutting through her daughter's self-flagellation. "The wild child that I never had. You and Olesya will reach an accord after a fashion, one day. After all, it's normal for siblings to fight.

As for the rest—when the time comes, I'll teach Nuawa that my daughters will not be treated this way."

The hallway lights flicker. We do not have forever.

Elizaveta looks up and smiles. "Your friends are fighting their own ways out. Find them." She takes hold of the doppelganger's hands. "If I had a third daughter, her name would have been Xinfang."

"It's perfect," Xinfang says. Swallows back tears, again. "Thank you."

"And as for you—" Elizaveta turns to me and rests a hand on my cheek. "I hear you have a beautiful new lover." She adjusts the collar on my suit, brushes away the dust of her copy's ashen death. Her smile is loving, genuine. "I want to meet her next time."

My voice hitches. "How are you here?"

"I contained Nuawa, imperfectly. And in the process, some part of me was contained by Nuawa. I have limited knowledge of what has transpired since my... passing? But what remains of me runs through their machinations and their misdeeds like a rat in the bowels of a ship, cleverness and luck my only armor."

"I love you." I say it this time. "I've always loved you. And I'm not leaving without you." This is her, I know it, impossible but real. I have made it this far; one more effort, one more miracle, and she will be restored.

Elizaveta pushes me forward. "I can't go with you," she says gently. "But come find me. Find me and when you do we'll leave together. I have every faith in you. And I love you. Remember that. You, Fahriye, are still the love of my life."

RECADAT

Dallas is terrified in a way that I have never seen her before. "We can't be here," she wails, grabbing me by the arm as she pulls us toward an exit, any exit. As she turns, she runs straight into a powerfully built butch with piercing eyes and hair that glows like the heart of a furnace.

"Dallas?" the stranger asks with real concern. "Where have you been? I've looked everywhere for you. I could not hear you; I could not find you."

"And yet here you are, Yves," slurs the woman from the back of the bar, oblivious. "Like a bad penny, or a shadow I just can't get rid of."

All three of us—Dallas, this woman named Yves, myself—swivel to see another Dallas lift her head, ruddy from alcohol and from having fallen asleep on the table. And then it makes sense: we're now in a version of Dallas' past, watching some scene of incredible import play out differently.

"Dallas, what's the meaning of this?" Yves asks. She reaches out to set a reassuring hand on Dallas' shoulder.

The tiger recoils, pale as a sheet. "No. No. I'm sorry. *I'm sorry.*" She stumbles back, crashing against the bar. Already, the knowledge that this is an illusion has fled from her mind. "I can fix this. I fixed this once before, I can fix it again. I can—I love you, Yves."

It's not my nightmare, so it's easier to see the kuroko shifting the set pieces, read the heavy-handed intrusion of tragedy for what it is. It's predictable, cheap horror movie tricks pulling at heartstrings, when a claw of nova light explodes out of Yves' chest.

Dallas is splattered with ichor, frozen in place. My sushi chef smiles back, and the last of its skin burns away to reveal incandescent light. "I did warn you, beast: you are going to die tired, unable to save anyone."

This time, I am not pinned; the heartbreak is not mine. But there's no door in this dream, no way through the rising brilliance. I reach out for the one shadow that remains—

—my hand touches bone and scales. My mind connects, ten thousand discordant souls snapping into place to remind me that I know this person. This is the demon Cecilie Kristiansen tortured, or at least a very convincing copy. Among the many violations inflicted on the demon, she—I—we tore from Yves the knowledge of how to become incorporeal; I used that very ability to escape my bonds at my first meeting with Dallas.

We are trapped in an illusion that is conspiring to make our worst pasts reality. Is it rewriting causality, altering time? I cannot know. But I *do* know that the demon under my hand is real—real enough, made flesh through foul magics, a perfect duplicate of an unwitting original.

And it is with that full knowledge that I relax and let the beast in my stomach uncurl, let the ravenous swarm that is me march forth, unhinge my jaw and consume all that is Yves.

I feel myself—all of myself, all the mandibles and wings and legs of the eldritch hunger Cecilie Kristiansen became, the curse that she bequeathed to me, the me that is now truer than any memory or any name—I feel myself gorge. Aphids devouring vineyards, ants swarming over carcasses, maggots born of spoilt meat: I am this.

The knowledge and might of a timeless being flows into me. Already, I can feel it starting to wane, my stolen power burning away under the light and heat of our enemy. But for a moment—for a moment, I have the power of a leviathan, and I can fell a god.

I knock our enemy away: not through a wall or a window but out of this dream and into another. Immediately the glare is reduced, and a tear-streaked Dallas, mouth agape, blinks in surprise. Across her face sparks anger the likes of which I have never seen, the unrivaled rage of the jungle's queen, and the next moment she is her true self, a tiger of blazing stripes and scything claws, chasing after her prey through the holes I have torn.

I follow, hurling myself to her side, wrapping her in my power, armor and guide through the destruction we bring to our jailer's mindscapes. Around us tumble the fragments of breaking dreams, collapsing nightmares—giggling families, grieving widows, snow of purest white and ash like coal, landscapes of flame and scenes of green, all of them falling around us. Who knows how many souls it torments in these halls. I shift my form again, and then I am a panther of smoke and fire, black and gold to her gold and black, and together we leap from shard to shard, hunting.

OLESYA

I have spent weeks insensate, delirious, slaved to the drives of my unchecked id. I wake and am not rested; I sleep but do not dream. And now, at the end of this marathon, strung out emotionally and frayed physically, I must

THIRTEEN: ALL ROADS LEAD TO RUIN

rise to the occasion and save the very women I have put at risk—and then, alone, take on the timeless enemy that has hounded my family for fourteen generations.

Fahriye Budak once told my sister that of any mage family, the Huas are the most adept at the impossible. I've let that woman down enough recently; I'm not going to prove her wrong about us—about *me*—one more time.

So I begin this mortal fight as auspiciously as one can: I sit across from my enemy and watch the scenes of torture and malice they are inflicting on those I love. The bank of screens shows what must be each person's most personal fear, though like all waking nightmares they begin harmlessly enough: Dallas is in a jungle, Fahriye is greeting my mother in an office, Recadat is sitting in a car. They even look happy. And looking at Elizaveta Hua, at the mother lost to me for so long, I can even imagine being happy too.

"The Melusine believes herself capable of realizing every fantasy. Each of these scenes is so close to healing your friends, making their lives perfect and without hurt. But one little change…" They twitch fingers of spindly glass, digits articulating like spider legs, and discordant notes enter the song. The jungle burns, a shield fails, a boon companion is murdered.

And yet…

"One of your prisoners is missing." I motion to Dallas' screen; the jungle is empty, the loggers and hunters looking for prey that has slipped their trap.

"An inconvenience. A jail is more than one cell; let her run and have a final fleeting hope. Her despair at the end of the hunt will be that much sweeter. And look—your twin has made an appearance." Sure enough, the Melusine lords over a downed Fahriye, only to turn and begin to fight another version of Nuawa.

On another screen, Recadat is gripping a table so tight her fingernails splinter. "They'll stop you," she's saying. "Those women will stop you."

"Do you see what I mean?" Nuawa mocks. "Such false bravado in the face of—hmmm?"

The tiger reemerges just in time to tackle Recadat away from a killing shot. I scoff as Nuawa's effort to appear in perfect, cruel mastery falters. "Is your prison not as sturdy as you believed, monster?"

A laugh like famine. "Again, my nemesis, hope is the sweetest of poisons. I miscalculated about what would ensnare the tiger. *This* time..." Dallas and Recadat tumble into a seedy bar; the demon Yves is there, and another version of Dallas. I know by instinct that this is the past—the moment their relationship died.

But then Nuawa's smug tone turns to disgust. "Oh, what *now*?"

Fahriye is headed down a hallway with my mother. "Nuawa is a brittle thing," Mother is saying, "strong but inflexible. Hit it enough times from enough directions—"

She is interrupted by a confrontation with my doppelganger. No, not a confrontation—a *greeting*: this copy of my mother embraces the Melusine as her own. "If I had a third daughter," I hear her say, a voice I have not heard in a decade, "her name would have been Xinfang."

"Enough of that," Nuawa growls; they flick their wrist, and the screens we are watching shatter. How easily their facade of control falls away to reveal the cold anger beneath, the hatred lurking behind their every word and deed. They intended this to be their crowning moment, and instead I have watched their prisoners escape, watched as they struggle to...

Hit it enough times, I just heard a version of Elizaveta Hua say, *from enough directions...*

I move before I consciously think, lashing out at the proxy of Nuawa in front of me. Another front in this war, another blow to strike; if I can distract them, draw their ire for just a moment, I can buy seconds for the others. Maybe one of us will find the purchase that becomes the fatal crack.

The response is immediate. Hemorrhage brightens the air, hot and sweet; I hear myself scream. My arm lands, distant, plopping wetly to the floor. The red blood splashing to the ground is the only thing that gives my white hell any sense of depth or form.

"So predictable," Nuawa almost snarls. "Pathetic, all of you. Just bugs. Lice. *Maggots.*"

"My sister lost her arm, too." The pain is almost unbearable; I remember

THIRTEEN: ALL ROADS LEAD TO RUIN

that this is Nuawa's world, and that my senses can be manipulated by their whims. I soldier on, clenching my remaining hand to steady myself. "Fighting Cecilie Kristiansen. It grew back, of course. Her demon is good at many things, and by the way she tells it, growing appendages—"

Nuawa kicks me in my stomach, and the force of it punts me across the floor; they advance through the river of red my tumbling body leaves behind. How crass their violence, once the illusion fails.

I spit, crimson pattering to the floor like the footfalls of cat feet. "My sister," I croak, "is as determined as me. As will be her daughter, who will have a daughter"—Nuawa grabs at my hair and brings my face down into something that approximates a knee; I cough up teeth alongside the blood—"and one of them will kill you. As long as you exist, there will always be a Hua."

My enemy is done playing with their food; they lift me by my throat, hand of bone and glass beginning to crush not my neck but my jaw. "Thank me, Olesya." Nuawa's face splits into a gash, a marionette's unhinging. "I'm going to reunite you with your mother. Once we're done here, I'll send your sister along too."

But it's a poor hunter who loses sight of their environment, even in the moment of the kill—and for our entire conversation, Nuawa has been stalked by the queen of the jungle.

Dallas lunges at Nuawa's back. It must have some sort of effect, because Nuawa snarls and begins to turn—in time for a shadow, the black of insect carapace, to fly at their exposed wrist. It's a panther of smoke, and I think for a moment that Yves has joined the fray.

But it transforms in midair, catching me in arms of corded strength and carrying me to momentary safety. It is Recadat Kongmanee—haler than I remember, with eyes that glimmer with a hint of topaz. "Olesya Hua," she says, breathing hard, "this is just a dream. You're as strong or as weak as you *want* to be. Put yourself back together."

I saw these two materialize behind Nuawa, spent several bone-shattering moments distracting our enemy as they closed the distance. Now Dallas and Recadat return the favor, buying me time to recover. Recadat throws herself back at Nuawa—the tiger and the panther twist around their larger foe, covering each other's flanks, nipping at Nuawa when they leave themself exposed.

But for all the hunters' strength, they cannot win against a hide of glass; talons and fangs can only do so much damage to timeless crystal. For all that I am damaged, they need *me*, and Recadat is right. Under Nuawa's torture, I lost sight of the unreality of this place. I look at the sanguinary stump of my arm and wish it whole; instantly it restores. Disconcertingly, my *other* arm continues to lie where it fell. But the metaphysics of this place are ours to command, too, and this prison was constructed from my soul—I run for the shorn limb and will it into a sword of bloodied steel. Macabre, but in this dream realm, it's literally the thought that counts.

Before I can charge into the fight, a door opens in the white expanse—and in steps Fahriye and the Melusine, shoulder-to-shoulder. The inspector does not hesitate: she runs at Nuawa and checks them with a braced shoulder. The blow connects with the sound and power of a freight train… but more importantly, I can hear the smallest tinkle of cracking glass, and in that instant we know Nuawa can be slain.

The Melusine—Xinfang—follows up Fahriye's hit with a laser-focused strike against the cracked flesh, and Nuawa roars in pain. They retaliate, a scythe of glass and shattered dreams slicing through the air where the Melusine stood. But she has teleported away in fireflies of gold—appears beside me, and then flashes away again, my hand in hers.

I will my thoughts to my twin sister. *I hear that you have your own name now, Xinfang.*

She laughs, and I realize that this is what my laughter must sound like; she pirouettes from a blow, and I realize I can move like this, too. *Maybe I should follow in my sisters' footsteps and pick my own business name, one day. But Xinfang's beautiful, isn't it? Xinlan, Xinyu, Xinfang. All of us a matched set, a happy little family.*

She dodges, too slow, but my golden silk is there, wrapping around the attack, twisting it off the mark. I smirk back, feeling the tiniest bit of superiority to my twin. She returns the same look; to be part of a family is to accept the thousand slights that mean love.

We continue to flit through the air, interrupting and vexing our foe. Dallas and Recadat feint and snarl, distracting; occasionally, Recadat will slip into her human form—gaunt and emaciated still, but fired to action by a will that now burns hot—and slash with borrowed quicksilver.

But it is Fahriye who inflicts the most telling damage, who does not stop, who does not give quarter. She moves with the grace of a ballet dancer and lands like an anvil, light on her feet and heavy with her fist. Nuawa tries to disengage, and Fahriye pursues.

"You took from me the woman I love," she says, voice harder than Nuawa's crystal, steel tempered by ten years of lonely pain. "You hurt children I gave my life to protect."

She adds nothing else, no other taunts, no other cries for vengeance. The sound of cracking, and then shattering; pieces of Nuawa scatter. So total is Fahriye's concentration, so complete is her focus, that her fists of stone again become flesh; she tears apart her knuckles, each blow driving shards deeper and deeper into her hands.

One more hit, and reality—snaps. We are no longer in a hall of white, but in a field of perfect grass, under the bluest sky. The scene is pastoral, bucolic; this is Eden, or something like it.

And in this perfection stands Chun Hyang, their hands stained where they have clawed at the grass and earth to find a way out; whatever twist to this world, whatever nightmare Nuawa trapped them in, it has left them with a hollowed expression. They don't even pretend at being our foe—quicksilver flies forth, only to curl into chains of adamant, lashing Nuawa down, preventing them from evading another of Fahriye's punches.

Again reality trembles before Fahriye's touch; now we stand in a grand hall fallen to ruin, the gore of two dozen dead flowing into a red carpet that leads to a dais and throne. Lussadh al-Kattan stands before it, one foot raised to the first step, wearing a martial uniform and holding a broken saber. She pivots to glare at the interlopers that have fallen into her dream, trying to process what she is seeing; hate and confusion fill her eyes in equal measure.

Fahriye starts, confused at what has transpired and concerned for her comrade. The mistake is almost fatal: Nuawa knocks her to the ground and sets about returning, blow for blow, the injuries inflicted.

I'm not going to let that happen.

"Al-Kattan!" I scream; the memories I share with Xinfang give me a sense of her sight and her way with blades. I throw the sword in my hand to her; she catches it on instinct, and the motion seems to clear whatever lingering illusion she was under. She sprints across the floor, blood splattering against her high field boots, and brings the sword through one of Nuawa's arms.

A strike on an open nerve, a flick of a tuning fork, a blow against priceless jade. The beast flinches, and with a pained wail the dreams collapse.

We fall; we surface—back to a rooftop in Sentosa, spilled food our only companion in a party long-since dead.

The area lies in ruins. Tables overturned and scorched, potted pines fallen over, pockmarks in the ground. Broken flesh everywhere, evidence of the Melusine's excess. Fahriye kneels in a crater of broken marble and metal, bits of glass smashed across the ground and driven deep into her knuckles. Blood and tears streak her face. I can read the shape of my mother's name on her lips, and an instinct seizes me to go to her, to say, *I understand. I am so sorry.*

By a thicket of fallen ferns, my tiger and Recadat lie sprawled, breathing hard like cats recovering from a mighty exertion. Both are naked, streaked in gore. Shredded leaves and flecks of glass adhere to them. Fahriye's companion—Lussadh—stands alone. Her fingers are still gripping the hilt of my sword, white-knuckled. A cut runs along her cheek, slowly seeping.

And my double...

She's materialized by me, closer by far than Dallas did, and she's falling apart. On her knees she pants, gold leaking through her eyes and fingers, cracks running through her torso and limbs as though she's a porcelain doll carelessly dashed. Her outline smears, and her suit is blotched, gray and black staining the platinum. "Fuck," she whispers.

"Take some of my power, Xinfang," I say without thinking. "Enough to keep yourself together."

THIRTEEN: ALL ROADS LEAD TO RUIN

"It's not over. It's not over yet," she mutters. One of her hands drops to her lap. Her left cheek is blackening, exposing white bone, which is itself on the verge of dissolution. Embers are drifting down her chest, orange against the graying clothes. "I'm not breaking down because I'm out of power." She laughs, and in it is an echo of ashes. "There's an explosion in my chest, and I'm"—a gasp, and she clutches at herself—"I'm trying to contain it. You have to get out of here. Nuawa is trying to manifest, or turn me into a bomb. I'll die before I'm their tool again."

I should run. Instead I kneel beside her and pull her close.

A snort of derision. "You've never shown your enemies mercy, Xinlan. Why start now?"

What can I say—that Xinfang is my confessional, my reflection? "I heard Mother. You're not my enemy. You are a Hua."

Her eyes flicker. Or, her eye. The other one has disappeared into the cracking, blackened ruin of her. "Sisters before everything else, is that it? Mother really raised you right. But it's pointless. Sorry. I'd like to have stayed around to see Viveca."

"No." My voice is flat, drained. I crush her to me tighter. "You're not going anywhere. I'm…"

She shakes her head. "Thanks for trying, Olesya."

Then she tears herself free of me, and bursts into flame.

The brilliance of something that isn't her—that was never born from me—keens above the rooftop. I glimpse its outline, its sneering mouth, as it rises over and consumes my double. The air warms, then heats. Stray tablecloths begin to crisp. It is unbearable; it is like standing before a forge.

"—my heart," Xinfang is shouting as her mouth splits and her jawline scorches, as flame spills through the cracks in her body. "Take out my heart and destroy it before that fucking thing can take form and start this all over again. *You* know how."

And I do. I will not hesitate: I do not want her to suffer, here at the end. She has made her decision; she has committed to the sacrifice.

Plunging into her chest is as easy this time as the first—easier, because she's opened herself to me, is no longer trying to protect herself. My hands meet hard, sharp crystal; it cuts into my skin, making me pay for this intrusion in blood. What I wrest out of her is a pulsating core of fire, ever-burning, all-scorching.

Professor al-Kattan, close by, knows precisely what she must do. Her eyes are brightening to the chromatic glint of a mystic quartz. She strikes, and the sword cuts true.

At once the heat extinguishes, and immediately the air regains its chill. Nuawa is gone.

In my arms, golden motes fade to gray, and then to nothing at all.

Epilogue

In the dream, there are three sisters of a great house. Together they live in a fine mansion, surrounded by the accouterments of wealth and power. The firstborn, the secondborn, the thirdborn.

Or, not precisely: Xinfang and Xinlan are the exact same age, down to the millisecond at which they were decanted. And they are not sisters but mirror images, cleaved apart by a knife of crystalline will.

Xinfang remembers the moment of her making as an agonizing separation. Being ripped out of the soul into which she was born, being told that she must stand as her own separate person now. Harsher by far than an extraction from the artificial womb—there, at least, she went into the hand of a loving mother, and she was allowed to scream.

(How did Olesya not notice, this act of half her soul being torn out and molded into something else? Perhaps that anger has informed Xinfang all along: the knowledge that her other half didn't experience the pain, didn't appear to ever care. Why should Xinfang alone *feel*? Why should she be the only one who hurts?)

She told Olesya/Xinlan that she would erase the secondborn, but it was more of a bluff, said in the heat of the moment, as vicious as she could summon. Xinfang cannot begin to imagine a life without her Viveca.

She wanted to make their mother proud. They could have protected the family together, protected Viveca/Xinyu together. More than anything, she wanted to bring Elizaveta Hua back. She could have succeeded, and they'd all be together again. A future unreeling before them, exquisite and perfect, one in which none of them has been touched by grief.

It would have, she thinks, been a good life.

Lussadh walks into the living room to find Fahriye packing. They have not cohabitated for long—a week, perhaps—though it has felt longer. But reality is not moved by perception, the Melusine notwithstanding; the proof is in how quickly Fahriye is filling the duffle, how easily she collects the detritus of their momentarily shared lives. Here one day, gone the next.

She waits for the former inspector to finish, which isn't long. But Fahriye remains silent for a long time afterward, her back turned to Lussadh, clearly lost in tumultuous thought. It isn't until Fahriye makes a wracked noise that Lussadh realizes she is trying to stifle sobs, her hands grabbing the bag so tight it has begun to tear.

"In the dream," Fahriye finally gasps, "I saw Elizaveta. She was exactly as I remember her."

"Lies," Lussadh says; she tries to make her voice as soft as possible. "Nothing we saw can be trusted." She does not volunteer what she saw, the contents of a vision tailor-made for her.

"No, you don't understand. This was not Nuawa, I'm sure of that. Some fragment of Elizaveta, the *real* Elizaveta, exists within the dreams. She was autonomous. She showed me how to move through the illusions. And she—she asked me to come find her."

Lussadh considers; Lussadh decides. "Since you're packing, you obviously don't mean to begin your search by consulting oneiromancers. When do we leave?"

Fahriye finally turns to look at her, shock on her tear-streaked face. "I can't—"

"You told me that Elizaveta got herself killed by running off to face Nuawa alone. You're about to do the same, and I'll be damned if I let history repeat—you may not have noticed, but I'm invested in your continued survival."

At this, Fahriye cracks the thinnest, most tentative of smiles.

"And I'm a retiree in a city currently under martial law *because* of a disaster this monster helped unleash. My schedule is open and my desire to bring the thing to justice great. The fifty-five-and-up racquetball tournament will have to wait."

"A terrible loss for Singapore's elderly community," Fahriye sniffs, trying for the safety of glibness.

"It's a doubles tournament and my partner will be out of town." This, finally, causes Fahriye to actually laugh; Lussadh's charm is undeniable, can break even the hardest of stone.

"But…" The truth that Fahriye cannot voice: that asking Lussadh to come feels like a betrayal of what they have shared here—the demolition of a still-setting foundation, tantamount to asking the new girlfriend to help woo the ex-wife.

Lussadh waves away the issue. "I don't think it's really Elizaveta. I think Nuawa is lying to you, baiting you to your death, a fate I must prevent. But even if it were Elizaveta, I will help you. I am not so childish that I would refuse you aid in saving the love of your life."

"She said she would like to meet you, in the dream. Even, I daresay, gave you her blessing."

"Bah," Lussadh retorts. "Now I *know* it was Nuawa; no way in hell would someone like Elizaveta Hua let a catch like you slip through her fingers."

"I'm just lucky she never met you—I think you're far more her type. All my heroism with a great deal more charm. More… princely."

The professor snorts. "Well, if you're right—and I have my reservations—and we find her, then I'll do my best to take her off your hands. So again I ask, Inspector: when do we leave?"

Returning to the estate, Olesya half-expects to find it in ruins, that in her absence some vengeful adversary might have come and torched the entire place down. That her actions will be punished by the entire residence spontaneously going up in flames. But it remains as she left it, her sentinels patrolling the perimeter, her snipers at their stations. She is saluted as she comes in.

During the drive, they were both silent. Olesya watched the city blur past, the destruction and debris that something with her face wrought: it will take a long time for Singapore to scab over, to begin the process of healing. Dallas was at the wheel—the tiger is, relatively, less injured.

Olesya keeps touching the arm severed in the dream, but it has healed perfectly, seamless. Not even a centimeter of raw skin. The memory of it tearing off remains vivid: the wet noise, the bone snapping. The shock to her system. Her intact, undamaged arm seems now like a phantom limb.

She tries not to think of Xinfang turning into flecks of light. She tries not to think of her mother telling Xinfang, *I'm proud of you. The wild child that I never had.* It is illogical to mourn, when the Melusine has done so much harm. And yet at the last, she felt—she felt as though she was watching a part of herself die, a part that should have gotten a second chance.

The two of them remain silent as they go through the corridors, until they reach Olesya's suite; finally, Dallas breaks the quiet. "You felt mercy toward her, at the end."

"It's more—responsibility. She *was* me, on some level, and I unleashed her, even without meaning to. She deserved more. I should have been able to give her a better existence. If I'd reined her in, somehow…"

"It's human to think of what-ifs," her tiger says gently, then pauses. "To be fair, a tiger thing too—I went over that a lot, when I threw that bracelet away."

"I don't have any excuses." Olesya tries to vocalize the accounting of it, the balancing of the ledger, the list of wrongs to put in front of a jury. But her voice stoppers. There is too much, and not enough she can say. "Everything I did during… all this. To you, to Kongmanee, to Chang'er even. She was just lucky enough not to be around to see it happen. And I—" *I am sorry* is simple, stupid, inadequate. Her throat thickens. "I don't know how to make this right."

For a time Dallas looks around, at the potted plants that hang from the window, several tropical specimens that descend from Elizaveta's collection. A few have begun to flower, tiny pink or white buds. "I completely wrecked my suite. Broke about everything. Shredded clothes you made me."

EPILOGUE

"That's not the same thing at all. Those are just objects."

"She's trying to tell you," says a new voice, "that Yves forgave her and you forgave the Melusine. There's a middle ground between acting like you never did anything wrong and flagellating yourself forever. You may have noticed, too, that Dallas is remarkably laid back. For a pretty face, she'll forgive almost anything."

Olesya stares at Recadat emerging from a pool of sunlit tiles, drawing herself straight as though she's been folded interdimensionally. Most likely she was. "How did you get back from Sentosa?"

"The usual ways." A shrug. "Been a while since we talked when you're lucid, Master Hua."

Dallas starts to speak. Olesya, her neck flushing, shakes her head. "It's fair to say. I have wronged you as well." This part is, at least, easy. Easier. "What would you have for restitution?"

The woman studies her. Recadat should have looked worse for wear, but she's never looked healthier, steadier to Olesya. There is a gleam to her eyes, unnatural and bestial, and her stance for once is without weakness. She's not leaning on anything for support. Though she is as thin as before, there's now an impression of robust constitution, one that will not fail under the slightest pressure from Kristiansen's legacy. Gone is the haunted look, the terror of herself.

"I would like some resources," says Recadat. "Money. Computers. Access to information brokers. A place to stay while I figure out how to restore a certain doctor to her previous career. It's something I swore to do, and I'd like to keep my promises."

"Done. And then?"

"And then I will see." A faint smile tugs at her mouth, a hint of fang. "In the meantime, I believe I should make myself scarce. No sense getting between marital matters." She hesitates. "I *did* fuck your tiger."

"Bragging, are we?" Olesya is deadpan, but she crooks an eyebrow.

"I'm laying it out. I don't want lingering embers of animosity to burn down *this* foundation, too."

Dallas, uncertain where the conversation is going, opts to stay very still and very, very quiet.

"I'm certain you laid her out alright." Then, more serious: "She's not *my* tiger. She is her own, and she may come and go, and lay with and come with, whomever she wants. Barring one exception."

"Not you," Dallas hurriedly adds. "Her sister."

"The one who is married to your ex, the demon. Of course, of course." Recadat makes it sound as if it is the most reasonable arrangement she has ever heard of. "Nevertheless, I will live out of my luggage for a few days, just in case."

Light again folds; Dallas and Olesya are alone again.

"I *am* your tiger," Dallas corrects. "Whatever has happened this past—has it only been a week?—does not change that for me, if it does not change that for you."

"Dallas, if there is to be a true accounting between us—if there are to be no lingering embers of animosity, as your panther put it"—Dallas does not argue against the appellation—"then I must be very clear: that *was* me. I cannot have you telling yourself that I was possessed, or driven to it, that she was somehow my evil clone. Everything the Melusine said, or did, or wanted to do—those were my fears and hopes and dreams that drove her. *I* hurt you."

"I know." Olesya holds her tongue, waiting for the tiger to gather her thoughts and continue. "When I met you, I wasn't drawn to your power or your beauty. There is an anger inside of you, an abiding fury, a need to hunt. I have always known that within you lives something like me, something of tooth and claw, and I love that part of you as much as every other."

Olesya purses her lips. "You make it sound as if I am a monster."

Dallas shakes her head. "You are as dangerous and proud as any queen of the jungle, and the capacity for incredible destruction lives within us both—more than that, it defines who we are. But what I can say is this: if a primal evil had stolen into my head and turned all my most savage thoughts into reality, everyone I love would be dead, torn to shreds before me. That in your moments of lucidity you struggled against your demons, that we have all walked away from this mostly intact, our enemies dead and new

EPILOGUE

allies made—that is a testament to both your incredible viciousness, but also your strength and your love. I have forgiven you. But it will take longer for you to forgive yourself."

This is everything she could possibly want, the total and comprehensive absolution. It doesn't mean she's been forgiven by *everyone*—a part of her dreads Viveca's return—but Dallas was the one she wounded the most. "I…"

Her tiger closes the distance and touches her forehead to Olesya's. "Once I've picked a mate, I do not turn away from her so fast." Her tongue darts out, light, licking around Olesya's mouth. "In the past, I've left too many women behind at the first sign of trouble. This time, I want to try something else."

Their kiss is slow, considered, almost shy. In such a kiss, new things can be made, a path to healing found. It will take time. It will be as laborious as guiding a garden into prosperous life. But both of them have chosen each other, and Olesya swears that she will make this work, will make this last.

Recadat has made good on her promise. Access to her memories and powers is still spotty, often intermittent, but the powers she absorbed—from Chun Hyang, from Nuawa's visions—has been almost therapeutic. She can now recall enough to get a sense of Orfea Leung's downfall, its masterminds and their methods. With S&C destroyed and High Command defunct, most everyone who would still have an opinion about the good doctor's career is either dead or out of the picture, and righting this wrong has no obvious opponents.

The process is quicker than she expects, if painful. Cecilie Kristiansen's larceny was widespread and multifaceted; with considerable, tooth-gritted effort, Recadat calls on the skills of a consummate forensic accountant, a middle-tier bureaucrat, various hackers and cybermancers. A few nosebleeds, a brush with catatonia, and several nights spent sobbing, curled in the bottom of a bathtub, crushed by the weight of a dozen, vividly recalled memories that are not hers, and Orfea Leung's medical license is restored, all records of her accusations purged.

"She will not appreciate this," Dallas grumbles, sitting on the tile floor beside the bathtub. She has stayed with Recadat through the trying nights, brought tissues for the nosebleeds, centered her friend when the memories were most vivid—the tiger has, as promised, helped Recadat hunt for the justice Orfea was denied. But she prickles at Orfea's dismissal, her unfiltered disdain: Recadat deserves better.

"I know. But it's not about her. It's about me." Recadat groans as she rights herself into a sitting position. "I just wanted to close this chapter of my life as cleanly as possible, for once. A little bit of vomit is worth the freedom from guilt."

"No, I get it. Lord knows how many terrible people I carried water for, all because they got me out of cages, metaphorical or no."

"And Olesya is not one of them." This isn't a question or an accusation, but a statement recited for Recadat's own sake, a reminder that vengeance upon Olesya Hua for her trespasses against Dallas is both unwelcome and unnecessary. That Dallas deserves better is left unsaid.

Dallas hears it in Recadat's voice, though. "I appreciate your concern for me, friend. I—it's been a long time since I had someone like you on my side." There is a reason that a grouping of tigers is called an ambush, Dallas thinks: short-lived, focused on the target, easily dissolved. This thing that has formed between them is inchoate yet, but there is real loyalty here, real love. "Please take my word that I am raw but healing, and that I have enough self-respect to know when I should leave."

"I'm proud of you." When Dallas jerks her head up, Recadat weakly shrugs. "Is that the wrong thing to say? You're something like ten times older than me. But you've shared with me the general contours of your relationship with the demon Yves"—neither has ever overtly acknowledged that in Nuawa's visions, Recadat witnessed the breaking point of that relationship, but the fact rests heavy on the conversation—"and it seems to me that you're doing things right this time. Not trying to force healing, taking it at your own speed. It is a healthy and mature step for you to take."

"It still feels like shit," Dallas mutters. "I'll be on edge and paranoid for a good while yet. But I love her, and she loves me. Leaving feels like it would be an unnecessary punishment, for us both. It's… complicated."

"Healing does feel like shit. Sometimes love does, too. Take it from someone whose bones will probably never set right."

Dallas stands. "Take a shower and clean up. I've got something I want to show you."

Recadat looks suspicious. "It's four in the morning."

"Oh, don't complain," Dallas teases. "Panthers are supposed to be nocturnal hunters. And anyways, by the time we get where I want to take you, it'll be six—even eight or nine, if you don't hurry and we hit morning traffic."

Dallas' car again, another wait. Recadat has a false memory of doing this with Thannarat, too; the strange, cursed gift of the Melusine's influence. The dream has not so easily dissipated. Her brain refuses to distinguish between the true and the false.

"I did some digging," Dallas says slowly, as if trying to calm a wounded animal. Perhaps she is. A peculiar skill set for a tiger to have, but then again, she has lived a long time. "The name on the lease is yours. Rent paid out of a bank account automatically, so it's just been… sitting here."

"Could be a trap," Recadat suggests.

"Even if it is, you have to know, right?" Recadat appreciates that in this moment, it is not *we*, only *you*; some pains cannot be shared, are for you to know alone.

Or maybe not. "I'd like it if you came up with me," she admits. "Just in case." The possibility, always, of being on the precipice. She knows Dallas will have her back, will pull her away from the edge.

It doesn't feel like coming home, but of course Recadat has never been to this apartment building before. Or rather, she retains no memory of ever having done so. For some reason she didn't even think she lived in Singapore—but then again, this city was where she woke up, shorn of self and recollection.

There are no cobwebs on the exterior of the door, no standing dust. Not a sign of entry in itself; this is a nice apartment in a nice part of the city, there will have been cleaning crews coming by to regularly sweep. Still, Recadat tenses, approaches the door like she is about to burst into a crime den. Instinctively, she even reaches for the gun that is no longer holstered at her hip—

The door is warded. And then she relaxes, turns, looks out over the landing at the cityscape beyond. Breath in, breath out. "They're my wards," Recadat clarifies. "Unbroken. Pre-Cecilie, even—even if I don't remember making them, I know the texture of my magic."

Dallas volunteers her services opening the apartment—no ward or lock can keep her out for long—and Recadat waves her away. But she doesn't turn back to the door, either; she's still looking at the skyline. She laughs, a scoff. "Down there is the park Dr. Leung found me in. I made it so close to home, and *yet*."

"Home is where you make it," Dallas says, and Recadat understands her meaning: that they can leave, that whatever is on the other side of this door changes nothing, that she can make of her life a completely new shape and a new home elsewhere.

"Thank you," Recadat says, and opens the door.

It's... an apartment. A normal apartment. Past-her had good taste in decor; the leather couch looks both classy and comfortable, the art that adorns the walls was chosen with a skilled aesthetic eye. Minimalist without being sterile. But she might as well be walking through a museum exhibit, for how little she recalls.

On the wall is a little shrine, incense long turned to ash and flowers wilted to brown stalks; a photo of an older lady, smiling. "I think that is my mother. At least now I know what happened to her."

Dallas motions to more photos on the walls. "Looks like you had a bit of a sentimental streak."

"I should tear out your throat for that," Recadat jokes; humor is still unnatural to her, but she's trying it on. And she can't dispute it: there's a photo of her at some sort of graduation, another of her and her mother; a celebration, with her and—

EPILOGUE

Her heart seizes. The colors are faded, but the person is unmistakable—long shaggy hair, tall and densely built, that wolfish grin. "This was my old partner," she says.

Dallas leans over and whistles. "I think I'd have liked her."

"Oh, you'd have crushed on her, hard. I did, only to find out that she was married and frustratingly monogamous. And gods, the drama that woman went through—her wife was haunted by this kitsune spirit, and…" Recadat trails off, touches her face to find it wet with tears, her smile almost painful. "Huh, I guess I remembered something new."

A last cursory look around. The bed is made, everything carefully put away; Recadat wonders if she had a sense of what was coming and sealed this place up as a time capsule to herself. If so, she's been shorn of most of the vocabulary necessary to interpret its signs, to read its portents. Newspapers clippings, unearthed decades later, referencing events that have no meaning or relevance to the present.

"I think I'm done," she finally announces.

"You don't want to… move back in?" Dallas' tone is carefully neutral.

"You said home is where you make it, tiger. This isn't my home anymore, and I'm not interested in making it my home again. At least not right now."

She pauses at the door. Mail has built up in a pile—no overdue notices, she realizes; past-her must have been meticulous with the autopay. Small blessings. Responsible, independent. Probably she had to be both exactly because she was so alone.

And there, slipped between the spam and the utility bills, is a postcard—bright and festive, a skyline she does not recognize, pierced by a tall observation tower. Johannesburg, South Africa, apparently. She checks the postmark—sent only two weeks ago—reads the message on the back, then hurriedly checks the postmark again.

R, the postcard reads,

Business took me to South Africa—you know what they say, I always get my man. Decided to make a vacation of it. Offer still stands, if you ever want to join me. Wife says hi, says she still owes you for your help "with that one thing the one time."

Heard some bad things about your job. Thanks for supporting my decision to quit when I did. Worried about you. Please let me know you're okay, usual ways. I want you to be well.

- T

Recadat stares and stares, trying to parse what she is reading. Finally, she turns to Dallas. "Do you think the Melusine could have really changed the past?"

Dallas shrugs. "Probably. But how the fuck would we know? It's all in the past."

Recadat smiles, then laughs, at the tiger's practicality. She shrugs too, slips the postcard into her pocket, and then closes the door on that chapter of her life.

Xinfang awakes to emptiness, darkness upon the face of the deep. This is a surprise: she should be dead.

Senses return; light separates from darkness. Above the firmament, and beneath the land.

No, not quite land. Stone—concrete. Debris.

With a gasp, Xinfang sits up: she is back on the roof of the Sentosa resort. It is dark, still in ruins; starlight twinkles down on a quiet, unlit scene of carnage.

"I've politely asked the first responders to give us some privacy," a voice says. A tiny flame flickers—the candle beneath a butter warmer—and Xinfang makes out a rough outline, a hint of purple limned with silver.

"This may come as a surprise," the speaker continues, "but I've never had crab before." A sharp crack as a leg is snapped in two; in the glow of candlelight, Xinfang catches sight of strong fingers, expertly freeing the succulent meat within

"Why am I here?" she asks. She died, fell apart; has now, impossibly, been reconstituted. It must be for a reason.

"The muscle memory on how to eat it is there, but the flavor of it? Its texture? No idea. It's very strange, what I retain from my constituent parts." A *hmph* of annoyance. "There's less in these shells than you might think. Unrewarding, for the effort. Are pistachios the same way? I'll have to investigate."

"Why the fuck—"

"Yes, yes, I heard you the first time," Chun Hyang complains, still focusing on their meal. "You're skipping past the fun stuff, like the *how*. It took me a considerable amount of—"

Xinfang summons her magic to her—a sputter compared to what she could muster when empowered by Nuawa, but still enough to threaten the mage in front of her.

"Enough of that. I'm trying to have a pleasant dinner." The mage lifts one butter-stained hand and rolls the wrist; the gathering magic immediately dissipates. "You're anchored to me now. I'm not the limitless battery your old patron was, but I can power you for long enough."

Xinfang holds her tongue after that, waiting them out.

Annoyed that their meal has stopped fighting back, Chun Hyang turns away from the crab. "You're here because I wanted to ask you a question." Their voice is as mellifluous as ever, but Xinfang can see the pinch around their eyes, the tightness that clenches their jaw. "I was pulled into the dreamscapes you crafted. You know what I saw; I need to know why you showed it to me."

"I—" Xinfang is confused when she searches her memory and finds no recollection of Chun Hyang's ambitions, their innermost hopes. "I don't, actually. That one must have been all Nuawa."

Chun Hyang draws a sharp intake of air through their teeth, and then gasps a strangled, abortive laugh. "Of course, of course. It could never be *that* easy."

Xinfang tests her fingers, stretches out her arms—she is here, as solid as her ephemeral body of light can be, if reduced in luminance. "Well, you went through all the trouble of bringing me back. You could at least tell me what you saw. I'm, quite literally, a captive audience."

"Nuawa, it would seem, showed me a perfect world. No pestilence or famine, no war. And this was not one of those dystopian perfect worlds, all dependent on a beaten child or an annual bloodletting. This, I could tell, was More's promised *no place*, pristine and truly perfect. And—and I wasn't in it."

"Excuse me?"

They continue, distress creeping into their voice. "Every name rectified in accordance with its purpose and identity, every person content in the fullness of their lives. And with the absolute certainty of a dream, I knew that I was not in that world. So I summoned you back into existence to ask *why*."

For someone like Chun Hyang, Xinfang realizes, this must have been the ultimate nightmare. Forged from the stuff of two paramount mages, certitude and power the life breathed into their quicksilver body, their entire worldview predicated on the belief that they are worthy, that they matter. That through them, and through them alone, can the world be made complete. And to see a world that was complete *without* them—

—well, Xinfang could empathize. What use does the world have for a third Hua sister?

Still, she can't help herself. "Oh, you don't need Nuawa to explain that one, Chun Hyang. It means you're a piece of shit and no one likes you."

A snort, a murderous glare. "I could very well say the same about you."

"The difference between us is that I know what I am."

"Well, it was a pleasure to finally make your acquaintance, Melusine, but—" They lift their hand. "I think it's time you go away again."

This time, it is Xinfang who reaches out; Chun Hyang's fingers flick open and closed, and then their hand slams against the table. They stare down at their traitor limb in shock.

"Looks like the connection goes both ways, motherfucker," Xinfang taunts. "You won't get to banish me *that* easily."

"Ah." A pause, and then Chun Hyang snaps open another crab leg. "It would appear, then, that I have deeply and royally fucked up, and we are now at an impasse. I might as well keep eating."

Xinfang stands and looks the city over—jewels of light as far as the eye can see, as numerous and as beautiful as the heaven above. Somewhere

EPILOGUE

among those precious treasures is her family—her sisters' estates, their lovers, people that she is shocked to find she might care for after all. What a feeling to be born back to.

They won't love her, not the way the specter of her mother did. They won't understand her, and they won't forgive her. Better, then, to keep her distance, to chart her own path. And how many experiences there are to be had, to be made hers—hers, as her own person, not an image of Xinlan.

Xinfang sits across from Chun Hyang, and the candle of a second butter warmer flickers to life. "I've never had crab, either," she says, and begins to break limbs.

Viveca is relieved, upon her return to the mortal realm, that she has been gone for only a couple months. Time flows differently between here and there: there was every chance she could have been gone for a year and more.

It's good to be home again. None of the security measures in her tower have been breached; every tripwire alarm has gone untriggered. Servitors, demonic and otherwise, report that nothing untoward has occurred, save two mistaken food deliveries, and those were chased off without event.

She stretches as she comes into her suite—it will be a delight in itself to sleep in her own bed again, enjoy these fine sheets the color of antique gold. She usually picks indigo or black, but Yves has had some say in decorating decisions recently, and the demon favors warmer tones. A few desk lamps, too, have shades of similar colors now. Previously Viveca was a creature of solitude, but she loves this: that Yves is coming to leave personal touches on their shared residence. The demon is even learning to cook, just for her. She likes licking sauces and morsels off Yves' fingers.

Soon she's going to have to contact her sister, share with her what she obtained in the other world. For now, though, she wants to take off her clothes and have a good bath. Yves is running one for her, the noise of the taps turning. A smile tugs at her mouth. Domestic bliss with a demon; what a concept.

Her wife is waiting for her in the bathroom, the tub full and steaming.

Yves' mouth crooks, just a glimpse of teeth and hunger. "Shall I join you, Ms. Hua?"

They fought well together, in the tournament that won them the grimoire that once belonged to Elizaveta Hua. Some residual excitement has lingered. Viveca pretends to think it over. "Oh, I don't know. Do you think it's big enough for the two of us?"

Yves raises an eyebrow. "If you wish to focus on ablutions, then of course I shall not bother you and leave you to your soap and shampoo."

She mock-pouts. "Of course not. Can you bring us something cold? Doesn't have to be alcohol. Imagine the warlock of her age getting drunk and drowning in her bath."

"I'd never allow that," her wife murmurs as the inky smoke of her clothes seeps away, leaving her chosen form gloriously naked. Viveca can't get enough of the sight—the sculpted bulk, the small perfect breasts, the curl of wiry hair between powerful thighs.

When Yves slides into the bath with her, she is warm, corporeal; Viveca leans into her and sighs, relaxing entirely against her demon's chest, the fine hard muscles of her demon's stomach. As much easy strength as tenderness, and shown to her alone. Or nearly alone, but she's not one to be jealous about the tiger. Faintly she wonders how Olesya and Dallas have been making house in these two months. Well, she will catch up shortly.

A second Yves, clothed, walks in with a tray of iced grapefruit tea. When she kneels to serve it, she also leans in to kiss Viveca on the mouth while the other body finger-combs her hair. Hands knead at her shoulders and hips, soothing away tension.

"You could," Viveca purrs, "touch other places too."

"Ms. Hua," says Yves, in stereo, "your libido could put a succubus to shame."

"I *have* kept a succubus around, you know, not that anything interesting ever happened. She was more of a secretary." She wiggles a little, guiding her wife's hand to her breast. "Besides, in real-world time, I haven't had you for two months. You can't blame me for being hungry."

At this, Yves does kiss the back of her neck, and also the front. Arousal is instantaneous. Viveca loves it most when her wife takes her with two bodies. There's so much more possibility then, so much new ground to cover. Her imagination gets ahead of itself. She thinks of asking whether Yves can split into three bodies.

From the other room, her phone rings. The warlock makes a face. "Could you get that?"

The clothed Yves sighs but dutifully leaves; returns with the phone in hand, speaker on. Viveca takes one look at the number and says, "Inspector Budak—you're calling from Armenia, of all places. Is everything okay? A vacation away from blood sausages and the Scottish chill?"

The line is quiet for a moment. "Master Viveca." Grimly formal.

It is, Viveca realizes, far from a social call. She sits up in the bath. "Did something happen?"

"Yes. No. Or—much has happened; it's hard to know where to begin. I'll catch you up, if no one has yet."

"Olesya," she says, abruptly cold despite the water. "Is she okay?"

"As okay as she can be. She's physically hale and her residence stands strong, if that's what you are asking, but..." There are noises in the background, a heavy thump, a creak of hinges. "There's something else you need to know. Something that I feel I should be the one to tell you."

Viveca twines her fingers into Yves'. Her pulse hammers. "What is it?"

On the other end, Fahriye takes a breath. It sounds, almost, like the gasp of someone who's narrowly escaped drowning.

"I think, Viveca, that your mother is still alive."

The jade hall has been warped into something cavernous and alien, a place where no human may venture, a place of beasts and gods alone. Ice coats every surface, and under its touch artistry and architecture have twisted and cracked, uneven sloping panels replacing the precision of yesteryear. It is the way of conquerors, to despoil that which they topple, to break every straight line and bend them anew.

What was once High Command is destroyed, irrevocably, with a finality that the magical world seldom witnesses. The Moloch was beaten to death in this very chamber; the Exegesis and Cynosure have been taken off the board, left in a condition that precludes their participation in affairs of state for the foreseeable future. The others—some dead, others fled, none raising a hand to aid another, their oaths to pursue the Rectification of True Names cast aside in the face of the Melusine's bloody coup.

And to the victor, the spoils: fragments of shattered lazuli have been molded into a rough throne, allowing the chamber's occupant to keep court in the carcass of her foes. Today, as ever, she has only her weapon in attendance.

"I was successful." Nuawa is lying to her, again. "I inflicted on the Huas and their retinue—"

"You are renowned for your strength, but you have returned to me in *fragments*."

And Nuawa has: their pristine form is laced through with hairline fractures, and around them orbit shards of light and glass broken asunder by Fahriye Budak's final assault. "It was a hard-fought battle. Our enemies—"

"When you accepted my terms," she interrupts, "certain promises were made. You swore to me that you would help end all our enemies. The Huas, the al-Kattans, High Command. And, I grant, you ably used the elder Hua as a scalpel to dismantle the latter set; I congratulated you on this weeks ago. And then, apparently, you thought your work over, my desires slaked?"

"The loyalties of the Huas have been tested and found wanting," Nuawa hisses. "Already, the elder daughter—"

"Congratulations, Olesya Hua is *sad*." The dismissal in her voice drips like venom. "The investment High Command coveted has regained her humanity and is now under the Hua aegis. Fahriye Budak has been unshackled from the restraints that kept her from investigating us, and she made a new ally in the process. Very soon, the younger Hua and her demon will return to this realm—our chance to burn the Hua estate in their absence has slipped from our fingers, on account of your clumsiness. You even managed to create a new Hua, somehow. Remarkable work, sword of the eternities."

EPILOGUE

Nuawa seethes. They are a thing of eldritch hatreds, of searing passions, of alien geometries that detest the shapes of this lesser reality. Someday, they will flense the flesh from every human skeleton, make of this earth an ossuary. And when that day comes, they will start with the woman in front of them.

She sneers. "You are dissatisfied with your treatment? You think I should show my sword more kindness? It's not as if you'll kiss my neck with a duller edge. I know you tempted the al-Kattan scion with a future where she, and not I, wields you to avenge past slights. Do you think she will hold you in a looser grip? Do you find my ice too unmalleable? I am not so stupid. I am not so shortsighted, either: of course you would fail."

"We have a setback, and you pretend it was the plan." Nuawa lets their tone shade into insubordination.

She stands with a laugh and descends from her throne—the ring of a collapsing glacier, the implacability of an oncoming avalanche. "You are a brittle thing, Nuawa, strong but inflexible. And when you want to break an unbreakable thing, you smash it against a fist of immovable stone. In this regard, Fahriye Budak never fails to disappoint." She reaches out and seizes one of the shards that orbits Nuawa.

There is an initial burst of steam, and for a moment Nuawa hopes their master has finally overreached. But glass cannot cut ice, cannot make it bleed; its brilliance is reflected back, as cold and hard. The mage opens her hand to show the fragment of Nuawa's power contained within her palm.

"One mighty blow was never going to fell the Huas," says the Winter Queen. "They'll die from a thousand dagger cuts."

Bonus Story: The Demon of the House of Hua

In my long hours in the archives, I have become something very like a thief. There is the knowledge that you are prying private lives open as you peruse the diaries, the family annals, even the ticket stubs marking long and frequent journeys. The people in these journals are long dead—save one—and eventually these papers must be returned to the descendants. Their owners never did surrender them to any collection. That they are here is by happenstance more than intent.

For now, I take pleasure in the yellowed papers—fine penmanship, excellent binding—whose memories are too removed from my time to coalesce. Such recordings in objects have a mayfly lifespan, fragile and transient; my psychometry reaches only so far back into the past. This collection is a rare find, at that, and holds the secrets of a notorious lineage: the Hua warlocks, from the sixth and seventh generations. A family whose fortune has, over time, risen and fallen and again and again—never a straight line toward ascent or descent, often destabilized.

To the sixth Hua of her line was born a sickly child, pallid of flesh and brittle of bone, destined to die before her first sunrise. From the dark of the woods came a demon of great cunning, who sought a deal: the life of a Hua, in return for raising an heir of intelligence and puissance. The demon assumed the sixth Hua would let the newborn expire—use its thimbles of blood to ink the contract—and start anew, develop and decant another infant. Instead, the Hua sacrificed herself, and in her death bound the demon to the task of bringing her child to greatness. A treacherous choice, from the demon's perspective; a tragic one, from that of the sixth Hua's widow.

BONUS STORY: THE DEMON OF THE HOUSE OF HUA

And yet, in the black soil of that bargain, something took root and came to flower.

Every life must end. But the words left behind will last. In this way we hear the voices of those who are long gone, and we commemorate: to remember is the most human act.

- *Professor Lussadh al-Kattan, Department of Theory and Epistemology, Shenzhen University*

Madhuri, wife of the sixth Hua warlock and mother of the seventh, does not care for her child's nurse.

To call the creature a nurse stretches the definition; it suggests nurturing, a maternal aspect. It suggests a contractual agreement between the parent and the nurse. In this case the contract is with Madhuri's late wife, whom the infernal being murdered.

"I didn't murder your wife," says the demon, for perhaps the tenth time, as they emerge from the nursery in which the little Hua sleeps. "You do realize that."

The demon, today, has chosen to manifest as a figure of lean angles in a layered crimson dress. Madhuri spends several seconds examining their form, seeking in the details any hint of mockery, any resemblance to the sixth warlock. Finding none, she says, "Had you not been *there* to offer your bargain, she would still be *here*."

"But your daughter wouldn't be," the demon counters, tactless in the way of all infernal breeds.

Madhuri has studied some of her wife's annals. She is no warlock, but she is developing an idea of rites and spells with which to banish a demon. As of yet she has not had an opportunity to put them into practice. "We could have found another way. My wife and I were women of resources." This, too, she has said before.

"Ah. The abundance of time left in the infant girl, that must have been why she leaped off the cliff. Surely your child could wait a few months while the two of you composed a solution."

Fury comes easily. Until now, she has never been an angry woman; she was always the still lake to her wife's raging river. "Fuck you."

The demon widens their crimson eyes. "So vulgar, from the mistress of the house. Nor am I seeking companionship at this time, I fear. Good night, my lady." They curtsy, as though they are a maid of the house in truth, and dissolve into a cloud of smoke and black whispers.

She enters the nursery. Her daughter sleeps, peaceful and hale. Looking like the smallest creature in existence, infinitely precious.

Madhuri does not touch her child. In the darkest hour of the night, she knows in her heart that she would rather have her wife back; that the warlock means more to her than the heir. The child she would have mourned, but another could have been made. Her wife and she could have raised a secondborn. But she never voices these thoughts aloud. They make her no better than the demon.

Her daughter makes a little noise in sleep. She stands there, looking down at this result of her wife's contract, and starts weeping. Silent, very silent, so as not to wake the child.

She is bathing her daughter, three days later. There is no servant left in the house and, even though Madhuri has the means (and relatives to reach out to, if it comes to that), there are only two beings in the world she trusts with her daughter's care: herself and—unfortunately—the demon.

It is while she is lathering the child's scalp that her daughter stops breathing.

The demon appears at once without being called. They reach for the child, touch a fingertip to her tiny throat, and in a moment she is restored: the respiratory interruption is a hiccup rather than the fatal strike it would have otherwise been.

Madhuri returns to shampooing the child, for all that her fingers are gone to ice. To the onlooker, she would seem the coldest mother in the world, barely perturbed by her child's brush with mortality. "What is wrong with her exactly?"

"Her body has limited interest in surviving. Sometimes humans are made thus. Innumerable infants perish every day." The demon tilts their head. "Shouldn't the child have a name?"

"What business is it of yours?"

"I have pledged to make her great," they say, reasonably. "Nameless mages don't make history. If you'll not name her, then I will."

"And give her a name unpronounceable by human tongues?" She carefully tips warm water to rinse out the shampoo—her daughter is rarely fussy; is almost preternaturally compliant—and takes the girl out of the tub. "She will be Rabhya, if only to prevent that."

Four-legged today, the demon settles on their hind legs. Two tails swish lazily at the marble tiles. "Very off-handedly done. Well, I shall not gainsay you; I'm sure you discussed the options with your late wife. It's my understanding that most parents name their children not long after birth. You strike me as having delayed it greatly."

"I doubt that you know much of humanity."

They make a low, rolling noise that human vocal cords cannot replicate. "I've existed much longer than you, enchantress. Little Rabhya is brighter than you think. She will notice what I notice."

Madhuri does not answer. She towels her child dry. She takes the child in arms, to prepare her for breakfast.

"Have you observed," the demon goes on, "that she never smiles?"

"I will not take child-rearing advice," she says over her shoulder, "from the creature that very much meant to kill my daughter, and which has never known familial warmth in their life."

But she is aware that the demon has a point, that little Rabhya sees more than is typical for a child her age. Madhuri knows herself to be an unloving mother, and she cannot change that in herself. When she looks at her child, all she can see is her wife's absence; all she can feel is the empty place in their marital bed, the empty place in everything.

Madhuri reaches out. She sends for her relatives. Some families use wet nurses for milk; she must be able to find a surrogate to offer maternal affection just the same.

Only one answers, a cousin of her age from her mother's side. All know what family she has married into, and most want little to do with the notorious lineage. Powerful for now, yes, but ever on the brink of disaster; to associate with the Huas is to gamble with one's life. Many mages are power-hungry enough—Rabhya is already receiving tentative offers of courtship, absurdly—but Madhuri comes from a family that puts sense before ambition. She was all but disowned when she wedded her warlock.

The cousin, a prim and proper woman famous in the family for her deftness with children, arrives in a dress whose fabric has been woven from clouds and sunset shadows: a method of transfiguration particular to the family, and which Madhuri has considered adding to the Hua's library—perhaps down the line, a Hua daughter will take it up. There are more than one progeny, on occasion.

In the nursery, the cousin greets the child, who flinches away at once.

"She's shy," says Madhuri, though she is concerned. Rabhya has never shown fear of the demon, a far more concerning entity than her cousin. "Not used to strangers."

"Most children this age are." The cousin kneels to be level with the child, who has fled to the far end of her bed. "Quiet, isn't she?"

In truth, Rabhya was months past the point where most children are expected to begin speaking; thus far, she has kept her own counsel. "Well," Madhuri says, all brittle cheer, "let's hope you can help change that, cousin."

"I'll sleep in her room—she'll get used to me faster that way. I'm surprised she isn't in your room, Madhuri. How does she fend for herself every night?"

Madhuri ignores the suggestion that she is a terrible mother, the unspoken, *How is she still alive?* "I hope you'll settle in easily. Ask me for anything." By which she means compensation too: the cousin has done less well than she, who has access to half the Hua wealth, the other half being reserved for Rabhya when she comes of age.

The cousin comes to take charge of Rabhya's meals, of reading to the girl, of taking her out to the garden. On her part, Rabhya does not warm to her new caretaker; she remains as silent as ever, as reticent. The only time she pays attention to the cousin is when she is read to. Then she is enraptured; then she absorbs.

Deep within each of the girl's pupils glitters a red pinpoint, no matter what lighting she is under. It shines in the dark. Madhuri pretends not to see it. The cousin remarks on it but once in a low voice to Madhuri, to which she snaps, "Some children are born with birthmarks, do you breathlessly inform their mothers when you spot them too?"

"Wedding into this house has given you a bad temper," the cousin chides. "Surely you'll consider remarrying?"

Madhuri stares at her, unblinking. She does so long enough that the cousin falls quiet.

In the privacy of her study, Madhuri sits alone, her face in her hands. She breathes through her fingers. There are necromancers she could consult. But she knows, the same as anyone else, that true resurrection is all but impossible—and not when the body has been so utterly shattered, the soul fled its housing for this long. At the moment of terminus, if the spirit is captured… but that was not done, and she never had that capability.

All she has are her wife's belongings and her useless enchantments and the tears she allows herself only when she is alone, behind doors triple-locked by iron and sorcery both.

Many times she, well-versed as she is in crafting images that do not exist, is tempted to recreate her wife: it would be a solid thing, too, corporeal and realistic. It would last for a time; it would speak to her as her wife did. She could find solace.

But each time, she tamps down this urge. The past is its own shackles, and she cannot sink into that quagmire—if she begins, she knows she won't be able to stop. She would lock herself in her private rooms to spend every day and every night with a ghost of her own making. Rabhya would never see her again, and what kind of mother would she be then?

The demon has known for some time, and so when they come upon Madhuri's cousin hunching over the child in her nursery, they are not surprised. For a few moments, the demon watches as the woman sheds her dress of clouds and dusk, and then sheds her skin. What stands in her place is a thing of ragged scales and lashing tongues and a hundred lambent eyes.

They sigh. It is any demon's fate in the mortal realm to send their own kind scurrying home. Though that state of affairs is not so different from their native country's—theirs is a warlike sort.

The demon traverses into the shadow behind the thing that is no longer Madhuri's cousin. They put their fist through the creature, which twists around, more in shock than pain.

"You," it snarls. "The warlock of Hua is long gone."

A second time they sigh. "Some contracts persist beyond death. Unfortunately. What is this about, in any case? You're acting on behalf of an enemy of the Huas."

It glares at them with its many eyes. It tries to move but, having been pierced by another demon, it cannot quite dissolve into black haze; for the moment, it is pinned. "She'll come to no harm. Another family wishes to raise this thing as their own, nothing more."

The demon pretends to consider, cocking their head this way and that. Then they seize at the substance of the interloper, begin tearing it apart: efficient as a butcher would carve up meat. "I fear that idea," they murmur mildly, "stands in quite a contradiction with my pact. Apologies."

They have forced the intruder to stay corporeal; some of the gore splatters onto the child, who is at once alert, and who begins to wail.

Madhuri appears in the nursery near-instantly, as though she's a demon herself, turning on every light in the chamber. She does not pause to make sense of the tableau before her; she dives for her daughter, taking her in arms. "You were supposed to keep her *safe*." Her voice is high, nearly a shout.

"I have." The demon is calm. They flex their hand; pieces of enemy meat slop onto the floor. "I did consider destroying it immediately, but I wanted it to play its hand first, or you would have accused me of attacking your

BONUS STORY: THE DEMON OF THE HOUSE OF HUA

cousin unprovoked."

Madhuri opens her mouth, ready to spit out a spell that would—at the very least—sear the demon, even if it amounts to no lasting injury. In her clutch, the child's fallen quiet. Alert to Rabhya's every shift, Madhuri fusses over her, checking for wounds. None, and no blemish save the blotch of blue gore.

Rabhya makes a noise, seemingly experimentally. She tries again, then a third time. After the fourth, she enunciates clearly: "Mother."

Madhuri looks down at the girl, who has been silent for so long; whom she has thought might grow up mute, whatever the demon's efforts and promises. "Rabhya?"

The child makes a small, considering noise, a little too adult. Her pronunciation of each word is deliberate and precise. "Mother Madhuri. It's all right. I was never in any real danger."

The demon makes a gesture, as if to say, *I told you so*.

"It's not all right," says Madhuri, her voice cracking. "I've been... I haven't—I'm sorry."

She holds her child close, and that night she takes Rabhya to sleep in her bed.

The demon appears in Madhuri's study, taking this time a form of sharp shoulders and narrow hips, clad in a suit the color of unoxygenated blood that looks as though it has been composed from industrial corners rather than fabric.

"The child wishes to call me *mother*." Their normally melodious voice bristles with indignation.

"Well," says Madhuri, "she has to call you *something*."

They seat themself and frown at her. "I thought you'd be irate."

"It's an appalling thought, but I'm a practical woman. Rabhya does what she pleases, one way or another." Her voice turns sly. "And there's not much you can do about being called mother, is there?"

A beat before they say, "You're enjoying this."

"Obviously."

"Good," the demon says, unexpectedly. "You should enjoy something once in a while."

Madhuri bites back a retort—that the demon is responsible for robbing her of the greatest source of her joy, that they have precipitated the starkest grief in her life, and how dare they offer that platitude now. Instead she says, "Why the suit? You've never put on such a look before."

"You didn't seem in want of a housemaid, so I decided to try the looks of a butler instead. A majordomo, perhaps."

"No matter your appearance, demon, I'll find you loathsome just the same. Don't bother."

"As you wish, my lady. I'll see to my charge."

She takes a deep breath. She leaves her study, and then her house.

The Hua estate is vast, the area around it forbidding: the gloaming woods, the dark cliff face and the jagged rocks beneath. It is there that Madhuri makes her nightly pilgrimage, the precise spot stained by her wife's blood. Time and the elements will cleanse the stone of Hua sacrifice eventually, but for now it is still vivid, even against the setting sun. The gravestone is elsewhere—also on the estate—but this is what she considers the true marker.

For a time she sits at the cliff's edge. She tells her wife about their daughter: how fast Rabhya is growing, how healthy she's become these days, and how it's not so long now before they will need to enroll her in a school. "She misses you every day," Madhuri says. "I always tell her you would have been proud of her. That you'd have adored her. That you'd go shopping with her for dresses and hair things. That you'd…" Tears steal her voice. She has gotten, slowly, better at controlling her emotions. She marshals her self-discipline every minute of every hour, even in private, because Rabhya will notice if her eyes are red and swollen. But the dam cracks every so often, and the loss floods. She lives within the wreckage of her wife's body. She inhabits the moment where she discovered what had transpired. And a part of her does not want out. To never move on, to never allow the wound to heal, that will be how she honors her warlock.

BONUS STORY: THE DEMON OF THE HOUSE OF HUA

It is late when Madhuri returns to the house and finds the demon in the kitchen, crafting dinner.

"What is the meaning of this?" she asks, sharp. This is an unexpected intrusion; Rabhya is asleep, and the house should be hers alone.

"Your daughter has gone to bed early," the demon answers, unperturbed. It is a useless explanation; Rabhya always goes to bed early, seriously announcing each evening that the first step on the path to greatness is a good night's sleep. "And you deserve a nice meal."

Something catches in Madhuri's throat. Her wife delighted in cooking; since her death, this kitchen has been as a sepulcher, unused. How else can one immortalize what has been lost? Grief turns parts of you as cold and hard as marble, and that is appropriate—the most fitting material for remembrance.

"You should leave," she manages.

Every part of the demon pivots to focus on Madhuri. She turns her face to stone, lets her eyes look back, as clear as ice. But too late; the demon has seen, she realizes.

"My apologies," the demon says, and the next moment they are gone, the kitchen again restored to pristine cleanliness, every tool replaced and every crumb of food vanished.

Somehow the emptiness and silence is even worse than if the demon had stayed.

"I spoke to one of your nieces," says Rabhya, who has already acquired that adult habit of assigning ownership away from herself when she is irritated or aggrieved: thus, *your niece* and not *my cousin*.

Madhuri's family has come around ever since the incident with the disguised demon, as a sort of apology: the real woman is well, and has agitated for the rest of the relations to relent, to send Rabhya playmates. And so in the last year, Rabhya has—for the first time—had company her own age. Some she has taken to, and vice versa. Most find the Hua heir too solemn, too watchful, a girl who seems to anticipate a momentous event at all times. On her part, she's kept quiet about her demon or the promises bound to her birth.

"All right," says Madhuri. "What did one of my nieces say?"

"She asked if you would remarry."

"I'll skin her mother alive." Gossip flows from the adults first, every time.

"Well, yes, you should." Rabhya looks gratified. "But *would* it make you happy?"

"No." This is said without hesitation. "Your mother was the love of my life, Rabhya. There will be no other. No woman may compare."

The girl folds her hands, prim. "You have to tell me how the two of you met someday. But Mother—" Here she pauses, as though trying to recall a rehearsed speech. "What would make you happy? You're so sad all the time. I'd like to change that."

"I *am* happy, my jewel. Because you are my daughter. Because you are brilliant and a good girl, and..." Madhuri sits up. "The demon put you up to this, didn't they."

"No one puts me up to anything. They and I are simply in agreement that you deserve to have a vacation, to do something for yourself. You should at least promise me you'll get a hobby, Mother."

Today, as she does every day, Madhuri wears mourning colors: a muted blue-black that carries with it the shimmer of a scarab's wing. The lines and cut of it are fine and elegant—she has not fallen into disrepair after her wife's passing. But the funereal character is undeniable.

I pledged to always remember her, she does not say. To begin to forget, to not hold the dead warlock's face in her mind's eye every day, is an act of betrayal.

"I'll try a hobby," she concedes. "But first, it's time for your classes. Let's see what kind of progress you have been making with the family library."

Later in the day, Madhuri ambushes the demon in the garden.

Among the pruned shrubs and foliage, they blend in, almost another shadow. But they have kept the outline of the suited silhouette, tall where

BONUS STORY: THE DEMON OF THE HOUSE OF HUA

the Hua warlock was short, narrow where the Hua warlock was plump. As if to create as much distance as possible, as if to cut the association.

"You have been putting ideas in my daughter's head." Madhuri does not try to moderate her tone: she means to bring forward an accusation.

The demon shrugs, almost imperceptibly. "She is a bright child. She doesn't need anyone's ideas when she has plenty of her own. Do you think she doesn't notice how dour you are?"

"I'm well aware that I'm not the mother she deserves—"

"On the contrary. If Rabhya were to have only one parent, it is good that it was you."

Madhuri opens her mouth, a thread of anger bright on her tongue. "Never speak ill of my wife," she snarls. "Never speak of her again, ever. I swear I will unmake you, irreversibly, if you so much as breathe her name."

"That is my point," the demon says. "Your wife was a great woman—unmatched in power, my superior in intellect, and heroic in the way only a mortal can be. She died for your daughter; despite my annoyance at how successfully she bound me with her death, I can only respect, truly, what she did."

Madhuri sets her jaw like a sprung steel trap, crushing any response between her teeth.

"But it is easy to die for a thing," the demon continues, their tone softer than Madhuri would like, filled with more emotion and understanding that anything inhuman should possess. "It is far harder to keep living for it, despite the pain."

"Also," the demon adds in afterthought, "if you intend to unmake me, you'll need to know my True Name."

"You have never given it." Madhuri spits at this affectation of intimacy, this playacting at care.

"And you have never asked."

"Your name doesn't matter to me. I don't—"

"Savita," they say. "It lacks the potency of a True Name, but if you speak it, I'll hear you all the same."

Something about that bleeds away her anger a little. No sane demon offers *any* name. "And for what cause would I have to call upon you?"

"Danger. Inconvenience." A long pause. "It has been a long time since you left these estate grounds, my lady."

So it has. She has become a recluse: she knows that too. Madhuri had a life, once, full and brilliant—the butterfly of her circles. And she has, on purpose, cut it all down, narrowing and narrowing her scope.

She has not set foot outside the estate since her wife broke on those rocks.

Knowing is one matter, acting another, healing a third still. And yet time advances.

Rabhya is with tutors now, preparing for classes soon—the beginnings of a life apart. Madhuri wants to forbid this, to keep her daughter safe and close, to build the ramparts of the estate so tall and wide that no one may ever come and go: just her and Rabhya and the demon—

She knows this is guilt, both for her wife's death and for the initial distance with which she treated her daughter. But she also knows that this feeling is not something she can fix, only avoid in the future, only work to and build around; no apology to make, except to chart a better course. Thus is the nature of scars.

The demon—Savita, Madhuri grudgingly acknowledges—has taken more and more to a corner of the garden, growing flowers of unnatural color and shape in a greenhouse that smells vaguely of cardamom. Perhaps the demon needs something to fill the hours, too, now that their charge has begun to take wing.

In boredom and in loneliness, Madhuri gravitates to this alien space. It gives her distance, she thinks: of course her wife would not be in this garden of unnatural blacks and reds, of course Rabhya would not be in this little slice of hell. The hostility of the environment is like absolution: no guilt, for just a moment—a space apart, for perspective.

And from this angle, it is obvious how unhealthy and parasitic it is, to keep her child at hand. How many parents have destroyed their progeny with absence, how many with smothering? Her wife sacrificed everything for this chance; Madhuri will not see it ruined because she took the safe approach, because she took the path that was easy and comfortable. Rabhya will run and grow yet, and Madhuri's own scars will need to break and move to keep up.

But it hurts. It hurts more than when her wife died, she thinks. And it is terrifying. Pruning, growing, shaping a life—there is no rulebook, no guide.

"It takes a light touch," the demon confides when they find her in the greenhouse, "for an uncertain outcome." Madhuri knows they are not speaking of only flowers.

A street of commerce: boutiques and cafes and restaurants. The most ordinary thing in the world, and yet Madhuri finds herself tense as she strolls down its length. She knows why—it hardly takes some doctor of psychiatry to diagnose the issue. She has grown used to isolation, to a life that is both restricted in scope and utterly predictable. No wild variables save the rare visitor. Even Rabhya's tutors steer clear of her.

Her heartbeat is elevated. Each couple she passes by cuts at her. They are arm in arm, or they are ever touching, or they wear matching pendants. Once she walked these streets with her wife just the same, a world unto themselves. Her wife dealt in dangerous contracts, yes, but this is a time of peace. Mages do not wage wars. Hardly any conflict happens outside personal feuds, little fires rather than an inferno. There was every possibility the pair of them would age in peace—there was no reason for them not to grow old together.

It is a wound, and it is also her resentment of the destruction of a life she thought assured.

The near-panic becomes intolerable: she cannot concentrate on any storefront, and yet she doesn't want to go home empty-handed. She wants to show her daughter that she is recovering; she wants to bring Rabhya treats.

She finds a secluded alleyway, and there says Savita's name under her breath.

The demon appears instantly. "My lady," they murmur. Then, taking stock of the area: "You don't seem to be in any danger."

She tamps down her embarrassment. "I want your suggestions on what to get Rabhya."

"Oh, of course." Their tone is mild. "It's just that I was expecting a bloodbath and came ready to carry out retribution. Let us see what we can get for the young mistress."

In public, Savita has made their form more humanlike and less wreathed in shadow, their flesh like polished teak, their eyes like twin topazes. And a handsome figure they cut: they draw gazes, and those that can tell Savita's true nature startle. Is the current Hua warlock not quite young? The previous one is long gone. What kind of child can perform such rituals so soon, to summon such a being as this? Madhuri takes note, plotting already how these rumors might help or harm Rabhya's future, how one can make use of them.

With Savita on her arm, everything becomes easier, simpler. She selects jewelry and dresses, with Savita's input. Together they choose baked goods and confectionaries: beautiful little macarons, tiny but perfect cakes, pineapple tarts, bespoke chocolates.

It is not like before; it is not like shopping with her warlock. But for the first time in so long, Madhuri feels—nearly—normal. She will not allow anything to erode the memory of her wife, but perhaps she can feel, if not happy, then at peace on occasion.

Something is the matter; Madhuri is struck by the same premonition she felt when her wife died, the same as those early nights when the weakened Rabhya would stop breathing.

"Savita?" she asks, and no answer comes. On instinct, she rushes to the demon's greenhouse. There, she finds the demon has collapsed in a corner of the garden—not a shape of flowing smoke and blood now, but a solid gray thing, the stuff of them sloughing away like paper curling in fire, like ash.

They are dying, or something like it—demons can't die, not in the mortal sense of the term. But she thought the same of her wife, once.

Madhuri grabs at the human-shaped mass, rolls it over on what might be its back. The child-rearing classes she took are useless in this space; how does one resuscitate a demon?

The answer comes to her immediately, of course. Simple, too; she knows enough of daemonology because all mages do, learned even more in her preliminary research on banishing this specific specimen. A garden shear has fallen near them; she grabs at it and tears at her palm. A deep and ugly cut, but rich and red with the stuff of life—she crushes her hand into a clenched fist and lets the blood flow, first into what she thinks might be the demon's mouth, then across the decaying flakes.

"Drink, gods damn it, drink," she demands, then begs. "Drink."

She's not in the garden, not now; not in her alien refuge, her wilted potted plant of a life. She's not even at the cliff edge, looking down—she's below, among the rocks, where she has never gone, where she never went, saying the things she never said and never meant to say.

"I'm sorry," she begs. "Please don't leave. I can't lose you. I can't lose you again."

Color returns, and around them all the plants shudder, as if shaken with a great intake of breath. "My lady?" the demon asks, confused.

Later, Savita explains they expended too much of themself—too long from home, too much of their parts dispatched to watch over Rabhya, and Madhuri, too. It won't happen again, they assure. They volunteer, too, to restore her palm; conventionally treated, it will scar, a ruddy and nasty blemish.

"No," she says, flinching away from the precipice—closing her hand over the rent flesh, over a heart that slipped.

Rabhya contemplates the small hill of her birthday presents before she declares, "Mother, I'm very spoiled."

The pile is primarily edible—sweets hand-picked by Madhuri and Savita on one of their shopping expeditions: spun sugared egg yolk, pastries in the shape of delicate roses and orchids, chocolates flavored with exotic ingredients. The rest are carved figurines, in ivory or quartz, and boxes of reagents for Rabhya's burgeoning art. Practical gifts.

"Indeed?" says Madhuri. In most material senses, of course Rabhya has everything she could possibly want. She is moderate in her temperament and never asks for more than is necessary, and there are mage daughters who live far more luxuriously, and whose moods are like little tyrants'. Madhuri is biased, but she judges her daughter better-behaved than most.

"Oh, I don't mean these, Mother—though I like them very much. I mean that I always get what I want." Rabhya deploys one of her rare smiles: it has the force of the sun breaking through cloud cover. "Such as you getting along with *them*."

Savita, it has occurred to Madhuri, has not given their name (for all that it is merely a synecdoche and not the True Name) to Rabhya. She wonders at this. "We've always gotten along, my jewel."

The child sniffs. "Please, Mother. I've been sapient since I was very tiny, and my recall is comprehensive. You could barely stand to be in the same room as them. Now you're shopping together for my chocolates. That's an enormous improvement. And I think you're even a little happier."

This leaves her at an impasse: to insist on her unhappiness would aggravate Rabhya into making further demands—a hobby, Mother; travel, Mother; spend more time with your family, Mother. To admit some measure of joy would be to agree that the demon has contributed to it. "We both love you, Rabhya." Not that she is certain Savita is capable of it. But Rabhya has affection for them, and thus Madhuri is invested in the idea that demons can love a human child.

"This isn't about me, Mother, it's about you. Well," the girl adds with an impish smirk, "I know what I see whether you confess it or not, so I won't keep pressing. The truth always tells on itself, doesn't it?"

It was one of her wife's favorite sayings; Rabhya is making quick progress with the warlock's journals. Madhuri makes a mental note to put away the ones with content too adult for her child, but by now it is impossible to ignore how much Rabhya resembles her warlock parent. The angle of her chin, the tilt of her eyes. And, in a strange way, Madhuri realizes that to allow herself to heal may not be such a betrayal after all. Here is the living legacy, that which her wife sacrificed herself for. Commemoration does not need to be through grief alone.

The gentle chop of regularity—knife through carrot, again and again, steel on wood.

"Tell me again," Madhuri demands, "that she is okay."

Rabhya has been gone close to a week now, the longest she has ever been away from the estate—invited by the extended family for a summer vacation. It will be yet another week before she returns. Madhuri has walked to the market every day; it is like dying every time, nerves of corded rope and breath that refuses to come. But it is better than the alternative. So she cooks, poorly and with no skill, to simply do *something*.

At her request, the demon across the counter stills, as if listening to a whisper from another room; for all Madhuri knows, that is what Savita's casting about is like.

"She is... fine," Savita says after a moment. Madhuri jerks her head up at the demon's tone; she swears it sounds almost cross.

"The young mistress has her wards up," the demon explains. "She was serious about leaving us *both* at home."

Madhuri stares in wonderment at the demon. She realizes that for all their power, they are worried, too, and are not used to feeling so impotent. How this eldritch monster has been brought so low, been made to feel and hurt in a way she understands; Madhuri thinks she might laugh.

She doesn't get a chance—the next moment, and the knife has sliced her finger open. It doesn't feel like anything, not yet, and the blood has not spilt; the blade is too sharp for her body to know it has been cut. "Ah, shit—" she starts.

And then Savita is *there*—tendrils of shadow and blood wrapping around Madhuri's wrist, lifting the cut finger up to lips that feel of fire and smoke.

The contact of tongue on her skin burns, not as a candle would, but as a live wire: her every nerve-end ignites. She gasps. Slowly they lap at the welling blood. Their mouth purses around the wound to suck, to draw forth the substance that courses through her veins.

When they look up again, their mouth is red and her cut is gone.

"Your blood isn't to be wasted," they say, as if what they've just done is the most natural thing in the world.

Her pulse roars in her ears. "It's just a little cut."

"Yes." They have not let go. Madhuri is conscious of how their touch grazes along the scar on her palm, as if drawn there by a magnetic force. Aware, too, that she has not been touched like this since her wife—has not been touched at all, in truth. But there is a knowledge here, a heat and a weight, that Madhuri had not been expecting. "I'd prefer you not be mutilated again on my behalf, though."

This is spoken with something that approaches the bounds of—Madhuri tries to decipher it: possessiveness? "I chose the scar, Savita."

"For that, I owe you."

A puzzling thing she's observed over the years finally clicks into place. "Is there a reason why you appear in all manners of forms to my daughter, but to me only in this one?"

They're quiet for a few heartbeats. "I was hoping you would notice."

Madhuri comes this close to snorting, and knows what that would sound like. She realizes that, in this moment, she'd finally be able to hurt this creature, say the right words and bring them low. It would be petty retaliation against what they have done to her family; yet it would pierce, lodging under their skin like a thorned sliver. She holds in her hand that possibility of injury.

"I…" She grasps for a suitable response. "I would have to consider it."

"Ah. Well, I was expecting you to banish me."

Now she does chuckle. "And what will I tell Rabhya, that I sent her other mother away because I felt embarrassed? First I have to eat. Why don't you help? I'm done cutting myself for the night."

Savita's outline pulsates. Anticipation, puzzlement, whatever else. "I thought I was not to touch anything in this kitchen."

"I'm asking now. Consider my earlier instruction revoked."

They prove, of course, the superior cook. The tom yum carbonara they turn out is exquisite, far outside the range of Madhuri's skill. But she observes. She intends to learn, and watching the demon at work is its own pleasure.

Much later that evening, she retires to her room and stays awake for a long time. When she determines that she cannot fall asleep, she sits at her vanity to brush her hair, to perfume her throat very lightly: the fragrance of star anise and an orchid to cut its sharpness. Once she is done, she looks over herself from this and that angle, forward and in profile. The nightgown falls over her figure in a way she thinks is charming still; she has remained trim, and by mage reckoning she is far from old.

She puts on a silk robe, and departs for one of the guest rooms.

The guest room lacks the grandeur of the master bedroom, but she does not want to carry out her intention there—*that* was her marital bed. And for a long time she remains indecisive, sitting at a long window that looks out to the canopies, craning her ear for the hoots of the owls. Then she paces, and then she thinks of returning to her suite, discarding this entire thought for the unwise fancy it is. She has not lit so much as a single lamp, shying away from committing that much.

But she has missed being held; she has missed the sensation of—the demon has shown her precisely what she has been without for as long as Rabhya has been alive. And perhaps it is a betrayal, perhaps…

"Savita," she says, barely above a whisper, half hoping the demon will not hear. Or pretend not to hear.

They manifest beside her almost before she's finished uttering their name. "My lady."

She clutches at her robe. Breathes in, breathes out. The flow of respiration seems to demand more than it should, rocking through all of her. "I thought you might not come."

"Considering what I got up to in the kitchen, that would send very mixed signals. I'm a creature of trickery, but in this regard I prefer to be direct."

"Do you often—?"

"Take human lovers?" Anticipating her as though she's a scroll spread wide open. "Very rarely."

The simplest choice would be to set aside the inadequacy of language; to lead them by the hand to the neatly made bed; to allow herself to be overwhelmed, and not think. But she must know. "Is it pity that you feel?"

"No, Madhuri, it is *respect* that I feel. For your patience with Rabhya. For your sufferance of me, who took your wife from you, even though I never meant to. For…" They trail off. One of their hands lays upon hers, feather-careful. "How can I describe to you the mechanisms of desire? The specifics of why I have a part of myself watch over you at all times, and I would wring myself dry to do so because it pleases me to look at you, to know you are hale and your heart beats strong; to see how you look in sunlight or moonlight, to see you about in my greenhouse? These things make me content. To me, your blood is beautiful. Your scent distracts me from being homesick."

Their form draws back from her, though they do not break their hold; quiet descends, as if all this has sapped the demon of their words, or as if they are—like her—a little embarrassed.

Madhuri finds a place where Savita is substantial; still smoke and blood, but tangible. She places her fingers on the side of their neck, slides up to their jawline, a face they may have sculpted to meet such rubrics that would please her. "Take me to bed. But be warned, demon, that I am quite rusty."

They kiss her scarred palm, once then twice, and a third time. "Then it will be a privilege, my lady, to help you relearn."

Savita lays her on the bed with easy strength, and when the clouds move the moon sheens them in their most humanlike aspect, the brown skin and well-made bones, the eyes that most resemble banked embers.

When they slide off her robes, Madhuri resists the urge to pull the silk back on, to cover herself once more. She hasn't been naked in front of another person for that long. Their touches are experimental, now firm, now light. They chase every curve of her body, charting each with fingertips, and then their mouth.

BONUS STORY: THE DEMON OF THE HOUSE OF HUA

Madhuri, exploring them in turn, expects something like flesh. She discovers instead petals that open like those of night-blooming flowers, buds large and small that have bloomed into being, quick and spontaneous as though the demon is fertile soil. She brings their hand to her cheek and finds the petals velvet-soft, fluttering slowly against her. "I like these," she murmurs.

"You do?" A quiet chuckle. "That is just as well. Let me show you—"

The flowers susurrate and glide across her skin, petals and long fronds that are not quite like fingers but are surprisingly dexterous. It is like being made love to by a garden. A sepal tickles her thigh; another furls and purses around her nipple.

Savita pulls her against them, both of them on their sides, facing each other. "I'll capture for you a fragment of moonlight," they whisper into her mouth, "so you alone of all mortal women will wear a gemstone no other has."

"I'm already wooed." She reaches between their bodies, finds what she wants; she guides them into her.

What sheathes inside her has no human analogue; it feels many-jointed and yet as supple as the petals of Savita's skin. They cup her hips, establishing a hold, moving slowly against her. Their part thrums in her, seeking and finding places that make her breath catch, that make her jolt against their hips. Petals lap at her neck, her breasts, her stomach.

It is delicate; heat builds in her, drawing tight, tighter. She gasps into Savita's shoulder, wrapping her leg around their waist, urging them closer, faster. They oblige. They bring her to the precipice, and guide her not to the fall, but to the flight.

The demon tells her, as they lie in each other's arms, about their first human lover. A priestess in Eridu, who believed Savita an envoy of her goddess. She taught them pottery, how to press flowers, how to bake bread. She scented them with fragrant oils.

"What bound you to our world then?" asks Madhuri. Demons have to be anchored by an object, a pact written in sacrifice; the priestess does not sound like a practitioner.

They smile, slight. "A promise. You mages have made much of daemonology as a precise science, but there is plenty that lies beyond your studies. You would be surprised what can keep a demon here."

She runs her hands down their long back, her fingers lingering here and there to stroke the petals. They are everywhere, and it makes Savita feel diaphanous, easily bruised; fragile, even though she knows they are anything but. "You'll have to tell me about that promise." She kisses their throat, her lips against what feels like a lily. "Someday."

Rabhya, coming home, takes one look at her mother, and says, "Ah."

"Now what does that mean, young lady?" Madhuri raises her eyebrow as she sorts through the mountain of things her daughter's brought back: new dresses, fishing gear, dried fish.

"Nothing, Mother." The girl pretends to look demure, but doesn't quite hide her self-satisfied grin. "It's just good to see you looking pleased."

Madhuri raises her eyebrow further, but lets the matter drop. "Your aunts and cousins, did they treat you well?"

"They were very nice. One girl pushed me into the lake, so I had an imp set her hair on fire. Nobody suffered lasting injury," adds Rabhya, "and it was a good opportunity to practice my command over familiars."

"Someone pushed you into the—you can't swim!" Madhuri has an idea of the perpetrator; already she is composing the message to send that girl's mother, a demand for restitution and correction of behavior.

"I can't." Rabhya shrugs. "I had a different familiar keep me afloat. I'm good at quick thinking, yes?"

"You could have *drowned*."

"But I didn't. I'm the warlock of Hua, Mother, I have to learn to fend for myself eventually."

Madhuri draws in a deep breath. She lets it out. "You're growing up too quickly."

"It's not your fault. Other Mother gave me an early development. I'll bring a girl home to introduce to you one day, and *then* you can say I've grown up too fast. Ah!" Rabhya claps her hands. "Before I left, I was looking through the family annals and came across the mention of a sword. Am I old enough to know about that now?"

"That you are," Madhuri allows. "I'll bring you to where it's kept tomorrow. It can't stay on the estate—I'll explain when we get there."

Her daughter nods, excusing herself to greet her demon parent. The door shuts behind her.

Savita makes no sound as they materialize; she is sensitive all the same to their presence, has learned to know their arrival by the most fractional shift in pressure, something very like a whisper of wind. "Don't worry," they say. "Another part of myself will be waiting for her in the library. I just had a whim, and I wanted to see it through."

"Oh?" She pulls them into her lap. Most of the time they are semi-corporeal, weighing little to nothing at all. A handful of feathers in her arms.

A shadowed smile as a rose blooms, sudden, on their throat. White petals that blush into pink, fresh and vivid. They pluck it—thornless—and tuck it into her ear. "There. I've been debating the choice of flower; you've never expressed a favorite. Roses are perhaps too common, but I thought this shade would suit you."

"It's lovely. But too girlish, surely; I'll be fifty soon."

"I've existed for eons. To me you will always be young."

"Ah, the perk of taking an older lover." Her chuckle cuts short when they nose her throat, inhaling deeply of her scent. "Rabhya just came back!" But it is a token protest.

"What of it?" They kiss her clavicle. "She'll be kept busy in the library."

"There's no bed in here." Madhuri makes her smile coy. "And this chair's too small."

"Oh, well." They wrap their arms around her waist and perform some demon contortion that allows them to slide off her lap and rise to their feet without losing their hold. They lift her a few centimeters off the ground. "Then I'll have to keep you against the wall, won't I, my lady?"

She laughs, breathless, as they do just that—pinning her in place, demonstrating every evidence that they have strength enough; hands enough too, it seems, to stroke and caress, to hike up her skirts. It feels scandalous, reminding her of adolescent antics in libraries, furtive trysts in school.

Soon, though, such thoughts evaporate; only her demon lover remains. Savita's lips mark her like a brand, their petals as attentive as ever. The one tucked in her hair nips at her earlobe. Being with them is like being gently overwhelmed; like being pulled into a warm sea, not to drown but to exult. It is not long before she is thrashing in their grip, her legs around them as they keep her upright, her fingers digging into their shoulder and the back of their skull.

Madhuri turns rigid, every one of her nerves strung taut. The warm and gentle sea has become a high and roaring tide.

They keep her aloft, comfortably held, as her sinews unwind and her breathing slows. She makes a low, appreciative noise into their palm. "You've ruined me for all other lovers. My wife—"

Savita stiffens, expecting perhaps a rebuke.

Instead she draws deep a lungful of air, gathering herself. Her warlock would have wanted her to have joy, to have peace. She is sure of that. "My wife used to joke about the pleasures of a succubus. Never did bring one into our bed, though."

"Why—do you prefer a succubus? Shall I invite one over to make your acquaintance, see whether her charms will entice you?"

She swats them lightly on the arm. "I was curious, as most mages can sometimes be, but now that I've had you I find my interest in succubi much diminished. Surely you are a being of such vast age and experience you don't need me to flatter your ego."

The demon lays her back on the chair, setting her down before resuming their place in her lap. "I'm possessive, my lady. I prefer that you think of no other demon."

It is stated so plainly, and yet it strikes her deep; yes, they have been drawn to her, have looked upon her and felt covetous, desirous. But to hear it said outright, to be not merely pursued but *singularly* pursued.

"What was your wife like? The warlock," Savita adds, as if she has ever had any other wife.

Madhuri tenses. They can feel it too. "A little odd to ask, Savita." After this long, the salt experimentally dusted on the scar; to test, perhaps, whether the injury can still be reopened. "What do you want to know about her?"

There is silence, and inanimation: Savita becomes very still, even the petals of their body, and for a moment she thinks they have turned away from the initial question—have conceded defeat, or a lack of readiness.

"In my realm," they say, at length, "the Huas have always been of interest—not the earliest humans who've made contracts with us, nor even because their contracts are so unusual in purpose or nature. But their clarity, their ambition, that tends to attract us. It was with this in mind that I appeared before her."

Scar tissue can be ripped open, she knows that.

"I made a choice, I offered a deal. A child that had no future for one that would stride the world like a colossus. A simple choice, unrefusable, and I would be bound to that legacy, to that power, forever." A chuckle, dry, like the sound of wind through desiccated leaves. "I mean, I say the words. I know that must have been what I wanted. But these years on, all I can see is the ruin my choice—*my* choice—has wrought. I cannot make amends for that. I cannot even give you the closure of taking the life of the monster that killed your wife; I am immortal, older than all the stars in the sky. So instead, I ask—what was the warlock Hua like? So that when I learn the answer, I might carry it inside of me; when every star has fallen cold, at least some fragment of your wife will outlive them all."

It is Madhuri's turn to be silent, to turn so quiet that perhaps her demon might think she has retreated from the conversation, has stepped to a distant place outside of it. "I loved her," she says, when the pause has stretched near its breaking point. "And your request is a selfish one, a balm for your conscience, Savita."

The demon is quiet, then nods once. "You are right, of course. How conceited of me. I don't deserve your secrets, especially not to assuage my own guilt." Though they could vanish into nothing, they opt to stand, to physically pull away from her; the artifice of humanity, worn so comfortably, too easily, too painfully. "I will take my leave now."

Madhuri reaches out and feels the demon solid under her touch, as if she is their anchor to the physical world. Perhaps she is; perhaps she could break one chain, snap one rope, and this final reminder of her wife's death would be gone from her forever. And she knows then that she does not want that.

"You don't deserve my warlock's secrets," she says instead. "They're not mine to give. But..."

Savita stands, attentive, but they keep a respectful distance now.

"Do you think you are the only one to have made a deal to gain access to a Hua?" Madhuri continues. "The affection I felt for her was genuine, but I would not have courted her if she were a fishmonger. I wanted to be part of her legacy, too—to leave something of myself behind, in the halls of her power. Does that make me shallow? Does that make my love for her less? And I, too, promised her a child; I may have even used the same words you did, on that cliff years ago."

"What fools we are," the demon replies.

Her grip tightens on them. "I will not forgive you for taking from me my warlock. That is impossible. But if you will stay, I'll tell you about how we met, and how I pursued her. Those are my tales to share."

They kneel, a supplicant. "Thank you." A fragment of a pause, then: "Thank you, Madhuri."

It is the first time that she recalls them ever having called her by her name.

The ancestral vault is located far from the Hua estate; by nature of what it contains, it is anathema to most of the family's servitors. The substance of it is brooding stone, buried partway into sloping earth. From the outside, it is invisible save to those with a tie to the house of Hua, and its gates are defended by such spirits that can bear the being imprisoned within.

It is Rabhya's first visit. She marvels at the tall arches, the glass cages, the grimoires. The Hua family is not always prosperous and powerful, but no matter the circumstances, certain heirlooms are always preserved, carried from vault to vault or entrusted to otherworldly beings. This to be handed off to the next heir. That to be preserved for the next twenty years because a war is coming. Each warlock must make her own contingencies, create her own bulwarks against disaster. Some pieces of thaumaturgic knowledge are so precious, so essential to the lineage, that they must be kept safe—ready to be passed on—at any cost.

Madhuri leads her daughter past obsidian chambers, shelves of decoy texts of little importance, encased valuables that have monetary but no arcane worth: ostentations to tempt a robber who gets this far, to distract them from the true treasures.

Deeper, deeper they go into the vault. The corridors dim, and then become too bright.

"It will attempt to speak to you," Madhuri tells her daughter. "Don't listen. And don't answer."

"Is it more dangerous than Other Mother?"

Madhuri spends a few seconds weighing the two. "To us, yes. Your other mother happens to want the best for you. This thing wants to see the entire Hua line burn. And its nature is such that it's anathema to demons; your other mother cannot defend you from it. Do you understand?"

Rabhya is a bright and daring thing. But she understands danger; she takes the warning with gravity. "Yes."

"Charms against heat and fire, daughter. The strongest you know. And another to protect your eyes—it won't be quite like looking into the sun, there, but it will be close."

In this, too, Rabhya obeys.

The chamber is fortified against interference from without and within. Volcanic stone, to withstand the heat. For the moment the air is bearable—the being has not yet woken, will ration its puissance as it notices who has come to visit. There is only one object in the chamber, suspended in the air, wrapped end over end by chains of enspelled tungsten. A sword, its blade the perfect white of purity.

The temperature rises. Two degrees. Five. Ten.

An eye opens, in Rabhya's mind. An intrusion of presence that whispers it is here for her alone.

"Ignore it," her mother says, knowing without needing to see or hear.

Daughter of Hua. The voice is warm, so warm, like a perfect summer day. Warm like what Rabhya imagines her warlock mother might have been, the memory completely lost, too early for her to retain. She was an ordinary infant then, not yet gilded by the demon's touch. *Do you wonder about your future?*

"Your legacy," Madhuri goes on, "is to keep this contained. To hold it; to not allow it out of sight or out of mind. That is the oldest compact to the name of Hua."

Rabhya nods. She does not answer the voice in her head.

One day you'll need to take up the mantle and burden of your name. One day, child, you'll be pitted against a world that despises you for your chosen art. Little by little, you'll lose what you hold dear. The whisper unfurls like a vexillum. *But I am power. That is why I have been contained so rudely. I can be your sword, sharper and stronger than any demon. Your enemies will never understand what I am and how you wield me, nor will they be able to resist.*

The girl stands very straight even as the heat climbs and sweat beads at the back of her neck, in the crooks of her elbows, behind her knees.

"I have seen enough, Mother," she says aloud. "I understand my duty. I will make our line proud."

When they return to the family estate, Rabhya falls ill with a fever: the first sickness she has suffered in years. But it is nothing, she tells both her mothers. Everyone comes down with a cold or such eventually. All she needs to do is sleep it off. They will see.

Madhuri jolts awake in her bed.

Movement from the other side of the mattress. This strikes her as odd: Savita doesn't come to bed with her, nor do they usually sneak in. Not that she would mind. Perhaps it could be the start of a new habit.

A slant of morning light falls across the indigo sheets. She really must have fallen into a deep sleep.

More movement, a rustle of bed linens; the mattress shifts. She opens her eyes to the sight of her wife smiling down at her. "Good morning, Madhuri."

For several moments, she lies frozen. But her wife does not dissipate into thin air; she touches Madhuri and her hand is solid, warm, flesh and blood.

"Is something wrong?" The sixth Hua's expression has creased in concern. "Are you not feeling well?"

Time trembles, spiderweb strands pearled with dew. Madhuri moves to answer, to say, *But you're dead.* Instead what comes out is, "Rabhya. Is she all right?" By now the pyrexia must have broken. It must have. She is so hale, now.

A low, thrumming laugh. The laugh Madhuri loved so much, the laugh she wished she could have bottled to ease the long, lonely nights. "Of course she is. Why wouldn't she be? Come on. I think we'll find her in the kitchen. I've already run you a bath."

Madhuri takes her bath, dazed, while her wife hums and shampoos her hair; scrubs her back and arms; fills the air with rainbow bubbles. The water is warm, the shampoo honey-sweet, and the warlock smells like lilacs.

It is as if she has woken up from a long dream of monochrome and winter scents; that now, at last, she lives in the vision of summer.

Rabhya in the kitchen, as promised, steaming pork bao and shrimp siu mai. She turns on her heels, grinning. "Good morning, Mothers."

For a second Madhuri stops. She finds herself on the verge of tears, until her wife puts a hand on her waist and says, "Let's set the table, why don't we?"

A table for three, under the beautiful morning: not too warm, not too cool. A perfect balance.

The day goes by like a dream.

(In the corridor, walking alone, she comes upon a trail of petals: red, white shading to red, all of them withered and burnt. She blinks, and they are gone. She's trying to remember—do they have a gardener?)

She is happy. She's light as air. There is no burden upon her, not anymore.

In the evening, they have a sumptuous dinner; each dish is so rich, so refined. The lushness of duck fat, smoked. The savory sweetness of pork marinaded and roasted in honey. Madhuri doesn't remember who cooked exactly. Her warlock? Most likely. They don't have a private chef. Food seems to appear, plated to perfection; the dinnerware clears itself. But then, her wife has many spirits and imps at her command. She hardly married into the house of Hua to perform domestic chores.

Come morning, they see Rabhya off to school—"They grow up so quickly," whispers the warlock—and then they go to a market. It's like a holiday: everything in the streets is festooned in bright clouds, there's a shop where they find jewelry perfect for each other, and for Rabhya too. Rose gold and silver so bright it looks as if a slice of moonlight has been captured in metal, tricolored tourmalines and citrines and pearls of the most striking shades. They try on necklaces, hold earrings to their earlobes.

In the mirror, Madhuri catches a glimpse of herself with eyes gone to crimson. Her image stretches its hand toward her, seeking or beseeching. But it's gone so quickly that she becomes convinced it is her mind playing tricks on her. Too much sun. Too much duck fat from last night. Some hidden, secret ingredient can bend the periphery of your vision. Spices have the oddest effect on the balance of humors.

She doesn't tell her wife. No point worrying the warlock. All is right; why tempt fate with a suggestion of wrongness.

They return home. She looks for the greenhouse, but cannot find it. Of course they never had one, of course. Just lawns of perfectly manicured grass, topiary shaped to crystalline perfection. Things are perfect; nothing can mar that.

Broadsheets are delivered to the estate. In them, a headline proclaims, the al-Kattan house—a family known for their seers—predicts war within the next few generations. "They're always doomsaying," the warlock says with a little laugh. "It won't reach us—I'll have demons veil our estate in obfuscation before I will allow such a thing."

"You'll have to teach me *that*, Mother." This from Rabhya, who raises her head for the first time from a thick tome; no broadsheets for her—she disdains them; too much gossip.

"Of course," says the sixth Hua. "Anything for my heir."

BONUS STORY: THE DEMON OF THE HOUSE OF HUA

Madhuri smiles and turns a page, and finds there in small print next to some item about a necromancer's wedding: *Look at your palm, my lady.*

The message disappears. And even if it had not, what could it possibly mean. Nevertheless she looks, reflexively. They're just her palms, whole, unblemished skin—

A flash: her own blood, gushing hot and bright, the smell of it mingling with soil and compost and floral greenness. The tip of a garden shear blackened with soil. Her own voice, demanding, begging—

Petals under her fingers, under her mouth. *I'm possessive, my lady. I prefer that you think of no other demon.*

She puts the broadsheet down. She is sitting in the dining room, surrounded by the people she loves more than anything, and in her mind is the image of jagged cliffs, the rocks below them stained by a singular death, a singular sacrifice. The one that secured Rabhya. The one that brought to her doorstep…

"Is something wrong, Madhuri?" says her wife, still cheery, effortlessly delighted and delighting. "You look a little pale."

Madhuri comes from a house of illusionists and enchantresses. By the time she was ten, she knew how to make something out of nothing; by twenty, she was adept at enveloping a person in a dream of her choosing. Perception is malleable. Even recall can be reshaped. All of a human's sense of reality is clay.

"My wife," she says, "you've been dead for more than a decade."

The table falls silent. Rabhya drops her book, her eyes wide. The sound of hard spine meeting the parquet floor.

The sixth Hua only smiles. "Why would you say such a terrible thing? Have I done something to upset you?"

"You aren't my wife." Madhuri stands, though she suspects—or knows—that elsewhere her body is lying prone, trapped in the deep luring coma of this beautiful, perfect dream. "I began mourning her long ago."

A spark, as though sunlight has been snared and brought into this dining room. It grows. The outline of the sixth warlock flickers and blazes; her eyes, too, have become gold. "But you don't have to, Madhuri. You could have all this. You don't have to ever fear or grieve ever again." The table's edge begins to crisp and smoke. "Why return to such a cruel, unrelenting world? Why go back to a life where there's a stone in your heart, and always terror in the wings? You fear loss, Madhuri Hua. You're afraid something will happen to your daughter one day, a threat from which you cannot defend her. But here, she will be in this house, with you, forever. Always safe, never aging."

Once she is aware, she can see the seams of the illusion: her will sharpens, tugging at them one by one, unstitching each as she finds them. It is her trade, after all. She should never have fallen into it. "That's not what I want," she says aloud. "My daughter will grow and thrive, and come into a life of her own, and power too. She will contain *you*, creature, as will her descendants after her."

Around them, the dining room creases and pulls as though the environs are mere fabric, a thin layer being pulled apart.

The creature that pretends to be the warlock—and who no longer pretends—gazes at her with eyes like summer's sear. "You think, merely because you have *seen*, that you will triumph. But I am more than you are, enchantress, and I'll hold you here. You'll never go back. And soon, very soon, I will be free."

Madhuri works faster. She can nearly hear the *snip* of her might, surgical, cutting through the embroidery of this place, of this unreality. The furniture is growing thin, two-dimensional. The ground is growing gray, turning to bare stone.

In the far corner, a shadow gathers. It pools, thick. It spreads, fast.

"I'm not the kind of being you are," she grants. "But I am not alone."

She reaches out; she trusts. A hand of shadow-matter and petals grasps hers.

The dream rips. And Madhuri wakes.

Savita's arms around her, and Rabhya next to her, groggy still, half-conscious. Her demon grips her and says, "Welcome home, my lady."

BONUS STORY: THE DEMON OF THE HOUSE OF HUA

Rabhya is out on the lawn with the demon. Through the window, Madhuri watches as the two talk, voices muffled by the glass. Her daughter is not her usual staid self, collected and cool, mature beyond her years; she is pacing, screaming, almost incoherent with a rage that is incongruous with her diminutive size. She stoops to tear up a handful of Savita's flowers, hurls them at the demon, takes a swing next, collapses against her guardian third, wracked with sobs.

Savita has taken their more human aspect for this bloodletting; they stoop now, wrapping an arm around their tiny charge. The other reaches down for one of the torn up flowers, which they put into Rabhya's hair.

A moment later, Rabhya pushes them away, clearly done with the show of affection. Her back is straight, her jaw set; with a final word, she turns and marches toward the house. In the evening light, Savita watches their young charge leave. They stand alone for a long while, and then they, too, turn, and head into their greenhouse. After a spell, Madhuri follows them.

She panics when she steps across the threshold; her demon is resting on a bench, leaning heavy against one wall. "I'm fine, I'm fine," Savita says, though their voice is hoarse and lacking its usual resonant timbre. "The runt is furious at me; she said I was *insufficiently attentive* to your and her safety. I just need a moment to recover from her piercing barbs."

Around Savita, their flowers have wilted—eldritch vines burned and petals desiccated, as if exposed to great heat or a merciless light. At this, Madhuri feels real terror—the vertigo of standing on the edge of a great precipice, on the cusp of a new tragedy. But this time she is ready; she plants her feet and bites her lip, hard and then harder still, until blood spills angry across her tongue. She runs a hand through the demon's hair, pulls their head back and into a fierce kiss. Fear, desire, relief—they pour out and mingle, until human and demon each are breathing hard.

And then, lightheaded, Madhuri collapses beside the demon, her head on their shoulder.

"Your blood," the demon rumbles, "cannot be the panacea for every woe I face."

"And why not? If blood..." She trails off, losing her train of thought.

Something about blood as a metaphor for all the struggles and triumphs in life, and how burdens can be shared. Or something. "Gods, what the hell happened, Savita?"

"You and Rabhya were in danger, my lady." Already, the stuff of the illusion is burning away—Madhuri can only remember a smile, a newspaper, a growing contentment that felt grotesque. "The entity bound to the sword trapped you in a memory—to trick you into freeing it, or to kill you, or hurt you, I know not. I tore into the place to pull you both out."

Madhuri jerks back to look at the demon. "In the dream or in reality?"

"In both—what use is a mind without a body?"

She can see it now: the hall of white light, anathema to demons—the one place Savita could not go, could not help her family. And yet—

"You could have died," Madhuri exclaims. This great and terrible monster, immortal and impervious, risked the infinity of their existence for... for her and her daughter.

"Yes, well." Savita dismisses the concern with a scoff. "The shame of losing my charge would have been truly unbearable; I would never have lived it down among my kin."

After a while, Madhuri speaks again. "It was more than a memory, Savita. It was the basest of trickery. The thing, it wore the face of my first wife, showed me a world where she lived and—"

Savita pulls her tighter; their shadow feels warm against her arms, like grass and petals and gentle strength.

"—and I chose you," she concludes.

"The entity is a danger to my kind; its imprisonment was the oath upon which the Hua name is built." Savita's voice darkens, and there is anger in it, a fury that Madhuri has never heard from the demon and will never hear again. "It is also the monster that tears at the foundation of your house. I swear to you, I will find a way to kill it. It will take generations, but in years hence I will deliver to your descendants a way to destroy it, forever, and preserve the Huas from this obligation."

"Enough of that, for now," Madhuri says, and the demon relents, again relaxing into her. "Just being here with me and Rabhya suffices."

BONUS STORY: THE DEMON OF THE HOUSE OF HUA

After a time, Savita takes her into their arms. As the demon carries her across the lawn to the lit house beyond, they ask, "Your *first* wife?"

During the years that follow, Rabhya comes to know and court a girl with sweet brown eyes. This girl comes from a family which undertakes the arts that cultivate and encourage the growth of orchards, farms, greenhouses. It is a specialized skill, and for all its mundanity the mage world depends on it: how else does one obtain persimmons in the dead of winter, or bright orchids any time of the year? A sort of quiet renown, an ill match for the house of Hua. But it's not as if Madhuri will forbid it, and Savita enjoys talking shop with this girl, all about horticulture and botany.

Many clans are displeased that the Hua daughter has snubbed their offers for her hand. Madhuri takes this in stride. The warlocks have always done what they pleased in contravention of polite society. It's only when the Hua star rises that other families are eager to offer the current heir suit. Fairweather association, fairweather marriage. To select a bride from among that lot is to invite a viper into the nest.

(Madhuri herself did not court her own wife out of the purest intentions, but then, all the more reason to want *better* for Rabhya. Hypocrisy, yes. She'd have respected Rabhya's choice either way—even if she had chosen to court a power-hungry thaumaturge—but she's glad Rabhya's intended is not one of those.)

The gentle, doe-eyed girl, then. She shows little trepidation at discovering Rabhya's second mother is not quite human—seems to find it logical, even, considering the Hua line. She accords Savita the gravest respect, and brings as a gift a flower cultivar of her own making: in appearance, a fluted thing with furled petals. In function, it devours insects and even very small rodents. Savita laughs, pleased with the creation; few vermin of this world bother their plants in any case, but they delight in meeting another gardener, another creator of peculiar flora.

The bride-to-be stays over for dinner. She compliments Savita's cooking without ever mentioning once that it is odd for a demon to be so well-acquainted with human cuisine. Rabhya can't stop grinning. Her hand often brushes the girl's.

The wedding comes a year after.

The ceremony is small, attended by Madhuri and Savita, and a handful of relatives carefully vetted and screened. Most sorcerers have particular ideas about demons. Bind them as your familiars and servitors, that's business as usual. Honor one as your mother, that's much too much, less a bridge too far and more an entire continent.

Each bride wears red, trimmed and lined in gold—the marital colors of the Huas, which is a lineage with sufficient wealth and pedigree to have established its own codes for such. The doe-eyed girl will take the Hua name, though not as a matter of course or because she comes from the lesser house; she genuinely likes how it sounds next to her given name.

Both she and Rabhya wear veils of gold; each lifts it from the other, laughing and giddy, as if they've seen their bride for the first time and are euphoric at the discovery.

Madhuri has not thought of herself as the kind of mother who would get teary at her daughter's wedding; too much a cliche. All the same she finds a discreet corner to wipe at her eyes. Her demon joins her, murmuring, "It seems but yesterday that the young mistress was a nursery runt."

"Don't you dare call her that to her wife's face." Madhuri half-laughs. "Is this the first time you've seen your daughter to her matrimonial feast?"

"By necessity, yes. I've never had any other. Spawn don't count. Demon marriages are… interesting, and mostly are a borrowed concept." Savita has taken a human-seeming form for the festivities, and she notices—not for the first time—the gray at their temples, the lines that have begun to form at the corners of Savita's eyes.

"I appreciate it, you know," says Madhuri, "that you go out of your way to look like you're aging. It makes me feel less urgently mortal."

Half a minute before they say, "It's not just looks, Madhuri."

"Whatever do you mean?" For the many decades of their acquaintance—of their relationship, later—she has always taken their forms to be fluid, cosmetic almost, shaped to suit their whim and the circumstance.

BONUS STORY: THE DEMON OF THE HOUSE OF HUA

"The contract that binds me—" They nod at the brides receiving their wedding gifts, being doted upon, being plied with sweets. "Remember that I was to raise her, and carry her to greatness?"

Something inside her freezes, for all the warmth of the day and the occasion. "But she's not... she's *grown*, yes."

"And greatly accomplished in her arts. She has achieved much that her forebears could not. By any metric, she is the warlock of her age. And that first pact that binds me to this world, it weakens year by year. What holds me here now is the promise I have made to you. *With* you."

"But," Madhuri says again, her throat closing to a pinhole.

"It means," they say gently, "that I will age with you, my lady. That when at last your body has worn down and the end is near, it will be my time, too, to depart from this realm. It's nothing to fear. I will grow old with you, do you see?"

She draws her breath. All her nerves, her muscles, are tremulous. "It's not the same. *You* are eternal, or something like it. But I will just... die. No trace of me will be left in this world."

"On that, you are incorrect. You will be commemorated by all who have known you. The young mistress. Her bride. And myself, as I return to my changeless land, where all is stasis. Nor will you end—you will slip into the earth for a time, and emerge again as flowers in due course. Sun will fall on you always, and water nurture you, and you will again know life."

"Now you claim to know the afterlife, the cycle of it all."

"I don't claim," they say. "I know. But I didn't say all this to sadden you, my lady. I'm only asking what you will do after the young mistress and her bride have settled in the estate. I thought, perhaps, you would like to travel the world with me."

Madhuri blinks rapidly and sips her glass of tea—jasmine and chrysanthemum, particular to weddings—to stall. "For how long?" And she does agree: her daughter and daughter-in-law would want the manor to themselves, at least for a time.

"For as long or short as you like. I'd like to show you the spot where my Sumerian priestess used to live."

She has stayed on these grounds for so long, in this one place. "Very well. We can plan our itinerary after the wedding. And—thank you."

"Whatever for?"

Toward the new brides, she lifts her glass. "For everything."

A month after the newlyweds have taken over a wing of the manor, Madhuri begins to pack.

"You don't have to, Mother," protests Rabhya. "There's plenty of space, enough for all of us."

"I know." Madhuri kisses her daughter on the brow—despite the years, Rabhya's remained short, and Madhuri still has a head on her. "And this will always be my home. But I haven't been away for so long. It's time I see the world and how it's changed since I married into this house."

"And," Savita shouts from the other room, voice filled with faux glibness, "I can finally entrust my garden to someone with a real green thumb."

The demon resumes talking shop with Rabhya's wife; the seventh warlock of Hua makes a pout and ignores her other mother. "I'll fret every day, you know that. You will write? I should send a few imps and hellhounds with you, just in case."

"Savita will be plenty. *You* know that."

"Yes, well, I have yet to pact a demon as powerful as Other Mother..." The girl sighs. "One day. The most potent of their ranks are so difficult to get a hold of. Maybe they should introduce me to a few True Names."

"They won't," Madhuri chides, but only half-seriously. Both of them know the protocols between warlock and demon.

"Where will you be heading?"

"Somewhere cold. Savita wants to see flowers that grow on the tundra."

The seventh Hua widens her eyes. "How will their bones and yours cope?"

"Try more of that, daughter, and I'll tell your wife all about your childhood antics—remember when you set fire to someone's hair?"

Rabhya giggles, then sobers. "I'm going to worry about both of you so much."

"My girl, we are old, not senile." Madhuri pats her daughter on the cheek. "It'll be fine, and we will be very safe. You should enjoy your marriage. And we'll bring back souvenirs."

"From the tundra," Rabhya says dryly. "Well, the two of you never had a proper honeymoon. Do you want us to see you off at the station?"

"Savita's arranged for a car, one of those newfangled vehicles animated like homunculi; it'll be an experience. You've said your goodbyes?"

"Yes." The daughter draws in a breath as though she means to say more, but she says only, "I'll miss you both. But if I keep talking, I'll also keep you here and you'll miss your train. I love you, Mother."

"Love you, too, Rabhya."

Another kiss on the cheek, and then Madhuri is off.

Her demon is at the manor gate, dressed in that suit they favor, red and black. A few petals hide in their hair, glimpsed at their throat; one has to know what to look for. They take her luggage, gallant, and help her into the car. Both she and they are quiet on the ride. Tension under the skin, anticipation—a new, glittering stage of their lives together, and not the slow twilight she thought life at her age would be.

"I'm very glad you're here," Madhuri whispers.

They crane their head toward her. "I appreciate it, but what brought this on in particular?"

"You're making this part of my life so different from what I imagined. I'm a widow, of some advanced years, mother to a daughter who's beginning her own married life. For most my age, it's a time of gray, gradual fading."

"You're not old," they say, gently chiding. "Truly. But the years we've spent together—the years we will spend together, still—are my most guarded treasure. The heart of my garden will always be you."

She blinks, rapid, in a bid to keep the tears from running. "I love you, Savita." It is the first time she has said this; it will be the first, she intends, of very many.

"And I you. It may be strange for a demon to say, but I do." They speak slowly, deliberately; Madhuri can see their petals vibrating with emotion. "My old ambitions, my great dreams of power... all have receded before you, have become trivial and pointless in the face of your reality."

"That will go to my head." Madhuri squeezes their hand, feels the petals bend but not crush under her fingers. "We're almost there."

The train station is not busy this time of the year, this season. Madhuri stops to buy dried foods, sausages and pork cracklings and crystallized fruits, for the journey. Savita may not need to eat, but she loves sharing snacks with them. They show their tickets to the conductor, and if anyone on the train—all practitioners, on a vehicle that cuts through and folds space—notices Madhuri's companion is not human, none appears to pass remark or even to stare. Perhaps later: in any place where so many mages gather, intrigue is always afoot.

But in this moment, she concentrates on her demon as they slot her luggage into place, as they make the cabin comfortable. They note the pull-outs that will become a bed and nod, satisfied, deeming it adequate. They check the train's readouts of temperature and imminent weather, and hang up a shawl ready for her.

She only stops them, once, to kiss them on the mouth. And then they settle in, arm in arm.

The first journey of many. The first step on the next chapter of their lives, together.

CODA

It is another time, another place, and a different demon is tending a garden. She is tall, black-clad; flowers grow bright and enormous around her, red spider lilies of unnatural luster.

She is waiting. Has been waiting, for some time. Temporality flows differently here, though, and she is a patient creature. Up to a point.

The air ripples as another being manifests, one of the few she permits into this glade. Yves inclines her head. "Aunt Savita."

The elder demon has chosen a form nearly as tall as Yves', though slighter, sheathed in a red suit. They have retained, too, the features they took upon

BONUS STORY: THE DEMON OF THE HOUSE OF HUA

so long ago, when they were attendant to the house of Hua and its widow. A touch of gray, like ash, still adorns their temples. "Your glade is doing well. A transplant from the mortals' world?"

"It would all have withered without your advice." Yves raises a table, a pair of seats. In actuality it is unnecessary—neither of them is truly bipedal—but for the moment, they have both assumed these shapes for a reason.

They sit. Around them, beyond the glade's perimeter, the sky howls. The noise does not disturb; it is their home, after all, and they are both inured. To them, it is the harmonics of nature. A spider lily unfurls and bursts into song, a rich mezzo-soprano.

Savita cants their head. "A human's voice?"

Yves looks bashful. "She doesn't actually sing, but I thought I would try to capture her voice." A long exhalation. The sound carries with it a deep fatigue, for all that demons are physically incapable of such, least of all in their home territory. "Especially since I might never see her again." One day, she thinks, she might teach these flowers to talk. It would be demented and pathetic, yet better that than to never hear her warlock's voice again.

"Fourteenth of the house of Hua," Savita murmurs. "How long it must have been for them; how the names of their forebears have become history. To me it feels like yesterday."

Her aunt has spoken, before, of the seventh generation and the widow in careful, limited terms; keeping the tales close to themself. Private and rationed. By all accounts, Savita lived in the mortal realm with the widow for many decades. Saw the seventh Hua from infancy to prosperous adulthood.

"She's lost my True Name." Yves arranges her hands, careful, on the tabletop. It is pure black, like most of her; is conjured from her substance. "Or rather I made her erase it from her world. It was necessary—the only method through which her sister could be healed. Only I... I wish I could see her one more time. A descendant of hers, many generations over, will find my True Name again. But..."

"You've been busy," says Savita. Then a faint smile, briefly showing teeth the color of rubies. "I remember, niece, when you mocked me for my sentimental sojourn in Eridu."

"Even for us, *that* was long ago. I was young and prone to foolishness."

The elder demon makes a gesture, letting the point go. "In due course, your warlock will herself return to the world. She will have a new name, a new life, and your paths could intersect once more."

Yves reaches to cradle a spider lily in her hand. Hell is changeless, anchored to its own stasis. Her glade alone grows, if slowly. Already she can feel herself calcifying, returning to her natural state, the parts capable of novel thoughts and actions sinking fallow. "It would be quite the wait."

"The seventh of her line was great in her time, having surpassed all that came before." Savita steeples their fingers. "Has the house become stagnant or regressed?"

"No. Viveca—Ms. Hua—is most capable, superb at her craft." She chuckles, but her amusement is abortive. "I nearly killed her when she first summoned me." Or at least was fooled into believing she had brought Viveca Hua this close to death's door.

Her aunt laughs. "And my lady found me responsible for her first wife's demise. Not entirely untrue. I did my best to make amends, yet I could never bring her first wife back. But my point is that, if your Hua is greater than even the one I helped raise, then she will find a way. Not centuries hence in her world, but very soon. She will move heaven and earth, and the other realms besides, to bring you back to her. When that moment arrives, you'll feel a tug on your soul. You will hear her calling out for you."

"You're sure of that?"

"Yes. That family is nothing if not stubborn."

Yves looks out, once more, to the results of her efforts. To this slice of earth among the inferno, this garden whose heart is and always will be Viveca Hua.

"All right," she says. "I will be patient."

A demon tends her garden. Her head twitches and her neck cranes back when she hears it: a voice she has given to the flowers so that they will always sing. But what she has created is a mere imitation, a pale shadow of the woman in the true.

This is the law of the worlds, and I challenge it; this is the path by which those of the infernal realm may cross into our earth, and I hold sway over it...

The words belong to a ritual most ancient, an echo of long-crumbled Sumer. They are not part of any modern warlock's grimoire. But Yves knows who is calling. She knows who has achieved, or is about to achieve, the impossible.

She rises. She prepares herself. The path will not be straightforward. All the legions of hell, these days, covet this contract. Her hands become claws, and her shadow lengthens, budding with hungry knives. She will conquer a thousand, and then a thousand more, to return to her rightful place.

A smile grows on her lips.

"I'm coming home, Ms. Hua."

About the Author

Maria Ying is both a fictional character and the joint pseudonym of Devi Lacroix and Benjanun Sriduangkaew.

Devi Lacroix can be found on her **http://devilacroix.com**, on Twitter, or on Instagram at https://www.instagram.com/devi_lacroix/

Benjanun Sriduangkaew can be found on her **https://beekian.wordpress.com,** on Twitter, or on Instagram at https://www.instagram.com/benjanuns/

Acknowledgments

Those Who Break Chains has been our biggest project so far—we couldn't have done this without you! Credit and gratitude to C.S. Cary for the High Command section in "Dull Roots, Spring Rain" and for coming up with the High Command members. Many thanks to Rien Gray and Julian Norton for helping us whip the manuscript into shape.

The body of fanfiction for our strange urban fantasy series continues to grow at incredible pace. To our fanfic writers, we're so grateful!

Other Works by the Author

Those Who Bear Arms
The Gunrunner and Her Hound
The Spy and Her Serpent

Those Who Break Chains
The Grace of Sorcerers
The Might of Monsters

Printed in Great Britain
by Amazon